Sons of Steel

BLOCKCHAIN

G. L. Keady

ALSO BY
G. L. Keady

DREAMRAIDERS
SONS OF STEEL
CHANNELLING BO

Axis Stone Mysteries Series

SUICIDE BLONDE
LEG MAN
SMUGGLER'S HOLE

The Sons of Steel Saga

FUTURES END
CYBERWARS
DARK ENERGY

First published in Australia in 2023
by Big Island Productions

Big Island Productions
PO Box 3027, Tuross Head, 2537, NSW, Australia.
www.bigislandprod.net

ISBN:
Print: 978-1-923038-24-0
Digital: 978-1-923038-25-7.

Edited by: Canon Doyle
Cover design and art: Brandon Evans-Keady

Time is a non-spatial continuum that is measured in terms of events, which succeed one another from past through present to future. Someone is playing a gigantic board game with time. We question whether it is an extra terrestrial or God … or if they are one in the same?

TABLE OF CONTENTS

CHAPTER 1
EPOCH

THE WAR WITH North Korea had left Japan topographically and mentally scarred. After numerous missile strikes, many of the larger cities on the west coast of Honshu had been totalled, ravaged by the resulting firestorms. The attacks had provoked an unparalleled response from the USA.

Twenty-seven years later, a new Japan had emerged, with a fresh, optimistic psyche. The same couldn't be said of the aggressor. North Korea was the scene of the first nuclear strike on a civilian population since Hiroshima and Nagasaki. Pyongyang had been obliterated. The country was eventually invaded by United Nations forces, and after four years of fighting North Korea was finally annexed by South Korea.

The western world had narrowly avoided confrontation with China, after the UN had pressured them to not assist the rebel nation.

The setting sun glistened on the water, like sparkling reflections from diamond facets. Together with the boredom of fishing for three hours without a bite, it was making Doctor Rick Malone feel sleepy. It didn't seem to be having the same effect on Doctor Gensan Hyashi. He was happy whether he caught a fish or not, just glad to be out of the lab for a day to chill in the wilderness of Lake Okutama, a trout fishery that allows fishing under license and a vital source of drinking water for Tokyo.

The appeal of fishing to Malone was simply that in 2047 it was one of the only recreational sports to remain free from the grip of digital technology. As an industrial chemist, he was no Luddite, but at times he needed to escape technology — especially living in Japan, where it was ubiquitous.

As the orange glow of the last light streaked across the mirrored surface of the lake, Malone's mind drifted to his younger days, fishing for rock bass with his father in Put-In-Bay, South Bass Island on Lake Erie in Ohio. He rubbed his stubbly brown beard, reminded of when he first arrived in Japan in his late twenties.

Dr Hyashi broke his reverie. "Malone-san, look at the sky!" he cried.

Rick looked up in time to see a meteorite with a long tail streaking through the darkening dome.

"It's going to land right beside us!" he said, excitedly.

Dr Hyashi logged onto the nearest radar through his organic virtual vision retinal implant, OVVA — VV for short. An image of a military radar sweep, only accessible by security cleared users, was projected in real time to his optical vision aid via the retinal heads-up display.

"I see no sign of it on radar," he said.

"It's too small," Rick said. "No bigger than a golf ball, I'd guess."

They both watched the object plunge into the water only a hundred metres away. What they couldn't see was as a small metallic sphere opening and expelling a payload as it sank to the bottom.

Dr Hyashi was speaking excitedly in Japanese to a colleague through his VV. Rick had lived ten years in Japan, but he'd by no means mastered the language. He could, however, pick up the gist. Hyashi was describing what they'd witnessed.

Rick packed up his fishing gear. The event was over, and it was getting dark. Time to call it a day.

Hyashi finished his conversation and began packing his gear as well.

"What did your colleague think?" Rick asked.

"Probably a piece of space junk," Hyashi replied. "He will check … there is a registry of all space junk orbiting Earth."

"I know," said Rick, stretching his back. "Aaaah, that's better. Pity there were no fish today—but it was good to get out of the lab."

"I must let the fishing centre know they need to increase stocks," smiled Hyashi. "The last thing we need is casting practice."

Rick chuckled, but his face tightened as he recognised something in the water. "Will you look at that?" he said.

Hyashi looked. There were fish popping up to the surface in numbers, all of them gasping as though they were drowning. Rick walked over to the bank, knelt down, and plucked a big rainbow trout from the water. It died in his hands. Hyashi brought over a torch and shone it on the fish. They were both shocked by what they saw—both eyes had ruptured.

"That's incredible!" said Rick, putting the fish down and wading into the water to grab another one, this time a white spotted char. He brought it over to inspect under the light. The condition of the char was identical—both eyes ruptured.

"This must be related to the meteorite," Rick hypothesised.

"More likely radioactive space junk," Hyashi countered.

"Plausible," Rick agreed. "I'll take these back to the lab and analyse them."

Hyashi looked at the lake. "I will not tell the fishing centre they need to restock," he said quietly. "Look at all the fish!"

There were at least a hundred of them, floating upside-down in the water.

"No," said Rick. "But I think you better let them know what's happened as soon as possible … this is the water supply for much of Tokyo. I'll take a water sample too."

While Hyashi collected his fishing box and rod, Rick filled two flasks with water, put them in his keeper with the two dead fish, and gathered up his gear for the hike back to their cars.

"It'll be interesting to see the results of that water sample."

"I do not think you will find much, Malone-san," said his companion. "Whatever killed the fish will probably be neutralised in a few hours. The real problem will be cleaning up the mess!"

Rick wasn't so sure. A gut feeling told him there was more to it than met the eye.

Twenty-five years earlier, Black Alice took a sip of coffee given to him by the President of Oceana's private secretary, Rita Vallins. The President, a large man with a round face, bald head, and bushy eyebrows, was sitting opposite Alice in the lounge setting of his plush Sydney office. Approaching 11 a.m., the sun was streaming in through the huge floor-to-ceiling windows, through which Alice could see picturesque Sydney Harbor.

A noted connoisseur of coffee blends, the President was anxiously awaiting Alice's opinion of the brew.

"Killer coffee," Alice purred.

The President relaxed back in his chair. "Glad you like it, Panama Geisha Coffee," he grinned, almost boyishly. "Sweet upfront, a hint of Jasmine and raspberry followed by the subtleties of mandarin and sweet apricot."

Alice had a look of amazement. "Yeah, I can taste all of that ... I suppose." He flicked the long plait that extended from the top of his otherwise mostly shaven head over his shoulder. He liked to keep a close-cropped Mohawk because he felt it complemented the Celtic tattoos that decorated both sides of his head just above the ears.

"It was recently revived from decades of obscurity," the president continued. "This particular coffee varietal only thrives in certain conditions. As a consequence, only a few farms in Panama can produce it."

"Must set you back an arm and a leg?" Alice chortled, knowing the President could pretty well afford anything.

The big man nodded. "About seventy dollars for two hundred and fifty grams, plus shipping, so a hundred bucks I suppose. Not excessive."

"Sure beats instant coffee," Alice joked with a chuckle. "Worth the coin I s'pose if you dig coffee, a bit like having a palate for good wine."

"You're a real working-class hero, Alice. I'm so glad you decided to tell me about the quest set for you by this alien entity, um, En-Ki … it's absorbing to say the least. I can't help but wonder what the implications for the world would be had you not been selected by some divine process to protect it or should I say protect us from malevolent forces."

"Oh, I wouldn't go that far, we still don't fully understand the quest … it's sort of an intuitive thing."

"I must say your explanation is more understandable than when our dear Doctor Secta tried to fill me in."

"Ah, you know these academic types, they're flat out tying their shoelaces."

The wallpaper behind the President abruptly changed from a tropical rainforest scene to a glacier, and it distracted Alice. "The wallpaper behind you just changed…" Alice said, a little shocked by it.

The President twisted his body to look at the wall behind him. "Oh that. One of Secta's inventions: programmable wallpaper … I think he set it up so that whenever his name is mentioned it changes mood … otherwise, it's supposed to detect the mood of the conversation and then adjust accordingly, brilliant stuff … brilliant man."

"Let's see," Alice said with a devilish grin and then growled, "Secta!"

The scene instantly changed to an aerial view over an active volcano.

"Yep, you're right. He's a trip … Do you know he programmed the security system to the door of his lab on Level 7 to say, 'Oh Yes,' when you stick your finger into the ID module?"

"Ha! That doesn't surprise me," the President said with a guttural chuckle. "Speaking of Secta, I'm informed he has nearly completed the new small particle collider."

"Yes, he and Professor de Luz reckon it'll be operative in a day or so. It's been a bonus having the physicist Robert James on board."

"We'll see when it works … it's all theoretical, you know?"

"Yeah, but these guys really know their stuff. I've got no doubt it'll happen."

"I hope you're right, Alice … it has cost eighty million dollars of taxpayers' money to build."

"Ah, that's nothing," Alice dismissed with a comical wave of his hand. "The returns will make that seem like pocket money."

The President's tight lips broke into a slight smile, amused by Alice's brazen persona.

"Speaking of returns, has the brains trust solved the problem of getting you back from your time travel treks?" the President asked.

"I spoke with Dr Hope about that yesterday. She reckons they're getting close to nailing it."

"Good. So where do you think the next expedition will take you?"

"I've no idea."

"Will you be giving up performing with the band?" President Ri asked.

"For the time being, pardon the pun."

The President chuckled. He had grown to like Alice. He found his wit, mettle, and honesty refreshing.

"There's a question I need an honest answer to," Alice said soberly.

"Go ahead, this meeting is for us to air our issues."

"Did you order the murder of my girlfriend, Stained Class?"

"Absolutely not," the President said emphatically.

There was a pregnant pause while Alice's eyes drilled deep into the President's soul, searching for confirmation of him telling the truth. Sometimes he wished he had Morri's psychic abilities.

Getting it, he said, "That's good to hear. Do you know she was murdered and that the order came from Honor's office?"

"I will personally investigate it, Alice. You have my apology … but it won't rest there, I assure you."

"Thanks, then promise me you'll keep the bitch out of my face, I don't trust her … Karzoff I can handle, he means well, but Honor is a ruthless sociopath."

"Granted … Just changing the subject to a question I have of you … Secta told me about how you had to deal with Gorrick and Zen in the future, and then of course that wicked character Anu Set on your last junket into the past. I'm still trying to come to terms with how Gorrick can exist in two different time periods at once … but that's not the question … what was it like to meet Nebuchadnezzar and Ezekiel? I read the report, which I might add was very comprehensive, but for you personally, what was it like?" he asked with keen curiosity.

"Incredible. There is no other word for it. I've met plenty of rock stars, celebrities, and even royalty, but none come close to those two … and not to mention King Zedekiah, Jeremiah, Zorlock, or Cannis … all of them extraordinary individuals struggling to survive in the most volatile of times … where life was cheap, punishment brutal, and war … beyond imagination and description, horrific in every sense. These people didn't use guns and bombs, fighting from a safe distance; they fought hand to hand with weapons that inflicted unimaginable physical damage … there were no doctors to heal the wounds, no hospitals … nothing to prevent infection … I could go on forever … All I can say, Sir, is that it was an experience that has fundamentally changed the way I think and feel about everything," he emphasised the last word.

"No doubt, no doubt ... that makes perfect sense, Alice. I can't express enough how much I respect you..."

"I believe that now we're on the same wavelength, with shared goals and aspirations, only remarkable things can arise from our collaboration and the utilisation of this extraordinary technology."

"Yes, I feel privileged to be in the company of the brilliance of Secta and Hope ... and now, of course, Professor de Luz. You are absolutely right, Alice, great achievements will result from our alliance."

He struggled to his feet and extended his pudgy hand for Alice to shake. "And Oceana is honoured to have you as its official time traveller, Alice."

Alice stood up and shook the President's hand. "Just make sure to stay clear of Gorrick and Zen, believe me, sir, along with Honor, I have no doubt they are the enemy."

Still gripping Alice's hand, the President squeezed a little tighter to emphasise his resolve. "I hear you, Alice ... I hear you."

The meeting had exceeded Alice's expectations. They had amicably discussed crucial matters that concerned them both and found common ground in resolving them. No longer would things be left to chance. Alice now felt confident that he had the President's full support. He trusted him, and that was a significant factor for the anarchist and former rebel leader of the Octagon: the most proactive and influential civilian anti-government movement in the nation.

The room was vast compared to Dr Secta's Level 7 lab. Secta took a moment to marvel at the incredible piece of engineering they had nicknamed Kairos, the Greek word for time, signifying the indeterminate moment that is right for something to occur.

Standing in the centre of the room, the upright circular teleporter that barely fit under the fifteen-metre ceiling had a circumference of ten metres. Around its perimeter were positioned an array of superconducting magnets, twenty-four in total, each one connected to a super generator powered by a nuclear reactor to produce twenty-five megavolts. Such a high voltage was necessary to accelerate particles to the speed of light within the magnetic array, leading to their collision and the creation of a minute wormhole.

Kairos was the brainchild of theoretical physicist Robert James. It aimed to replicate the functionality of the Large Hadron Collider at CERN, a twenty-seven-kilometre ring of superconducting magnets that could propel beams of protons and ions at velocities approaching the speed of light. With modifications to James' blueprint by Dr Secta and Professor de Luz, they anticipated that Kairos would perform similarly to the Desertron Super Collider facility in Texas, which Professor de Luz had formerly overseen and had previously been used to successfully send Alice back in time to the sixth century B.C.

The control booth was located at the far end of the room, behind a large Perspex window that shielded the occupants from radiation and other potential hazardous effects arising from the use of ultra-high voltage. After all, it was an experimental setup and inherently risky.

Secta crossed the black rubberised floor of what they referred to as the studio event room and entered the control room through a double blast-proof set of doors. Seated behind the console was Dr Robert James.

CHAPTER 2
THE WOLF

IN HIS LATE thirties, Robert James was the archetypal scientific boffin. A modern haircut shaved on both sides of his head with a mop of brown unruly hair on top, wearing a brown corduroy jacket over a Pink Floyd T and old blue jeans. He swivelled his chair around from the six computer monitors he'd been studying to face Secta.

"I reckon we're nearly ready to give it a whirl," he said confidently.

"I'll summon the Professor, Hope and Alice. If all goes well then we'll do the grand demo for the President and the rest of OTT tomorrow."

"No problem, just give me half an hour to complete a systems check of the software."

The door from the main lobby opening interrupted the conversation. Secta looked around not expecting anyone.

"Good morning, I thought to drop by for a personal update, considering I have had so few since ze building of ze device commenced," Honor said contemptuously.

"I'm surprised you could find the place Honor," Secta said facetiously. "We have after all been here almost 24/7 since the project was approved and this is the first time you've bothered to visit."

Garbed in a smart navy-blue business suit, the SS styled black uniform and corporate insignia had been superseded as part of the

Oceana image makeover. She ambled over to the main console brooding with an air of antipathy and leered at James.

"And you are?"

James rose gentlemanly to his feet.

"This is the physicist who designed Kairos, Doctor Robert James," Secta said congenially. "Robert this is Fanny Honor, chief security officer of Oceana Time Travel."

James offered her his hand but Honor didn't take it and instead gave him the once over like he was wearing something of hers.

"I see," she said indignantly. "Kairos … and vot is ze meaning of zis?"

"It's the Greek word for time Ms Honor, meaning the indeterminate moment that is right for something to occur," James said, a little unnerved by her attitude.

Secta detected his discomfort and said whimsically, "Pay no attention to Honor's indifference Robert, her people skills are boorish at the best of times."

Honor brushed off Secta's criticism like it was merely lint on her skirt. "Ven will it be tested … zis Kairos?" She said scornfully.

It was blatantly obvious from her disrespect of the project that she wasn't content with her new position at OTT and the changes that had been made within Oceana.

"In about—" James was about to say but was cut off by Secta.

"Twenty-four hours. I will email you an official invitation."

She looked around at everything as though evaluating it for auction. "So, describe to me vat you expect to happen?" she said turning sharply and glaring at Robert.

"The time traveller will enter the booth over there," he gestured at the small booth on the left side of the control room. The target will be inside a dispensing capsule here." He sat down and pressed a key on the keyboard in front of him and a drawer opened in a device on the console that looked like a DVD burner. "Kairos is activated. The selected particle, be it a proton, electron, neutron or other, will then be fired into the accelerator. The nodes around the outside of the circular frame of Kairos are powerful magnets that will increase the speed of the particle to the speed of light. At a given instant determined by the program, the speeding particle and target object will collide generating a miniscule wormhole through which the time traveller in his atomic form will pass."

"I assume ze target object is date validated for ze wormhole to reach?"

"Yes, in the same way as the Texas Desertron was used for the last mission," Secta added.

"And ze return?" Honor inquired, expecting the problem to still be unsolved.

"We are still refining the return process but for now, if we use a dated trigger as you mentioned, we would simply use a second one to reopen the wormhole at a predetermined date and time for the traveller to return through," Secta explained.

"So on return ze traveller would step back out through ze circle?"

"Yes, that is correct." James concluded.

"Thank you, I vill expect your invitation," Honor said brashly.

Secta watched her stride to the door pull it open and step through, all the while shaking his head at her curt attitude.

After the door closed behind her, she removed a small recorder sampler from her inside coat pocket and deactivated it at the press of a button. It had recorded all the information she needed for a report to Zen. Being a double agent was liberating for her, it was giving her the means to exact revenge for her perceived betrayal by the President—it was payback.

She stormed past the vacant reception desk that she knew would soon be filled by Viktoria, the former receptionist from OTT that she suspected of being Secta's spy and she as a subsequence had sacked.

There were only a few patrons in the main bar of the London Pub in Paddington, Sydney, one of them was Alice. He was sitting alone at the bar when a guy wearing a black leather jacket, black jeans and a red beret crept up behind him and said, "How about an autograph big boy?"

Alice swivelled, "Ratsso!" he exclaimed cheerfully, jumping up from his bar stool to embrace his bass guitarist in a big bear hug.

They sat down. Al ordered Ratsso a beer from the barmaid.

"Real good to see you mate, been a while," Ratsso said.

Al nodded with sly grin, if only he knew. "How are the boys?" He said avoiding the subject of where he'd been.

"Slut's got an offer to join another band, Needs the skins."

"I can dig it," Al said warmly. "Last thing I wanna do is hold any of you back from earning a crust. Can't promise when we'll get back to gigging."

"No worries from me mate, I'm sweet, always got an earn, but you know Slut, gets cranky when he hasn't got a gig."

"Yeah, I know. What about the gig with Mal up front, didn't it work out?"

"Can't get enough gigs mate. Fans come to see you not Mal."

"Yeah s'pose so, I'm much sexier," he scoffed.

Ratsso chuckled. "Yeah … Did Mal tell you what happened at the last gig?"

Al took a swig of his beer. "Nope, haven't caught up with him yet."

"Right O, well, this hot looking chick turns up backstage askin' for you. Said she knows you and all, well sort of—"

Al frowned, "Knows me? What's her name?"

"Wyetta Walker."

The surname hit a nerve with Al, "Walker?"

"Yeah mate, said she's your sister."

Al was stunned, but before he could react, he got a call from Secta. Mid-afternoon on a Monday meant they had the bar to themselves. Al finished the call and quickly downed his beer.

"Duty calls," Alice announced with a wry grin.

"Bugger, you're off already? One for the road, mate?" Ratsso asked.

"Nar mate, I'll have to take a rain check mate, I need to have my head together for a meeting … "I'll have a chat to Mal about Slut playing regular with the Units, Blue's already their drummer."

Ratsso smiled, it was the obvious answer. "Top idea."

"I'll give him a bell and let you know what he says, then you can lay it on Slut," Al said as he stood ready to leave, as did Ratsso.

Ratsso looked Al in the eye and said with regard, "Cool … are you alright with all this stuff Al, you know, working with Oceana and all? … It's not like you to work with the enemy."

"I know what you're saying mate, never imagined I'd be doing that … but hey what I'm doing has real purpose … makes a difference to the world. The President is a changed bloke since the assassination attempt … I'm pretty optimistic about the future."

He decided not to elaborate as much as he would like to. He'd just love to tell Ratsso about his journey into the past, his fight with the Golem, stealing the Ark of the Covenant from the Temple of Solomon, gladiatorial combat in the area, En-Ki—it was like a good sci-fi movie … but he'd made a pledge to Secta, the President and to himself to keep his time travel experiences secret, only his best buddy Mal Function was privy to it all, and that was mainly because Alice had passed on the leadership of the Octagon Peace Movement to him.

"Whatever turns you on man," Ratsso said. "You know what's right … just remember there's a mass of fans out there that don't just dig your music but they believe in you as a bloke … you're their role model mate."

They embraced in a man-hug, good mates … together they had travelled the dusty back roads of outback Australia touring, trodden the same floorboards on stage, toured the world, and experienced all of the ups and downs of a band coming from rehearsing in a broken-down old weatherboard garage in South Sydney, to being one of the most famous bands in the world.

Al held his friend at arms-length and looked into his eyes. "Find us a new manager Ratsso, someone we can trust, have him or her audit Wilson. When I fired him as the manager it was because I had serious doubts about his integrity, now I'm sure he's been ripping us off. I'll get onto the record company today and have dosh credited to Blue, Slut and you from the band's Bitcoin account. That'll keep you's going ... Okay?"

"Mate, you don't have to—" Ratsso started to protest.

"Hey Ratsso ... shut your face, that's how it will be ... cool?" Al interrupted with a cheeky grin.

"Thanks, man ... you know you're the best, don't ya Al?" Ratsso said thoughtfully.

They walked outside together, and Al hailed a cab. As it pulled up Al shot Ratsso his customary wave. "Chaa!"

After giving directions to the cabby, Al rang Mal. It was a typical sunny day in Sydney. In the distance, he could see the harbour sparkling in the noonday sun.

"Mal, just had a beer with Ratsso. Said some chick thinks she's my sister. Secta? Okay. I'll catch up with you later."

The traffic was moving well, so it was a quick trip to the city. All the way, the thought of someone masquerading as his sister was playing on his mind, but even so, there was an element of doubt—maybe, just maybe, he did have a sister.

When the taxi pulled up at a set of traffic lights at the corner of Bent Street in the city, Alice inadvertently looked across at a car stopped at the lights on the opposite side of the road. It was a black Pajero with dark tinted windows all around, however, he could clearly see the driver and passenger through the windscreen. The couple were arguing, and to his surprise, he recognised the passenger was Honor, but he didn't recognise the man behind the wheel. His gut was telling him that there was something dodgy about what he was witnessing, so he pulled out his cellphone, opened the camera, zoomed, and snapped a couple of shots of the feuding couple. Reviewing the shots, he chuckled at the rage he'd captured on Honor's face in one particular shot, and as a joke, he emailed it to Secta with the caption: "Honor about to bite some guy's head off!"

When Alice entered Kairos reception at underground Level 9, he found Viktoria settling in behind her new desk. "Hey Vik, how goes it?"

She looked up and smiled at Alice, dressed in his black jeans with a skull and crossbones belt buckle and a black leather jacket over a touring AC/DC T. She loved his rock 'n' roll get-up; it was easy to tell it came naturally to him ... not put on like some other rock stars. Even his hairstyle was original. But above all, it was always Alice's eyes that got her most—they were warm and friendly ... smiling even if his face wasn't.

"Good afternoon, Alice. I see you're dressed for the auspicious occasion," she said facetiously.

He sat on the edge of her desk and folded his arms. "And what occasion is that, Vik?"

"The big Kairos test, of course. Secta is in his new study with Hope and the Prof ... they're a bit nervous about it all, I'd say ... Go right on in."

Alice slid off the desk and opened the door beside the control room security entrance.

When he entered Secta's study, it looked the same as the old one, only bigger. Secta was pacing the floor, while Hope and the Professor were seated in the lounge setting.

Secta stopped pacing when Alice entered. "Alice, Alice, sit down, sit down ... do you want coffee?"

"Nar, I'm right, Secta," he said, as he leaned down and gave Hope a peck on the cheek and then affectionately patted the Professor on the back.

Secta looked worried. Dressed in his favourite three-quarter-length black coat with a Chinese collar, his high forehead with his widow's peak black hairstyle and trailing ponytail made his face look more pallid than usual. Figuring it was probably only nerves like

Viktoria had suggested, Alice turned his attention to the Professor. "You must be excited, Vic?"

"A big day, Al. The time has finally arrived to put Robert's theory to the test."

"It'll be fine. I, for one, am dizzy from all the computer models we've run ... none of them suggest that anything could go wrong," Hope said.

Secta looked gravely at Alice once he was seated and said, "That's not what concerns us, Alice. It's the photo you sent me."

"I thought you'd get a laugh out of it ... that draconian look on Honor's face arguing with that bloke is absolutely priceless," he said, making light of it.

"It's nothing to laugh at, Alice. That wasn't just any ordinary bloke beside her in the car, that was the Zen operative Zanza Kew, the bastard who only months ago tried to assassinate the President and got off Scot-free," he scowled.

Hope glared at Alice. "And the question is, what the hell was she doing with him?"

"I sent the photo to the President," Secta said, back to pacing the floor.

"Good, I spoke to him about Honor at the meeting this morning. Told him she's implicated in the murder of my girlfriend, and to keep her out of my face because I don't trust her," Alice told them.

That captured Secta's attention, and he stopped pacing. "What did he say to that?"

"He promised an investigation. I expect he'll first consult Karzoff. Boy, won't that photo throw a cat amongst the pigeons."

"The problem as I see it is she's a high-ranking member of OTT, and the photo suggests she could well be a double agent, passing off everything we're doing to Zen," Vic said gravely.

"Damn, never thought of that," Alice admitted.

Secta was reminded that Honor had visited the facility for the first time earlier that day, complete with a chip on her shoulder. That prompted the thought that she may have met up with Kew to report what she'd seen.

Silence had befallen them ... they knew the Professor was right. The accusation was validation of Alice's suspicion of her.

"She jumped ship before with that bastard Set," Alice snapped. "So what are we going to do about it?"

"Nothing," Secta said, taking a seat. "We proceed as though we know nothing."

"Having to be constantly looking over our shoulder for her," Hope grumbled.

"Well, it could be argued it's better to know what she is up to than not," Vic stated wisely.

"The wolf you know, huh?" Alice growled.

"Yes," Secta echoed, "the wolf we know."

CHAPTER 3
KAIROS

WHEN VIKTORIA INFORMED Secta and the others that Robert James was ready for them in the Kairos control room, the mood instantly changed. Excitement replaced the bitterness over Honor's perceived betrayal.

They filed into the control room and took seats behind Robert at the console.

"Hey Robert, we're hanging for the show," Alice said cheerfully.

"If you hear a knocking sound, it's just my knees," Robert joked.

"No need to worry, Robert. It's only a test," Secta said, placing a reassuring hand on the younger man's shoulder. "Crank it up, my friend."

The room was surprisingly void of gadgetry. There were only a few devices on the console: six flat-screen monitors, a central keyboard, and a few other pieces of digital hardware. This was because the majority of essential equipment was housed next to the traveller booth at the left end of the control room, facing Kairos in an atmosphere-controlled, dust-free secure technical systems room. This was where the brain of Kairos, with its own independent nuclear power supply, functioned: the Cray XC-70 Supercomputer with Dragonfly Network topology. Computation at light-speed meant it would effectively run the software program Robert and Vic had written for the particle accelerator collider integrated with the two atomic injectors—one for the target destination particle, the other for the dematerialized time traveller. Once triggered, these specific injectors were synchronized to activate in a nanosecond because the wormhole created at the hub would only exist for that length of time. This was the one element the scientists were anxious to increase because such a short duration of the wormhole window seriously cramped the return parameters.

Robert had already prepared the program. He hit the button to trigger it, and when a whirring sound commenced, all of them had eyes glued on Kairos in the studio event room.

"Thought you would've learned by now to have all of the sound effects happening, Secta ... still a bit of an anti-climax," Alice joked. "Maybe I should compose you a metal track to underscore it."

"Good idea, Alice. I was planning to add loads of flashing lights and sci-fi sound effects once we're content with its functioning," he joked.

"Hey listen, Secta, I heard from Mal you got a visit from someone claiming to be my sister ... As far as I know, I—" He was abruptly cut short by everything around him coalescing into a wavering mirage. "Whoa!" he yelped, jumping up out of the chair. "I'm having an episode, time is shimmering—"

"Quick, get into the booth," Secta ordered.

Hope rushed over to help Alice into the booth and then closed the door behind him. She watched his physical form wavering in and out of phase and then in a flash. "He's gone!" she squawked.

"But there's no destination target!" Vic said, alarmed.

Robert swivelled in his chair to face the others with a grave look on his face. "A wormhole has opened."

They all exchanged a look of consternation. Then, pacing the floor, Secta seemed to get it and said emphatically, "Quick, Robert, it must be En-Ki ... hit send, mark the coordinates."

Robert checked the accelerator and then replied in a panic, "The wormhole shouldn't be open ... the accelerator isn't even up to speed!"

"Do it anyhow, or he might be lost!" Vic ordered.

Against his better judgment, Robert hit send and dispatched Alice through the wormhole, which immediately shut down soon as he passed through. The control room fell into an eerie silence. Hope peered through the booth window.

"His clothes were left behind again."

Vic erupted, "Thought I dang-well fixed that!" His Texan-accented drawl stronger than usual.

"Where's he gone?" Robert muttered, shocked.

"Run a scan of his atomic marker through the remnant radiation, it will give us a result," Secta told him.

"Yes, sir," Robert said and immediately initiated the program.

It only took a few minutes before the program returned an answer.

"Here we go," Robert said, snapping the others out of their reverie. "You were right, the target was generated by an erroneous marker ... and the GPS target was ... thirty-five point six, eighty-nine five degrees north, one hundred and thirty-nine point six nine, one seven degrees east ... the year is 2047 A.D., and those coordinates are Tokyo, Japan."

Alice materialised inside an apartment. It was night, and he was naked. When he realised it, he cursed, "Damn! I thought you'd bloody fixed that!"

It was a large modern living room with big ceiling-to-floor balcony windows. Through them, he could see the lights of a city. It wasn't difficult to determine, by the holographic signage, that he was in Asia—his guess, by the orderly appearance, was Japan. The apartment seemed vacant, which suited him fine because he would need to find some clothing.

He ventured into the main bedroom, where the light came on automatically. Everything looked neat and in order—the king-size bed was made—there were no clothes strewn about. He thought perhaps the apartment belonged to a woman and worried that if it did, he would have to hit the streets dressed in drag. He entered the walk-in wardrobe and, to his delight, found a pair of black denim jeans, an acceptable black T-shirt with a star motif, and a leather jacket—exactly the sort of gear he would expect to wear. Figuring his host had class, he checked a closet for a shoe rack and found a bunch of lab coats, just like he'd seen Hope and Secta wearing. A further hunt disclosed an excellent collection of boots and shoes. He helped himself to a pair of ankle-high black Cuban-heeled boots, a pair of white cotton socks from a drawer, and a pair of undies. With everything fitting like a glove, his growling stomach ordered him to check out the refrigerator for some tucker.

But that was where the fun ended. When he entered the kitchen, he found a dead body face down in a pool of blood on the floor. When he kneeled down and rolled the body over, he retracted with a start. The man was in his mid-thirties, his face was bloody, and where his eyes should have been, there were two black, bloody empty sockets— his eyes had ruptured. By his estimate, the well-dressed man hadn't been dead long, as rigor mortis had only just set in, so maybe four hours. He looked around for signs of a struggle and found nothing, only a smashed mug in a puddle of coffee on the kitchen floor. It looked as though he'd been drinking it when he just keeled over. Aware he was leaving fingerprints, he decided to limit what he touched.

A further search of the apartment took him into a study where, on the desk, he found a clear plastic tablet. He touched it, and it booted up. It was instant, and that amazed him. He immediately saw the date: July 17, 2047.

"So, I'm in the future again," he mumbled to himself as he clicked around. He marvelled at the speed of the processor. He came up with a name, address, and job description of the owner: "Dr Rick Malone, Unit 24, 2075 Sunshine View Building, Setagaya, Tokyo. Senior industrial chemist at Nihon Inc., originally from Cleveland, Ohio, USA."

He opened the most recent mail and found one sent only six hours prior. It read:

"Dearest Sonoko, I am led to believe, by my own recollection, that a pathogen has entered my mind through a water sample I touched, and my life is somehow being edited. It's the only way I can explain what is happening to me. Headaches and nosebleeds have come today, with brooding, waiting, and knowing that whatever is living in my mind is biding its time for an opportunity to ambush me. Rick."

It was a disturbing message, and if Alice figured to find out more, he would need to locate this person Sonoko. First, he checked more mail and found one that Rick had sent to a Dr Hyashi. It mentioned a water sample he'd taken from Lake Okutama that had returned a negative result from tests—no pathogen. But it said Rick was still convinced there was a contaminant in the water; it was just that so far, it was undetectable. Alice wondered if it was the same water sample he'd mentioned in the note to Sonoko.

He went back to the body and searched Rick's clothes for a wallet; he would need money. It was in an inside pocket, along with a miniature cell phone. Sitting on the lounge in the ambient light of the city through the windows, he thumbed through the wallet, finding no money, only odd-looking cryptocurrency credit cards. He figured that cash was probably redundant in 2047, so he pocketed the wallet and then checked the phone for Sonoko's number ... found I t... Dr Sonoko Tanaka. He dialled her.

A sweet voice answered with a Japanese accent, "Hello, Rick?"

"Hi, Sonoko, this is a friend of Rick's from Australia, um, Doctor Alice—" he thought to call himself a friend and a doctor so as not to put her off.

"Pleased to meet you, Doctor. Why are you calling on Rick's phone?"

"We need to talk."

"Oh, when? I am free tomorrow afternoon?"

"Now," Alice insisted.

"Oh, is it urgent?"

"Yes, very."

"Is Rick okay?"

"No."

"Oh dear ... okay—"

He detected a little panic in her tone. "Don't worry yourself; I will explain when we meet. Where would be good for you? Oh, please take into consideration that I don't speak Japanese, and I only arrived here from Sydney tonight," he lied. His implant language translator allowed him to speak and understand almost any language, including Japanese.

"Where are you now?" Sonoko asked.

He looked out of the window and sighted the only neon sign nearby in English, "I'm staying at Sakura Hotel, Hatagaya."

"Oh, that is near Rick's apartment. I will meet you in the lobby in twenty minutes."

"Okay, see you then," Alice said.

"Wait, how will I recognise you, Doctor Alice?" she asked.

"Don't worry, we'll find each other," he said confidently.

Alice decided to walk to the Sakura Hotel in Hatagaya since he didn't have cash for a taxi. It was fresh outside, with a cool breeze, even though it was summer. Luckily, he had chosen a leather jacket.

Keeping his mind set on a direct path to the hotel, hoping he wouldn't get lost, he entered a series of small laneways. When he emerged onto a main street, he was amazed to find a plastic track suspended from the buildings. White plastic globular pods, containing up to four passengers, whizzed along the track. The Skypods were autonomous, silent, and travelled about six metre apart. There was an elevated track on both sides of the road. The lack of automobile traffic indicated that the pods were the preferred mode of transport. Alice had always imagined Tokyo, like many Asian cities, to be filled with neon lights. However, he found it interesting that now all signage was holographic and floating in the air. Even traffic lights were holograms.

The Sakura Hotel turned out to be a little further away than he had estimated when he saw it from Malone's apartment. Nevertheless, he managed to reach the rendezvous point within the allocated twenty minutes.

The lobby of the two-star hotel was small, resembling more of a café than a hotel lobby. He stood there like an ornament, under the close scrutiny of the two staff members behind the reception counter. Their stares made him feel like a flasher waiting for a victim, so he stepped outside the front door to wait, fearing they might call the police for loitering. As he reached the sensor-activated sliding glass doors, he almost collided with a pretty Japanese woman hurrying to enter. She had golden blonde hair worn up, and was dressed outrageously as if she had just come from a heavy metal gig. Alice was impressed.

"You wouldn't be Doctor Sonoko, would you?" he asked tentatively, fairly certain she wasn't.

"Doctor Alice?" she said, surprised, and offered her hand for a shake, wondering why a doctor would have a short-cropped Mohawk and a tattooed scalp.

The issue of Malone's death was so sensitive that he sought to be compassionate, in case they were lovers.

"I have to be honest with you, I'm not staying here. It was just the closest rendezvous point that had a sign in English I could read," Alice admitted.

Sonoko gave him a warm smile. "That's okay. I know a quaint café along the street. Let's go there, shall we?"

While walking along the pavement, Alice looked up at the pods. "Brilliant transport system."

"The Chubu, yes, it is very good. Without it, traffic would have choked Tokyo to death years ago. You say you are a doctor?"

"No, that was another lie... I knew you are one, so—"

"You thought that since I didn't know you, it would be best to establish some sort of medical bond?"

"Yes, nicely put. I apologise for all the smoke and mirrors, but you'll understand soon."

She didn't seem put off by Alice's admissions.

"So, you are a friend of Rick's?"

"No ... um—"

Again, she accepted another lie. He was beginning to feel like an outright cad. They arrived at the café just in time to save him from struggling to explain himself.

Named Henri's, it was a French-style, bohemian alfresco coffee shop. Dim lighting and walls plastered with copies of poster art by the 19th Century French post-impressionist artist Henri de Toulouse-Lautrec gave it an old-world appeal that made him feel quite at home.

They took a table under a suspended tennis light in the corner of the room. Out of the eight tables inside, only two others were occupied. A young waitress approached and handed Sonoko a menu, then spoke to her in Japanese. Alice studied the waitress's hairstyle: her head had been shaved into spirals of short hair that had been dyed with graduated colours from top to bottom.

Alice was amazed to find that he understood Japanese. He realised that Secta must have included it with the other languages he had loaded into his translator implant prior to his last mission. However, he decided to keep his ability to interpret and speak the language a secret for the time being. He thought it might come in handy if someone was talking about him or saying something in their tongue they didn't want him to know. He wondered if it was paranoia that led him to make that decision, but then dismissed the thought as being paranoid.

Since learning that Alice wasn't a friend of Rick's and that just about everything he had told her so far was a lie, Sonoko naturally became even more suspicious of him.

When the waitress left, Sonoko's eyes narrowed, and her lips compressed into an angry grimace. "Why have you been lying to me, Alice?"

He leaned back in his chair, looked her in the eye, and said, "Look, I'm sorry, but this is a delicate situation. I need to ask you something before I tell you everything. Is that okay? Please try to trust me. I mean you no harm."

"Okay, proceed," she said, relaxing her grimace.

"Were you and Rick an item?"

The question flustered her. "If you're asking if we were lovers ... no. We were just friends. We work at the same company, Nihon Inc. We have been workmates for two years."

Her answer was a relief to him, as he could now dispense with pussyfooting around the gruesome details of Rick's death.

"Okay, prepare yourself because this ain't pretty. When I arrived tonight at Rick's apartment, I found him on the kitchen floor dead, with his eyes ruptured."

He was surprised that she handled the news so well and guessed it was the scientist side of her. She reminded him a little of a Japanese version of Doctor Hope.

"Okay ... so now you need to explain why you were in Rick's apartment."

He realised that didn't look good, he was becoming more sketchy by the moment. It could easily be misconstrued that he had broken into Malone's place and attacked him.

The waitress returned, and they ordered coffees. Then Alice continued.

"Look, my name is Black Alice, and I work for the Government of Oceana. Do you know the place?"

He noticed that Sonoko was in a kind of daze, as though she was reading something behind him. He turned sharply to look at the wall behind him but saw nothing other than a Moulin Rouge poster. When he looked back at Sonoko, she was still staring into space.

"You're a heavy metal singer, and you're nearly sixty years old. Please explain why you look a lot younger. Being Japanese, it can be difficult to tell the age of a Westerner, but I think there is quite a discrepancy."

Alice was cornered. There was no other way out than to admit everything. "How do you know that?" he asked.

"We Japanese have retinal implants that feed a virtual image to both eyes. We call it a VV... I have just accessed a complete dossier on you. And yes, I know Oceana, formerly called Australia."

He had been outdone. His implant's historical database would be of little use to him in 2047. It had only been updated until the time he left.

"A heads-up display?" he questioned.

"Yes, my eye movement permits the use of a virtual hand to navigate the internet and many other databases. I expect you do not have this technology in Oceana ... but then again, you wouldn't know, would you? Time traveller, Black Alice?"

CHAPTER 4
ASHES TO ASHES

THE NEWS OF the incident had rocked the President. "So, are we to assume there was intervention by this alien character En-Ki?"

"Alice mentioned he'd told you about En-Ki ... the short answer to that is yes," Secta said, taking a sip of coffee. "We've tracked his atomic marker, we know where he is and the year, but not why he's there."

"So where do we go from here?" the President asked.

"We know Kairos is a success, and that's a massive plus ... but really, all we can do now is wait," Secta said.

The President looked uneasy. He leaned back in his big armchair, staring up at the ceiling, and said gravely, "My major concern is Honor."

"Yes, that was definitely Zen agent Zanza Kew she was with..."

He locked eyes with Secta. "This is a massive breach of security, Secta."

Secta noticed the programmable wallpaper on the wall behind the President change with the mention of his name. It was now a flyover scene of the idyllic Tuross River on the South Coast of New South Wales, its blue waters glistening in the sunshine.

"If she is, as we must suspect, a double agent for Zen, then that places the entire OTT operation in jeopardy. I must say, I've known her since she was a cadet, and it bowls me over to think that a person so devoted to her job and loyal to Oceana would double-cross us. What in God's name could have caused her to turn?"

"It has to be the undermining of her authority in OTT, Ri ... that's all it can be," Secta said gravely, reverting to the President's Christian name because of the sensitivity of the situation. He knew the revelation of treason would have an emotional effect on him.

"A fall from grace, you say ... yes, I can understand that. Honor is a proud girl, and I did note that her attitude wasn't positive at our last meeting."

"I just put that down to her dislike of me, but it had to be something far deeper than that."

"Do you think we can trust Karzoff?" the President asked.

"Yes, he displayed his good intent by shooting Anu Set in Jerusalem."

"Good, then I'll call him ... we need to get to the bottom of this right now."

"I agree," Secta affirmed.

The President spoke to his secretary, Miss Vallins, through his communications implant to summon Karzoff.

A few minutes later, the red-haired man arrived, dressed in a dapper navy suit. The President motioned for him to take a seat in the lounge setting. Secta wasn't used to seeing Karzoff dressed other than in the austere uniform of the secret police.

"Karzoff, I have summoned you to answer some questions regarding your superior officer, Honor," the President said soberly.

Karzoff sat forward on his seat, keen to oblige. "Yes, sir."

"Are you aware of her having any problems with the current set-up at OTT?"

He thought about it for a moment, then replied, "Yes, I would venture to say she is not amenable to the change in her rank."

"Can you please elaborate?" the President asked.

"I think since the departure of Anu Set and the change to the relationship with Zen, she was expecting to take over Set's position of governing OTT. May I be frank, sir?"

"Yes, go ahead."

"Instead, Secta was given control, and she put that down to favouritism."

"I see," said the President thoughtfully, unaware that he was making a steeple with his fingers under his chin, as he did when being contemplative.

Secta spoke up, "So she didn't consider that someone had to take control of the building of Kairos?"

"No, I do not think so. She concerns herself more with the non-technical issues. I do not understand what is troubling you about her. She is habitually unsatisfied but eventually comes around. Some people are less able to quickly adapt to change than others."

"That makes sense, Karzoff. I am going to give you an order that you may find difficult to execute ... you are to place Honor under your surveillance and report directly to me."

A surprised expression broke on Karzoff's craggy face. "And what will I be looking for, sir?"

The President and Secta exchanged knowing looks. Secta nodded at him.

"She is suspected of being a double agent, Karzoff."

The news rocked him. "With whom? Zen?"

"Yes," Secta acknowledged. "We believe her contact is Zanza Kew."

The President handed Karzoff his cell phone, displaying the photograph Alice had taken.

Karzoff studied it and then looked at each of them, somewhat stupefied.

"That is indeed Zanza Kew with Honor in the photograph. When was it taken?"

"This morning," Secta said.

"You realise how dangerous this makes your mission, Karzoff. This man is an assassin," the President emphasised.

"Who else knows about this?" Karzoff asked sternly.

"Alice, it was he who took the picture ... Doctor Hope, Professor de Luz, and Doctor James, that's all," said Secta.

A nod from the President, and Karzoff stood. "Then we must keep it to those people only for now. She must not get any idea that we are onto her. You can trust me to handle this, sir," Karzoff pledged.

"I expected no less from you, Karzoff. Thank you," the President said.

Karzoff nodded to Secta and then left the office.

"That's an awful lot of responsibility for him to take on, Ri," Secta said, slowly shaking his head.

"We have no choice, Secta," the President affirmed.

A devilish look appeared on Secta's face.

"What are you thinking, Secta? I know that look."

"I'm thinking of feeding Zen a red herring to put them off Alice's scent."

"Go on," the President encouraged.

"What if we were to confidentially leak to Honor that we intend to use a moon rock to open a wormhole for Alice to explore the dark side of the moon?"

"Would that achieve the purpose?" the President said, his bushy eyebrows curtaining his eyes.

"Yes, I think it would," Secta said, holding his chin thoughtfully. "And at the same time, it would put Honor's allegiance to the test."

"So we keep Alice's unexpected mission a secret between us, then?"

"I think so, for the time being," Secta admitted.

The President thought about it for a moment, once again forming a steeple with his fingers under his chin.

"Wouldn't that be difficult with the proposed exhibition launch tomorrow? It will be tough explaining Alice's absence."

"Leave that to me. I'll let you know what to say if you're asked about him."

Alice had no problem conversing with the staff of the Sakura Hotel where he stayed the night. His translator/responder worked just fine. After checking out in the morning, he headed back to Henri's Café to rendezvous with Sonoko for breakfast.

The sun felt warm on his face as he strolled along the street, watching white globular Skypods silently passing overhead, and others travelling in the opposite direction across the street. It was threatening to be a hot day, so he peeled off his leather jacket and slung it over his shoulder.

Sonoko was waiting for him at a table when he arrived, but he wasn't convinced it was the same person—she was no longer blonde.

He stopped at the table and asked, "Is that you, Sonoko?"

"Good morning, Alice."

He pulled up a chair opposite her and said, "Your hair?"

"I like to change the colour according to my mood, so today it is brown."

He gave her a quizzical look. "So, what mood is brown?"

"Oh, serious, I guess you could call it."

"And is that from the news I delivered last night, or—?"

"A little, but mainly from the news I heard on television this morning. There have been many deaths in Tokyo from ruptured eyes. It is feared to be an epidemic."

"Do they know the cause?"

"No."

"Then we need to look at Rick's research into the water. Maybe he was onto something," Alice suggested.

"We also need to report his death. You can't just leave him on the floor of his kitchen."

"I know, but first we need to go to his apartment and download the contents of his laptop; otherwise, the police will take it."

"I can do that from the cloud ... no, all we need from his apartment is his private access code to his work terminal, and I know where that will be."

Alice leaned back in the chair and studied her. She had large almond-shaped brown eyes bordered with long black eyelashes. Her face was finely featured and pear-shaped, with full, ruby red lips. She had long, slender fingers with beautifully manicured nails painted to match her lipstick. Her small, high bust and hourglass figure caught his attention. While she was checking the menu, he glanced under the table at her shapely legs with cute sandaled feet. They were beautifully manicured with red lacquered toenails. She wore a lightweight white cotton dress that was fitted at the waist and flowing, patterned with strange geometric designs. The dress came to just above her knee, with short sleeves and a neckline that plunged to her cleavage. It was a different look from the rocker he had met the previous night.

They gave the waiter their breakfast order.

"I read the mail Rick sent me again when I got home last night. I think it is definitely related to this epidemic. I think Rick had discovered it."

"I also saw a note to a Doctor Hyashi, you know him?" Alice asked.

"Yes, he is Rick's fishing partner. Once a month they would go to the Lake Okutama Fishing Club together ... Doctor Hyashi is a member ... it is very exclusive."

"Rick mentioned a water sample he'd taken from Lake Okutama that had returned a negative result—no pathogen, but he was still convinced the water was contaminated, only that it was so far undetectable."

"I think you are right, the facts must be linked. Rick suspected there was a pathogen in the water, I wonder why? If there is, it would explain the epidemic because Lake Okutama supplies much of the drinking water for Tokyo?"

Alice was impressed by the sharpness of Sonoko's deductive reasoning; it made sense she was a scientist.

"Would the water be checked daily?" Alice queried.

"Yes, it is, but it seems what Rick discovered is undetectable. He would know he was a very good chemist. We will need to contact Doctor Hyashi ... he might also be infected."

After breakfast, they went to Rick's apartment. Alice took the key card from Rick's wallet to activate the elevator and then to open the apartment door. He wasn't sure of the state of Rick's body, so he asked Sonoko to wait at the door while he checked.

It was eerie for him to enter the apartment knowing there was a dead body, especially of a person who had died under suspicious circumstances. He sneaked up on the kitchen, prepared for the worst, and was shocked by what he found.

He called out, "Sonoko, come and look at this!"

She left her sandals in the shoe rack just inside the doorway and then rushed barefoot to find Alice in the kitchen standing over Rick's remains on the floor.

"But—" Sonoko gasped with a frown, staring at the black silhouette in the shape of a body on the kitchen floor.

"It's like he dissolved," Alice said, mystified. He picked up a wooden ladle from the benchtop, knelt down, and shovelled around the black powder that was all that remained of Rick.

"It's like dust ... his body must have internally combusted or something."

"No, I think not. There is no sign of burning on the kitchen cupboards or floor. A body burns at eighteen hundred degrees Fahrenheit; it would have left a sign."

"You're right, a temperature like that would have burnt the place down."

"It must be chemical or bacterial decomposition," Sonoko posited.

She took her handbag that was slung over her shoulder and produced a resealable plastic bag from inside, knelt down beside Alice, took the ladle out of his hand, scraped some of Rick's remains into the bag, and sealed it.

"I will test this," she explained.

Alice straightened up, ambled into the living room, and sat down in an armchair. He looked out through the balcony windows at a different scene than he remembered seeing before. Things always look different in daylight. Sonoko followed him and sat in an armchair opposite, crossing her legs.

"Do you think you were sent here to solve this mystery?" she asked conversationally.

Alice thought about it for a moment. It was a question that was playing on his mind as well.

"Possibly. If that is the case, then there must be a significant danger of it becoming a global epidemic, and I'm to play a role in stopping it ... but I'm no scientist, and that's what's needed here."

"Well, I am, but I will need help from someone much more qualified."

"Would that be Doctor Hyashi?" Alice quizzed.

"No, I don't think so. He is only an industrial chemist, I think a food scientist. From what Rick had said about the pathogen being undetectable, what is needed is a scientist of nanobiotechnology."

A name instantly sprang into Alice's mind.

"I know just the guy, but he's in another time: Doctor Secta."

"Perhaps you should think about getting him here. Can you get a message to him?"

"Now that would be an interesting challenge."

Sonoko got up and left Alice deep in thought while she went to the study to find Rick's Nihon Inc. lab access code.

Awaiting the arrival of the President, the OTT team had gathered in the control room for the demonstration of Kairos. Honor and Karzoff were in the teleporter studio, looking at Kairos, while Viktoria was taking drink orders from Secta, Professor de Luz, Hope, and Robert James.

"It feels uncomfortable knowing she's passing everything to the enemy. Look, she's taking shots of Kairos on her phone," Hope said.

"Don't worry, they won't come out," Robert said with a wry smile. "I've bumped up the radiation level around Kairos to interfere with digital cameras."

Hope grinned and playfully elbowed Robert in the ribs. "Aren't you a clever-clogs then?"

Viktoria handed the President a small cup when he entered the control room.

"Good morning, sir. Doctor Secta said you would enjoy a cup of Café Cortado from Argentina."

He took a sip and smiled. "Oh, absolutely splendid, my dear. A fine brew."

The lights dimmed slightly with a minute power outage. Secta frowned.

"That shouldn't happen. We're on our own circuit to the reactor here."

"Secta!" Robert called out from the console. "Kairos is activating of its own accord again!" The power outage had come from elsewhere, a sign something was taking control of the Cray XC-70 computer.

"Quick, get Honor and Karzoff out of there!" Secta said.

Without hesitation, Robert hit a button on the console and spoke sternly into the desk microphone. "Honor and Karzoff, evacuate the teleporter studio immediately ... immediately!"

They all watched through the control room window as Honor and Karzoff rushed for the security door. Kairos had initiated the collider program, and the soft whirring sound of activation was evident. Robert was studying the monitor displays, perplexed by the program's self-activation. Secta stood behind him with de Luz and Hope, all wearing befuddled expressions on their faces.

Nonchalantly sipping his coffee, the President wandered over beside Secta and inquired, "What's going on?"

CHAPTER 5
BACKSLIDER

THE LIVING-ROOM SHIMMERED, as Alice instinctively knew it would. It seemed to him he was now capable of causing a vortex to open by just thinking about it.

With Sonoko still in the study, he had the privacy to do what was needed. He finished scribbling a note on a piece of A4 paper, then he spat on it, circled the saliva, marked it "spit" and then waited for the vortex to open.

"A wormhole is opening," Secta told the President.

"I see, to what designation?"

"We don't know Ri, it has opened of its own accord ... we had nothing to do with it."

"Fascinating."

Honor and Karzoff were now safely inside the control room intently watching Kairos with the others.

From the centre of Kairos a piece of paper appeared out of nowhere and floated like a poorly made paper aeroplane until it landed on the ground. Then Kairos shut down. Everyone in the control room was on their feet in stunned silence.

Secta eventually broke the abstraction by opening the security door rushing out and fetching the piece of paper.

"What could it be?" Karzoff murmured to Honor.

Though hearing him Honor was busy flicking through the pictures she'd taken of Kairos on her cell phone, "Probably a piece of rubbish caught in the machinery or something. What ze hell happened to ze photos I took?" she grumbled irritably.

Secta returned to the control room and unfurled the paper. He chuckled as he read out what was scrawled on it forgetting Honor was present.

"The note is from Alice. It says ... I'm in Tokyo ... it's 2047, arrived naked ... thought you fixed that!" A chuckle went round the room. "He continued, there's a terrible pandemic here, need you now Secta. It threatens the world. Then there's the word spit circled with an arrow pointing at it."

Hope held out her hand to Secta and he passed her the note. "He spat on it to use in the accelerator to open a wormhole to him."

"Clever boy," the Professor said.

"How did Alice get to 2047?" Honor questioned.

It was then Secta realised his error in reading the note out aloud. He had inadvertently exposed the truth instead of the cover story he'd planned to give Honor. Thinking on his feet he explained, "Okay, everyone sit down please. Yesterday, while doing a systems check on Kairos, just as it did then, it fired up of its own accord. Alice was here and figured it was no accident ... that it had been orchestrated. So he entered the wormhole and it closed behind him. Until now we only had a vague idea where he went, what year or for what reason. Now we know." Secta fired the President a knowing glance and then carried on, "I don't think there's any point in continuing the exhibition, it seems Kairos took upon itself to show off enough for you to get the idea of how it works. Anyone have any questions?"

"Yes," Honor piped up. "If ve are to assume Alice is in Tokyo in 2047, vat benefit to Oceana is zat and do you intend to do as he requested and join him ... oh, I also vant to know vy ze digital photos I took of Kairos from my cell phone haff not come out?"

Secta had anticipated her questions. "Firstly Honor, at this early stage we don't know any more about the mission than what I just read you from Alice's note. Secondly, the question of me joining Alice in 2047 will have to be discussed, so I cannot answer that for now … finally, the reason your photos failed to materialise is because photos of Kairos are prohibited … from a technical standpoint the radiation from the Kairos electromagnetic field would have affected the photographic process."

Honor pulled an indignant face, "Vy vud photographs taken by a board member of OTT be prohibited?"

"There are no exceptions to the rules Honor … there isn't one rule for you and rules for others. Kairos requires the highest security clearance, you should know that … security is after all your job is it not?" Secta added facetiously.

"Zat is exactly vy I should not be subject to ze rules of others," she argued.

"I agree with Secta, Honor … we cannot take the risk of OTT classified details falling into the hands of Zen. The matter is not up for debate," the President said sternly, terminating the discussion.

Honor scowled and then stormed out of the room.

The President nodded for Karzoff to follow her.

Karzoff had to run to catch the elevator. The doors were closing and he only just managed to slip inside to join Honor, who was seething.

"What is the hurry?" Karzoff enquired. He could tell by her body language and face she had boiled over. Always volatile under circumstances where she felt her pride had been assaulted, it was a good chance to pump her for information.

"I do not need to take zat sort of humiliation from anyone," she snapped.

"You know as well as I what they said was correct. Why do you want photographs of Kairos anyway?"

"It is not about vat I vant, it is about ze privileges zat comes with my rank … seems to me I haff been stripped of zem … for vat reason?" she snarled.

"So, were you only testing them?"

"Zat is correct. Look Karzoff, ve haff been shut out of zis operation since it began. Left off memos, not included in design meetings, obstructed from making enquiries, and now iced out of a mission. Vy should I not be distressed about zat, hmm?"

"Because most of it was technical and did not concern us. Like today, either some sort of technical glitch caused the device to activate or it is being remotely operated … if that is the case then it presents a breach of security."

"Zen zat should be our concern, should it not? Ve head up security, our responsibility vud be to investigate zis but zat is not ze case … vy is zat?"

"I … I do not know," Karzoff stammered. "Perhaps with some of the things that happened in the past you have lost their trust."

He was out on a limb posing such a scenario and expected a sharp retaliative bite in reply and got it.

"Such as vat! Vat haff I done zat could haff caused a loss of confidence in vat I haff to offer?" she snapped.

"You sided with Anu Set in Jerusalem, remember?"

The elevator stopped at the Oceana car park level. It was a secure elevator so they needed to change to another to reach OTT on the twenty-fourth floor of Oceana HQ. Karzoff stepped out and pressed the call button. Honor walked off into the car park.

"Not going to the office?" Karzoff called after her.

She didn't reply just kept on walking. He suspected because she was so angry she'd be making a beeline to dump it all on Zanza Kew. This was his chance … he had to tail her.

The look on the President's face was priceless, astonished by Honor's impudent attitude. They were still in the control room discussing what to do about Alice.

"We need to resolve this matter with Honor as soon as possible, we can't have dissension in the ranks," the President said genuinely. "It endangers everything we are doing."

"Irrespective of Honor, we must focus on the letter from Alice, it's not like him to be so grim … the situation must be dire," the Professor submitted.

"You're right Vic, it's not like him at all. I don't think you have much choice Secta," Hope submitted.

"Will the saliva give you a fix for a wormhole to Alice?" the President asked.

"It will but that's not the concern, the problem for Secta is how to get back," Robert explained.

"Surely if it was good enough for Anu Set to be dragged back through the vortex hanging on to Alice's legs you could do same…" the President asserted.

Secta got up and began pacing holding his chin. "You're right Ri … I know … look, I'm not hesitating for any reason other than to make sure Kairos is secure."

That caused a ripple of disquiet amongst them. The President formed a steeple with his index fingers under his chin. "Are you worried about Honor?"

Secta stopped pacing, turned and glared at the President, "I'm worried about sabotage Ri."

His statement was unsettling. Since the assassination attempt, none of them envisaged Zen might try to sabotage Kairos.

"It makes sense. Honor is the perfect plant to put an end to OTT. We are a threat to Zen's world domination plans. They've tried to compete with us by sending Anu Set after Alice and failed … if I was Gorrick I'd be looking at destroying Kairos and doing it while Alice and myself are on a mission — that way he would eradicate a trilogy of endothermic feathered vertebrates utilising a singular particle of naturally-occurring crystalline composite."

The President lowered the steeple, frowned and uttered, "I'm sorry Secta I didn't get that."

"Zen would be killing three birds with the one stone," Hope clarified.

"Oh, I see," he said, getting a handle on Secta's warped analogy. "It makes sense … blow Kairos up and trap you and Alice in another dimension … that would certainly put an end to it. So, what should we do?" The President questioned.

"At the moment all our hopes are pinned on Karzoff," Secta said mournfully.

"God help us," Hope grumbled.

"God help him," the President echoed. "He's not just taking on Honor, he's taking on Kew and the might of Zen."

Honor surprised Karzoff by emerging at street level and then hopping into a black Pajero that was waiting for her. When the car pulled out into the traffic, Karzoff looked for a taxi to give chase. He was lucky, one pulled up to let a passenger out and he grabbed it. The cabby was happy to tail the black Pajero up ahead; it added colour to his otherwise mundane day.

"You a gumshoe or sumfin mate?" said the cabby with a cockney accent.

"Afraid so," Karzoff admitted, enjoying playing James Bond.

"Bit odd you being undercover 'enall, what with hair like that," he chuckled.

"The red hair is part of my disguise … now concentrate, I don't want you to lose the Pajero."

"She'll be right Gov, I'm your man for spook work … what is it MI5 or Oceana SS?"

"I'm not at liberty to say," Karzoff said smugly.

They followed the Pajero onto New South Head Road to Rushcutters Bay, where it turned left into New Beach Road.

The driver indicated taking a park on the right side of the road.

"Pull up here," Karzoff ordered.

"Looks like they're going into d'Albora Marinas mate."

The cabby was right. Once the Pajero had angle-parked, Honor and Kew emerged. Karzoff fumbled for his cell phone and snapped a bunch of shots of them crossing the road and entering the Cruising Yacht Club of Australia, beside d'Albora Marinas.

"Takes knowing someone with plenty of dosh to get in there," the cabby said with a snide chuckle.

Karzoff handed him a hundred-dollar bill, "Here, keep the change."

"You sure you wanna stay here wiffout any wheels? Here..." he handed over a business card. "I'll be in the area so ring me if you need picking up, alright?"

"Alright ... yes, I will ... thank you."

"No worries, mate."

Karzoff got out, waited for the cab to move on, and then went and found himself a park bench to wait on. With an excellent view of the Yacht Club and its exit, he sat down and sent the photos to the President.

The President was standing at the elevator chatting to Secta when his phone alerted him to a message. He checked it.

"It's a text from Karzoff ... he's at Rushcutters Bay Park, Honor is in the Cruising Yacht Club ... he sent photos. Well, will you look at that?"

He showed Secta a photo on his phone.

"That's Zanza Kew. Now we know why she wanted the pictures of Kairos," Secta said. "I think you better get him out of there, remember Karzoff killed Anu Set, Zen might well be looking for revenge."

"You think it might be a setup?" the President questioned worriedly.

"I think so."

"I'll ring him right away," he said, concerned.

Karzoff's phone rang; he reached into his pocket but before he could get it, he felt the cold steel of a snub-nose pistol barrel on the back of his neck.

"Hand me the phone, Karzoff."

"You will not shoot me here in broad daylight," Karzoff said bravely.

"Want to bet on it."

Karzoff believed him and handed over the phone. Kew took it and immediately hurled it twenty metres into Rushcutters Bay.

"Now get up, keep your hands in your pockets, and walk towards the Pajero."

"Where is your partner in crime?"

"She's enjoying an aperitif."

"Are you going to kill me?"

"Yes."

"Why?"

"For killing Anu Set," Kew snarled.

As they stepped onto the road to cross, a car roared out from a parking space and hit Kew, knocking him onto the ground without injuring him. Karzoff wasted no time in diving into the back seat of the car. His cockney taxi driver friend trod on the gas.

A flute of champagne in her hand, the summer sun beating down on her face, Honor lounged back in the comfy armchair on the aft deck of the luxurious Sunseeker Manhattan 63 power cruiser, taking in the unobstructed view of Sydney Harbour, including the Opera

House and the Harbour Bridge. It was the prized end mooring at the Cruising Yacht Club; Gorrick wasn't the kind to settle for anything less. Dressed in his weekend casual boating attire, Armani head to toe, Gorrick sank into a chair opposite her and took a sip of champagne.

"You certainly know how to relax," Honor said, making small talk.

"Lifestyle becomes habitual after a while."

"If you can afford it, I expect it would."

He put down his glass on the table between them, removed his sunglasses, closed them, and popped them into the breast pocket of his jacket, folded his fingers together, and then locked eyes with Honor. "I just heard from Kew ... he was hit by a car and Karzoff escaped."

Honor's face paled, and her lips tightened, "Is he—?"

"He's fine, it would take more than that to damage Kew."

Relief broke on her face. It wasn't like her to care for someone, but she did for Kew, and that was even a surprise for her.

"Which leaves us with a dilemma. Oceana now knows you are working with us."

The thought chilled her; she had hoped the deception would have lasted longer than that.

"Zus rendering my usefulness questionable, I presume," she said dispiritedly.

Gorrick let out a small scornful laugh, "I suppose you'd expect that, but you underestimate the extent I value your counsel."

Her thin lips curled. "It is of great comfort to know one is appreciated."

Gorrick picked up his flute and raised it in a toast, "To our success."

Kew arrived sporting a penitent look on his face. He stood in front of Gorrick, "I'm sorry, sir."

"Sit down, Kew, we were just discussing where this leaves us."

Kew pulled up a chair next to Honor. She hadn't seen him looking ruffled before. Dressed immaculately in a navy-blue suit, white shirt, and a pale blue tie, his clothes didn't reflect what he'd been through; only his attitude did: he didn't like to fail, and thus contrition was written all over his face.

CHAPTER 6
PATHOGEN

ALICE KNEW THAT Secta would have received his note. He expected, because of his saliva sample, that a wormhole would soon open to deliver Secta, and he was gambling that it wouldn't be at Rick's apartment.

Sonoko had found Rick's lab access code. There was nothing more they could do at the apartment, so they left.

On the street, Sonoko pointed out all the low-level flying police surveillance drones. The city was so well-covered that few crimes went unnoticed. Then it dawned on Alice that the police would have him on record visiting Rick's apartment twice.

"I know what you're thinking. When Rick is reported missing from work tomorrow, the police will be informed, and they will see you on surveillance footage," Sonoko said.

Alice looked up again while they were strolling along the sidewalk, and he saw a drone swoop over them. "Yeah, the thought has crossed my mind."

"Don't worry. With no immigration record of you entering Japan, they won't find you in the database ... besides, they will have enough on their hands with the pandemic. I want to take the sample to the lab for testing..."

"Mind if I tag along?"

She thought about it for a second. It was now a matter of necessity to trust him. "Okay, it is closed on Sundays, but I have access. We'll catch a Skypod. It will take only twenty minutes to the lab from here."

The pod ride from Hatagaya followed route 431. Sonoko had chosen a dual-seater pod and programmed it to take the most direct route to Shinjuku Chuo Park where Nihon Inc. was located. The Skypod guidance program interfaced with Sonoko's VV and locked onto the desired destination, deducting the fare from her cryptocurrency account.

"How does the pod recognise me?" Alice asked.

"A sensor alerts the system that there are two passengers, and an algorithm charges the one with the VV. Otherwise, it apportions the fare according to the destination."

"Clever. So a VV is an OVVA ... Is it a WiFi connection?"

"Yes, all of Japan is connected with free WiFi."

"Happening."

Elevated above roads and houses, sometimes rising up to twenty stories, the view of Tokyo from the pod was at times spectacular. The lack of traffic congestion on the roads below was most noticeable to Alice.

By 2030, in Japan, fossil fuel transport had been totally replaced by electric vehicles. However, the people preferred an efficient public transport system, so the pod commuter system was built. The fully automated system took only four years to construct. Made of enzyme-bonded plastic and powered by solar energy, it was cost-efficient, faster, cleaner, and more reliable than any other form of transportation. Of course, at the same time, the subway efficiently transported many more passengers underground. But the public preference was for Skypod because the big earthquake of 2035 had trapped and killed thousands of passengers in the Tokyo Metro. In sharp contrast, no harm had befallen any Skypod travellers; the pliant enzyme-bonded plastic rail and pylon supports simply swayed with the tremors.

Alice was astounded by how many drones were in the sky at any one time. "Don't those drones ever crash into one another? It must be a hell of a job controlling them."

"They're fitted with sensors that detect obstructions, and they're powered by an RF frequency."

"What? Broadcasted power?"

"Yes, it is called RPT, which stands for resonant power transfer: the wireless transmission of electricity or energy from a power source to an electrical load without connectors, across an air gap. The basis of a wireless power system involves essentially two coils—a transmitter and a receiver. The transmitter coil is energized by alternating current to generate a magnetic field, which in turn induces a current in the receiver coil."

"What does resonant mean?"

"Resonant frequency RF refers to the frequency at which an object naturally vibrates or rings—much in the same way a tuning fork rings at a particular frequency and can achieve maximum amplitude," Sonoko explained.

"You seem to know a lot about it?"

"It was the subject of my PhD."

Alice saw an aircraft landing at Narita Airport and was fascinated by it. The plane had a long double-decked cylindrical fuselage with long wings upswept at the ends and a V-shaped tail with one huge fan enclosed in cowling. "Check out that wild-looking plane."

"That is an electrical transcontinental aircraft," Sonoko said.

"Electrical?"

"Yes, battery-powered. The entire aircraft skin is made up of solar tiles."

"Fantastic."

The pod was moving silently at thirty kilometres an hour, and then after five minutes, it began to slow. It branched off the main track and then entered a multi-story building sporting a large neon sign that read: Nihon Inc.

As it docked at a platform, the gull-wing doors automatically opened.

"This is our stop, the private platform of Nihon Inc.," Sonoko said, getting out.

Alice looked up the name Nihon on his translator database and found that it meant "Origin of the Sun," which was one of the original names for Japan before it was changed to Nippon.

Sonoko checked them through a security door into the complex that, with aseptic stainless-steel walls, floors, and ceilings, and a lack of any decorations at all, felt overly sterile and austere to Alice.

As they arrived at the end of the corridor, Sonoko walked directly at a stainless-steel wall. Alice panicked and was about to stop her, thinking she might be distracted by reading something on her VV... but the wall sensed her approach, and a doorway opened in it like magic. Amazed by the sensory technology, Alice followed her through.

"You guys trust technology a hell of a lot more than the people of my time. If that door failed to open, you'd have a bleeding nose."

Sonoko chuckled. To her, it went without saying that she trusted technology. Her world thrived on it, and she knew nothing else—of course, it was going to open.

Alice was reminded of how, at the turn of the century, the advent of handheld digital devices had led to total connectivity to the Internet, social media, and portable personal computing. But it was blamed for a massive change in lifestyles, the breakdown of family values, and a decrease in social interaction. With what he had witnessed in 2087, where a world war had destroyed connectivity worldwide, satellites, and all forms of power transmission, society had been reduced to primitive tribalism that struggled to sustain itself. That was the net result of an overdependence on technology. He worried that in 2047, they were heading in that direction.

Alice followed Sonoko into a completely different environment. The laboratory was equipped with a vast array of digital and traditional chemistry paraphernalia: flasks, glass tubing, and Bunsen burners.

"This is where I work. Rick's lab is two up from this one."

Alice cruised around, checking out the gear. "So, what do you mainly do?"

"Testing ... mostly government contract work. We can chemically analyse almost anything here."

"Such as?"

"Well, let's say the health department suspects a contaminant in a certain seafood. Then we would be given the job of certifying it safe or otherwise."

"I see. So would you have tested the water Rick was concerned about?"

"No, the water department checks the Tokyo water supply at least a dozen times a day. As the senior industrial chemist here, Rick had the right to test whatever he felt needed testing. But for the most part, his focal point was high-level contract work."

She opened a device that looked on the outside like a microwave and emptied a small quantity of the powdered remains of Rick onto a small Petri dish inside it, and then closed the door.

"This will give us a readout of the composition of the black dust."

"How long does it take?" Alice asked.

"Thirty minutes."

In another part of the city, a young man staggered down a dark alleyway lined with blue plastic industrial garbage bins. He was moving as if he were drunk. But he wasn't. He bounced off a bin like a pinball, and then his legs gave way, and he toppled over. Crawling on hands and knees with his head down and a long string of saliva dangling from his chin, he desperately tried to compose himself by taking deep breaths, but it didn't help—something was trying to possess him, and he was losing the battle. The pressure inside his head had become so intense that he felt it was going to explode. His heart was pounding as though he had just run a marathon. His VV cut off for the first time in his life, making him feel totally insecure and vulnerable. Then something in his brain told him to raise his head and howl like a wolf at the moon—only he wasn't a wolf, and there was no moon. The whites of his eyes had become bloodshot, his wan complexion cracked into a rictus ... and then the pain and confusion in his mind ceased as quickly as it had begun, replaced by only one instinct, one single desire, one driving force that overrode any other: the need to procreate. He slowly rose to his feet ... he was no longer a well-mannered seventeen-year-old student ... he had transformed into a wild animal.

A massive abnormal overproduction of testosterone had surged through his entire body, overpowering him with hypersexuality and generating an irrepressible predatory urge to copulate. A supercharged beast had been spawned—a beast totally out of control. The only thought in his mind was to find a female, and fast.

Not far from the male student, a twenty-year-old young woman with a shock of long fluorescent purple hair emerged from a Seven Eleven convenience store. She was dressed in an hourglass-shaped red plastic micro mini and wore red pumps. This area was the oldest prefecture of Shinjuku, known for its high-rise apartments, narrow alleyways, and the famous red-light district.

The young woman in the red plastic micro mini was a sex worker. She lived in a tiny apartment in one of the nearby skyscrapers and worked the streets at night.

She staggered as though the heel of her shoe had given way and then leaned against a Skypod pylon to check. The heel was fine, but she still felt dizzy ... it was as though her menstrual period had arrived, but it couldn't have been since she had it only a week ago. Suddenly, her adrenal glands released a massive overdose of testosterone, causing her to lose her rationality and feel seriously disoriented. She tried to access her VV for help, but the neural connection failed for the first time ever.

Her fingers weakened, and she let go of the shopping bag. It dropped onto the pavement, and a bottle of fish sauce smashed inside, leaking out and filling the air with the stench of rotten fish. She put her face in her shaking hands and took deep breaths, confused by the loss of physical and mental control. Just as she was about to lose it, she screamed and then froze, spellbound. After a moment, she slowly lowered her hands ... they were no longer shaking ... whatever had been affecting her had won the battle and taken control. Her eyes grew bloodshot, and a macabre grin broke on her thin, pale face. Blinded by an overwhelming desire, she took a few tentative steps but was unable to keep her balance, so she stopped and kicked off her shoes. Barefoot, she felt more like the animal she had become. This wasn't some driving primal arousal disorder or promiscuity ... it was an insatiable need to breed.

She walked trance-like along the footpath, and other pedestrians passing by observed her as just another half-drunk prostitute making her way home at 11 a.m.—an all-too-familiar scene for them.

Lured like a moth to a flame, she came to an alleyway and entered. The narrow lane was littered with blue plastic industrial garbage bins. When she reached halfway along, a dark figure slowly rose from behind one of the bins. It was the young male student— she was seeking him, attracted by his pheromones.

Like a ferocious animal lurking in its lair, he struck out, and in a flash, dragged her into his den. During the act, his face flushed red— his eyes began to swell and swell. He tilted his head up like a wolf ready to howl at the moon. His bloodshot eyes bulged way outside of his eye sockets ... then his face contorted into a rictus of agony ... two loud pops, and his eyes ruptured, spraying clots of blood and black retinal ink over the girl. He collapsed and lay twitching, dying.

She had absorbed his very life force, which increased her strength to ten times that of a normal person, almost superhuman. Done with him, she irreverently cast him aside, and then rose as though empowered. Her hunger sated, she climbed in behind the bins and used both sets of clothing to form them into a nest.

The alleyway fell silent ... the only evidence of the event was the dead body of the student lying on the ground in a contorted pose, his head resting in a pool of blood. A clawed hand reached out from between two blue rubbish bins, gripped the bloody hair of the dead victim, and unceremoniously dragged him along the ground behind the bins, leaving a trail of blood. She would remain in hiding with the dead student until sundown and then make her escape under the cover of darkness.

CHAPTER 7
CHAA!

CHEMICAL COMPOSITION ANALYSIS, under spectroscopy using magnetic resonance to explore atoms in the molecules of Rick's remains, had registered an unexpected reading. Sonoko then used elementary analysis to confirm the element she had discovered, resulting in verification that it was Propynylidynium: an element not found on Earth.

Alice had nodded off to sleep on a couch in the laboratory. He woke with a start and looked around, confused and quite lost, then remembered where he was and relaxed. After stretching, he rubbed the sleep from his eyes and sat up, feeling refreshed from the short nap.

Wearing a white lab coat over her clothing, her hair up, and her eyes fixed on the hologram output from an electron microscope, Sonoko looked like the archetypal scientist.

"Have I missed anything?" Alice asked.

"You've been asleep for two hours," she said without looking away from the 3-D image. "I didn't want to wake you ... Do you know you snore?"

"No, I was asleep," he joked. He walked over to her and peered over her shoulder at what she was doing. "Anything?"

She looked up at him. "Yes, look at this."

He peered at the 3-D image and yawned. "What am I looking at?"

"See those little black dots?"

"Yes."

"What you're seeing is magnified one hundred thousand times."

"Far out."

"I think those black dots are a rare element called Propynylidynium that is not found on Earth."

"Are you saying it's alien?"

"Do you remember what Rick said in the message to me?" She accessed her VV database. "'I am led to believe by my own recollection that a pathogen has entered my mind through a water sample I touched, and my life is somehow being edited. It's the only way I can explain what is happening to me. Headaches and nosebleeds have come today with brooding, waiting, and knowing that whatever it is living in my mind is biding its time for an opportunity to ambush me.' He could be suggesting this element Propynylidynium is in the water and that it had bound with another element to create a pathogen."

"So if you're right, how did this stuff, propy-whatever it is, get in the water?"

"I don't know, but maybe Doctor Hyashi does. I called him yesterday and left a message. I'll try again."

Viktoria was seated behind her desk in the new OTT reception and looked up when Mal entered through the sliding glass doors with a young lady.

"Hey Vik," Mal announced in his cavalier manner. "Meet Wyetta Walker, Al's sister. She'd like to apply for a job in security. Secta said to bring her to you for an interview. Got time?"

Viktoria smiled. "I always have time for you, Mal. Hey Wyetta, pretty name. Didn't know Al has a sister."

Chewing gum and dressed Goth, Wyetta said, "Neither does he. Anyway, call me Vee."

"Leave Vee here, Mal. I'll get her started on processing. It'll take an hour or so."

"Have you shut down Honor's security clearance and access codes?" the President asked Karzoff.

"Yes, sir, and I sequestered her computers and nullified her access to everything. Her apartment is under surveillance, but she is unlikely to return to it."

The President looked at Secta, seated on his right at the boardroom table.

"I've initiated a lockout on her MCI and programmed an intermittent two-kilohertz tone to be broadcast in one-second bursts every three minutes. It will cause her to have the implant removed," Secta explained.

"Ooo, squealing ... that would drive you round the bend," Hope said with a wry smile.

"It's not meant to torture her, just to ensure she has the mastoid implant removed," Secta clarified.

"Fair enough, but I do like the idea of it causing her some grief, if I might say so ... So, we come to the reason for convening this meeting at such short notice," the President said, scanning the faces of Secta, Professor de Luz, Karzoff, and then Hope. "There are four issues I believe require our immediate attention. Firstly, the question of a replacement for Honor at OTT ... Seeing we now have, shall I say, a more democratic form of governance, I put these issues to you for a vote. I would like to nominate Karzoff as the head of OTT security. Please raise your hand if you are in accord. It will need to be unanimous ... Karzoff, you will abstain."

Uncertain of how the others would react, Karzoff waited anxiously.

Secta and the professor raised their hands, while Hope, remembering some of the more unsavoury times she'd personally spent with Karzoff, hesitated. All eyes were on her.

Images of Karzoff torturing Hope in the safe house flashed through his mind. He wanted the job but was mentally coming to terms with accepting that Hope might choose to vote against him.

She looked Karzoff in the eyes. "I have more reason than any of you not to raise my hand, but I am prepared to accept that when Karzoff tortured me, he was acting under Honor's express orders." As she raised her hand, she added, "I trust I'm making the right decision, Karzoff."

Karzoff let out a sigh of relief and then rose to his feet. "I thank you all for the trust you place in me, and I will not let you down." He was so thrilled and humbled by their belief in him that tears welled up in his eyes. He sat back down, pulled out a handkerchief, and wiped his eyes.

"The next issue is who will take Karzoff's old position, to be his 2 IC. Any recommendations?" the President posed.

Secta sat back in his chair, chewing the end of his HB pencil, and then said confidently, "I submit Miss de Cock."

They all exchanged a look of agreement and raised their arms.

"You're happy with Miss de Cock, are you, Karzoff?" the President asked.

"Yes, sir. She already has level one security clearance, so she can be appointed immediately," Karzoff said confidently.

The President had beaten him to the punch. He was already talking to Miss Vallins. The door opened, and Viktoria de Cock entered, garbed in a beautifully tailored business suit with her blonde hair worn up.

She stopped just inside the door and said gracefully, "You summoned me, sir?"

The President, Karzoff, Secta, and then the Professor rose to their feet with good manners.

"Miss de Cock, you have been nominated to take the vacated position of assistant security agent to the newly appointed senior directorate of OTT security, Karzoff. Will you accept the posting?"

She looked shocked. "Absolutely, sir. Thank you," she said excitedly.

"Good, welcome aboard." He applauded, and the others joined in. "Please take a seat beside Karzoff." He waited for her to sit and then continued, "The third issue is what to do about Fanny Honor?"

Karzoff stood and said, "Sir, I will brief Miss de Cock on the subject, and we will put together a proposal for your consideration regarding this matter." He resumed his seat.

"Good ... Finally, a pressing question we need to resolve ... Black Alice and the issue of whether Secta will abide by his request. What say you on this matter, Secta?"

"Of course, I will follow Alice. We're currently resolving the matter of wormhole targeting using Alice's DNA. Hope?"

Hope stood and explained, "Alice's atomic marker was in the saliva on the page he sent us. Doctor James is now programming the coordinates that will target the wormhole to the exact time and place. We need to avoid a repeat of what happened to Secta on his last mission, where he entered another body ... In this case, it could be Alice."

"Yes, I think it would be more effective if I stayed myself," Secta said with a chuckle.

Hope continued, "The Professor, however, has come up with the means of avoiding that."

"It will still have about a twenty percent risk," the Professor clarified, "however, I'm confident that if I lower the resonance cycle for Secta, his reconstitution on the other side of the wormhole will not clash with Alice's."

"All gobbledygook to me, Professor, I'm afraid, but if you say so. Do we have a go, and if so, can I rest assured of Secta's safety?"

"I think so. As far as the process is concerned, sir, the rest will be up to him and Alice," the Professor submitted.

"Good, when will you be ready?" the President asked.

"In about three hours, sir," Secta affirmed.

"That soon! Fine... How amazing that in only a few hours, you will arrive in Japan in 2047. What wonders will you find there, Secta?"

"I only hope I can help Alice stop whatever it is threatening the world," Secta said gravely.

Hope particularly noted that there was none of Secta's wit or sarcasm attached to his answer; he was deadly serious. She, for one, understood that Alice would never have asked for Secta if he had not considered the situation dire.

Viktoria half-raised her hand for the president's attention, and she got it. "Sir," she said tentatively. "If I might, I'd like to raise the question of Alice's teenage sister, Vee."

The President looked surprised.

Honor was sitting in the reception area of Zen Sydney headquarters, calmly reading a magazine. Gorrick had summoned her for a meeting. Her MCI (mastoid communications implant) suddenly went down and was replaced by a loud, obtrusive two-kilohertz tone that almost knocked her out. She immediately knew what it was and dived for her cell phone, calling Zanza Kew.

""Zanza, it is Honor, yes I know I am here waiting … listen to me … Oceana has sabotaged my MCI, yes a loud tone came through … I zink Secta has programmed it to occur intermittently … oh, probably just to piss me off. I need to haff it extracted do you haff such a facility here? Oh good, I vill vait for you." She put her phone away and sat waiting for the next high-frequency jolt, cursing, "Damn you, Secta!"

After a few minutes, the door to Gorrick's office opened, and he came out.

"Kew called me," he said casually. "I've booked you on level three to have your MCI removed. We'll fit you with our OSCI, a far superior system," he told her. "This is, of course, confirmation that Oceana now considers you public enemy number one. So," he held out his hand to shake, "welcome aboard, Honor. You're no longer a double agent ... You are now a Zen operative."

Her traitor mouth was trying hard not to smile. Just as she reached out to take his hand and shake, her auditory senses were hit by another two-kilohertz blast from her MCI. This time, her knees buckled, and she collapsed.

Gorrick quickly caught her before she hit the ground. He gently laid her on the couch and then called level three on his OSCI. "Send a hospital gurney with an attendant to boardroom reception ... For Agent Honor OSCI refit, yes, she has collapsed."

The scientists gathered in the Kairos control room were anxious. The air was thick with tension, almost palpable. This would be the inaugural use of the new software and hardware to dispatch a traveller through Kairos, and what was more, the first time they would use DNA targeting that had only been developed as a stopgap measure.

Sitting in a chair being prepped by the Professor and Hope, Secta appeared remarkably calm. Doctor James was busy at master control, configuring the pre-launch.

"How are you feeling?" Hope asked Secta.

"Fine, just nervous about arriving in my birthday suit."

"Hopefully, Alice will be in a position to find you something to wear," the Professor suggested with a chuckle.

"Kairos should deposit me right next to him, wherever he is. Let's hope he's not in a restaurant or walking down the main street of Tokyo," Secta chortled light-heartedly.

The door opened for Viktoria and Karzoff to enter.

Viktoria's hand closed on Secta's shoulder, and she said warmly, "Good luck, my dear. Be careful, won't you."

Secta gently tapped her hand on his shoulder. "I'll give it my best shot."

Hope detected, for the first time, that there was more to their relationship than she had originally thought or even considered, and that was a good thing.

Karzoff was busy looking over Robert's shoulder and didn't notice the chemistry between Secta and his new sidekick, Viktoria.

Robert swivelled on his chair to face them and announced, "I'm good to go here."

For the first time, Hope noticed an anxious grimace on Secta's face. "Are you sure you're all right with this, love?" she said warmly, offering him an out.

But there was no way he was going to take it. "Ready to rock," he responded enthusiastically.

Hope had a syringe, tested the contents, and then injected Secta's right arm with the demolecularizing agent. Once finished, she gave him a big loving hug. The Professor gave him a high five, and Viktoria gave him a peck on the cheek.

"Good luck, Secta," Karzoff said kindly.

"Good luck, boss. Don't worry about Kairos, all systems are go," Robert said to instil confidence.

Secta stood up. "Bye all, I'll give your best to Alice."

Just then, the President entered the room. "Secta, I didn't want to miss this ... Is everything set?"

"Yes, we're ready to go," Secta said calmly.

The President shook Secta's hand. "Good luck, my friend."

"Thanks, Ri. Can I bring you back anything from Tokyo 2047?" Secta said jovially.

"Just you and Alice."

"As Alice would say ... Chaa!" Secta said with a wave of his hand and entered the dispatch cubicle.

CHAPTER 8
ELEMENTARY

"I WANT TO know everything she knows about Oceana, everything ... Is that up your alley, Kew?"

"Yes, sir, but there is something that requires your immediate attention. Honor was meeting you to report on the progress of OTT's Kairos project."

"Go on," Gorrick said, sitting back in his armchair and crossing his legs, his mood relaxed by the sound of the waterfall three metres away from his chair, gently bubbling in the hollows of the spacious luxurious office. Behind him was the towering Blue Gum Eucalyptus tree, soaring three stories to the glass skylight ceiling, through which rays of sunlight streamed like ribbons.

"Alice has been dispatched to Tokyo in 2047," Kew said.

"You mean to tell me that thing is up and functioning?" Gorrick grated. Oh, how he hated being beaten to the punch by Oceana.

"Yes, sir ... But as well, he sent back a message to have Secta join him to resolve, quote, 'a terrible pandemic that threatens the world.'"

Gorrick slumped back in his chair, sporting a grimace of defeat. "These people are a lot smarter than we give them credit for... They continually beat us, even when we have good intel... Something needs to be done about that. This Kairos time travel contraption will undoubtedly affect our strategy. When is Secta going after Alice?"

"Honor didn't find that out, and after what happened, they'll probably shut it down so tight we won't be able to find out until after he's gone."

"Honor knows where it's located, yes?"

"What are you thinking, sir?"

"I'm thinking someone needs to go after them."

"That didn't work last time with Anu Set."

"Yes, but that was into the past. This is into the future, where we have Zen operatives to provide assistance."

"Ah, I see... In Japan?"

"Everywhere," Gorrick said emphatically.

"If you're looking for a volunteer, sir."

"I'd expect nothing less of you, Kew," he said, leaning forward in his chair and speaking conspiratorially. "Once Honor is out of surgery, get with her and plan it. But, Kew, I don't want a repeat of what happened with Anu Set, you hear me?"

"Nor do I, sir," Kew said, getting up to leave. "So, my orders are to take out both Alice and Secta?"

"No, what happened last time proved there's value in keeping Secta alive. Alice is the danger man, kill him... And no botch-ups like what happened with Karzoff, understood?"

"Yes, sir."

Kew was content with his orders. This was the opportunity he'd been waiting for. He very much wanted to succeed where his predecessor Anu Set had failed. All he needed was someone on the inside of OTT to send him into the future without the knowledge of the others, someone he could control... And someone who knows the ropes.

Forty-five-year-old Daichi Yamamoto was driving home from Lake Okutama in his driverless SUV, with his kayak strapped to the roof racks. It had been a strange day kayaking alone on the lake.

There had been many putrid dead fish floating in the water, and as he was taking his kayak out of the water, he slipped over and nearly drowned. It took him ages to dry, but he felt sick from gulping down so much of the lake's water.

Driving through the traffic, he was feeling agitated. Out of nowhere, a guy on a motorbike cut him off, forcing his vehicle's sensors to pull his car over sharply. He snapped, turned the auto-drive off, and then burnt rubber, taking off after the biker.

It was dark, and Daichi was working up a sweat. He felt something driving him to get retribution, something more than just road rage. He sighted the bike up ahead, sped up, and weaving in and out of traffic, caught up with the biker and forced him onto the side of the road.

Full of aggression, he skidded to a halt, leapt out of the car, ran over to the biker, who was removing his helmet, wondering what the hell was going on, and proceeded to bash the living daylights out of him.

A motorcycle cop passing by caught sight of Daichi beating up the young biker and quickly pulled over. He climbed off his bike and rushed over to the scene.

Like an out-of-control wild animal, Daichi dropped the biker, who was a mess, and turned on the cop.

A passing police patrol car sighted the fight and screeched to a halt. Two officers got out of the car and ran to the assistance of the motorcycle cop.

They tried to attract Daichi away from the badly beaten motorcycle cop, to Taser him... When they got him clear, the cop with the Taser fired. It was a good shot; the Taser electrode ball hit Daichi in the chest and stuck... The officer turned up the juice, but it had no effect. The second officer quickly drew his Taser and fired. He also got Daichi in the chest... Two Taser balls were enough to demobilise a raging bull, and they were amazed when Daichi continued to stumble towards them like Frankenstein's monster, shaking from the shock of the Tasers but unperturbed.

Bang! The motorcycle cop fired his Glock 19 at Daichi and kneecapped him. But dragging his shattered leg behind him like a wounded wild animal, blood everywhere, Daichi continued to come at the two cops.

The motorcycle cop fired again, and this time took out the other knee, but Daichi just kept on coming, driven on by some kind of blind animal instinct, crawling along the ground with saliva hanging in strings from his snarling mouth like a rabid wolf.

The cop who had fired the first Taser jumped Daichi and, dodging his snapping jaws, managed to cuff his hands behind his back. Daichi's eyes began to swell... Bigger and bigger, ballooning out of the eye sockets. The three cops recoiled from the stricken man. The eyes burst with a spray of blood and tissue. The cops stared in horrified disbelief at Daichi sitting on the ground with both his legs twisted the wrong way, his knees totally shattered, blood and black slime running down his cheeks, strings of thick saliva mixed with blood hanging from his mouth and chin, but still alive... Then, his face froze in a rictus, and Daichi collapsed, dead.

Sonoko couldn't get directly to Doctor Hyashi but managed to set a meeting with him for 6 p.m. at Café Henri. She and Alice were hopeful the doctor might be able to shed some light on what happened with Rick Malone at Lake Okutama.

It was just after 5 p.m. Sonoko tidied up the lab and then dumped the data from the tests she'd completed onto her VV.

"There is a newsflash, twenty more deaths from ruptured eyes. Whatever it is, it is spreading fast," Sonoko said gravely.

Alice was sitting on the edge of a bench, waiting for her to finish packing up. The room wavered, and he had to steady himself from falling. "Whoa! Something's—" When he looked at Sonoko, she was standing frozen, about to say something, her finger pointed at him. A small vortex appeared about a metre from the floor and oscillated...

After a moment, it began to increase in size. Realising what it was, always keen for a prank, Alice picked up a sticky notepad from the benchtop, went over to Sonoko, and began sticking them all over her face and hands, giggling as he did it.

Out of the blue, a person popped out of the vortex and landed with a thump on the floor. Alice stopped plastering Sonoko and looked down at the skinny white naked male battling to cover his private parts.

"Secta! See, I told you... The fall is a bummer, and you still haven't fixed the birthday suit arrival." He peeled Sonoko's white lab coat off her and handed it to Secta. "Don't worry, it'll be a few seconds before she comes back online," Alice said. "Boy, am I glad to see you."

Secta struggled to his feet, took the dustcoat from Alice, and slipped it on. "Ah, that's better. So, where are we, Alice?"

"We're in the lab of Doctor Sonoko Tanaka here. It's a chemical stroke drug company called Nihon Inc. She's some sort of industrial chemist. We were running tests on the residue of a body I found when I arrived. I'll fill you in on it in a minute, but first, in about five seconds, I'll have some explaining to do to her."

He was spot on; the vortex closed, and Sonoko immediately sprang to life. She began frantically pulling the sticky notes off her face. "Argh! Did you do this? You—"

Alice and Secta were cracking up. Sonoko realised Secta was there, wearing her dustcoat, and she froze, this time remaining conscious.

"Who are you?" she asked politely.

Secta approached her with an extended hand to shake. "I'm Doctor Secta ... Alice summoned me from the past to give you a hand."

"He's the guy I figured we needed to solve this thing. He's a genius."

They shook hands.

"Sorry I had to borrow your lab coat; the time travel process removes one's clothing."

"He arrived naked; lucky you missed it," Al joked.

It took the next half an hour of explaining to bring Secta up to speed and for him to absorb the spectrographic analysis Sonoko had completed of Malone's remains. He knew the element Propynylidynium and agreed it was extra-terrestrial. There wasn't much more they could do until they had questioned Doctor Hyashi. Sonoko knew of a department store nearby where they could stop to fit out Secta with some clothes, so they left the lab.

A short Skypod ride took them to the department store. Secta was in his element in the pod, surrounded by all the technology Japan lived and breathed. The four-seater pod stopped at an off-ramp after the short five-minute ride. The gull-wing door lifted automatically, and Sonoko climbed out onto the enclosed platform at the entrance to the store.

The interior of the department store was something to behold— for Secta, anyway. There were aisles and aisles of every kind of item imaginable for sale, and not a salesperson or attendant in sight. If an item were selected to buy, the cost would simply be immediately deducted from the buyer's crypto credit account via their VV. The application of implant technology delighted Secta.

As soon as he had the chance, Alice pulled Secta aside and admitted that he hadn't let on to Sonoko that his translator allowed him to speak and understand Japanese. Experience had taught him to keep that benefit up their sleeve for now. Fitted with one as well, Secta agreed.

Checking himself in a mirror, Secta looked quite dapper threaded up in the trendy attire of the time. A grey lightweight suit produced from a fabric neither Secta nor Alice could identify: a sort of cross between linen and a plastic weave. When Secta checked the label, he was impressed to find the fabric was called muscle fibre, which consisted of an exoskeleton of electro-active fabric that was light, durable, strong, self-cleaning, and never needed to be pressed. Worn over a light white T-shirt of similar fabric, the suit coat was reminiscent of the 1960s with its Nehru collar. The major difference was that it sealed closed at the front without buttons or Velcro because the fabric was magnetised.

They arrived at Café Henri a little late and found Dr Hyashi holding a table. He was a small man of around forty, with a sour look on his round face. His good manners had him stand to receive them. Despite his dour looks, he was quite affable.

The terrible news of Rick's death shocked him. Speaking in Japanese, Sonoko had to appeal to his friendship with Rick to keep him at the meeting—once he'd learned of Rick's demise, he wanted to leave, figuring it best left to the police. Sonoko promised they would keep his name out of it to protect his reputation. She convinced him to give them an account of the Okutama fishing venture with Rick. He acquiesced and reiterated the story about the tiny meteorite and how Rick had taken a sample of lake water and two dead fish to test because he believed the meteorite was responsible for the fish kill.

When Alice heard that the eyes of the fish had ruptured in the same way Rick's had, he was certain the presence of Propynylidynium in Rick's ashes was enough evidence that the meteor was indeed the culprit. But Doctor Hyashi wouldn't agree. He told them that in his authoritative position with the Chemical division of a large international company responsible for advising the Japanese Government and the Water Board on such matters, he had assured them that the fish kill in Lake Okutama was in no way related to the current outbreak of the unknown virus.

Secta asked if he'd told them about the meteorite, and he admitted he hadn't. When Alice asked why, he claimed that, in his opinion, it was irrelevant and in no way associated.

Secta wasn't satisfied with his rationale; he felt Hyashi was hiding something.

The meeting concluded. Hyashi stood and bowed while presenting his business card to Sonoko, held in both hands. She graciously accepted the business card, and he departed.

Alice and Secta were in total agreement. "I'm not sold on his blag," Alice got in first to say. "This thing about the meteorite is seriously suspect."

"His qualified opinion seems to lack any qualified research. I think he's trying to shelve the incident for some reason... There's more to this than meets the eye," Secta claimed.

"What do you think, Sonoko?" Alice asked.

"I don't know, Alice. He certainly didn't react to my test results."

"But he did react when you told him Rick had died from eye rupture," Secta posited.

"Why wouldn't he want to investigate the death of his buddy, especially dying the same way the fish had? I don't get it. How could the authorities not relate the Lake Okutama incident to the pathogen?" Alice argued.

"Because they don't want to," Secta said, grasping his chin with his hand.

"What do you mean by that, Doctor Secta?" Sonoko asked.

"Just call me Secta... Maybe the authorities are trying to contain panic. For example, if it were known there was a pathogen in the Tokyo water supply, hysteria would almost certainly break out. I mean, it will anyway, eventually, but for now, they might be trying to buy time to deal with it by containing the truth."

"Doctor Hyashi will surely inform the police of Rick's death," Sonoko said glumly.

That sparked a thought for Alice. "Would my fingerprints be on an international security database, Secta?"

"I don't think so unless you have a misdemeanour you haven't mentioned. Why?"

"Because they'll be all over Rick's apartment like a cheap suit. Next thing, I'll have the cops on my hammer ... especially if they determine the prints belong to Black Alice. Sonoko checked me on her OVVA database and found out that I'm a time traveller attached to OTT... How's that?"

"Ah, so the OVVA is known as VV... It stinks of Honor... Oh, that's right, you don't know. The day after you departed, we ran a test on Kairos for the President. Honor was there and tried to take photos. When she realised they failed to come out because Robert had generated a digital shield around the facility to prevent photos from being taken, she blew her stack—I suppose you could say it was the last straw—she felt humiliated at not being trusted to take pictures and stormed out. Suspecting her, the President immediately put Karzoff on her tail."

"This is even after the photo I took of her with Kew?"

"Yes, Karzoff saw her meet up with Kew, waiting for her in a car outside Oceana, and then followed them to Rushcutters Bay. While spying on them going into the Royal Motor Yacht Club there, Kew snuck up behind Karzoff and tried to bump him off. Karzoff got away but with proof Honor is a double agent. The President immediately ordered her cut off, and she was promoted to public enemy number one. As a result, I sabotaged her implant with a high-pitched tone to force her to have it removed, which was fun. So, with her now officially a Zen agent, she would have almost certainly tried to sabotage OTT, and that would mean exposing you—hence publishing your digital profile on the net. We'll be able to fix that once we return."

"Fine, but that doesn't help me now... So, therefore, you'd expect her to fill Zen in on all she knows about Kairos? Plus, she will have told them I'm on a mission and where? Did she see the note I sent you?"

"Yes, she did."

"So we can assume Gorrick knows all about you coming here, and he will be sending someone after us, if he hasn't already, like he did with Anu Set on the Jerusalem mission. I'd put my money on it being Kew."

"Well deduced, Alice. You'd make an excellent detective," Secta admitted. "Oh, by the way, your sister Vee has applied for a job with Oceana security."

"I don't think I have a sister, mate," Alice said with a frown. "She'd be an imposter."

"They'll put her through all the security rigors; we'll find out."

Sonoko was listening intently to the conversation but struggling to grasp it. They were speaking fast and using words with an Aussie accent that made it difficult for her. She glanced at the business card in her hand and said, "Did you mention Zen, Dr Secta?"

"Yes ... but I didn't mean the Buddhist religion," he said dismissively.

"Zen Corporation," she said knowingly. She flashed the business card at him. "Doctor Hyashi's business card states he is the Senior Research Scientist for Biomechatronics Inc, a division of Zen Corporation. I thought maybe it might be the same Zen."

Secta took the card, read it, and grimaced. "If this is the same Zen Corporation, then it would certainly explain why this is being kept under wraps." He showed it to Alice.

"That's their ten-point star logo, all right... So, they're probably behind this. I can't believe it. When will they ever give up?" Alice complained. "If you're right, Secta, this could get pretty tough. You going to be able to handle it, mate?"

"I don't think we have much choice in the matter, Alice. By the way, have you thought about the fact that if we went to Sydney right now, we could meet up with ourselves, provided we're there, of course?"

"What do you mean?"

"In this time travel instance, we already exist elsewhere, albeit much older."

"Oh, I see... So if we contacted us, maybe we'd know how we solved this," Alice suggested.

"But we haven't solved it yet."

"Now you're doing my head in, mate," Alice complained, finding the paradoxes of time travel difficult to grasp.

CHAPTER 9
THE FUTURE

IN A DARK alleyway, out of sight on the ground behind two blue industrial rubbish bins, was a black shadow reminiscent of a police forensics chalk outline of a body at a crime scene. The dark shadow was all that remained of the young male student whose eyes had ruptured after inseminating the young prostitute.

Her name was Mirai, which in Japanese means 'the future.' Safely back in her small apartment, she had a deranged look in her eyes. She was sitting on the tiny kitchen floor, blood all over her face and dripping from her chin, feasting on a fresh liver—the liver she had removed from the student in the alleyway.

And she wasn't the only pregnant female doing exactly that. All over Tokyo, young women all under the age of thirty, after having been inseminated, were in hiding. It was similar to how a female Black Widow spider goes to ground after killing the male that had impregnated her. In the case of these women, they had all extracted the liver from the body of the male they had killed after fertilising them. The liver would be consumed as sustenance for the accelerated growth of their foetus. Chemically programmed, none of the impregnated women would leave their lair throughout the entire gestation period.

"Where would Rick keep his test results?" Secta asked Sonoko as they left the café.

"On his computer."

"Can you access it for the results of the fish and water tests?"

"Yes, I have the access code. But I cannot do it remotely; we will need to return to the lab."

She led them to the Skypod platform where they joined a queue.

"What are you thinking?" Alice asked Secta.

"I think the meteorite was the delivery mechanism for the pathogen ... and I don't think it was natural."

"Do you think it was man-made?" Sonoko asked.

"Yes, or alien ... and I'm expecting Rick's test results to confirm that."

After a short wait, they boarded a four-seater pod, and Sonoko programmed it to take them to the industrial estate. The pod had a holographic display of the current news, and even though it was in Japanese, both Secta and Alice understood that the pandemic was spreading through Tokyo like wildfire. The situation had become so grim that the Japanese Government was contemplating enforcing martial law. A spokesman from the Nippon Health Department warned they were in the process of placing the entire city under lockdown until the virus could be identified and dealt with. All flights in and out of Tokyo had been cancelled, as well as ships, trains, Skypods, cars, trucks, and any other form of transportation. Self-isolation for all citizens was ordered. They had the previous experience of the COVID-19 pandemic in 2020, which had spread around the world, killing millions and lasting three years. It had crippled economies. The death toll in Tokyo this time had already reached two thousand and was rising. Hospitals had been inundated with patients carrying symptoms. The supporting live broadcast images were terrifying: shots of individuals sprawled out in the street in a pool of blood with black holes where their eyes had been.

There were angry and frightened relatives of victims being forcefully restrained by the police from approaching their dead loved ones. Hysteria had broken out all over Tokyo. Shops and businesses were closed, and panic buying in supermarkets had left the shelves bare. Now there was looting and rioting.

The Government official ordered, "If you know someone with any of the following symptoms, you must report them immediately to the nearest crisis centre: intolerable headache, fever, nosebleed, loss of reasoning, sudden disorientation, or sudden loss of VV signal. There is a crisis centre in every prefecture."

"This pandemic is spreading fast," Alice told Sonoko, still acting ignorant to understanding the language.

"Yes, the government is voting to enforce martial law. All of Tokyo is now under strict quarantine, there is no way in or out ... it is very serious, over two thousand dead, and more dying every minute," she said gravely.

Alice sensed her distress and took her hand. "Do they know anything more about the pathogen?"

"No," she wiped tears from her eyes. "They know very little. The man talking from Nippon Health Department is my uncle."

"Then it is important you contact him. We are going to need his influence to get through all the red tape to beat this thing," Secta said earnestly.

Because there was no sign of Doctor Rick Malone, who had been reported missing by the landlord of his apartment and Doctor Hyashi, police forensics were sweeping Rick's apartment with DNA and fingerprint detectors. Both devices had the ability to automatically match findings on IAFIS, the Integrated Automated Fingerprint and DNA Identification System. The system took only seconds to find a match on the international database. The result of the scanned set of prints found was that they belonged to an Australian national named Black Alice, who, according to his birthdate, would be aged over sixty. The investigating officer from the Tokyo Metropolitan Police force, Detective Inspector Atomu Shintaro, acted immediately upon the data by contacting the Department of Immigration, on his VV, to determine the arrival date of Black Alice in Japan. The prints made Black Alice a witness in the missing person's investigation.

DI Shintaro didn't expect to get a negative result from Immigration: no arrival was registered. He immediately suspected that Black Alice had arrived in Japan under a phoney passport and was therefore elevated to the prime suspect in Malone's murder. He obtained a photograph of Alice from thirty years ago—there was nothing current—and sent it to the police graphic art department for them to age to sixty. Once it was done, it was circulated to all field operatives. Shintaro then put out an APB for Alice's arrest.

DI Shintaro suspected Doctor Malone had been murdered, and it looked like a hit. He knew from his Interpol profile that Alice was a former agent of the Oceana Government, and therefore suspected it could very well be a case of international industrial espionage.

At a luxury modern home in Rose Bay on the foreshore of Sydney Harbour, an attractive woman with blonde hair, in her mid-thirties and dressed smartly in a grey business suit, was saying goodbye to her eight-year-old daughter Aurora. Standing next to the BMW parked on the sloping driveway to the house, she hugged the pretty blonde-haired child. Looking on and smiling was her Filipina au pair, Mira.

Wife of Doctor Robert James, head physicist at OTT, Dianne James was leaving for her Edgecliff office, not far from Rose Bay. A partner in the law firm Turner, James, and Green, she specialised in intellectual property law.

Dianne released Aurora to Mira, got into her BMW, and drove off past a black Pajero parked on the opposite side of the road with two occupants.

Zanza Kew hopped out of the Pajero and walked over to Mira, who was leading Aurora by the hand back into the house.

"Excuse me, ma'am, can you help me please? I'm looking for Mrs James," Kew said cordially.

The thirty-year-old Filipina clutched the little girl close to her and said defensively, "I'm sorry, sir ... she just left."

"Oh, okay, was that her car leaving for the office?" Kew asked.

"Yes, sir."

"I have a package for her, maybe I can leave it here with you. Can you sign for it?"

"Yes, sir."

"Okay, follow me, and I'll give it to you."

Mira took Aurora into her arms and followed Kew to the rear of the Pajero parked in the quiet street. Kew pressed a remote, and the rear hatch opened. Mira could see a woman sitting in the passenger seat inside. When Mira came close enough to the hatch, Kew pounced and covered her nose and mouth with a cloth containing chloroform. Mira panicked, and the more she panicked, the deeper her breaths and the more chloroform she inhaled. Her legs buckled.

Honor was out of the vehicle and at the rear in time to take Aurora from Mira's weakening arms. Kew removed the cloth from Mira's face and was about to give it a fresh dose of chloroform for Aurora when Honor stopped him.

"No, she is calm," she leaned down to Aurora. "Are you okay, Aurora? We are the police, and we will take you to your mother. Mira is in trouble for something she did in the Philippines, so we had to arrest her. Do you understand?"

"Yes," the little girl squawked, unsure.

Kew loaded Mira into the rear of the Pajero and shut the hatch. Honor got into the rear seat with Aurora and secured her seatbelt. Kew climbed in behind the wheel.

It had been a quick and effective abduction. The street was so quiet none of the neighbours had even noticed.

Robert James was alone in the Kairos control room when he received a call on his cellphone from the kidnappers. His face paled, and he fought back panic when he learned if he failed to do what would be asked of him or spoke to anyone, both Aurora and Mira would be killed. Without hesitation, he agreed and asked for the demand.

"You will use Kairos to send someone safely after Black Alice and Doctor Secta."

"How do you know about that?"

"It is not for you to ask questions. You do as you're told ... you understand?" the male voice said harshly.

There was a rustle on the phone as though it was changing hands.

"Daddy?"

Robert jumped out of his chair at the sound of his daughter's voice.

"Aurora, darling ... yes ... I'm here, are you alright, love?"

"Yes, daddy. I want to go home."

"Okay, darling ... you will—"

He was cut off by Kew. "If you want to hear your daughter's voice again, James, then you will do exactly as I say ... do I make myself perfectly clear?"

Robert's heart sank with confirmation this was very real. His daughter's life was being threatened, and only he could save her. "Yes, yes, I will do anything ... just don't hurt her ... them ... please," he implored. "But I've got to tell you ... I can't send anyone through Kairos on my own. There is a process ... um, the subject needs to be injected with a specific formula to be dematerialized first. I only operate the teleporter ... I have nothing to do with the subject's preparation process."

"Who does?" Kew snapped.

"Doctor Hope or Professor de Luz."

The call terminated.

"Hello ... hello?" Robert slipped his phone into his pocket and then sank into his chair dejected. There was nothing he could do but wait. He couldn't even tell his wife. He knew, as a mother and a lawyer, she wouldn't be capable of sitting on her hands and waiting. She would go directly to the police, and he believed that would be putting his daughter's life in danger.

Mal Function came out of the Coogee beach surf feeling refreshed. The swim had done him the world of good, relieving the hangover he'd contracted from a big night out drinking the previous night. With the late morning sun beating down on him, drying the saltwater from his freckly skin, he jogged over the warm sand to where his towel was waiting.

He noticed that a stunning girl with long black hair in a striking red string bikini sunbaking nearby, reading a book, was wearing a watch.

"Hey, love," he said pleasantly, "can you tell us the time, please?"

The thought struck him that she was so pretty and shapely she might be a model.

"That's got to be the worst pick-up line I've ever heard," she asserted.

He gave her a cool glance. "It would if it wasn't true ... you are wearing a watch ... which, I might add, will leave an impression on your skin that might not be so photogenic."

"Oh," she sounded disappointed and quickly checked her wristwatch. "It's, um, eleven forty-five ... sorry ... it's just ... well, thanks," she said apologetically, removing her watch.

Mal slipped his shorts over his budgie-smugglers, threw on a T-shirt, picked up his thongs, and shook the sand off his beach towel, ready to go. But he couldn't resist getting in the last word with the pretty girl. He ambled over to her.

"Are you from here ... Sydney?"

"No, Melbourne," she said in his shadow, and acting a little self-conscious.

"There's a club in town called The Jungle Bar. I'm performing there tonight at ten. What's your name, and I'll leave it on the door in case you feel like steppin' out."

"Geez, you've done that before ... very smooth," she purred.

It was then he realised she was a little more mature than he first thought, and that made her even more intriguing.

"Plenty of times."

"Kris Fisher," she offered up with a gentle smile.

He shot her an air kiss and then trudged off on the yellow sand headed for the promenade.

CHAPTER 10
TIKAD

DOCTOR HOPE WAS seated at a round redwood table under a big green beach parasol on the balcony of her penthouse apartment overlooking Coogee Beach, reading an OTT dossier when the intercom sounded. Dressed casually in blue baggy denim shorts and a white midriff top, with her long blonde hair worn up, she picked up the remote for the intercom from beside her cell phone on the table.

"That you, Mal?"

"Howdy Ho Doc! It is but moi!"

She chuckled at his habitual exuberance. "Coffee's ready, come on up."

She pressed the remote to open the lobby entrance door and to give him access to the elevator. It also unlatched the front door of the apartment.

The coffee was brewed, so she went to the kitchen, popped the plunger coffee pot onto a serving tray along with two mugs, packets of Stevia, and a plate of homemade Anzac biscuits, and then carried it out onto the palatial balcony. She filled the two mugs with coffee and was reclining in her chair when Mal arrived.

"Hey," he announced in high spirits, reached down, and gave her a peck on the cheek.

He flung his towel over the back of the chair and sat down.

"How was the water?" she asked.

"Magic, thoroughly recommended after a night of such magnitude."

She handed him a mug of coffee. "You had a gig last night?"

"Yeah, a private party over the north side ... too much bubbly."

He took a sip of black coffee and snatched a biscuit from the plate. "Any news of Alice?" he said, half muffled by the biscuit in his mouth.

"There's plenty of news to tell you ... Alice is in Tokyo."

Mal chomped up the biscuit and then swallowed it with a surprised gulp. "Tokyo? Hmm, nice biscuit."

"Made them myself ... Yeah, in 2047... we were testing Kairos, and it opened of its own accord, so Alice decided to enter the wormhole to find out why."

Mal's face froze with astonishment. "2047... Tokyo... far out! Opening of its own?"

"Yes ... we're still not sure why. So then Al sent back a message to us asking for Secta to join him to help solve a terrible pandemic sweeping Japan."

"A what?"

"A contagion ... a plague."

"So did he?"

"Yes, Secta entered Kairos yesterday ... and there's more ... Honor was finally found out ... she's a double agent," she said with her eyes narrowed, like she'd known it all along—well, at least she had suspected it.

"You're kidding me ... playing both sides, eh? A switch hitter ... always reckoned she was suss. So, what happened?"

"She's been elevated to Oceana enemy numero uno. She's working for Zen."

"Those bastards ... Karzoff take her place?"

"Yes, and Viktoria."

"Cool, she deserves it. You sure Karzoff is kosher?"

"Yes, Zanza Kew tried to kill him."

"What! I see, so that at least proved he's not on their side."

Hope's cell phone rang. She picked it up from the table, checked the ID, and looked at Mal, surprised. "Speak of the devil, it's Honor!"

"Hello," she answered tentatively and then put it on loudspeaker.

"Doctor Hope, have I interrupted you?"

"Why would that matter to you?" she said bluntly. "What do you want, Honor?"

"I ... I did not know who else to turn to. I have been set up. Ze accusations against me are false."

"That's better left for the authorities to determine, not me."

"I was just hoping to get some support from you."

"What on Earth would give you that idea, Honor?"

Mal got up and wandered over to the balcony balustrade to take in the stunning view of Coogee beach in the midday sun. The ocean was azure blue and sparkling under the cloudless sky—people were sunbathing, swimming, riding surfboards: an idyllic Sydney summer's day. He noticed a drone about one hundred and fifty metres up in the air, flying in his direction. It was a bigger drone than he'd seen before, and the thought struck him how dangerous military drones must be, being so silent. They could easily stealthily creep up with ease on an unsuspecting target.

Still on the phone, Hope got up from her seat and headed for Mal at the balcony rail.

"Yes, I'm going to the balcony rail now. What do you want me to look at?" In reaching Mal, she pulled a quizzical face at him, to the phone.

Mal figured she was confused by Honor's rhetoric.

"Do you see ze TIKAD drone hovering off your balcony?" Honor said slowly ... deliberately.

Hope looked at the drone, then at Mal, then they both looked sharply back at the drone that was now hovering only twenty metres from them, just as Honor had described.

"Yes," Hope replied tentatively, her brow wrinkled.

"Do you see ze camera on its underbelly?"

"Yes ... what's this about, Honor?" Hope growled angrily.

Honor snapped back, "Shut up and listen very carefully! Beside ze camera, which is feeding me live vision of you ... is slung a semi-automatic handgun. If I wish, I could shoot you and Mal Function dead right now ... if you move, I will shoot. To demonstrate..."

Bang! A puff of smoke came from the gun barrel on the drone, and the coffee pot on the table exploded.

"Jesus!" Mal shouted, ducking.

"Zat was a warning shot. Now do as I tell you, or so help me, I will not hesitate to shoot both of you dead."

Hope was shaking so much she had to hand the phone to Mal.

"What do you want, bitch?" Mal snarled into the phone through gritted teeth.

The intercom sounded.

"Press ze remote to permit entry ... now!" Honor shrieked.

Mal nodded to Hope.

She went over to the table and pressed the remote.

"Hope, return to the balcony. Put ze phone on ze ground next to your feet, Mal."

They did as they were instructed.

"Now, both of you stand with your back to ze drone, with your hands gripping ze rail behind you."

They did as they were told.

Two men, brandishing guns and wearing black balaclavas, burst into the apartment and rushed out onto the balcony. They stopped, with guns trained on Mal and Hope, and one of them ordered harshly, "Hold your wrists together in front of you to be cuffed!"

They obliged.

"What is this?" Mal growled.

The second man holstered his pistol, pulled two pairs of handcuffs out of the pocket of his hoodie, moved in, and then quickly cuffed Hope's hands together. As he went to cuff Mal, he was surprised by Mal throwing his arm around his throat, turning him, and using him as a shield against the other man with his gun on him.

Bang! A shot rang out from the drone. Mal's knees buckled, and to Hope's horror, he went down. The hooded assailant with the gun grabbed hold of Hope. "Leave him," he barked at the other guy. "He's no use to us."

"You bastard, don't leave him bleeding like that on the floor," Hope squealed.

"Shut up!" He bent down, snatched up Hope's phone from the floor, and said to Honor, "All done here, good shooting."

"You haff no idea how much I enjoyed it," Honor said.

Kew and his accomplice whisked Hope out of the apartment.

The drone banked and flew off, leaving Mal on the balcony floor to bleed out from the bullet wound in his back.

Sitting at the Kairos console, wringing his hands, Robert James had been on the edge of his seat for hours, waiting for a follow-up call from the kidnappers. When his cell phone eventually rang, the jolt almost ejected him from his chair.

"Hello?" he said frantically, sitting forward.

"This is what is going to take place," the voice at the other end said. "You're going to prep Kairos for a mission that will launch at exactly sixteen hundred hours today. You will tell no-one, and you will permit no-one access to the control other than myself. You will program Kairos to send me to the same coordinates as Secta. If anything happens to counter this, your child will suffer. Do you understand?"

"Yes, yes ... but I told you before ... the traveller needs to be—"

Kew cut him off. "That has been arranged. Sixteen hundred hours."

"If I do this, when will my daughter be returned? Hello—"

The call had been terminated. Robert hadn't really expected an answer. He got to work programming Kairos.

It would be relatively easy for Kew to enter the Kairos facility, having Hope's security clearance. However, getting past the vast array of wireless CCTV cameras strategically positioned about OTT presented a much greater challenge for him. But his training as an agent provided him with the answer: the obligatory spy equipment of the day—a lithium battery-powered, handheld UV90 CCTV camera, UHF, RFID, VHF professional jammer.

Kew and his offsider escorted Hope into the facility, and just in case he missed a camera, Kew was wearing a facial disguise, which was Honor's handiwork.

It went smoothly, and they soon entered the control room. When Hope entered, it was three forty-five, and Robert was waiting after completing the prep sequence for Kairos. Right behind her, Kew quickly stepped aside and motioned to the guy following him.

"This man is armed, and he will shoot if any of you make a false move. Where is the formula, Hope?" Kew ordered.

His accomplice, a smaller man than Kew, his hand in his pocket obviously holding a pistol, sat on a stool with his beady black eyes trained on Hope and Robert.

"It is kept in the RX refrigerator through the door beside the cubicle," Hope said.

"Okay, I'll go with you ... James, is everything prepped?" Robert nodded nervously, his eyes flashing on the man on the stool.

Hope led Kew inside the cold room and then returned a moment later, holding a vial and a syringe.

"Get your goon off the stool and sit on it," Hope said maliciously, not intimidated by them.

Kew ignored her bravado, removed his black flak jacket, and then gestured for his buddy to get off the stool. He took his place and rolled up his sleeve.

Hope glanced at the tattoo on his bicep, a screaming skull impaled on a dagger.

"Before you jab me," Kew said bullishly, "We're holding James's eight-year-old daughter. If anything goes wrong, my buddy over there will trigger a remote, and little Aurora will meet her maker ... and then he will shoot both of you. Is this the correct formula? Check it, James."

Robert got up and went over to them. Hope handed him the vial. He checked the label. "Yes, it's correct."

Kew presented his tattooed bicep to Hope, "Okay, shoot me up."

"Before that happens, when do I get my daughter back?" Robert questioned nervously.

"Once my associate here is satisfied that I've been safely dispatched. Give me the phone."

His associate pulled a phone from his pocket and handed it over. Kew dialled.

"Hi yes, everything is go ... I'll hand you over to my assistant, and once he's satisfied, you can make arrangements with James for him to collect his kid and the maid ... Okay, I will." He handed the phone back to his partner in crime.

Cool-headed considering the risk he was taking, Kew said, "Let's get this show on the road."

"Remove all of your clothing, they won't pass through the wormhole."

Kew wasn't at all shy and stripped down. Hope saw there were a number of Satanic tattoos on his chest.

Robert quickly rechecked the telemetry on the launch sequence, and once satisfied, he announced firmly, "Countdown initiated."

Hope withdrew the needle from Kew's bicep and then led him to the cubicle and locked him inside.

Left on his own with the noise of the apparatus increasing along with the stress level, Kew's buddy began to fidget nervously. With a patina of sweat breaking on his forehead, he pulled his pistol and aimed it at Robert's back for Hope to see. A whirring sound began to oscillate, climbing in pitch until it flattened out at an uncomfortable level for him. He nervously glanced across to the cubicle window and Kew inside, then, in the blink of an eye, Kew disappeared.

"He's gone!" he almost yelled in a panic, waving the pistol about.

"Calm down, he's on his way to the future," Hope snarled.

The noise wound down.

Robert flicked a few switches on the console, and the room fell silent.

"That it?" The man with the gun snapped, still looking uncomfortable.

"Yes, he's gone ... you can tell Honor now, she's on the phone waiting, remember?" Hope said facetiously.

He raised the phone, "It's me, Kew's gone ... yes, I suppose it went right, how would I know, I'm not a scientist. Okay, I'll put him on." He handed the cell phone to Robert.

"Hello Honor, I was told you'll make the arrangements for the return of my daughter now that I've done my part." He switched the phone to speaker for Hope to hear.

"After our man has safely left ze premises, I vill contact you to make ze arrangements."

The call ended, and Robert handed the phone back to the man with the gun. He put it back in his pocket and, keeping the gun trained on them, carefully picked up Kew's clothes. He then backed out through the door. Once he had gone, Hope dived for her phone.

"What are you doing?" Robert snapped.

"Calling Karzoff."

Robert jumped up, snatched the phone out of her hand, and stopped the call.

"If any move is made, I was warned my daughter would be harmed. I don't trust Honor, please, Hope ... leave it be until I have her and Mira, the au pair, safe and sound."

Hope nodded slowly; she understood.

CHAPTER 11
THUNDERSTRUCK

SENIOR INSPECTOR HYUNBO Kim of the International Division of Interpol entered the office of DI Shintaro at Tokyo Metropolitan Police Headquarters. Though asked in English by Shintaro's desk sergeant to take a seat, Kim, a small man in his thirties with slicked-back hair and wearing a tailored blue suit, remained standing. When offered a coffee, he glared stonily at the young female sergeant and shook his head ever so slightly. Despite his reputation for ruthlessness and bad manners preceding him, experiencing Kim's rudeness in person left the sergeant noticeably rattled.

After a few gruelling minutes in the same room as the imposing man, she felt relieved when Shintaro asked over her VV to usher Inspector Kim into his office. As Kim was a Korean national, both men were forced to use English to communicate.

Shintaro offered him a respectful bow of his head, but Kim snubbed the formality and took a seat in the small lounge area designated for meetings in the modestly decorated office. Shintaro, an affable and well-mannered man with a rugged appearance and a broad face that, unusually for a cop, regarded the world with considerable amusement, ignored Kim's ill-mannered jibe and moved from behind his desk to sit across from him.

"Did you want coffee or tea, Kim-san?" Shintaro inquired politely.

Kim ignored the question and snarled, "I'm sure by now you have researched Black Alice and found out he must be over sixty years of age."

"Yes, but anything is possible in this day and age."

"We have more information in our database about him than you have access to. That's why I was requested to join your investigation."

"So desu ne ... our intelligence suggests he is an agent of Oceana. Is that true? What kind of threat can a sixty-year-old man nearing retirement pose?"

"The answer is not multiple choice, Shintaro," he barked arrogantly. "Black Alice is a time traveller and a founding member of Oceana Time Travel, or OTT. There is an international directive for his arrest."

"On what charge?"

"Murder."

"Murder?" Shintaro said, stunned. "And who made the charge?"

"You know I cannot disclose that ... let's just say it's a very powerful global corporation."

"So, that explains why there is no record of his entry into Japan. But we have no evidence linking Black Alice to the death of Doctor Malone. In fact, it seems more likely that Malone was one of the first to be infected by the current virus sweeping the city."

"Our intelligence suggests that the virus was probably released in Tokyo by Black Alice, but not the same Black Alice."

"Aso desu ne... But why? And what do you mean by 'not the same Black Alice'?" he asked, surprised.

Kim gave him a cool glance. "While Black Alice is here, he is also in Sydney. I suspect the Black Alice here is from a different time and is not sixty years old."

"That is astonishing ... is it even possible?"

"That's what I'm here to determine. What else do we know about this virus?"

Shintaro proceeded to share all the information he had on the contagion—how it seemed to only affect men and how they died in two different ways. If they were over thirty, their eyes would rupture within twenty-four hours of contracting the virus. If they were younger than thirty, the infected men would be driven by an insatiable desire to rape young women. After inseminating the victim, their eyes would rupture, and they would die in agony.

"What happens to the women?" Kim inquired.

"We haven't been able to determine that yet, but there have been no reported fatalities."

"And what did the chemical analysis of the remains of these male bodies reveal?"

"Nothing. After the eyes rupture, the bodies seem to internally combust, leaving only dust," Shintaro explained.

"And what about the analysis of the inseminated females?"

"How would we know? No female has come forward to report being raped. Our only knowledge comes from the few witnesses to such an attack. Our scientists theorise that the virus might be a genetic mutation resulting from the Pyongyang nuclear explosion. It is known that radiation has caused genetic damage and increased mutation rates in many organisms in the Fukushima region following the meltdown thirty-six years ago."

"Yes, but there is little convincing evidence that organisms have evolved to such an extent as a virus," Kim argued.

"If it were possible that the Pyongyang explosion was responsible, it might also explain your interest in this case. After all, you are Korean," Shintaro pointed out.

"No," Kim barked dismissively.

Both men took a moment to collect themselves after Kim's angry response to the North Korean question.

"I must say the explosion hypothesis carries more weight than your claim that it was released by this Oceana time traveller, Black Alice. Oceana has been a strong ally of Japan for over a hundred years. It is not feasible that Oceana would jeopardise that relationship," Shintaro said emphatically, growing weary of Kim's abhorrent attitude.

"I said Black Alice might be from another time. Besides, with the world's population becoming unsustainable, there are those with hidden agendas to trim the population. The most practical means to achieve that would be to exterminate the male youth. I have statistics if you're interested. Don't get me wrong—we are not blaming Oceana. But we do believe Tokyo is a test run for an intended global pandemic."

Shintaro grimaced, realising that if Kim was right, the survival of mankind might well be in their hands.

Kew landed with a thump on the grey rubberised floor from the vortex, exactly where Secta had landed. He sat up and surveyed the room—it was clearly a laboratory. Needing clothes and finding himself alone, he got to his feet and made his way toward what he assumed was a storeroom. Inside, he found a variety of Hazmat suits, along with breathing apparatus, laboratory dustcoats, gloves, and sterile footwear. He would have to make do with the available protective clothing since there was nothing else to choose from.

Three labs down the corridor from Kew, in Doctor Malone's lab, Alice, Secta, and Sonoko were suddenly interrupted from reading Malone's files on a computer terminal by an alarm.

"We have a security breach!" Sonoko exclaimed, startled.

"Are there no security guards?" Alice asked.

"No, everything is automated, and it's Sunday. There's no-one else here."

"Leave it to me. You keep reading, and I'll go and check it out. Can I enter and exit the doors without you, Sonoko?"

"No, I must go with you."

They left Secta studying Malone's notes and set out to investigate the breach. Sonoko paused in the corridor, her face wearing an odd expression.

"What's wrong?" Alice asked.

"Because I have security clearance, I accessed the internal CCTV network through VV to see where the breach is, and there's someone in this wing. I'm frightened, Alice."

Alice placed a comforting hand on her shoulder. "It's okay, I'm here."

Her words lifted Sonoko's spirits, as she had no experience dealing with this type of threat.

"Is there more than one intruder?" Alice asked.

"I think there's only one ... no, there are two, but they're in different places!"

"Too bad I don't have a weapon."

"There is a janitor's room nearby. Maybe we can find something there."

"Good, lead the way."

They hurried along the bland grey corridor, which felt to Alice like a stainless-steel tube connecting sections of a space station. The seclusion reminded him of the Avalon bunker but felt even more claustrophobic. There were no windows, few doors, and the anaemic lighting—bright yet incandescent—created an aseptic atmosphere. It was impossible to tell whether it was day or night outside.

The sound of their footsteps on the rubberised floor echoed off the metallic walls with a strange reverberation as they quickened their pace. They arrived at a T-section, and Sonoko, monitoring her VV, led them to the right.

"The janitor's room is just ahead," she said, slightly out of breath.

Alice couldn't see a door, so he went along with Sonoko's lead. She stopped, faced the steel wall, and then, using her VV finger, activated a hidden door. It slid open seamlessly and silently.

"How did you know there was a door there? Oh, right ... man, it's weird seeing you do stuff on your VV that I can't see—it's like magic," Alice commented.

"Yes, I often forget what that must be like," Sonoko replied.

They stepped inside the small room, and Alice immediately searched for something to arm himself with. He found a toolbox, opened it, and grabbed a hammer. "This'll do," he said, slapping it in his palm as if he were preparing to bash someone's head in. Sonoko winced at the thought.

Sonoko suddenly became alert. "One of them is coming our way!"

They stepped back out into the corridor. "Which way is he coming from?"

Sonoko pointed to the left. "He's at the end of that corridor. It leads to the commissary."

"Alright, stay behind me. Are you sure it's not just an employee?"

"Positive. My VV would have given me an ID."

"Okay."

Alice held the hammer at the ready while they hugged the corridor wall, heading toward the commissary. Halfway there, Sonoko received another alert. She touched Alice on the shoulder and whispered, "The other intruder is behind us."

Alice kept moving but whispered back, "We'll have to confront them one at a time."

As they approached the commissary, they began hearing the sounds of furniture being angrily thrown about. Unlike the hidden entrance doors they had encountered earlier, the door to the commissary was open. Alice stopped just before it and took cover, peeking around the doorjamb. A chair came sliding across the floor and smashed into the wall.

Alice could see that the person responsible for the chaos was a young man built like a sumo wrestler, determined to wreck everything in the room. Taking a deep breath, Alice stepped into the doorway.

"Hey there," Alice said calmly, surprising Sonoko with his perfect Japanese.

"What are you doing?" Alice asked.

The young man froze, his eyes flashing with hostility. It was clear even from a distance that he looked desperate and unstable. Alice recognised the look from people addicted to methamphetamine, commonly known as ice. He knew that after taking ice, the brain could become overloaded, leading to sleeplessness, symptoms of psychosis, and often paranoia, which could escalate to violence.

Alice bent down and carefully placed the hammer on the floor, out of sight. He straightened up and took a couple of tentative steps toward the young man.

"My name is Alice. What's yours?" he asked in Japanese.

There was no reaction from the young man, so Alice moved a few steps closer. Just as he stopped, Sonoko appeared in the doorway behind him, triggering the intruder. He threw the chair with all his might at Alice, catching him off guard. Alice ducked, but the steel leg of the chair clipped the side of his head, knocking him over. His head hit the ground hard, and knocked him out.

Sonoko let out a frightened squawk, but before she could turn and run, the young man pounced on her, ripping at her clothes with a crazed determination. Driven by an insatiable urge, he dragged her screaming onto the floor.

Sonoko clawed at his face, kicked, and kneed him, but her efforts were futile. His arms and hands jerked in a violent dance, seemingly beyond his control. Suddenly, he froze and let out a primal scream, resembling a wolf's howl. Then, his head jerked violently to the side at an unnatural angle. His eyes rolled back in their sockets, and he collapsed on top of Sonoko.

Trembling uncontrollably, Sonoko looked up past the body on top of her at Alice, who stood over them with the bloodied hammer in his hand. Despite struggling to remain conscious, a stream of blood trickling down the side of his face from a deep forehead wound, Alice had fought through the darkness of unconsciousness, regaining his senses just in time to strike the attacker across the side of the head with the hammer.

Alice extended a hand to Sonoko and helped her to her feet. They looked down at the unconscious young man, who began twitching more and more, convulsing and shuddering as if something inside him was trying to escape.

He sat up abruptly, his eyes opening wide and staring at them with insanity. Blood gushed from the gaping hammer wound in the side of his head. Then, his eyes began to swell, as if under extreme pressure. His head shook violently, and his face contorted in a gruesome expression of death as his eyes bulged to six times their normal size. With a sickening sound resembling the simultaneous popping of two corks, both eyes exploded, spraying a mixture of dark slime and blood onto Sonoko and Alice. They stood there, thunderstruck.

"He was infected by the virus," Sonoko said, her teeth chattering nervously.

"I've never seen anything like it. He was going to rape you," Alice said, horrified.

Sonoko grimaced at the thought. While they were still staring at the body, they heard the sound of someone running in the corridor, followed by a loud bang and an alarm.

"The exit door!" Sonoko exclaimed.

CHAPTER 12
SATO-SAN

ALICE TOOK OFF like a bat out of hell after whoever had gone through the exit door. When he reached it, he found the source of the bang and the triggered alarm: the glass door had been shattered. He stepped through the frame onto the flat rooftop, which was dark but illuminated by security lights on poles around the perimeter. In one of those pools of light, he spotted a man in a yellow Hazmat suit running. Realising he couldn't catch up, Alice watched the man disappear into the night before returning to Sonoko, who was waiting by the damaged door.

Sonoko was covering her ears to block out the cacophonous alarm. With Alice's return, she used her virtual finger on her VV to silence it.

"Argh, that's a relief," Alice exclaimed.

"I stopped it. Did you see who it was?" Sonoko asked.

"Yeah, a dude in a Hazmat suit."

"It couldn't have been an employee; his ID would have registered on my VV. We better get Secta. We'll have to leave now that the alarm has been triggered. Security will be here in about ten minutes."

On their way back, they checked the body, but all that remained was a black smear of ashes on the floor.

"Just like Malone," Alice remarked.

There was no time to linger as they needed to leave the building before security arrived. They rushed to the lab to find Secta. A few minutes later, the three of them were catching their breaths as they hurried to board a four-seater pod from the building terminus. Sonoko programmed it to take them to her apartment.

Seated across from Alice, Sonoko frowned when she said to Secta in Japanese, "Did you find anything in Doctor Malone's notes?"

Alice instantly realised that he had blown their cover by speaking Japanese to the rapist.

"I'm sorry. I wasn't convinced we were on the same side, so I was keeping our ability to speak your language a secret ... like a card up my sleeve," Alice admitted.

"Are you now assured we are on the same side?" she asked curtly.

"Yes, again, I apologise."

She glared at Secta, incensed by the betrayal. "Can you?"

"Alice and I have implants, similar to your VV. Actually, I hesitate to admit it, but they were the forerunner. It's called an MCI, a mastoid cochlear implant. I invented it, actually. It contains a translator that enables us to understand and converse in a number of languages, including Japanese."

"That is a brilliant invention, Secta, but why hasn't this technology been made available to everyone by now? Has it been kept a secret for only Oceana operatives to use?"

"I have no idea. You'll have to ask my other self in Sydney. He would be more up to date than me," he said, jokingly. "And yes, I did find what I was looking for in Malone's notes. The element Propynylidynium you found in Malone's remains was also evident in the fish and water samples."

"That almost confirms your hypothesis that the meteorite is the delivery mechanism for the pathogen," Sonoko said.

"Presumably, but we need to go to the site and check the water. I borrowed this from the lab, Sonoko. I hope you don't mind," he said, showing her a small handheld device.

"Not as long as we return it," she replied. "Isn't that used for atomic particle fluid analysis?"

"Yes, it's lithium battery-powered. It's a clever little thing, only recently invented, I assume. There was no such item in our time. I've calibrated it to detect Propynylidynium in any fluid after adding a few drops of this," he held up a small vial of fluid. "Luminol, a chemical used by forensic investigators to detect trace amounts of blood or sperm at a crime scene. I tested a lot of agents, and when I mixed Luminol with the water sample, it showed the presence of Propynylidynium. Malone's search for it was only cursory since he didn't know what he was looking for. But he did use Luminol to fluoresce particles in the water and found them, though he failed to identify Propynylidynium. We need to go to Lake umm ... and test the water immediately to see if the contaminant is still there. I believe the virus might be masked by Propynylidynium."

"Lake Okutama," Sonoko corrected.

"Yes, and test the water immediately to see if the contaminant is still there. I believe the virus might be masked by Propynylidynium."

There was silence as the three of them contemplated Secta's claim that Propynylidynium was intentionally used to mask the virus.

"All that sperm..." Alice murmured.

"What sperm?" Secta asked.

"From the guy who acted like he was possessed—"

"Like a zombie," Sonoko added.

"Yeah, there was an abnormal amount of sperm."

Secta held his chin deep in thought. "Perhaps the virus caused an overproduction of sperm to ensure fertilization of his victim. This might be..." he trailed off.

"Might be what, mate? You're mumbling?" Alice asked.

"What if the virus is trying to reproduce? What if it's attempting to create human hybrids by attaching DNA to male sperm and inseminating it into female eggs? That could explain why the male hosts are driven like mindless zombies to find females to inseminate."

"And then their eyes explode?" Alice questioned.

"Was that immediate after he—" Secta stopped abruptly.

"Almost," Sonoko confirmed.

"He was of no further use to the pathogen. Maybe he only gets one shot to inseminate his target, and then he is discarded."

"Unbelievable," Sonoko said in amazement.

"Yes, presumably," Secta said, his mind working at an incredible pace. "Um, I need to test the sperm. Is there any of it on your clothes?"

"Yes, we're nearly at my apartment. You can test it there," Sonoko said.

The pod pulled up at a small, elevated platform that was annexed to a multistorey apartment block. In fact, there were multistorey apartment blocks as far as the eye could see in the dark. Though there was ample street lighting and lights from holographic advertising and from buildings, there was an inky darkness due to the overcast sky. Alice felt a chill, not from cold but from a feeling of impending doom. He noticed a lack of life on the streets. It was early evening and there was hardly any traffic … it all felt a bit strange.

Sonoko led them into her apartment building and the elevator. They rode to the 33rd floor and then traversed a narrow corridor to her apartment door.

The apartment was small, like a bedsit. Alice and Secta removed their shoes and with their knee joints protesting sat cross-legged on tatami mats on the floor.

"Welcome to my humble apartment. It is very small, only for one tenant. I only sleep here; otherwise, I am at my lab working."

"Sonoko, can you give me the garment with the semen on it and two glasses of water please?" Secta asked.

She removed her dustcoat and handed it to him, then brought two glasses of water.

"Why two?" she asked.

"One to test the semen and the other to test if your water is contaminated."

Sonoko went into the small bathroom to change her clothes, and Secta began conducting tests.

First, he tested the tap water, adding it to a small cup on the sampler and then three drops of Luminol. The gauge read zero.

"The water is free of Propynylidynium. Sonoko, does your water come from Lake Okutama?" Secta asked.

Sonoko emerged from the bathroom wearing a simple green knee-length dress and a beige cardigan, her long hair neatly tied back. Alice found her appearance lovely.

"No, the water here comes from the Tonegawa and Arakawa Rivers."

Secta nodded and emptied the cup. He then wet down the suspected area of Sonoko's lab coat that contained the rapist's sperm and gently squeezed a sample into the cup on the device.

"The Luminol will fluoresce the sperm blue, but if Propynylidynium is present, it will fluoresce orange."

When Secta added three drops of Luminol to the cup, it immediately fluoresced blue.

"Ah, you see, sperm is present."

After thirty seconds, several small orange dots appeared.

"There! Propynylidynium in the sperm! This could be a paradigm shift in genetics. What we might be looking at here is genetic modification on a massive scale. We need to check the water at Lake Okutama tonight," Secta declared.

"The Tama and Tone Rivers are the main water sources for Tokyo, fed by the Tama River. Lake Okutama is part of Ogouchi Dam, from where the water is taken. It is piped to the Tokyo Metropolitan Bureau of Waterworks nearby in Shinjuku-Ku," Sonoko explained.

"How do you know all this?" Alice asked.

"She's reading it off her VV," Secta answered for her.

"I can take you there in the morning," Sonoko offered.

"No way. We need to go now. Surely someone will be working the night shift. Can you message them and find out how I can run some tests before any chemicals are added to the water?" Secta requested.

"Okay, give me five. It is better for me to message them," Sonoko said.

Secta shrugged his shoulders.

Alice whispered, "Text them."

It didn't take long before she received a reply. "Okay, you can meet Mr Sato. He is the night duty chemist. I will take you there now."

"Oh no you won't, not after what happened with that rapist. You're not going anywhere, babe," Alice demanded.

"How will we get there? We don't have VV, so we can't pay the pod fare," Secta said.

"A pod will take you directly there from here and return ... I can program it for you."

"Cool," Alice said, beaming a grin.

"So, if I understand you correctly, you are here from the past to hunt down this Black Alice character who is also a time traveller from the past and the Moriarty of Zen. You suspect this Black Alice is in Tokyo to sabotage our objective, whatever you presume that to be?"

"That about sums it up, sir," Kew said, while standing at attention.

Gorrick turned from the huge ten-metre penthouse ceiling-to-floor windows from which he had been looking down fifty stories at the Tokyo CBD below and glared at Kew, who was still dressed in Hazmat protective clothing. The massive office made Gorrick's amazing Sydney penthouse office suite back in Kew's time look ordinary. Seeing Gorrick face on, Kew was struck by how this Gorrick was an exact replica of his Sydney boss from the past.

"In fact, sir, little of this was up to me. My orders came directly from Gorrick."

"Yes, I see. I understand how seeing me now could make that confusing for you. Leave it with me, Kew. I'll contact Gorrick in Sydney to confirm your mission, and then we'll speak again. In the meantime, I'll have you taken to a hotel and," he gave Kew a scrutinising once-over, "dressed appropriately."

The only thing Kew noticed discernible about the two Gorricks was that the Tokyo Gorrick had the unmistakable hint of British public school in his accent.

As Sonoko watched the pod carrying Alice and Secta dissolve into the darkness of the night, she received a message alert. It was from DI Shintaro, the officer investigating the disappearance of Doctor Rick Malone. He was requesting a meeting to ask some questions. Sonoko wasn't surprised by the contact. She had been expecting it after Doctor Hyashi had said he'd be notifying the police of Rick's death. She also expected her fingerprints to have been recovered from the crime scene at Rick's apartment, which would also have earned her a call. She agreed to rendezvous with Shintaro at her apartment in an hour.

The pod dropped Alice and Secta off at a platform outside a big warehouse-like building in Shinjuku-Ku: a shabby and badly rundown old industrial section of the precinct. Surrounded by a high fence topped by razor wire and lit only by the odd pole light, the dark building looked quite sinister.

At the entrance gate Secta found an intercom and pressed the call button. Expecting them, Mr Sato answered and then buzzed them in.

In his small office, Sato was a plump little round-faced man with an overabundance of manners. After all the bowing and scraping, he offered Alice and Secta a seat and then retired behind his grey-painted metal desk. They conversed in Japanese.

"How can I help you, Secta-san?" Sato asked.

"I have brought a device to test a sample of untreated water from Lake Okutama."

"We test all the water supply daily, is there some problem?"

"No, we just need to satisfy ourselves there is no pathogen in the water from that particular area."

"I see. Well, no problem," he stood. "If you would follow me please, I will take you to a pre-treatment junction."

"Thank you, Sato-san," Secta said, getting to his feet.

They followed Sato through a labyrinth of gloomy corridors, down two flights of stairs, and into a tunnel through which ran a number of massive pipes that carried water into the treatment plant. They followed the pipes along the tunnel until they finally came to a rusted old red door.

"Pretty creepy down here," Alice whispered to Secta.

"This is the junction of the pipeline from Lake Okutama into the plant. There is a valve in here," he said, opening the old door and switching on a light inside, "where you will be able to obtain a sample." He produced a small torch from the top pocket of his grey dustcoat and scanned the tiny room with the beam until he stopped at a tap bearing a sign in Japanese, which obviously designated it from Lake Okutama. He collected a flask that was parked on the floor, filled it from the tap, and then handed it to Secta.

"This water is direct from Lake Okutama without any treatment, except on very hot days when some chlorine is added automatically into the pipeline at Ogouchi Dam. But there has been no chlorine added in the last three months."

"Good," Secta said, handing the flask over to Alice to hold while he retrieved the testing device from his pocket. They stepped back out into the tunnel where the light was better.

Secta took the flask and filled the cup on the device. He then added three drops of Luminol. They waited anxiously for the chemical to register, but nothing happened.

"A negative reading. There is no Propynylidynium in the water, so we can safely assume there is no pathogen. But to be certain, we will need to test the water in the lake itself because that's where the meteorite landed," Secta told Alice in English.

"Did you say meteorite?" Sato said in English.

Secta hadn't expected Sato to understand him. Now he was forced to explain some of his theory.

"Yes, a few days ago, two scientists fishing in Lake Okutama witnessed a meteorite land in the lake. Within thirty minutes, there were dead fish floating on the surface," Secta admitted.

"Yes, I know about the fish kill. We were ordered to shut down the water from Lake Okutama for two days for the dead fish to be removed."

"Didn't such a huge fish kill seem unusual?" Alice asked.

"Yes, but it is not my job to question."

"Other than the fish kill, was there anything else odd about the event?" Secta asked him.

"Yes," Sato admitted. "All fish were male. I thought that very strange."

"Presumably. It is important to establish there is no pathogen still in the waters of Lake Okutama," Secta said pressingly. It was further proof the pathogen only attacked males.

"I understand. Do you think the epidemic in Tokyo is linked to the meteorite?" Sato asked.

"Presumably. Well, that's my hypothesis," Secta qualified.

"But water is carefully analysed every day. Surely, if a pathogen was present, it would have been detected in testing."

"Not necessarily. You would not be testing for the rare element Propynylidynium. I have found it in early samples of the dead fish and the water. I think it is masking the pathogen virus."

"Then I will drive you to Lake Okutama myself. It is critical you test water."

"Thank you, Sato-san."

CHAPTER 13
WATER

ROBERT JAMES WAS seated beside his eight-year old daughter Aurora in the office of the President of Oceana. The President looked grimly at Karzoff who was also seated in the lounge setting next to Viktoria and then at Doctor Hope.

"It is frightening to imagine what this poor child must have gone through," the President said genuinely.

"I was okay but Mira was upset," Aurora said pluckily.

A smile cracked on the President's otherwise stern face, "Brave girl ... and who is Mira?"

"The au pair sir. She was kidnapped with Aurora," Robert said.

"I see. Fine, you can leave us now Doctor James. Goodbye Aurora, I'm very glad you're all safe and sound."

She gave the President a big hug. He smiled watching the two of them leave but once the door was closed behind them his face soured.

"I want Honor brought in and charged with kidnapping, it is a capital offence. As for her accomplice Kew, we now have the problem of him being in the future, I expect with a licence to kill Alice and Secta. Do we not have some means of warning them?"

"Let me work on that sir," Hope suggested. "Perhaps we can find a way of getting a message to them just as Alice managed to get one to us."

"And what of our security measures, it's unacceptable that someone can just walk right through it all into the Kairos control room. In addition, what happened at your apartment Hope and at the James home ... none of this should have been possible, get onto plugging those holes Karzoff and Viktoria. We can't have this sort of thing happening."

"Yes sir," they both agreed in unison.

It was obvious by the look on his face that Karzoff wasn't confident in taking on Zen.

"Do you have a problem Karzoff?" the President asked.

"I think the kidnapping is more a police matter sir. They are more familiar with dealing with such things."

The President sank back in his chair to think and it creaked in protest of his size.

"You're right, I will talk to the commissioner, though I'm not on the best of terms since trying to replace him with Zen a few months back. Where the hell would we be now if that deal had gone through?" he said shaking his head.

"Zen is a formidable enemy sir, it might take more than the police to arrest Honor. I am reminded of how easy it was for Zen's lawyers to get Kew a repeal for his assassination attempt on you," Viktoria said earnestly.

"Yes, yes, you are of course right Viktoria. Gone are the days of the Government just shutting the bad guys down, everyone has rights these days, plus we live in an era of alternative facts ... at least back when I was growing up there was no grey area, you did what you were bloody-well told," the President complained.

"Kids are even taking their parents to court these days sir, school teachers are afraid to discipline their students ... there's so much political correctness it makes you want to throw up! God knows what society is coming to ... I wonder if it's the same or worse in 2047?" Viktoria questioned.

"It will be interesting to find out when our time travellers return, if they return," the President said, with a look of consternation. "First, we need to deal with Honor, but I am intrigued as to why Zen went to all this trouble to send Kew after Alice and Secta, any thoughts?" The wallpaper changed at the mention of Secta's name.

"They did try it before when they sent Anu Set into the past after Alice but that failed," Karzoff reminded them.

"Yes, but that was to do with Zen wanting the Ark of the Covenant, this is a totally different scenario," Hope claimed.

"They must somehow feel threatened by Alice," Viktoria suggested.

The President's gaze wandered up to the ceiling, "What if Zen is behind this epidemic ... this pathogen?"

"But how would they know that when it's in the future?" Hope submitted.

It was a two-hour drive from Shinjuku-Ku to Lake Okutama in the Nishitama District. Both Alice and Secta were sound asleep when Sato pulled the electric car into the poorly lit car park. As soon as it stopped Alice and Secta woke up.

"You must have needed rest, you both slept all the way," Sato said with a grin.

Secta was on the front seat and yawned, "I could do with more. So, are we here?"

"Yes, welcome to Lake Okutama. There is a track you can see in the headlights that leads down to the water. It is a place for fishing."

"Looks pretty dark out there," Alice groaned still sleepy.

"I have a torch. I will lead the way," Sato said.

Alice wasn't wrong, it was inky dark. The track snaked down a steep wooded incline that every now and then had steps cut into it. After twenty minutes of stumbling along the path Sato's torchlight flashed on a post and rail gate obstructing further passage. A sign on the gate appeared to be a warning.

"What does it say?" Alice asked.

"Please not to worry ... it is just a warning for hornet nests. The hornets are the biggest in the world here but they do not come out at night."

"And the other sign?" Alice said pointing at a larger warning sign plastered on the trunk of a nearby tree.

Sato flashed the torch at it. "Oh yes, this is a warning about Japanese black bear. There are many here and often appear on the hiking trails."

"Bears? And they don't come out at night either, right?" Alice questioned.

"No, I am afraid they do come out at night," Sato said with raised eyebrows.

The thought of black bears in the dark sent a shiver up Alice's spine. Secta was also visibly shaken.

"Oh dear... Um, I can't believe how quiet it is, you'd expect to hear something, crickets, cicada's, owls ... something," Secta said, nervously looking about the thick forest for bears.

"And what's that smell?" Alice said.

"Yes, something is dead," Sato confirmed. "This is all very strange. The ravine here is very famous for the sound of insects, but there is nothing."

He climbed over the low fence and then held the torchlight on it for Alice and Secta to negotiate it.

"It is not far from here to the water," Sato said assuredly.

After another ten minutes of slipping, sliding, and stumbling, they reached the bank of Lake Okutama. The lake surface was like a mirror, not a ripple. The clouds parted and moonlight struck the lake.

"How beautiful," Sato said, his breath taken by the scene.

Secta was only interested in the task, the moon was providing him better light so he went to the water's edge and filled the cup on the device.

Alice was staring up at the heavens through the parted clouds at the vast canopy of stars and asked, "Hey Secta, what date is it?"

"Fifth of August," he muttered, thinking the question trivial.

"Do you remember Turk telling us that an alien spaceship lands in Tokyo?"

Secta was focused on the device and the job at hand. "Sato-san, can you bring over the torch please? Um, yes, Alice, I remember Turk and Nerdo saying something about it being the first recognised close encounter, why?"

"Because if it's true, then it's going to happen in three days, on the eighth of the eighth."

Secta looked up startled, "Gee, you've got a good memory Alice ... you're right, and we'll be here! What made you think of that?"

"Just thinking it's a good spot for a meteorite to land and then looking up at the stars."

Secta looked at the device and said, "The reading is negative."

A loud rustle in the bushes behind them caught their attention.

"What the stuff was that?" Alice barked, on edge.

Sato walked in the direction of the noise flashing the torchlight about.

"It might be a bear," Sato said matter-of-factly.

"Okay, I'm done here, let's leave the bear to his woods," Secta said hurriedly, keen to get out of there.

But Sato was staring at something in the bushes.

"Come on Sato-san, what's up?" Alice asked.

"I'm using infrared on my retinal implants ... I can see something big watching us from the bushes," he mumbled spookily.

"Right-o, let's get out of here then," Alice said bullishly.

Sato snapped to it and led them back up the steep gradient. It was tough going made worse by the fear of a bear attack and the phantom rustling noises they could hear from the dark woods on both sides of the narrow pathway.

Puffing out of breath Alice said, "Hey Sato, is there a take-away on the way back to Tokyo?"

"Yes, yes ... I think so Alice-san. You are hungry?"

"He loves chicken nuggets ... has to order them from the kid's menu," Secta said with a chuckle, and that brought a giggle from Alice and Sato.

A loud angry growl erupted from the bushes to the left of them. Sato stopped them and quickly flashed the bushes with the torchlight. The beam wavered about with his shaking hand.

The trees were eerie in the torchlight branches looked like withered, clawed fingers. A black shadow streaked through the beam and growled, it frightened Sato so much he dropped the torch.

As he bent down to pick it up, from out of the darkness, a bear attacked. Standing on its hind legs, it was taller than Sato. It snarled and drooled saliva, coming at him with its long, sharp claws extended. Sato tried to back away, but the ferocious bear grabbed him. An earth-shattering scream came from Sato when the bear hugged him and then dragged him to the ground. They rolled around ... the sound of its teeth gnashing at Sato's hands while he tried to protect his face was frightening. The beast struggled on top and then straddled Sato, slashing at his body with its claws and snapping viciously at his face. He didn't stand a chance.

Alice dived for the torch, grabbed it, and then quickly shined it at the battle. What they saw in the torchlight was absolutely horrendous: the ferocious bear was virtually ripping Sato to pieces.

"It's going to kill him, Alice!" Secta yelled.

Alice caught a glimpse of something in the light beside the path: a steel dropper supporting a newly planted tree—a weapon. He rushed over, yanked it out of the ground, and raced back to Secta, handing him the torch.

"Hold this on the bear!"

With a trembling hand, Secta shined the torch on the bear. It was a brutal scene. A mass of blood, lacerations, and stripped flesh had Sato limp, unconscious, and at the mercy of the beast.

Alice strode bravely over to the bear, took aim, and with an almighty swipe, belted the snarling brute across the side of the head with the metre-long metal spear. It opened up its head big time, and blood gushed out. Its paws fell limp ... it dropped Sato, and then keeled over onto the ground, where it lay twitching. Alice wasted no time and speared the dropper into the creature's chest.

Secta kept the torch on it. The beast fell silent and still—then suddenly, its eyes opened wide and began to swell, bigger and bigger—its mouth opened wide in a snarl full of sharp teeth but no sound came out—and then to their horror, both eyes ruptured.

Secta looked away. "Oh, that's gross."

"Same deal as with the dude at the lab ... it was trying to rape Sato," Alice said.

Secta recovered, screwed up his nose, and observed, "Presumably it's infected from eating contaminated dead fish."

It was a gruesome sight. Sato had literally been torn to pieces. Steam was rising from his eviscerated gut, slashed open by the beast's razor-sharp claws.

Secta knelt down beside Sato's body and felt for a pulse. He shook his head. "He's gone. We'll have to leave him here; we can't manhandle him all the way back to the car. It's a crime scene anyway."

Puffing out of breath after the fight, Alice nodded. "Okay, Sonoko can call the cops once we get back."

"I'll get his key card." Secta dug around in Sato's pockets.

Sonoko opened her apartment door to DI Atomu Shintaro and Hyunbo Kim. After introductions, they sat down to talk. Sonoko was more than happy to answer Shintaro's questions, but her instant distrust of Hyunbo was made obvious by her body language whenever he addressed her. Shintaro recognised Kim's attitude problem and, figuring he had poor people skills, tried to work around it.

"So, this Black Alice phoned you to meet after he found the body of Doctor Malone?" Shintaro said calmly, respectfully.

"Yes, that is correct," Sonoko answered quietly spoken but cooperatively.

"And you say he is trying to solve the case of Doctor Malone's death and has a Doctor Secta assisting him?"

"Yes."

"Why do you think Black Alice decided not to call the police?"

"Because when we went to Doctor Malone's apartment, his body had gone ... all that was left of him was a black mark on the kitchen floor, and Black Alice thought without a body, he could be blamed for the doctor's death."

"And that didn't strike you as being odd?" Kim asked sternly.

"No, it made perfect sense."

With a cool glance, he asked her, "Are you attracted to Black Alice?"

"No, I am not," she asserted.

"Oh really, then why are you protecting him?" Kim snarled.

"I am not protecting anyone."

He gave a brittle laugh. "Of course you are ... otherwise, you would have called the police yourself ... wouldn't you?"

Shintaro had had enough of Kim's badgering and said warmly, "We're not here to blame you for not calling the police, Miss Tanaka. I apologise for that suggestion. I would just like to meet with Mr Alice and Doctor Secta so that we can get to the bottom of this. I don't want this to be a murder investigation when I personally believe it is the result of the virus sweeping Tokyo."

"The evidence is irrefutable, Black Alice is spreading the pandemic," Kim asserted.

"Oh, what rubbish! He and Secta are doing more to solve the mystery of this virus than you or anyone else. If I were you, I'd be trying to help them, not harass them. Doctor Malone died from the virus; I've seen another man die in the same manner, and his body combusted ... I am sure you are already well aware of this. Trying to blame these men is absurd ... and just how is that going to help stop the virus anyway? You are just wasting precious time," she said spiritedly.

"Do you know Black Alice is a time traveller?" Kim snapped in rebuttal.

"Yes, which even gives more plausibility as to why he is here: to help solve this terrible pandemic, can you not see that?"

CHAPTER 14
HYBRID

THE AUTONOMOUS EV took them all the way back to the Waterworks at Shinjuku-Ku without Secta having to lift a finger to drive. Alice was sound asleep in the passenger seat when they arrived, which gave Secta the dubious task of having to wake him. He could never get used to the way Alice woke with a violent jolt from a deep sleep; it made his heart skip a beat, expecting to get punched in the nose.

It was then a matter of them catching a pod from the terminal and punching in the code number Sonoko had provided them to program it back to her apartment block. Everything went according to plan, and they entered the apartment at 3 a.m.

Peering through narrowed eyes, still half-asleep and dressed in a long white robe, Sonoko told them, in between yawns, of her visit from the law. However, she woke up very quickly once she had finished, and Secta imparted the horrid story of the encounter with the bear and Sato's grisly demise. They turned in for the night, agreeing to make fresh plans over breakfast in the morning.

Twenty-one-year-old personal bodyguard Gaku Suzuki was in the bathroom of his Tokyo city apartment, shaving. Looking in the mirror, he could hardly recognise himself. His steroid-enhanced body looked fine, but his eyes had changed; they looked a different shape, and his eyebrows were far bushier than they were yesterday. His beard was tough, making it difficult for the beard liquifier gel to dissolve the bristles. His overall face shape seemed somewhat Neanderthal compared to normal, his brow appeared to be a little more exaggerated than usual. He wondered if it was a side effect of the intravenous steroid jabs he'd been giving himself over the past two years. The phone rang, distracting him, and he dismissed the notion. With a white towel wrapped around his waist, he irritably wiped the residual gel off his face with a hand towel and then stalked into the bedroom to answer his cell phone. He wondered why he hadn't been called on his VV, and then realised, to his surprise, that it wasn't functioning. How odd, he thought. When the voice on the other end of the line testily ordered him to explain why he was running so late, he reacted completely out of character and growled at the caller like a wild animal and then terminated the call. It was past 5:30 a.m., and he was only fifteen minutes late.

Returning to the bathroom, he checked his face again in the mirror and noticed his beard had already grown back.

Running seriously late, Gaku entered an office block to collect Premier Ito in order to escort him to a press conference scheduled for 5:30 a.m. Ito's secretary greeted Gaku with a serious berating for being late and warned him that the Premier was also fired up. When Gaku entered the Premier's office, Ito immediately launched a tirade at him. At first, Gaku handled it, but then, all of a sudden, he snapped. He exploded with anger and, like a wild animal, delivered Ito an almighty king hit that dropped him like a sack of potatoes, shattering his jaw. Then, with the older man on the floor at his mercy, Gaku punched him to a pulp.

Alerted by the commotion going on in her boss's office, the Premier's secretary charged in and upon seeing her blood-drenched boss lying lifeless on the floor, let out an unearthly scream. Her reaction was immediately curtailed by a punch so hard from Gaku that it almost took her head clean off her shoulders. She lay on the floor unconscious. With his navy-blue suit and white shirt soaked in blood, Gaku left both victims and casually strolled out of the office as though nothing had happened. Twenty minutes later, the tea lady discovered the carnage and alerted house security. They found Gaku Suzuki on CCTV entering the offices and then leaving, covered in blood. They contacted the police, and they issued an APB on him.

From a patrol car, two cops recognised Gaku from the description issued and reported it. They were immediately warned Suzuki was extremely dangerous and to approach him with caution. Backup was ordered. Gaku easily eluded the cop car by entering a Shinjuku Gyoen, a spacious park with wide lawns, trees, and ponds, famous for its Cherry Blossoms.

Sitting on a park bench with his head in his hands, he questioned himself, "Why do I feel so weird?" He looked up and saw a pretty young girl jogging. He sniffed the air ... his nostrils flared ... the scent made him want to procreate. He jogged after her.

The pathogen had triggered a massive overdose of testosterone into Gaku's nervous system, which was now driving him like a mindless animal in heat. Only a few paces behind the girl and closing on her, he was just about to jump her when she unexpectedly stopped to chat with two other joggers. Gaku jogged past. She would never know how close she came to being attacked. Gaku was now being driven out of control by the unquenchable need to mate. He noticed a young woman walking a French poodle on a leash. In a hurry, she was dressed in a tracksuit with her raven hair tied up. She was running late to rendezvous with her driver on the other side of the park. But before she could get there, she would need to pass under a small bridge and then take the path up a hill to the car park at the top where her car was waiting. There were many Cherry Blossoms in full bloom, and they gave Gaku good cover for him to wait in ambush, just the other side of the bridge. As she emerged from under the bridge, he reached out and grabbed the poodle, snapped its neck with a quick twist, and then pulled the horrified woman toward him by the leash that was attached to her arm. He was way too strong for her to take on and easily brought her down onto the ground. She tried desperately to placate him, consenting to him, but he was too far gone; she just had to capitulate.

With her eyes squeezed tightly shut, she endured the terrible attack. Then, her eyes opened wide. Her facial expression changed ... she had become just as much an animal as he. She kicked him off her and sat up, possessed with the alien seed, and it had control of her every thought.

Gaku looked up at the sky as though he was going to howl triumphantly ... but instead, his lips drew back, and he bared his teeth in great pain. His victim just lay on the grass, propped up on one arm, watching his eyes swell ... and swell ... until they were the size of hen's eggs. Then, as his face contorted into a terrified rictus, his eyes burst, sending a spray of blood and gore down his cheeks. Gaku Suzuki collapsed on the ground, dead.

Morning arrived all too soon for them, with the sun streaming in through the windows at 6 a.m. The three of them had slept on tatami mats on the floor in the small room, which was fine for Sonoko. She was used to it. However, both Secta and Alice struggled with aching backs from the hard floor.

Walking like a pair of geriatrics, they accompanied Sonoko into a café on the ground floor of the apartment block.

"Feel like the walking dead this morning," Alice groaned.

"I think if we don't stay in a hotel tonight, I'm going to end up a cripple," Secta admitted, gripping his back as if he had lumbago. They found a table and sat down. The café was full of young people.

Alice leaned across the table and spoke confidentially, "We need to do something about having money on trips. It makes it difficult being broke."

Secta reached into his pocket and produced a small resealable plastic bag. With a smug grin on his face, he opened it and took out a tiny scroll of paper, then unravelled it.

He whispered, "I had this in my mouth during the time travel process. See, it's a draft for 200 Ethereum. I assume cryptocurrency is still valid, Sonoko?"

"Yes, Ethereum and Bitcoin are the two most favoured. Two hundred Ethereum is a lot of money, more than half a million US dollars!"

"Good grief, I didn't expect it to be worth that much!" Secta erupted.

"There's a Bitcoin cash and deposit auto-teller over there. It will take the note and credit you."

"How does that work?" Alice asked.

"There's a code on the note that authenticates the transfer of the said amount from an OTT account I had Viktoria set up before I left," Secta explained.

"Cool. Let's hope it hasn't been closed over time," Alice joked.

"Yes, you will need to provide ID to set up an account. Do you have any?" Sonoko asked.

"No. So what we will do is transfer it all to your account," Secta said.

"And then I can give you both supplementary cards."

"Exactly."

"It is a lot of money. I've not had anything like that much in my Bitcoin account before," she said with a giggle.

They ordered breakfast, and then Sonoko took Secta to the Bitcoin machine into which he deposited the note. Sonoko set up a sub-account for Alice and Secta and then, following Secta's instructions, deposited twenty Bitcoins in each account. The machine spat out debit chips for Secta and Alice.

Secta gave Alice his chip at the table, and their breakfast arrived.

Sipping his coffee, Alice said, "Okay, what do I do with this chip?" It was no bigger than a dime.

"Hold it on your wrist for 30 seconds for it to print an invisible tattoo that will last twelve months. Then put the chip in a safe place. When you want to pay, just wave your hand near the sensor. But in most cases, sensors will read the tattoo from a distance," Sonoko instructed.

Both Alice and Secta followed her guide.

"Cool," Alice said. "So, what's the next move then?"

"Sonoko will need to make an anonymous call to the police to report Sato's death. Are you okay with that, Sonoko?" Secta asked.

"Yes, no problem. But I think you need to speak with DI Shintaro. Otherwise, you will be running from the law. It would be best to talk to him without the presence of Agent Kim, the Korean from Interpol. He blames Alice for the pandemic, but Shintaro does not."

"Good shout. Since we don't have a mobile phone, and we're not fitted with a VV, could you call him and arrange a meeting, please?" Secta asked.

"Sure, where?"

Secta glanced at Alice for his thoughts.

"Here is as good a place as any," Alice suggested.

Kew was waiting at Zen reception for an 8 a.m. meeting with Gorrick. After the previous meeting, he wasn't too sure what to expect from him. In effect, he felt confident he could proceed without Zen's support, but in reality, he'd be better off with it. For him, the task was simple: find and kill Black Alice and Secta.

The pretty Japanese receptionist was busy lacquering her fingernails when she got word over her VV to admit Kew.

"You can go in now, sir," she said warmly.

Radiating a surly attitude like a beacon, he offered her a deadpan nod in reply, then rose from his chair and entered the office.

Gorrick was seated facing his direction in the lounge setting next to the Japanese-style bridge over the small stream that ran through the beautifully maintained garden setting. Dotted with amazing Bonsai trees, lawns, and exotic plants, it felt more like he was outdoors than on the fiftieth floor of a Tokyo skyscraper.

Needing to cross the bridge to reach Gorrick, he glanced down at the stream abundant with an incredible collection of big, long Ginrin Showa Koi and giant Golden Koi.

The sunken lounge setting was on an island surrounded by the meandering stream.

Dressed in a cream suit, Gorrick gestured for Kew to sit in the empty lounge opposite him. The U-shaped lounge setting could seat six, while Gorrick was seated in an independent plush armchair.

"I spoke with Gorrick in Sydney, who confirmed your mission. As a result, I have authorised the highest security clearance for you." He leaned forward with something in his hand. "Give me your hand."

Kew reached out his hand. "What's this?"

"You will see," Gorrick replied, irritatingly obtuse. "Now turn it over and bare your wrist." He stamped it with a metal gadget. "I just inserted a microchip under your skin. It will give you access to all Zen facilities. It will require secondary validation, which will be arranged after our meeting. Now, before you meet my other operatives, I want to bring you up to speed on our current program. It directly affects your mission because your mark, Black Alice, is involved."

They had finished breakfast, so Sonoko took the opportunity to have a few queries clarified and asked, "Secta, how did you manage to locate Alice in this time?"

"Alice has a genetic marker I implanted in his DNA that allows a technical device to track and locate his coordinates in space and time."

"How was he sent through time?"

"We open a wormhole using a big, science fiction-looking gadget called Kairos, to a specific time for Alice to travel through. He leaves behind a strong quantum signature we can accurately target. The software program our physicists developed quantizes those elements to provide us with the telemetry."

"I hope you understood that, Sonoko, 'coz I sure as hell didn't, but it works," Alice said with a cheeky grin.

Just then, a man entered the café whom Alice took to be a cop at first glance.

"Is this your friend?" Alice asked Sonoko, who had her back to the entrance.

She swivelled round in her seat and, catching sight of DI Shintaro, stood and offered him an ever so slight bow of her head.

"Good morning, DI Shintaro. May I present my friends, Black Alice and Doctor Secta?"

Shintaro graciously bowed his head to them. Alice and Secta stood and shook hands with the inspector, who was tall for a Japanese and quite handsome for a cop. They all sat down.

"Can I order you a coffee, Shintaro-san?" Sonoko asked, welcomingly.

"Yes, a flat white, please. Thank you, Miss Tanaka."

While Sonoko was getting the coffee, they attempted to ease the awkwardness of the meeting.

"I expect Miss Tanaka has told you I issued an APB for your arrest, Mr Alice?" Shintaro said.

"Just call me Al. Yes, and I understand why, given the circumstances of Doctor Malone's death. Of course, I didn't know about the APB, or I would have contacted you."

"DI Shintaro, we are here to provide our expertise to solve the pandemic that threatens not just the population of Japan, but the entire world. I am a scientist, and I'm convinced we are dealing with genetic modification on a massive scale," Secta explained.

"That is why this morning I cancelled the APB on Black Alice. Miss Tanaka explained the situation to me, and though the explanation still leaves some unanswered questions—"

"Fire away," Alice said.

Sonoko returned with the coffee and took her seat.

"Such as, how did you both get to Japan, and why does an older version of you exist in Sydney right now?"

"We are time travellers, Detective Inspector. We came from nearly thirty years ago on a mission to solve the pandemic," Secta explained.

"If you are from the past, which I do not doubt, how could you know there is a pandemic occurring in Japan now?"

Alice reclined in his chair and folded his arms. "Good question. A force that determines threats to mankind, which require my help, directed my mission here. Once I identified the extent and danger of the threatening pandemic, I contacted Secta back in my time for his scientific assistance, and he followed."

"I see. Please understand it is very difficult to accept this?"

"Yes, of course. But I think if you trust Sonoko, then she will confirm from her experience with us that we are not from this time, and we have the best intentions," Secta added.

"Yes, that is so," Sonoko asserted.

"Then let us put all that aside. We need to focus on the problem. How can I be of help?" Shintaro asked.

"Excellent. We know the virus only attacks young men ... and—"

"No, that is not correct. We have determined that women under the age of thirty are also infected. The only difference is they do not die after they are inseminated; they just disappear," Shintaro corrected.

"It's even worse than I thought. I didn't think women were being infected," Secta said dispiritedly. "At least we've determined the pathogen is no longer in the water, so the infections will decrease."

"That also is not exactly accurate, Doctor. Infection can be transferred by a bite from an infected male," Shintaro advised.

"Vampires ... bloody hell, what next?" Alice grumbled.

"Hmm, this transference of the virus by bite totally alters the paradigm," Secta muttered to himself, perturbed by the revelation.

Shintaro added, "We have had many cases of women over the age of thirty or women incapable of reproduction who have died from the virus in the same frightening manner as men."

"Why do they disappear after being impregnated?" Alice queried.

Sonoko had the answer. "To wait out the gestation period and then to give birth, I expect."

"Makes sense, but for what ... nine months?" Alice questioned.

"Maybe the gestation period is much shorter ... think of it ... if this is an alien invasion as I suspect," Secta theorised. "Women are being impregnated with genetically modified sperm containing alien DNA, to give birth to hybrid human/aliens."

"So this is what you suspect, Doctor?" Shintaro said, astounded by the assumption.

"I'm afraid so. I still have no proof, but that will come soon enough if we can capture a pregnant female and do tests," Secta declared, convinced of his hypothesis.

"Then that must be our priority," Shintaro concluded.

Kew was now up to date on Zen's agenda. Now he understood why it was imperative for his mission to succeed.

"So, all that stands between success and failure is Black Alice and Doctor Secta?" Kew said.

"That is correct, and why I am going to provide you with assistance. You will meet them now."

As he spoke, the doors opened, and a nuggetty Asian man in a sleek blue suit doing his best impression of a mobster entered, crossed the bridge, joined them, and took a seat.

"Kew, this is Agent Hyunbo Kim from the International Division of Interpol."

Kim nodded as coldly to Kew as he did in return, and then the doors opened again. There were loud footsteps on the tiled floor from the much bigger man that had entered. This guy walked with complete authority and power. As he was making his way across the bridge, Kew thought he recognised him, but then dismissed the thought as absurd. That all changed when, just as the man was approaching them, Gorrick made the introduction.

"And this is our senior agent, Anu Set. He will be your right hand."

For a man that rarely displayed emotion, Kew slowly rose from his chair, speechless. Before him was the man who had been killed in his time and then reanimated as an android. Questions were racing through Kew's mind: Is this Anu Set a real human or an android?

CHAPTER 15
SNATCH

❝ JUST AS SHINTARO was getting up to leave, the owner of the café turned on the holovision and made an announcement.

"The President of the North American Block is about to make an important announcement."

Shintaro took his seat again. "Better stay to see what she has to say."

"Maybe the pathogen has broken out there," Alice said.

The insignia of the President of the United States floated in 3-D in the middle of the room, which then cut to a middle-aged black woman seated with no background, just floating in mid-air. She looked matronly. Alice was wrong; the President had gone on air globally to make a presidential admission to the presence of aliens visiting Earth. She admitted there had been a government cover-up on the subject for decades and that UFOs had been visiting Earth for thousands of years. She continued, stating that in the last century, the U.S. Government had had numerous bilateral meetings with several alien species for the sole purpose of mutually exchanging technology. Then, in order to contain any possibility of panic and to put citizens' minds at ease, she affirmed that there had never been any evidence of hostility from any of the known alien species. She kept it brief and, in closing, said that more information would be made public over the next few days.

"Wow," Sonoko exclaimed, aware that the patrons of the café were now sizing each other up with suspicion. Who's an alien? What do they look like?

"Well, that has been long overdue, hasn't it?" Shintaro stated firmly. "We have so many files of unexplained UFO sightings over Japan." He stood. "It changes very little, of course ... I will confirm a meeting for later today with the chief forensic scientist at the Met. By the way, we are expecting the Government to declare martial law today, so get supplies you need because the city will be shut down by dusk."

"How will we get around?" Alice asked.

"Special permit. I will have permits sent to your VVs," he said in closing.

"Wait," Secta squawked. "We're not fitted with VVs."

Shintaro stopped and thought. "Of course, no problem. I will have permits for you and Alice forwarded to Miss Tanaka. You'll just need to keep her with you."

"I could think of worse things," Alice joked.

Sonoko blushed.

With a slight bow to them, Shintaro was out of there.

Sonoko stood up and excused herself to go to the bathroom. Secta glanced at Alice with a look of consternation. "Timely for the President to make such an admission only days before the UFO lands in Tokyo."

"You're not kidding. A coincidence, I don't think. I reckon there's a lot more to this than meets the eye," Alice said cynically.

"I'd say it was designed to lessen the public hysteria for when the UFO lands here ... conditioning."

"Conspiracy theories spin my head out," Alice admitted. "I need some new threads, and we need to check into a hotel with real beds before the city goes offline. What say you?"

"I agree. I felt like I'd been put on the rack by the Spanish Inquisition last night. Let's knock that over first thing this morning."

Alice suggested, "Might be a good idea to get Sonoko a room next to ours, seeing she's now our official custodian."

"Yes, good thinking."

"We forgot to tell Shintaro about Sato," Alice said.

"There wasn't much we could do about that, was there?"

"Hey, did you check out the laser shower in Sonoko's bathroom?"

Secta grinned. "It was the first thing I tried there. An unbelievable sensation having a waterless shower, and incredibly hygienic ... obliterates bacteria."

"Man, when I hit the button, I expected a blast of water, not a hundred red laser beams. Dug the tingling sensation, though. I felt super clean once it was done."

A waft of perfume caught Alice's attention. He looked up at Sonoko, who took her seat and said, "I just received a message from Shintaro that he has been told by the police forensic division that they have captured an infected male and female, and she is suspected of being pregnant."

"Hmm, that'll make the meeting this afternoon very interesting indeed," Secta said.

Alice nodded vaguely, still taking in Sonoko's perfume and wondering whether he was becoming attracted to her.

Hope was in the Kairos control room with Professor de Luz, working on a means to get a message to Alice and Secta and not having much luck when Robert arrived.

"The added security measures are a bit of a pain," Robert admitted.

Both swivelled on their chairs to face him, and de Luz said, "It's for the best. You should be the first to agree."

"Yes, I suppose so. What are you working on?"

"We've been at it for hours trying to find a way to get Alice and Secta a message to warn them about Kew, but we've come up with a blank," Hope said dispiritedly.

"The problem is if we send a wormhole to the last coordinates, how can we be sure they'll be there?" the Professor explained.

Robert's facial expression changed with an idea. He quickly pulled up a chair in front of the main computer monitor and said excitedly, "I've been working on an algorithm that will allow us to direct the wormhole to either Alice's or Secta's atomic marker."

"Yes, we've looked at that, but we would need the quantum signature for the wormhole telemetry, and that would only target the last coordinates," de Luz asserted.

"Only if we use Secta's quantum signature coordinates ... Alice is a totally different matter ... we didn't generate them, remember ... we sent Secta to him?"

"You're right. We haven't been thinking laterally. The answer was right under our noses," Hope admitted.

"All we need to do is use my algorithm to set the quantum signature to Alice, and we'll have the telemetry," Robert chirped confidently.

A few minutes of data entry from Robert, and the Cray supercomputer spat out a set of numbers.

Robert swivelled his chair and faced Hope and the Professor. "Right, all we need now is the message in a bottle, without the bottle."

"I don't know about that. A bottle is silica; I think it would travel," the Professor pondered.

"Let's test that hypothesis next time. For now, we should stick to a conventional note," Hope maintained.

The concept of Robert's algorithm was for the wormhole to locate Alice wherever he was in real-time. The opening would then give them a small window through which to dispatch the message.

Shintaro was at his office desk when Hyunbo Kim knocked and entered. Shintaro looked up to greet him and could see chaos in the open-plan area beyond the glass windows of his small office.

"Good morning, Kim-san. Take a seat."

"There is madness on the streets and in your offices," Kim said blandly.

"The force is preparing for martial law. I personally don't see how it will help. Things are crazy enough," Shintaro said, pinching the bridge of his nose and squinting, stressed. He got up from behind his desk and joined Kim in the modest lounge setting.

"I understand you lifted the APB on Black Alice. Why?"

Shintaro was beginning to take exception to Kim's abrasive manner. He fixed his eyes on him and said sternly, "Because I believe it is an unnecessary waste of manpower ... there are far more important things for us to attend to."

"I take it from your attitude that I can no longer count on your support in hunting him down."

Shintaro stood up and shot the smaller man an icy stare. "Like I said, I have more important things to attend to." He'd had enough and was terminating the meeting.

Kim was incensed; it was written all over his face. "Very dismissive of you, Shintaro. As I understood it, I am supposed to receive your full cooperation."

"And you have had it, but with my workload about to increase, I am afraid you have not got it any longer," he lied. It was obvious to him Kim was a time-waster.

"Fine, I'll put that in my report to your superiors."

"Put whatever you like in your report. Now, if you wouldn't mind, I have work to do."

Kim got up slowly and made his way to the door. He stopped and turned to face Shintaro. "I will pursue the interrogation of Miss Tanaka. I am certain she has contact with Black Alice and his accomplice," he said, spoken like a true despot.

As Kim closed the door behind him, Shintaro wondered how he knew about Alice's accomplice, Secta, considering he'd never mentioned him. This compelled him to suspect Kim of an ulterior motive behind his false accusation that Black Alice was behind the pathogen. But he had no evidence of what that ulterior motive might be.

↯

Happy to be garbed in better-fitting threads, Al had his feet up on the coffee table in his swank five-star hotel room and was digging into a box of chicken nuggets. The suite was sandwiched by adjoining rooms occupied by Secta and Sonoko, respectively.

Sonoko opened the door to her juxtaposed room, wandered in like a lost soul, and sat down opposite Alice on the two-seater settee of the three-piece lounge setting. He offered her the box of nuggets, and she took one.

"I found out more about you, Alice," Sonoko said conspiratorially.

"Yeah?"

"Well, being a bit of a fame junkie, I was impressed to discover you were a famous singer."

"What do you mean 'were'?" he barked, as though offended that in 2047 he had been relegated to a has-been.

"Sorry, I did not mean to make light of your fame. I even listened to two of your albums, 'Endangered Species' and 'Sons of Steel'."

Alice smiled, glad his music was still in circulation.

"I toured Japan twice, I think," Alice tried to recall.

"Yes, once in 2004 and again in 2010," she confirmed.

"Hey, you know more about me than me."

"Do you know ... oh, wait a minute, I just received a text from DI Shintaro. He said the meeting with forensics is set for 4 p.m. at the Met, and he will send a pod for us."

"Does he know we are here?" Secta asked.

"Of course, he has my VV tracked," Sonoko said. "He also said that terrible Korean man who works for Interpol, Hyunbo Kim, wants to talk with me. He thinks I know where to find you, Alice."

"Who is this guy?" Alice groaned. "As if there isn't enough crap going on without some Interpol flat-foot on my butt."

"And he is not a very nice man. He came to my apartment with Shintaro," Sonoko added with angst.

Alice stood up and walked over to the big sliding glass doors that opened out onto the small balcony. He surveyed the view: the Tokyo CBD and a sky full of clouds. For midday, the sky was very dark and foreboding.

"Looks like a storm's coming," Alice observed.

Secta joined him. "Hmm, cumulonimbus incus, a typhoon perhaps?"

"Yes, there is a typhoon warning, but it will not hit Tokyo until around 5 p.m. Normally, typhoons are very weak by the time they reach Japan, but this one is strong. There has been an increase in typhoons over the last few years due to global warming. It will bring acid rain for sure."

"It's a wonder the acid rain doesn't eat away the façade of buildings," Alice said.

"It does, so they are coated with ant-acid-resistant polymer," Sonoko explained.

"Sounds to me like the typhoon will tie in with the martial law announcement. Perhaps this is the calm before the storm," Secta said.

His metaphor wasn't lost on Alice, both of them uncertain as to how Tokyo and the world were going to react to the arrival of the UFO.

"Well, I am going to order some food since the nuggets failed to hit the spot. Anyone else for a munch?" Alice said, rubbing his belly.

Hyunbo Kim used a tracking device to locate Sonoko's VV. He suspected she was holed up with Alice and Secta at The New Imperial Hotel in Shinjuku.

He entered the lobby of the hotel, stopped, and called her.

"Miss Tanaka, this is Interpol Agent Hyunbo Kim. I need to speak with you ... as soon as possible, please. Where are you located?

We can meet there ... Yes, I can be there in fifteen minutes. I am nearby. The hotel café?... All right."

Thunder rolled in the distance, announcing the typhoon was on its way.

Kim made his way to the café, ordered a coffee, and sat waiting for Sonoko.

CHAPTER 16
STAKEOUT

66 **I AM WORRIED** about this man. I do not trust him," Sonoko confessed to Alice and Secta.

"He's after me ... why don't I just confront the bastard?" Alice snapped. He was tired of the cloak and dagger routine and wanted to resolve things quickly.

Secta got up from the settee and began pacing the room, deep in thought. "I think that's a good idea, Alice."

"Alright, Sonoko, you go down first and try to find out why he considers me so important. Then I'll ambush him and give him the old bum's rush. Can you handle that?"

Sonoko giggled. "Yes," she replied. She found Alice's lingo, bravado, and the mischievous look on his face when he was plotting most amusing, but also comforting.

"Done. You go down, and I'll join you in about fifteen minutes," Alice said, walking Sonoko to the door.

Secta slid open the balcony doors and stepped outside to gaze at the stormy sky. It looked even more ominous than before. The air had grown humid, causing a patina of perspiration to form on his skin. A deathly silence hung in the air, occasionally shattered by distant rolls of thunder. The electrostatic air made his skin crawl.

"Secta!" Alice urgently called from inside. When Secta returned, he found out what had excited Alice. A small vortex was floating in the air just above the coffee table.

"Watch this," Alice said, demonstrating by tossing an empty coffee cup into the air. It froze mid-flight. "Pretty funky, huh? That's what I've been telling you about. Time slows down for everything except a traveller when a vortex opens."

Their train of thought was abruptly interrupted when a paper airplane emerged from the vortex and landed on the coffee table. In a flash, the vortex vanished, and the coffee cup unfroze, gently landing on the carpet, still intact.

Alice picked up the paper airplane and unfolded it. A wide grin spread across his face. "It's from Hope ... She says, 'Kew kidnapped Robert's daughter and threatened to kill her if we didn't send him after you. Honor shot Mal ... he will survive. We had no choice but to comply. We suspect Zen sent him to kill both of you. They must have reason to go through all this trouble. We have no idea what it is. We sent him twenty hours ago ... it took us that long to figure out how to send you this message. He has no way of returning. Robert got his daughter back safe and sound. The President ordered Honor's arrest. Be careful, Kew is dangerous. Love, Hope.' I wonder if this Interpol guy has something to do with Kew's arrival?"

He handed the note to Secta. "This complicates matters, Alice. But hey, they did an impressive job figuring out how to send us a message through time using a paper airplane, of all things."

Alice settled on the arm of the settee. "You've always suspected Zen's involvement ... I think this note confirms it. There's no other reason for Kew to be here."

Secta paced the room, his hand on his chin. "But how could they know? We're in the future. Zen could only know that you asked me to join you in stopping the pathogen." He stopped pacing. "We must assume they don't want us to stop the pathogen for some reason."

" I reckon this might be tied in with the UFO? Like, how come there's an epidemic that could wipe out the world going on here in Tokyo and right at the height of it a UFO decides to make first contact ... coincidence or not?"

"Yes, Alice, I have to agree with you."

Alice exclaimed, "Bloody hell! Sonoko!" He rambled, rushing towards the door, with Secta following closely behind. "I forgot all about her!"

Just before reaching the café, Alice halted Secta and said, "Wait here while I do a recce. I'll give you a hoy when it's cool to join us."

Secta nodded and waited while Alice entered the café.

The Imperial Rock Cafe, as the name implied, was adorned with rock 'n roll memorabilia and roughly resembled the Hard Rock Café decor from Alice's era. The ambient rock music barely audible, brought out the muso in him but at the same time annoyed him. He despised elevator music.

He scanned the dimly lit room, finding only a few customers occupying a handful of tables, with no sign of Sonoko. After a couple of minutes of searching, he returned to Secta.

"She's not there," he grumbled, wearing a grim expression. " I reckon the bludger has snatched her."

Secta grasped his forehead and tightly closed his eyes. "Damn, damn ... the bastard!"

He looked at Alice as though he might explode but then regained composure and resolved, "We should contact Shintaro."

Upon entering their hotel room, they discovered a note slipped under the door.

"Don't need psychic abilities to guess what this is," Alice remarked, picking up the note. They moved further into the room, and he read it aloud. "Seems like it's a day for notes. It says, 'You will be contacted in 20 minutes. Follow instructions, or Miss Tanaka will die. Do not involve the police.' So, what do we do?" he pondered.

In unison, they both declared, "Involve the police."

After a tedious phone exchange, Alice managed to reach Detective Inspector Shintaro at the homicide division of Tokyo Metropolitan Police. Sometimes, modern technology proved more of a hindrance than a help. He explained what had happened, and Shintaro instructed them to stay put until he arrived.

Time was running out. Alice stood on the balcony, the wind blowing against his face. It had intensified since his last venture outside, and the sky had grown even darker. In the distance, intermittent sheet lightning illuminated the heart of the approaching massive purple thunderclouds. Thunder rumbled, serving as a warning: a typhoon was on its way.

The house phone rang.

"Should I answer that?" Secta called out from inside.

Alice strode back into the room, his expression determined as if he had absorbed some of the brewing storm's anger. "No, leave it to me." He sank into an armchair, picked up the hands-free phone from the side table, placed it on speaker, and answered, "Hello, who is this?"

"Never you mind," a gruff voice at the other end replied arrogantly. "Are you Black Alice?"

"Yeah, what's this about?" Alice retorted grumpily.

"A pod will arrive at the hotel exactly at 1 p.m. in fifteen minutes. If you miss the pod, she dies. You will come alone. If anyone accompanies you, she dies. Got it?"

"Yeah."

"When the pod arrives at the destination, wait to be contacted. Understood?"

"Yeah."

The call ended.

"I don't like it, Alice. You're unarmed, and Shintaro isn't here..." Secta began but was interrupted by a knock on the door. Secta opened it and was relieved to find Shintaro.

After a quick briefing, with time running out, Shintaro and Secta accompanied Alice to the hotel's Skypod platform on the third floor.

Within minutes, right on schedule, a pod arrived. Shintaro opened the gull-wing door of the four-seater and quickly checked the dashboard monitor, which flashed the name "Alice." It was the correct pod. Stepping back, he extended his hand to Alice. On his palm sat a capsule. "Swallow this, please, Alice," he whispered conspiratorially.

"What is it?" Alice whispered back before popping the small brown capsule into his mouth without swallowing it.

"It's a GPS tracker. It will allow me to track your location. Don't worry; it will dissolve within twenty-four hours and cause no harm..."

Alice swallowed the capsule.

"And here..." Shintaro handed Alice a small pistol. "This is a Beretta Nano Stun-gun. It fires chemical discharge darts, accurate up to twenty metres, and has unlimited shots."

Alice accepted the weapon, small enough to fit in the palm of his hand, and concealed it inside his jacket.

"The Beretta is made of carbon fibre, undetectable. It's only issued to the police."

Alice nodded and climbed into the pod. Despite his frayed nerves, he signalled a brave thumbs-up.

"Good luck, mate," Secta said, his expression filled with concern.

Two silhouettes stealthily entered the room, one larger than the other. The two agents on stakeout were only expecting one person.

The smaller silhouette flicked the light switch up and down several times, but nothing happened.

"Damn!" Honor cursed. "Ze power must be cut."

A powerful light suddenly flooded the room. Shielding her eyes with her hand, Honor growled, "Vat ze?"

The person holding the 3,500 Lumen spotlight demanded, "Raise your hands!"

A hand holding a pistol appeared in the light, aimed at Honor, encouraging her to comply.

The larger person with Honor suddenly lunged toward the light. The gun fired, but it couldn't stop the person's advance.

Karzoff received the shock of his life when he recognised the big man as Anu Set, the man he had killed in Jerusalem just a few months earlier.

"But you are dead. How is this..." Karzoff began, but Set's swift hand knocked the spotlight out of his grip, sending it crashing onto the lounge.

Honor quickly assessed the situation and slowly backed out of the room. Viktoria, armed with a gun, spotted her fleeing and chased after her.

Karzoff ducked down behind the settee, hoping Set wouldn't be able to find him in the dark. However, the android was equipped with infrared retina implants, enabling him to detect the body heat of a human target as a large glowing blob in the darkness. Set reached over the settee, grabbed Karzoff by the throat, lifted him over it, and unceremoniously dumped him onto the couch. Karzoff grabbed the nearby light and flashed it in Set's face, hoping to blind him.

In the bright light, Karzoff could see that Set was no ordinary man. Somehow, he had been resurrected. Set didn't shield his eyes from the light; instead, they glowed an unnatural red, reminiscent of a wolf caught in the headlights of a car. His facial skin had an odd plastic-like sheen, lacking any normal human expression. He appeared machine-like. As Set reached down to grab Karzoff, Karzoff struck him across the face with the metal torch, leaving a deep groove in his cheek. The ugly wound didn't bleed. Karzoff caught a glimpse of shiny metal beneath the exposed flesh and realised he was facing an android.

Unaffected by the injury, Set wrapped his enormous hands around Karzoff's throat and squeezed.

Karzoff's eyes bulged, his legs kicked frantically, and he punched at Set's face, but his efforts were in vain. He was losing the fight, the strangulation sapping his strength. With his face turning the same colour as his hair, Karzoff gasped for his last breath, his body going limp.

The silence shattered with the loud crack of a gunshot. Set released his grip on Karzoff and staggered. A second shot struck him in the back of the head, causing his face to explode with the force of the bullet's exit wound. At close range, a 9 mm gunshot creates quite a mess.

The large man collapsed to the floor.

Viktoria holstered her Glock 17 and then checked on Karzoff. He lay sprawled on the lounge, clutching his throat, gasping for air, but alive.

"You all right?" she asked.

"Yes, barely," he wheezed, squinting up at her. "Thought I was about to meet my maker. Thank you."

"No problem," she said, looking down at the lifeless body at her feet. She grimaced at Set's damaged face, or rather, what remained of it—half of it was gone, revealing a mass of arcing circuitry.

"Is that thing a robot?" she asked, suddenly realising the truth.

Karzoff struggled to sit up, wincing in pain. "That was Anu Set, the man I killed a couple of months ago in Jerusalem. He has been resurrected by Zen, using cybernetics to transform him into an android."

"Seriously?"

Karzoff coughed and spluttered as he slowly regained his composure. "What happened to Honor?" he asked.

"She's been living here long enough to have the perfect exit strategy."

"Call Hope," he rasped. "Have her send over a body bag. I think she and the Professor will want to autopsy my old friend here."

Outside her apartment block, Honor hurriedly hailed a taxi. She wasn't willing to wait around for Set; now it was all about self-preservation. She hadn't anticipated being ambushed by Oceana agents at her apartment, and she wondered how they had known she would be there and at what time. As she entered the backseat of the cab, she fumbled for her wallet inside her coat pocket, opened it, and retrieved her Kairos access card. It suddenly became clear to her— they had been tracking her by reading the embedded microchip in her card, using GPS.

"How clever of you," she murmured to herself. Then, an idea struck her. Leaning forward, she slipped the card under the rear of the driver's seat, wedging it tightly into a groove where it wouldn't easily be found or dislodged. Pleased with her clever move, she settled back into the seat and muttered with a mischievous smirk, "Now you can follow a taxi around for ze next few days." She cockily gave the order to the driver, "Pull over and let me out."

CHAPTER 17
HOIST

THE **POD STOPPED** at what Alice estimated to be an abandoned industrial complex. Standing on the small platform three stories above the ground, with decaying old warehouses below him and ominous storm clouds rolling in the backdrop, it resembled the set of a dystopian science fiction movie.

Alice glanced down and spotted a message scribbled in white chalk-like graffiti on the black tarmac platform.

ALICE, GO TO GROUND LEVEL. WAIT AT FRONT GATE

He followed the instructions and made his way to the four-metre-high heavy-duty wire mesh front gates. The fence, topped with razor wire, enclosed the entire rundown complex. A sign on the gate displayed the obligatory red X icon, indicating Prohibited Entry. However, what caught Alice's attention was the small print at the bottom, stating 'by order of Zen Inc.' A chill ran down his spine as he realised he had been set up. Before he could react, the lights suddenly went out.

When he regained consciousness, he found himself naked, his hands tied above his head, and his feet secured to a fixture on the floor. His head throbbed from the blow he had received. The pungent smell of oil filled the air—he was in a garage. His hands were fastened to a yellow hydraulic car hoist, which held him upright a metre above his head. Blinking to clear his hazy vision, he surveyed the surroundings. It was a large vehicle servicing area with several hoists and a workbench running along one side. The wall above the workbench was adorned with tools. The place was grimy, but it appeared to still be in operation, unlike the exterior of the building suggested. At the far end of the rectangular space, he spotted an office with someone moving inside.

"Hey, you!" Alice yelled out, his voice echoing in the vast space.

The person looked up and made their way towards him, their footsteps scratching against the grease stained cement floor.

The man, short but solid, dressed in a dapper blue suit, stopped in front of Alice. "So, you are the famous time-travelling Black Alice," he remarked.

"Yeah, and who are you?" Alice snarled.

"Hyunbo Kim."

"Thrilled. Now, how about unhooking me from this freaking contraption and discussing this in a more civilized manner?"

"Sorry, Alice, but this is as civilized as it gets," Kim replied.

He pulled a device from his pocket and held it up for Alice to see.

"From the moment you entered the pod, the GPS tracker Shintaro gave you to swallow became inert. Such is the technology of the day. But all transmitters have blind spots, so to avoid any possible detection, it's best to be sure..."

He moved the scanner over Alice's bare stomach until it beeped, indicating a spot of interest.

"Ah, there it is," Kim remarked.

Using a felt-tipped pen from his top pocket, he marked a spot on Alice's stomach, just below his navel.

"Good," Kim said, pleased with himself.

"What the hell do you think you're doing, man?" Alice exclaimed.

Kim fumbled in his side pocket and produced a menacing pointed stainless steel prong, approximately twenty centimetres in length, with a plunger at one end. As he held it up, he squeezed the plunger, causing a small claw to emerge from the pointed end and open. When he released the plunger, it clutched.

"What the stuff do you think you're going to do with that thing?"

Dangling from one of the four metal pylons supporting the hoist was a remote control for operating it. Kim took hold of it and pressed a button. The hoist's servo activated, causing it to rise thirty centimetres, stretching Alice as if he were on a torture rack. He screamed in agony.

Kim halted the hoist, leaving Alice held in an excruciating stretch.

"Why are you here?" Kim asked.

"Argh! To stop the plague—" Alice began.

Kim walked around to face Alice directly, holding up the prong.

The severe stretching caused Alice's muscles to spasm.

Kim positioned the sharp tip of the prong on the marked spot and pushed it forcefully, breaking the skin.

"Argh!" Alice bellowed in agonising pain.

"Secta's going to love this when he gets back," Hope said, her voice muffled a little by the green surgical mask covering her lower face.

"They've definitely got a head start on us with cybernetics. This thing makes Secta's android guard look like a toy," the Professor joked.

They were in an autopsy room, all stainless steel and sterile. On the dissecting table in front of them with a body brick under his back to prop it up was Anu Set. A single vertical cut had him open from the pubic bone to the middle of the neck. There was no deviation around the navel because he didn't have one. Hope had used shears to open the chest cavity and was still holding them in her hand after she had finished hacking it open. Professor de Luz was holding a bone saw he had used to open the ribs and expose the organs—again there weren't any.

"Remove the body block and put it under his neck, let's open the skull I'm keen to see the CPU," Hope said.

Though Set's face had been mostly obliterated leaving a mass of circuitry the main processor didn't seem to be there, Hope figured it was in the cranium.

"Hard to believe he was once a living, breathing person."

"Hard to believe he was once a living, maybe not breathing android," the Professor countered jokingly. "He's got no lungs, no wonder he couldn't speak."

"Zen knows we've got him," Hope said. "He was connected to the Zen cybersphere. Even though Honor would have told them, he would have gone off-line as soon as he was shot because lucky for Karzoff, the bullet took out the power supply."

The Professor slipped the block under Set's neck to support the head, while Hope swapped the shears for an electric cranium saw. She slipped on a pair of goggles and then switched the small circular saw on. After a few seconds of whirring she had circled the skull with a neat cut. She put down the saw and removed the cranium.

"There we go, look at that. About twenty-five percent organic and the rest cybernetics." She moved some wires and circuitry aside to uncover the central processor. Just as she did the President entered the room.

"Good afternoon," the President announced happily. "When I heard about Anu Set here I just had to come for a look see, you don't mind do you?"

"No sir, sorry he's a bit of a mess but it's not gory ... no blood and guts," Hope said.

The President stood beside the Professor and stared at the android in awe. "This thing is amazing, if only Secta were here."

"If he were he'd be concerned by how far ahead of us Zen are in cybernetics," the Professor claimed.

"Yes, I spoke with Karzoff and Viktoria an hour ago and they told me Set moved like a normal human being, that's incredible. But Karzoff said it couldn't speak."

"Yes, there are no speech sub-routines, I don't think they've developed them, maybe on purpose—perhaps they don't need it to speak or there's just isn't enough room in the cranium to fit more software. I've just located the CPU, look," Hope said.

They moved beside her at the head of the table and looked at the small metallic object she held in her gloved fingers. It was still attached by wires to the head.

"The CPU, a positron neutral transmitter processor ... fast, and a very expensive, this little sucker would set you back close to a million bucks." She took a magnifying glass from the mobile tray table beside her and peered closer at the CPU.

"So, it could hear and think but not speak ... just how fast is it? ... The speed of a domestic computer?" The President queried.

"Much faster sir, about the speed of a supercomputer, not quite the Cray that runs Kairos but fast ... hmm, the small print on the processor says, made in Japan by Zen Inc.," Hope said.

"Good grief, this entire thing must have cost what, millions?" the President exclaimed.

"Absolutely," de Luz confirmed. "It's streets ahead of everything else in the world and that's of real concern. They've solved the rejection problems between cybernetics and organics, the next step for them will be the RF series of Warbots that Alice and Secta had to deal with in 2087."

"Goodness knows what else they might develop before then," the President said gravely. "I suspect Alice and Secta might find out, being where the CPU was made."

"What do you think that is?" the Professor said, pointing at an object inside the cranial cavity.

"I think that is the Holy Grail, Professor, a solid-state persistent storage flash drive ... the main memory. The RAM would have gone as soon as the power went down." She looked up at the two men, her face glowing with excitement. "When this is decoded, it could very well reveal some of Zen's dark secrets."

A gunshot echoed, and Hyunbo Kim froze, the nasty device in his hand drawing a trickle of blood from Alice's abdomen. He withdrew the prong and turned to face Shintaro, who was standing just inside the big sliding front doors with his gun trained on him.

Backed up by four SAT (Special Assault Team) cops and with Secta standing beside him, Shintaro shouted, "Drop that, Kim, and put your hands on your head."

"This is Interpol business, Shintaro. You're way out of your jurisdiction."

"It is you who is out of your jurisdiction, my friend. This is Tokyo, and it is my town, not yours ... now drop it or I will drop you."

Kim dropped the prong and submitted with his hands on his head.

Still straining, Alice called out through gritted teeth, "Secta, lower this bloody thing before I pop my cork."

The cops covered Secta as he lowered the hoist. Shintaro cuffed Kim. Alice was getting dressed and said, "I feel about twenty centimetres taller." He walked over to Kim and got in his face. "Seems your smart-ass jamming device failed to block the GPS."

"No, he blocked it all right, Alice," Shintaro admitted. "We followed your pod and then read the instructions on the platform, amateurish for an Interpol agent."

Kim snarled.

"Right now would be the appropriate time for you to tell us where you have Miss Tanaka," Shintaro told Kim resolutely.

A loud clap of thunder was magnified in the hollows of the garage; the typhoon was near.

"I warned you not to call the cops," Kim growled at Alice.

"Okay, if that's how you want to play it," Shintaro said as he pulled a small device out of his pocket and aimed it at Kim. When he pressed the device, it emitted a high-pitched squeal so loud that Alice and Secta had to cover their ears with their fingers. If the two SAT officers hadn't been holding Kim's arms, he would have collapsed on the floor. His eyes rolled back in his head, and he began to convulse, as if suffering from an epileptic seizure.

"What the hell was that?" Alice complained.

"I disabled Kim's VV, so he can't contact his confederates."

"What confederates?" Alice queried.

"The ones holding Miss Tanaka hostage."

Secta and Alice exchanged knowing looks; the situation reeked of Kew and Zen.

"Take him away ... charge him with kidnapping," Shintaro ordered the SAT leader.

They manhandled the prisoner out through the door and into a waiting riot vehicle.

"So how do we find Sonoko?" Alice questioned Shintaro.

"We'll use a retinal scanner on Kim back at the Met. It will retrieve image fragments of the last twelve hours from his memory. Don't worry, it will reveal her location."

"The typhoon is getting close," Secta said.

"Yes, and there will be a declaration of martial law in an hour. Military gunships will be deployed on the streets with orders to shoot to kill anyone suspected of being contaminated. A curfew will be imposed. The GP will have four hours between 10 a.m. and 2 p.m. to attend to their needs outside of their homes," Shintaro said gravely.

They strolled towards the exit doors.

"That, along with the typhoon, will make things very difficult," Secta remarked.

"Indeed, it is believed there are now thousands of infected male psychopaths on the streets, spreading the virus through their saliva. We have no alternative but to exterminate them," Shintaro said dispiritedly.

They stepped outside and watched the SAT electric-powered Bearcat silently drive off. Alice glanced up at a sky that seemed darker than before. Additionally, the wind had picked up, and the air was charged and oppressive.

After closing the entry gates behind them, they made their way to the staircase leading to the pod platform. Alice was the last to reach the staircase, and just before climbing them, he caught sight of something out of the corner of his eye.

"Hey! You!" he yelled and took off after the fleeting figure.

Shintaro and Secta stopped halfway up the stairs and looked back down at Alice darting in between the derelict buildings, chasing after someone.

"Alice, wait!" Shintaro bellowed.

But Alice was determined to catch whoever was running away from them and kept on going. He ran into an alleyway and stopped. Scraps of broken timber, busted bricks, shattered glass, twisted metal, and other debris were strewn all over the floor of the dark lane that ran for thirty metres between two three-storey ramshackle buildings. Then, from the shadows of larger pieces of discarded building materials stacked against one side of the laneway, stepped a figure, then another ... and another. Three of them—it was a trap.

Drooling saliva and snarling like trapped feral cats, the closest guy, the one Alice had been chasing, backed up by the other two, prowled threateningly towards him. He looked like a vagrant, dirty, with unkempt matted hair and tattered, torn clothes. He was barefooted.

Alice decided to take no risks and went for the Beretta. He took aim with the gun in both hands and waited for his target to be in range. He intended to stun him, figuring that might scare off the other two. As the other two emerged from the shadows behind the one closest, Alice could see that one of them was wearing a camouflage sniper's veil and was obviously not a vagrant. As far as Alice could tell, he was in his twenties. The other one was around the same age but looked even more like a pariah.

The first guy was now within range for Alice to fire a shot. He could tell by the deranged look in the young man's eyes that something was seriously wrong. A strange gurgling noise was coming out of his throat, and he was gnashing his teeth as though his only thought was to sink them into someone.

Alice fired, and the dart sank into his target's chest. It stopped him momentarily, but it had little to no effect. The n-pulse should have locked up his muscles and disabled his nervous system, but it hadn't. He just kept right on coming. Now only five metres away and closing in, Alice began to panic. So, he squeezed off another shot, this time aiming for his face. The dart hit him in the cheek below his right eye. Again, it stopped him, but only briefly. The other two were getting closer, their snarls growing louder and louder. The situation was looking grim for Alice.

The closest zombie lunged at him with clawed hands, snarling and spitting, his teeth snapping, attempting to bite him. Alice quickly pocketed the Beretta and threw a powerful left hook that connected with the zombie's chin, snapping his jaw with a loud crack, like a branch breaking. The creature's mouth dropped open, and drool mixed with a stream of blood hung in a long string from his shattered jawbone. But even such a brutal knockout punch failed to stop him; he just kept coming, clawing, grabbing, and scratching at Alice's face.

A loud bang resounded, and a bullet took the top off the vagrant's head, spraying blood into the air. The zombie stood motionless, his face frozen in a macabre rictus. His eyes began to swell, bulging larger and larger.

Alice knew what was going to happen next, so he quickly ducked out of the way. Both eyes ballooned and then popped ... his legs immediately buckled, and he crumbled to the ground, twitching. Four more shots were fired in quick succession, taking out the other two zombies and exploding their heads, painting a surrealistic pattern of blood and brain matter on the walls of the lane.

"Excellent timing, Shintaro," Alice chuckled gratefully. "And for the record, this Beretta stun gun thingy isn't worth shit against these bloody zombies."

"I meant to tell you that, Alice. Sorry," Shintaro admitted.

Secta knelt down beside the body of the young vagrant to examine him. "Phew, this bloke hasn't had a bath in a while!" He moved over to the others. "Hmm, all three of them infected with the virus."

"We call them Putaro ... it means homeless. But the one wearing the sniper's veil is different. Leave them. We should move on; there could be more of them around here."

As they made their way to the platform, Secta asked, "Do you have a homeless problem in Tokyo, Shintaro?"

"Inequality reigns, as it does in all big capital cities ... there is the super-rich, the slaves, and the jobless. The gap is so vast. The rich subjugate the workers, keeping wages low so they can line their pockets with unreasonable wealth. Consequently, jobs become scarce. As a direct result, in the last twenty years, the streets of Tokyo have become filled with Putaro. Not just old homeless bums, but young men and women ... Revolution has been in the air, not only in Japan but everywhere."

"Nothing changes," Alice said remorsefully, recalling his hit song from another era, "Organic Panic." "It just gets worse."

Shintaro continued while waiting at the platform for a pod. "When the virus first broke out, before it was recognised as a virus, it was considered to be the start of the expected revolution. The violence, the killings, it was all blamed on those less fortunate. The fat cats at the big end of town were content to have us, the police, hunt down their detractors and clean up the streets. Now I fear the situation will be exacerbated by martial law."

"Ethnic cleansing," Alice groaned, looking up at the big purple, rolling thunderheads overhead. The typhoon had become a metaphor for what was looming, and he had seen it all before, not only in his own time but in other eras: in 2087 in the aftermath of the

Cyberwars, and in Jerusalem in 587 B.C. with the persecution of the people of Jerusalem, and now in 2047. It was a sorry but familiar story of mankind, and until humankind ceased territorial exploitation, the species was sure to ultimately implode. Alice had learned from personal experience that a society based on greed, religious dogma, and oppression is unsustainable.

They climbed into the first four-seater pod to arrive at the platform, and using his VV, Shintaro programmed it to take them to the Met.

"Are you a socialist, Shintaro?" Secta asked.

"No, my friend, a realist."

Secta looked out of the window at the city below and said forlornly, "It seems that in 2047, with all the changes and undeniable improvements automation and consumerism have brought to the proletariat's standard of living, it hasn't changed the financial power structure, which still rules the human race."

Nodding in agreement Alice growled, "Yeah, no matter what era, government is about as effective as a chocolate teapot."

CHAPTER 18
ZEEMAN-Y

THE SUNSET WAS magnificent from the balcony of Professor de Luz's Darling Harbour luxury apartment. Hope leaned on the balcony rail, relishing the breathtaking view from the thirty-sixth floor. From there, she could see the Sydney Harbour Bridge to the northeast, Darling Harbour below, and the Parramatta River snaking to the northwest. The Blue Mountains and the setting sun were due west, while Botany Bay and the beaches were visible in the south. She smiled at the sky and took in a deep breath of the fresh summer breeze, which was blowing her long blonde hair out like a streamer. The Professor handed her a flute of champagne.

"You look a picture with your hair blowing about backlit by the setting sun, cheers," he said.

They touched glasses and sipped their drinks.

"You know how to tickle a girl's fancy, Professor. What are you doing for company now that you're pretty much a local?"

He walked her over to the round table of the outdoor setting, in the centre of which stood a furled umbrella, and motioned for Hope to sit at one of the six deck chairs. He pulled up one for himself. "Oh, because I work unconventional hours, I have a service that delivers me the fetish I require when I feel the urge," he said with a sly grin, then subtly changed the subject. "Hope, I asked you here to tell you what Robert and I managed to decode off Set's flash drive," his Texan accent cutting through, perhaps because Hope had referred to him as a local, and he preferred to keep his Texan uniqueness.

"Excellent, I was worried it might have been damaged or had some sort of protective erasure mechanism."

"No, it was fine, but it took us about twenty hours to crack because it wasn't based on code but algorithms."

"How is that different?"

"Algorithms are a finite number of calculations or instructions that, when implemented, yield a result, whereas code is a way to provide instructions directly to a computer. In essence, algorithms are a series of different operations to be performed in a certain order, very different from code. The flash drive used a binary heap, as opposed to sorting a different data structure. This is more efficient when you want to find the smallest or largest element in a sequence. Essentially, you don't need to be able to code to create an algorithm any more than you need to know how to read music to write a song. It is the abstract step where algorithms enable us to find patterns via clustering, classification, machine learning, and any other number of new techniques underpinned, not by code, but by algorithms. This new step is needed to find the patterns you or I can't see. Like the spectrum of light, where there are wavelengths that the human eye can't see, there are patterns we can't see beyond certain volumes of data. The volume over which we can't see patterns is big data."

"So are you saying Zen has used big data binary algorithms instead of code, and that is revolutionary," Hope summed up.

"Alien, even. As far as I know, the IT and AI world are a long way off using algorithms in such a manner ... as a driving platform for AI."

"Both Alice and Secta suspected Zen or alien collusion."

"There's more ... the flash drive contained details of sequenced pre-programmed triggers ... we were stumped by the data, but maybe you can make sense of it." He handed Hope half a dozen A4 pages clipped together, while retaining his own copy.

"Read this through and give me your thoughts," he said.

"Well, straight off the bat, the first page has to be instructions," Hope deduced.

"Yes indeed, it appears to be commands inputted from an outside source that were then wet-wired into Set's nervous system."

"So, he was programmed online from an outside source."

"Yer damn right he was."

She flipped through the pages, speed-reading them. "This on page three looks interesting ... it reads like a tweet. Directive access open = ZeemanY72.8@137.6W."

The professor found the equation in question. "Yes, Robert and I thought this one over a lot. We think they are coordinates to a place, but we couldn't determine where."

"I think you're right, but the clue is Zeeman. From memory, I think he was a Dutch physicist who had something to do with the splitting of the spectral line into components."

"Yes, well done, Hope. I'd forgotten that ... in the presence of a magnetic field."

"But there was something more about him ... wait, Zeeman-Y," she punched it into her iPhone. "Ah, there you go, the Zeeman crater. Y lies across the northern wall, reaching almost to the relatively flat interior floor. Zeeman Y is the northern wall of a crater."

"Where?" the Professor queried.

"On the dark side of the moon."

He whipped his glasses off and pinched the bridge of his nose between his fingers. After a moment's contemplation, he peered back at Hope. "Well done."

"No problem, now we know Zen has a moon base," Hope said.

De Luz stood and then strolled over to the balustrade. "This probably confirms the alien intervention hypothesis. Alice and Secta claimed it existed but hadn't been able to prove it. They're probably coming here because we're going there. Over the next few years, the moon will have bases on it."

"Why would Set have been sent code from a secret moon base?" she pondered.

"Because the algorithms are written by aliens, and they want them kept secret."

Hope got up and joined the Professor, who had wandered over to the balcony rail and was watching the moonrise.

"I guess you're thinking what I'm thinking," she said. "These aliens are responsible for Roswell, UFO sightings, abductions, and have been colluding with governments and the likes of NASA for years. Zen must be their Earth base, and Gorrick, as Alice always maintained, is likely to be an alien."

"And they're genetically engineering androids to ultimately occupy the planet," the Professor added. "We know that from what Alice and Secta witnessed in 2087."

"What if a component of their future stratagem is to release an alien pathogen to exterminate a huge chunk of Earth's human population?" Hope said, aware it wasn't just a hypothesis.

This time the pod journey wasn't as enjoyable. Under darkening skies, they could see small fires burning in the streets below. At one point, when they crossed the main road of a suburb, there were hundreds of looters smashing shop windows, lighting fires, and fighting each other.

"Because everyone is connected by VV, the news of martial law has travelled fast. The people are already reacting to it," Shintaro said gravely. "We'll be lucky to make it safely to the Met." Shintaro messaged ahead to advise the forensic scientists that they were running late.

The Met was chaotic. The martial law announcement had sent the police force into meltdown. Shintaro led Alice and Secta through a main corridor packed with officers dressing in their riot gear. They entered the elevator, and Shintaro selected the designated floor by VV.

"Martial Law has sent the place into overdrive," he said, stating the obvious.

The seventeenth floor was far less frenzied. They entered the meeting room.

Three scientists in white lab coats were seated at the board table, which could easily have seated twenty. Shintaro introduced Alice and Secta to the three grim-faced middle-aged scientists who nodded like glove puppets.

Alice felt like he was being scrutinised like an auction item nobody wanted to bid for. "I ought to be getting used to this," Alice thought ... but he wasn't, and that was far more painful than any irony.

Skilled at dealing with suits, Secta took over and bowed appreciatively. "Gentlemen, thank you for meeting with us today. Please accept our humble apologies for our delayed arrival," he said diplomatically.

His charm did the trick, and the shroud of reservation exuding from them seemed to vaporise, and they cheered up. After quite a long elucidation, the three scientists had a clear understanding of why Secta and Alice were in Japan and Secta's knowledge-based overview of the problem that confronted them. It was time for the scientists to respond. Doctor Yashida, the most senior of them and the stuffier, stood and explained much to Secta's delight that they had captured a pregnant female, and tests had resulted in determining the gestation period would only be ninety days. It was unheard of for a human foetus to develop adequately in ninety days and survive; the shortest being around twenty-two weeks or one hundred and fifty-four days.

The doctor triggered an interactive 3-D hologram projector, and an image of a solid molecular structure materialised, floating in the air above the black board table.

Alice gazed up at the ceiling, looking for the source of the hologram, and spied three small white globular capsules attached to a ceiling tile beaming a triangulation of lasers that converged to strike a circular metallic disk, the size of a quarter, flush-fitted into the center of the board table, over which the 3-D hologram floated. He was intrigued, having once been a hologram himself.

Secta was also impressed by the technology, in particular, the high resolution of the image. "So, I presume this to be a blood sample from the pregnant girl?" Secta solicited.

"Yes," Doctor Yashida affirmed. "As you can see, there is nothing abnormal about the blood."

Secta stood up and started pacing the floor, characteristically gripping his chin with his hand. He was making mental computations. "Can you show me a sample of the foetal blood, please?"

"Yes," Yashida said, and aimed a remote that changed the image. "Again, there is nothing abnormal. No virus, not even a remnant of a virus."

Secta ignored Yashida's scepticism. "I think the virus might mutate into a nucleotide within the host's DNA."

The scientists shook their collective heads in disagreement with Secta's hypothesis.

Secta stopped pacing and asked, "Is it possible to magnify the image?"

Yashida reluctantly aimed the remote and zoomed in on the molecular structure.

"Keep going," Secta requested.

One cell exploded into the DNA polymer, and the zoom stopped there.

"No, further ... much further," Secta said with excitement, like he was on an expedition into a lost world.

"I will have to recalibrate, one moment," Yashida said annoyedly while messing with the remote.

The oldest of the scientists, Professor Ito, who had so far been relatively quiet, spoke up irritably, "You are wasting our time, Doctor Secta. What could you expect to see that we haven't seen already?"

"There," Yashida announced, and again aimed the remote at the image. He pressed the zoom, and the image was magnified by increments until a small anomalous molecule appeared parked on a strand of DNA.

"Stop!" Secta said animatedly. "That's it ... exactly what I was looking for."

Alice's taunt lips curled into a wry smile, confident that Secta was about to blow their minds.

Secta pointed at the small dark red cell. "That, gentlemen, is a molecule of Propynylidynium. It is an element from outer space, and it is masking the virus. Please zoom further, Professor Yashida."

His attitude changed to more positive, Yashida obliged, and the cell opened up under magnification to reveal a completely new molecular structure.

"What is that?" Yashida said in awe.

Floating in 3-D was a structure of blocks.

"I know exactly what that is," Secta said confidently. "It's a blockchain. Each block includes the cryptographic hash of the previous block in the blockchain, linking the two. The linked blocks form a chain. The iterative process confirms the integrity of the prior block, all the way back to the original genesis block. It isn't an anatomical virus affecting the hosts ... it is a digital virus ... a blockchain that I'd suggest is of alien invention."

The three Japanese scientists were now on their feet. Gone were the dour faces, replaced by total astonishment.

"The first blockchain was conceptualised by a Japanese known as Satoshi Nakamoto in 2008, at Zen Corporation laboratory in Tokyo," Professor Ito explained.

"Did you say Zen Corporation?" Alice questioned, with a sharp glance at Secta.

"Bingo!" Secta exclaimed.

The three scientists and Shintaro looked at Secta quizzically.

"Sorry ... presumably a word from before your time ... what I meant to say was astounding," Secta babbled.

"You will have to excuse me gentlemen, I have been summoned by my superior," Shintaro said solemnly, got up, and left the room.

Shintaro knocked on the door to the office of Superintendent Nakamura, then entered. The top-floor office was considerably more elaborate than his humble hovel down on 5th floor homicide.

Seated behind his desk, Superintendent Nakamura, in his fifties, was overweight and balding, with an affable demeanour. "Take a seat, Shintaro," he said with a gruff voice.

"Yes, sir," Shintaro said stiffly, and selected one of the two chairs facing the Super.

The Super's face soured as he glared at Shintaro, "You have arrested Interpol Agent Hyunbo Kim for abduction."

"Yes, sir. He abducted Miss Sonoko Tanaka as a hostage to lure Black Alice into a trap. I filed a report by VV to the database."

"Yes, I have read it, however, Agent Kim claims it was in the line of duty that he arrested Miss Tanaka in order to capture Black Alice, whom he claims to be responsible for the virus."

"Sir, Black Alice is on the tenth floor, meeting with scientific forensics department heads as we speak, helping us to solve the epidemic. He is not responsible for anything other than unselfishly giving us his total assistance. Kim's claim is absurd. If Kim was acting in accordance with the law, why would he refuse to divulge the location of Miss Tanaka?"

"This matter has attracted the attention of Commissioner General Watanabe," Nakamura said sternly. "He is asking for an explanation and is demanding Kim's immediate release."

"Not until I've scanned him for the location of Miss Tanaka, sir."

"You're a good cop, Shintaro. I trust your judgment, but I am ordering you to release Kim immediately."

Shintaro stood abruptly, his lips tight, his eyes staring beyond his superior officer, unable to look him in the eye ... he had his orders, and like a good cop, he would execute them.

"As you wish, sir," he said, bowing his head slightly. He then turned on his heel and strode toward the door, inwardly piqued by Nakamura's lack of support.

As he reached the door, the big superintendent said calmly, "After you have scanned Kim and determined Miss Tanaka's whereabouts, of course."

A wry smile broke on Shintaro's face.

CHAPTER 19
BREAKOUT

WHEN SHINTARO RETURNED to the meeting, Professor Yashida had just conceded to Secta's request to inspect the pregnant captive girl. They were all getting on like a house on fire.

Alice asked to accompany Shintaro to observe Kim being scanned, while Secta and Yashida inspected the female detainee. The four of them took the elevator to the basement where Secta and Yashida went to the forensic stockade, and Shintaro and Alice continued along the clinical corridor until they reached a door marked ES for examination scanning.

Inside the small room, there was a large studio one-way window to observe the scanning in the even smaller room on the other side. Three chairs faced the window, and there was a small console. Shintaro offered a seat to Alice. A few moments later, Kim was led into the other room through a different doorway by a prison guard accompanied by a doctor in a white lab coat. Kim was forced to sit in the only chair, which reminded Alice of pictures he'd seen of an electric chair. An apparatus attached to the back of it locked Kim's head into a fixed position, staring upwards towards the ceiling. His hands and feet were coupled to secure fittings on the arms and legs of the chair. The doctor then fixed a set of horrific-looking stainless-steel clamps onto Kim's eyes to pry open the eyelids, making him look like the victim of a bizarre experiment in a B-grade science fiction movie from the '60s.

The doctor opened a small eyeglasses-like case and took out a syringe. After testing it, he proceeded to inject Kim's eyeballs with a fluid. The screams of pain caused Alice to wince, but when he recalled what Kim had intended to do to him, strung up on the hoist in the garage, he began to enjoy the man's suffering.

With both eyes injected, the doctor and the guard left the room.

There was a small digital unit and a monitor on the console in front of Alice and Shintaro. The doctor entered the room with them and took the third chair in front of the unit. He turned it on and fiddled with a couple of dials.

Two red laser beams shot from the ceiling directly into Kim's retinas. It would have been blinding, and Kim struggled in his seat, obviously in a great deal of discomfort. A black arrow pointing down appeared on the monitor, which incrementally turned blue, the colour rising up the arrow. After thirty seconds, the arrow was completely blue, signifying the task was complete.

The Doctor swivelled around his chair and said to Shintaro, "All done, sir, you can review it at your leisure."

"Thank you, Doctor Kobayashi," Shintaro said, taking the doctor's place at the controls.

The doctor left and then appeared with the guard in the other room to unfasten Kim from his restraints. They helped the wobbly-legged man out of the room.

Shintaro turned a knob, and low-definition pictures flicked across the monitor like a film or a video being fast-forwarded.

"We are looking here at the last seventy-two hours of Kim's visual memory. The techs call it virtual memory because it's an algorithm generating the pictures from nerve signals at the back of his eyes coupled with his retinal implant. Do not ask me how it works, but it does, as you can see. Here, he is looking at you strung up on the hoist."

"Yeah, well, let's not take a screen grab of that, it's not exactly flattering," Alice admitted.

Shintaro scrolled back, and images flicked past with a time reference at the bottom of the screen. When he saw a flash of Sonoko's image, he stopped it and said with a smile, "There we are."

Secta peered through the small viewing window in the door at a teenage girl huddled like a frightened cat in the corner of the tiny cell. He turned to Doctor Yashida, "Is it safe to go inside?"

"No, not without a guard," he said, referring to the officer standing beside him.

The officer opened the door and led Secta and Yashida inside.

The girl was sitting on the floor with her knees up to her chest in a puddle of her own excrement. She looked up sharply at Secta and snarled. Her face was pale, her hair matted, skin dirty; she was in a terrible state, and most of her clothing was torn.

Yashida explained, "She does not speak, acts like a feral animal, brainless. If you try to touch her, she will bite and claw at you with the ferocity to kill."

"Hmm, protecting her foetus. So, what do you feed her?" Secta asked.

"She will not eat or drink. I do not know how she survives except for the liver."

"What do you mean liver?"

"She had bitten one of the officers that apprehended her and infected him. He's in the next cell, will not live long. We anesthetised her so we could do a pregnancy test. While she was out, we pumped her stomach to test the contents for drugs and so forth and found huge hunks of liver she had consumed raw."

"So the liver has been keeping her alive. It's not unusual for pregnant women to have a craving for raw meat," Secta said.

"Yes, but it was human liver. We think it belonged to the contaminant that had inseminated her. We think whenever a female is inseminated by an infected male, like a black widow spider, she kills the male and then consumes the liver to provide her sustenance to last the short gestation period."

"And then what?"

"You mean once she gives birth?"

"Yes."

"We do not know yet. She certainly will not be producing milk to feed the baby."

"How far gone is she?" Secta asked.

"We think two weeks, but we can't be sure. However, one thing is for sure, if we cannot get her to eat, she and the baby will die within days."

The young girl hissed and spat at Secta.

"Do not let the saliva hit you; it could contain the pathogen," Yashida warned.

"Show me the contaminated officer."

When they stepped out of the room into the corridor, they heard a commotion—yelling and banging—all hell had broken loose. From an adjoining corridor, a prison guard flew through the air and slammed into the wall as though a giant had tossed him there. He lay still on the floor, dead, his bones shattered, and blood puddling on the floor from a massive crack in his head.

Two men brandishing stun guns burst into the corridor. Secta recognised them immediately; it was Kew, and of all people, Anu Set!

Kew sighted Secta and took aim at him. But as he pulled the trigger, the doctor stepped out into the line of fire from the cell Kim was imprisoned in and took the hit. He went down.

Before the guard could react, Set grabbed him in a vice-like grip and snapped his neck with a sharp twist. He let the dead body slump to the floor beside the unconscious doctor. Then he grabbed the metal door to the prison cell and ripped it clean off its hinges. Attracted by the noise, another guard rushed from behind Secta and confronted Set. The guard was big and looked a match for Set. A fist like the front end of an express train crashed into the guard's ribcage, three ribs snapped and pushed inwards, puncturing his lungs. Set grabbed his head and smashed it against the concrete wall. A trail of blood smeared the white paint as he slithered limply down the wall onto the cement floor, dead as.

On their way to meet Secta and Yashida, Alice and Shintaro appeared behind Kew and Set. When Alice saw it was Kew, he stopped dead. Then when Set turned and faced him, Alice's jaw dropped open in disbelief.

"You! What the hell are you doing here, you're dead?" Alice bellowed.

"You're the one that's dead!" Kew yelled back, raising his gun and peeling off a round at Alice that only just missed.

It was Shintaro's turn; he drew his pistol and fired at Kew, but he too missed.

Kew could see Secta wasn't armed, so he rushed him, on the way firing off a shot at Doctor Yashida, who collapsed stunned.

Kew grabbed Secta around the throat, spun him around as a shield, and yelled at Shintaro, "Right, free us a passage out of here, or Secta dies right here and now!"

Alice glanced sharply at Shintaro, who was poised to take another shot. "He'll do it, I know this mongrel."

Shintaro took what Alice said on board and yelled back, "All right, all right, but if you do not free him safe and sound outside the building, I will order SAT snipers to take you out. I have already put a team on standby out there. You hear me?"

Kim knew Shintaro would have used his VV to do that. With swollen eyes from the injections and clamps, he muttered to Kew. "Normal procedure, Shintaro would have done that."

"Okay, Shintaro, you have a deal, but Kim goes with us," Kew served up in reply.

"You're welcome to him," Shintaro returned serve with interest.

Alice grinned at Shintaro, "Alright!" he growled approving the guile of the man.

With Set and Kim behind him leading the way and still holding Secta around the throat, Kew backed along the corridor, all the while with his gun trained on Alice and Shintaro, who were following at a safe distance.

Set came to the emergency exit, opened it, then held it open for Kew. Once through, he locked it from the other side.

"They will lock the exit," Shintaro said hurriedly. "We need to back around the other way. Follow me, quick."

They rushed back the way they'd come past Doctor Yashida on the ground, sitting up scratching his head, dazed. He looked at them, confused as to why Alice and Shintaro would be in such a hurry.

They reached the street outside, puffing out of breath, and found Secta having a casual chitchat with members of the SAT team as though nothing had happened. Kew, Set, and Kim had vanished.

Alice patted Secta on the back, "Glad you're okay, buddy ... but what the hell is Anu Set doing alive in 2047?"

"Last person I expected to see, Alice, but you know what? Throughout the whole escape charging through the Met... he didn't say a word or even mutter a sound."

"Does that mean something, Doctor?" Shintaro queried, holstering his weapon.

"There was something about his eyes..." Secta pondered.

"He ripped that metal door right off its hinges!" Alice exclaimed.

"I think he's an android, it's the only explanation," Secta concluded.

"Explanation of what?" Shintaro said confused.

"Bloody hell, I fought him a couple of times when he was human and let me tell you he was a handful then ... now if he's an android, we're going to need an army to beat him."

"We both witnessed him killed back in our time," Secta explained to Shintaro. "He was a special agent for an organisation we have proof is conniving to exterminate mankind, and we suspect responsible for this pandemic."

"But did you not tell Yashida you believe it is of alien origin?" Shintaro questioned.

"Yes, and so too is Zen Corporation."

"Zen Corporation?" Shintaro said surprised.

"Wait a minute, that island where Sonoko is being kept?" Alice remembered.

"Yes, the Tokyo Bay reclaimed island facility, Zen Island belongs to Zen Corporation, a most politically influential organisation here in Japan."

"Ah, the thick plottens," Secta said jokingly, leaving Shintaro with a furrowed brow wondering what the hell the phrase meant.

CHAPTER 20
WALKERS

THE CLUB'S DARKENED oak panelling and high-backed leather chairs gave it the appearance of a place that could have dated back to the late 19th century. Honor sat in a big leather wing chair, positioned in one of the bay windows, which offered an unobstructed sweeping view of Sydney Harbour. This was a club that, for over a century, had been a male bastion, and she felt privileged to have broken that tradition with an invitation into its hallowed halls to meet him. She was alone, and the room was empty, with the pungent aroma of pipe tobacco hanging in the air, adding to the old-world ambience.

He arrived a tad late but made a grand entrance. Resplendent in a white gabardine suit, the type traditionally worn by English gentry when visiting the subcontinent, at six foot four with short-cropped white hair and pallid skin colour, he could easily be mistaken for an aristocrat. Gorrick sat in a chair opposite Honor.

"Good morning, Honor. I ordered freshly brewed coffee on the way in. I assume you take it?" he asked.

Removing her sunglasses, she smiled automatically at him, the smile turning mildly flirtatious. "Absolutely, sir … why select ze Royal Automobile Club in preference to meeting at your office?"

"Because my office block is under surveillance, and this place is not. Were you tailed?" he said curtly, his mood dark.

When she realised his seriousness, she curtailed her coquettish attitude. "No," she said bluntly.

"A good disguise, the short-cropped hair ... the executive business suit ... large sunglasses," he said, staring at her with one raised eyebrow.

It was then she noticed for the first time that he didn't blink.

"It pays to blend in on ze street."

"Is your accommodation satisfactory?"

"Yes, but it would be wiser, I think, if I was out of ze CBD for a while. There is too greater risk of being recognised."

"That is precisely why I summoned you," his affable tone transformed to brusque. She could feel something ominous was coming.

"Firstly, the botched attempt to get your possessions from your apartment cost Zen a two-point-seven-million-dollar android." He glared at her coldly to add emphasis. "Then, to top that off, the two-point-seven-million-dollar android has fallen into the possession of the enemy and is likely to be reverse-engineered."

Honor's mood chilled as though she'd been doused in liquid nitrogen. She started to speak, "I sincerely apologise, sir, I did not expect—"

Gorrick cut her off sharply, "Too late for apologies, Honor, but I concede it wasn't entirely your fault. Set's programmers should have known better. I'm not here to chastise or punish you. I consider you a much more valuable asset than that ... I want you—"

He was cut off mid-sentence by the arrival of a suitably attired waiter. His white-gloved hands held a silver service tray upon which he balanced a silver coffee pot, porcelain cups and saucers, cream and sugar in containers. He quietly, without expression, poured the coffees and then served them.

They helped themselves to cream and sugar. The coffee pot and additives were left on the small round Edwardian coffee table between them, and the waiter took his leave, all with a degree of pomp and ceremony that Honor detected Gorrick relishing.

"As I was saying, I want you to get Set back, and I want it done quickly before they completely dismantle him and begin reverse-engineering. Surely you know where they would have taken him. I'm giving you free rein on resources. I don't expect you to do it personally, use your knowledge of Oceana to coordinate it. Can I expect your full cooperation?"

"I embrace ze challenge, sir. Fortune favours ze brave," she said audaciously.

"Good, so arrange to abduct de Luz, and I also want Secta. I want everything he learns from 2047 before Oceana can benefit from it."

"But sir, Secta is off-world on a mission," she posed, her eyebrows raised questioningly.

He held up his hand to stop her. "I know … but they will need to bring him back, won't they, if they want de Luz to live."

"But sir, with all due respect, ze President will not trade Secta for de Luz."

"Well, we'll see about that … at least it will force them to bring him back. Now, as for your accommodation, I have a house in Point Piper on the harbour. It has the highest security." He took a key card from his inside coat pocket and handed it to her. "This will provide you access to the house and the guest room, it will also access the spare car in the garage for your use. The house is totally online controlled from my office with CCTV throughout. There are two live-in maids who will see to your every need. Come and go as you please."

Her flirtatiousness returned. She felt a pang that sharing the same house might give her an opportunity to seduce the man she had come to revere for his cold charm and intellect. She felt they were similar: much maligned, misunderstood, capricious, and unconventional. Then the thought struck her that he might be gay.

"Do you not have a partner, sir?"

"No."

"Are cameras in ze bathrooms?" she questioned.

"Yes."

"For you to watch at your discretion?" she pouted.

"Yes."

"Hmm, when can I move in?"

With Kim released, they needed to move fast to rescue Sonoko. But first, Secta wanted to examine the captured infected male, so it was decided to leave him with Doctor Yashida to do that while Alice and Shintaro went on the raid.

Shintaro quickly assembled a SAT team, and they boarded Bearcats for the drive to Zen Island in Yokohama Bay.

It was dark and eerie driving through the city streets, deserted of civilians but not gunships—they were everywhere. Shops had been set ablaze, looting and vandalism were rife. Cars had been overturned in the streets, and many of them were left burnt-out shells. In one place, the plastic pylons from which the Skypod rail was suspended had been so badly burnt they had melted. The pod system was out of order. The city had become a war zone.

On several occasions, they had been forced to stop to wait for a street battle to finish before moving on. In each case, it didn't end well for the infected pariah. Overhead, the sky was full of silent drones—some for the military, some for the police. Some were for surveillance only, while others were capable of accurately taking out a target.

Walkers, as the soldiers had nicknamed them, were mindless of their opposition, which made them an easy target for skilled snipers guided by surveillance drones. The streets were littered with the corpses of walkers. It was like target practice for the soldiers. Safe within their gunships, they could easily pick off walkers as they emerged from hiding places, because they just kept walking towards the gunships, oblivious to the threat. Even after horrendous injury, such as having an arm blown off or their face obliterated beyond human recognition or riddled with bullets, irrepressible, brainless, and robotic, they just kept coming—programmed by a parasitical microbe that cared not whether its host lived or died.

Alice looked away from the window at Shintaro, seated beside him on the back seat of the Bearcat. "This is sick. They don't feel a thing. It's like a turkey shoot."

"It's best to think of them as dead already, I'm afraid. There's no way back once they've been infected. They're just brainless empty shells you're seeing. You need to remember they're walking weapons not much different from the suicide bombers that plagued your time."

"I hear ya … there won't be many young blokes left in Tokyo once this is over."

"That is true. I am worried that it is taking us too long to get to Sonoko. With Kim free they will be expecting us."

"Yeah, I thought of that too, I reckon we're heading right into a trap," Alice said.

Shintaro leaned forward and said to the SAT leader on the front seat, "We cannot have any more delays, go around all this."

He turned to Shintaro, "We'll try sir but it's everywhere. I'll get a feed from the police drones en-route, that might give us a clearer passage."

Shintaro reclined back in the seat, "That might help. I just got a text message … the pregnant girl has died."

"The prisoner?"

"Yes. Apparently, she bit through her wrists and bled out, nothing anyone could do. That will at least provide Yashida and Secta the opportunity to study the foetus."

"I don't think so, she'll combust into dust very quickly."

"One moment … you are right Alice … I just received another message, that is exactly what happened. Damn, an opportunity gone begging."

Secta peered through the small viewing window in the cell door at the infected male prisoner inside. Attendants had fitted him with a straightjacket to prevent him injuring himself or anyone else. He was huddled on the floor in the corner of the empty room brooding.

"Pity about the girl but at least we have this chap. How did they manage to get him into the jacket?" Secta asked.

"It was an effort. They shot him with enough tranquiliser to anesthetise a horse and it slowed him just enough to slip a bag over his head to stop him biting and then got the jacket on him. I have taken a blood sample for you to study."

Secta turned from the door and faced Yashida, "Yes, that would be good but I also need a fresh sperm sample."

"Here, he's all yours," he said, holding up a can of spray.

"What's that?"

"Spray on latex surgery gloves, you peel them off after you have finished."

Keen to see this new invention, Secta held up his hands for Yashida to spray, seconds later when it dried he was wearing thin latex gloves.

"Brilliant," Secta said with a grin, as Yashida gave him a small glass vial.

"For the sample," Yashida said, and then nodded at the guard standing close by who opened the door and led Secta inside the dimly lit room.

Back in the corridor with the cell door closed at back of him, Secta looked a little rattled.

"Are you all right?" Yashida questioned, picking up on his vibe.

Secta held up the vial. "Let's get this to the lab for a look see."

A few minutes later Secta and Yashida were in the police forensics lab looking at a 3-D holographic representation of the sperm sample from a digital electron microscope.

Secta sat back in his chair folded his arms and said, "There it is the Propynylidynium molecule masking the blockchain virus. Look at the rate it's reproducing, incredible—every single sperm produced contains at least one strand of the blockchain virus."

"And look there is a rogue cell attached to each blockchain that was not in the foetal sample."

"Yes, you're right. You know I think that might be the detonator," Secta professed.

"What do you mean by detonator?"

"It causes a chain reaction to kill the host once it has detected successful impregnation, injury or danger. Perhaps it detects adrenalin."

Yashida peered quizzically at Secta, "Are you suggesting this blockchain molecular structure is sentient?"

"Yes, and I think once mating is completed the rogue cell there causes the brain to shut down, the eyes to rupture, death and then spontaneous combustion to wipe the slate clean of evidence."

"Fascinating."

"Only theoretical of course," Secta said with a wry smile.

The convoy of two EV Bearcats slowed to traverse the long four-lane causeway that reached out twenty kilometres into the darkness of Yokohama Bay like an illuminated finger. Ahead of them at the end of the causeway stood an austere complex, several four-storey buildings capped with a huge dome, which was totally out of context with the buildings.

"Fancy looking setup ... weird having that dome on top," Alice said offhandedly, "looks more like a temple."

"The richest company in Japan, I suppose that allows them to do what they want," Shintaro said with distaste.

"Where do they get all their wealth?"

"They provide private security ... produce medicinal drugs, a finger in so many pies I think is the expression you use."

"So what do they produce on the island?" Alice asked.

"I don't know. They built it ten years ago ... a reclamation. According to the schematic on my VV there is a container wharf, warehouses and an office block."

"Modest for Zen."

"There is a height restriction here because of the proximity to the airport. Zen headquarters is in downtown Tokyo. This is just admin, warehousing, laboratories, shops and apartments for the workers I believe."

"So, it's a little self-contained Zen city?"

"Yes, I guess you could say that."

After the convoy had crossed the causeway they were stopped by an automated security checkpoint with a barrier gate.

"You'd think they'd have the checkpoint at the start of the causeway," Alice posed.

"They have been monitoring us all the way, if they wanted to stop us they easily could have by activating roadblock spikes."

"So they are a law unto themselves," Alice presumed.

"Yes and no. They cannot prevent us entering, they know I have a warrant."

"So they know we're coming?"

"Yes, but maybe not why."

"I think if Kew, Set, and Kim have anything to do with it they'd know all right," Alice said knowingly.

"I guess so, holding Miss Tanaka here against her will certainly does not give me much confidence in Zen's perceived integrity."

The SAT Alpha leader, Riku Watanabe, turned from the front seat and with the leathery voice of a rugged old campaigner told Shintaro, "Sir, Zen is denying us entry."

Alice peered at Watanabe and identified a take-no-prisoners look in his eyes. Exuding experience, the scars that dissected his eyebrows bore evidence of many a scrap in the pool halls of life.

"Put them through to me," Shintaro growled testily.

Within minutes the barricade opened for the convoy to pass through.

His eyes intense, Shintaro issued directions over his VV and the Bearcats soon pulled up outside a block of warehouses. He then ordered the four SAT standard officers in the second Bearcat to stay put while he, Alice, Watanabe, and an elite officer went to reconnoitre the objective. Directed by images captured from Kim's memory and replayed on his VV, Shintaro was looking for landmarks, a task difficult in the dark. The only light was from overhead sensor-activated security lights positioned every thirty or so metres along the warehouse façade.

"There is a tree up ahead stop beside it," Shintaro ordered. "There … it matches the tree in Kim's memory scan. That warehouse door over there is the entrance." He pointed at a big sliding door.

Alice looked up at a CCTV camera above the door in question, "That camera will ensure us a welcoming committee."

The door was locked but after a quick word on his VV a loud click informed them they'd been provided access.

CHAPTER 21
KEEPER

SENSOR LIGHTS ACTIVATED inside the warehouse as soon as they entered. The enormous space was filled to the ceiling with boxes stacked on pallets. Robotic forklifts waited in the aisles like mesmerized metallic insects. In the gloomy shadows cast from the sparse overhead lighting, Alice felt as though he'd stepped into a colossal beehive, half-expecting a giant Queen bee to appear at any moment.

Alice was brought back to reality by Shintaro's voice. "We need to find a way through this maze to the elevator... follow me this way."

They hurried along a narrow corridor and eventually arrived at the doorway to the elevator lobby. One was waiting for them, so they took it to the 3rd floor.

The door opened to a sterile hospital-like passageway, which they navigated until they reached a door marked A3-76. Shintaro stopped them at the door.

"This is where she is. Riku, you and Kaito lead us in."

"Arm up," Riku told Kaito.

The press of a button switched their handguns from stun to conventional bullets. The Glock 33 pistol was equipped with switchable parallel magazines. One loaded with six 30 mm stun darts, the other six 9 mm hollow point rounds. They held their pistols up in both hands, ready to enter the room.

On the count of three, Riku pushed open the door, and they stormed in. What they found inside was totally unexpected. It was a long rectangular room with 2 x 2-metre containment cells along both sides. Each cell accommodated a pregnant woman. At the very end of the room, an unconscious female had been tethered to the floor, her legs and arms spread-eagle.

Riku gave an all-clear sign to Shintaro waiting at the door, and he and Alice entered. As soon as they were inside, the door closed behind them. Alice turned quickly and tried it. They were locked in.

An amplified voice bellowed, "This room is shielded to prevent incoming or outgoing messaging; your VV's have been disabled. We are monitoring your every move."

They searched the ceiling and found CCTV cameras.

The voice continued, "You will find Miss Tanaka at the end of the room. Also, at the end of the room are cells containing infected males, and this sound…" There was a loud clunk, and the voice continued, "means the doors to those cells are now unlocked. Shintaro and Alice, you are armed with stun-guns while the two SAT officers have twelve rounds between them—I have released exactly twelve infected males, so I hope you're good shots. Good luck."

"Wait!" Alice yelled. "What's all this about? If it's me you want, then just say so, there is no need for the others to risk their lives."

Infected males began stepping out from the cells, snarling and drooling.

Shintaro ran a hand through his thick black hair, a gesture he seemed to revert to when he was anxious.

"Answer me damn it!" Alice shouted. But no reply came.

The first walker out was drawn to Sonoko.

Alice was riled up, "Gotta stop that bloody thing!"

Before Alice could get to Sonoko, the first walker was joined by three others. Alice ran at them but pulled up just short, realising he was well outnumbered. The four walkers stopped beside Sonoko, looked down at her distastefully, and then, to Alice's surprise, bypassed her and came after him.

Riku wasn't about to waste any time and strode defiantly towards them with his gun raised, gripped in both hands. Kaito copied beside him. When they reached Alice, only a few metres from the walkers, Riku opened fire. Bang! Bang! Bang! Bang! He made each shot count with 9 mm bullet holes in their foreheads. Their legs gave way, and they went down with their heads exploded.

By now, the remaining eight walkers had emerged from the cells and were staggering zombie-like towards Riku, Kaito, and Alice, their arms out in front of them, their hands clawed, their mouths snarling, drooling, and their teeth gnashing. Kaito was showing signs of panic and fired off three quick rounds at them. The first shot missed, the second caught a walker in the shoulder, and the third scored a bullseye in the target's forehead. Riku knew the misses had put them at a disadvantage. He fired two shots and took out the two walkers Kaito had missed.

"Hold your fire until the rest are close," he ordered the younger officer. "We cannot afford another miss."

Alice and Shintaro were busily untying Sonoko.

With the downed walkers at their feet, Riku noticed the remaining five walkers were getting perilously close to Alice and Shintaro, much too close for comfort. He glanced sharply at Kaito to check he was okay. Sweat had broken out on the young man's forehead—a sign of alarm.

"Steady Kaito, we can do this," Riku said assuredly. "You have three shots left; I have one… we need to make them count."

After a lot of desperate fiddling, Alice finally managed to free Sonoko's legs.

Shintaro was almost done liberating her wrists when a walker came up from behind and lunged at him.

Riku wasn't expecting such a sharp movement from the walker. He took aim but couldn't get a bead on him.

"Move closer," he ordered Kaito.

But just as the young officer took a few tentative steps towards Shintaro, one of the downed walkers, still alive, grabbed his ankle.

Freaked out, without thinking, Kaito fired two shots into its head, exploding it. Now they were in real trouble.

Alice rushed the walker Shintaro was struggling to get off his back. Its teeth gnashed at the side of Shintaro's face, any second it would inflict a deadly bite.

Alice knew not to punch the walker in the mouth; its teeth would open up his knuckles, allowing infected saliva to contaminate him. So he pulled the stun gun from his pocket and used it to bash in the back of the walker's head. It took half a dozen powerful whacks before its head caved in, its knees crumbled, and it collapsed.

The remaining four walkers were right on top of them.

Riku checked Kaito … he had frozen with fear, so he snatched the gun out of his hands, raised it in his left hand, and took out the closest walker, right between the eyes. Three to go, one shot … then with Kaito's gun in his right hand, he unloaded the remaining bullet into the next walker's head; there was a great spray of blood, and it collapsed in a heap. But he was out of ammo, and the two remaining walkers were coming at them.

Shintaro had an idea and acted quickly. He ran over to where the CCTV camera was positioned on the wall and, taking aim, cast his stun gun at it as hard as he could throw. With the precise aim of a baseball pitcher, the gun smashed the camera lens.

Riku took on the next walker—clenched the gun in his right hand, and then let go an almighty punch with it into its snarling face. The punch miscued slightly, and his fist plunged into its teeth, shattering its jaw, but it didn't stop it. Replicating Alice's move with the stun gun, he wound up and struck out, sinking the butt of the pistol deep into the left temple of the walker's head. With the pistol protruding macabrely out of its temple and blood streaming in a crimson river down its left cheek, the walker grabbed Kaito and fastened its teeth into his exposed neck.

Kaito screamed as the walker pulled its head sharply away, taking a large chunk out of Kaito's flesh. Kaito collapsed.

Riku saw red and without any thought of self-preservation, let fly with an almighty onslaught of punishing punches that pulverised the walker's face into oblivion. When he'd finished and the walker lay twitching at his feet, he turned to Alice and Shintaro. His face and uniform were saturated with infected blood. He knew it was all over for him; he would be infected. But before he could think about it, there was still one last walker to deal with.

Alice had shaped up to take on the last walker, but Riku yelled at him, "No, Alice, I'm infected, leave him to me … there's an aircon grill in the ceiling you can reach from the top of the empty cell. Climb up and open it; I'll take care of this one."

Alice didn't argue; he knew Riku was right, it was all over for him. Leaving Shintaro holding Sonoko, he quickly scaled the two-metre black bars that finished at a truss, a metre and a half below the ceiling, and reached up to the grill. A solid push, and it lifted. Now it was a matter of how to get Sonoko up to it.

Kaito was on the ground, groaning. Riku kneeled down beside him and put a caring arm around the young man's neck. Then, with a sharp rotation of his hands, he snapped his neck—a mercy killing. He rose slowly to his feet and with a look on his face that could melt steel, flew at the remaining walker.

Sonoko was coming around, but very groggy.

The last walker was the toughest-looking. Well-built and full of energy, he and Riku fought like a pair of gladiators. During the fight, Riku caught Shintaro's eye and yelled, "Go, get out of here!"

Shintaro helped Sonoko over to the cell and hoisted her up to Alice's waiting arms. Then, as Alice pulled her up, Shintaro scaled the bars to join him on the truss.

Together they manhandled Sonoko up and in through the open air-conditioning duct.

Down below them, Riku was grappling with the walker when he abruptly stopped. His face contorted, and he began to drool, infected by the virus.

"Do you get ads on your VV?" Secta asked Yashida.

"No, advertisements were outlawed twenty or so years ago."

"But if someone knew how to contact you…"

"My handle?" Yashida clarified.

"Yes, your handle … couldn't that person hack your VV?"

"No, it's peer to peer, like the dark net or the deep net … and the phone aspect of it is controlled by each individual's i-Keeper."

"An i-Keeper, what on Earth is that?"

"Basically, an algorithm empowered by your knowledge to act like a virtual servant to do your bidding, we call it VV."

"Ah, virtual vision, so your i-Keeper monitors all you see like a gatekeeper?"

"Exactly, you can change the name … I think back in your day when Apple existed, an early version of it was called Siri."

"Yes, it was. Can you speak to it?"

"In real-time, yes, the same as Siri, but it is not a politically correct practice in public, so most use the mental interface with one's thoughts."

"Excellent," Secta exclaimed. "How long has this been around?"

"Just before the Korean War."

Secta looked back at Yashida, shocked. "The Korean War … That was in the early 1950s?"

"Sorry, I should have said the new Korean War … It began in the early 2020s and finished when the USA nuked Pyongyang."

"Nuked?" Secta blurted out stupefied.

"Yes, it was the first time a nuclear weapon had been used on civilians since World War Two."

"Unbelievable … I would have expected them to have resolved that issue peacefully. What about the Middle East?"

"Don't start me up, that place would be unrecognisable to you. Syria, Iraq, both annexed by the USA and Israel, Russia in another cold war with the West … a war with Iran is definitely looming. But enough of all that ... tell me about how this time travelling works?" Yashida asked.

"There will come a time when we will be able to send anything through a wormhole, to anywhere, including other planets," Secta told Yashida. "For now, we have a few teething problems to conquer, such as we can only send organics through, and there are inherent problems returning to our time, but we'll eventually solve them."

"What about that age-old problem of potentially affecting history with your interference, do you take that into consideration?"

"Yes, we use the prime directive," Secta affirmed.

"And what does that entail?"

"Fundamental to time travel, the Prime Directive is the embodiment of one of the most important ethical principles: non-interference with other cultures and civilizations. At its core is the philosophical concept that time travellers should refrain from interfering in the natural, unassisted development of societies, even if such interference is considered well-intentioned."

"Perhaps if it doesn't interfere with the prime directive, you could contact yourself in Sydney to find out how much you've advanced the time travel process in all these years."

"You know," Secta thought out loud. "That just might be worth a try. How about I e-mail myself a message?"

"No, that might not work; e-mail is obsolete, everything is now peer to peer on the deep net. Give me a minute to look up your handle on the FBI register," Yashida suggested.

Secta went back to studying the holographic output of the blood sample from the captive infected male on the super electron microscope.

"Got it," Yashida happily announced, "It's the word Hud ... strange word?"

"Hmm, yes, well, that actually makes sense. Morrigan Hud."

"Why is that a person?"

"Yes, it will be when she's born about twenty years from now," Secta said with a chuckle.

"Take that terminal over there," Yashida said, walking Secta over to a desktop array. It consisted of a circular metal disk thirty centimetres in diameter countersunk into the centre of a bench with a chair parked in front of it.

Secta looked for the computer. "Is this a computer terminal?"

"We call it a desktop array these days," Yashida said with a smile.

Using his VV, Yashida activated the unit, and a holographic keyboard appeared on the benchtop.

"There, I'll leave you with it, just hit the spacebar to start."

Secta sat in the chair and followed the instructions. A small holographic light materialised twenty centimetres above the metal disk.

"Oh, and then type in the word search, to open a browser," Yashida said while studying the holographic blood sample.

On hands and knees in the dark crawlspace, Alice, Sonoko, and Shintaro were now outside of the VV shielding. Shintaro knew straight away because his heads-up display activated his i-Keeper. He quickly sent a message to the SAT backup unit waiting for them to prepare for evacuation.

"I don't know about you guys, but I feel a bit claustrophobic in here," Alice admitted through clenched teeth. It was hard going: the crawlspace was only a metre square, dark, and with a very unpleasant odour. Shintaro was leading, followed by Sonoko, and then Alice.

"I am finding it difficult as well … I still feel very dizzy from whatever they injected me with," Sonoko mumbled.

"Do not worry, another twenty metres or so, a sharp left, ten more metres after that, and there is an exit point," Shintaro said. "Beyond that, a fire escape."

"How do you know all that?" Alice questioned.

"My i-Keeper accessed a blueprint of the building to find a way out. It is good my VV is working again … is yours Sonoko?"

"Yes."

"They cannot track me, but they can track Sonoko. We need to shut it down; otherwise, there will be a welcoming committee for us at the exit."

"Can she do that ... just shut it down?" Alice asked.

"No, but I can have it shut down ... there, it's done."

It took fifteen minutes for them to reach the exit point. By the time they'd lowered themselves down into the corridor below, they were filthy, worn out, with skinned throbbing knees.

Alice arched his back and moaned, "I wouldn't be an air-conditioning mechanic for all the tea in China."

Shintaro opened the fire door. "Two flights of stairs, and then we run for it to the front doors. You up for it, Sonoko?" His voice echoed in the dimly lit stairwell.

She nodded affirmatively; however, to Shintaro, who was used to reading people's faces, the worried look in her eyes betrayed her positivity.

Alice looked down, "There's a sensor CCTV camera on the next level. How are we going to get rid of that?"

"We do not, Alice; it would let them know we are here. If we get rid of the light and keep our backs to the wall, we might just get lucky." He pulled a Swiss Army knife from his pocket, opened a spike, reached up, and stabbed the LED light. The next light was two floors below, so there was enough light to see but too dark for the camera.

They made it down the stairwell and exited into the warehouse with all the stacked boxes they'd entered through. Unfortunately, they didn't know the final door to the ground floor triggered an alarm in the security monitoring room as soon as it was opened.

"Right, we have a hundred-metre dash to freedom. Take a deep breath, Sonoko," he looked down at her bare feet and knew it was going to be difficult for her. "You right, Alice?"

"Yep."

"Follow me then," Shintaro said, and then took off at a moderate pace along the aisle leading to the front doors.

Halfway along the aisle, thirty metres from them was a stationary robotic forklift. A small red light blinked to life on its turret.

CHAPTER 22
LEAP OF FAITH

SECTA WAS THRILLED to be talking to a holo-projection of himself twenty years older. There was plenty they could talk about, but being pragmatic scientists, they focused on the critical issues.

"We're looking good at your age..." Secta in Tokyo quipped to the Secta in Sydney.

"We do love a little flattery, don't we? I can't talk long for two reasons; firstly, it's dangerous to cross the prime directive line. I shouldn't tell you too much about us ... and secondly, I have an important meeting with the Professor in ten minutes— imagine when I tell him you've contacted me. Where is Alice?"

"He's on a mission to save an associate, Miss Tanaka, who has been kidnapped by Kew and, of all people, Anu Set."

"Ah, yes Set ... He's an android replicant. It seems there are clones of him in a number of countries ... be careful of him. The version you have there would be superior to the one we had to deal with here."

"So, what do I need to know from you?"

"Most importantly, you can't let Kew return to your time, or he will assassinate the president."

"I see ... okay, got it."

"That's it. Goodbye and good luck."

"Just before you go old son … a personal question … am I still with Viktoria?"

"Yes."

The hologram faded. Secta sank back in his chair and muttered a little perplexed but at the same time contented about Viktoria. "That was positively weird. I should have asked him about Hope … odd he didn't mention her."

"It is not every day you get to talk to your senior self, Secta. I am surprised the laws of physics even permitted it," Yashida said.

"So am I … so–am–I, my friend. Can you get a message to Shintaro to tell Alice that Set is an android replicant and extremely dangerous?"

"Done."

The size of a VW Beetle, the forklift—a bland square block of red-painted metal with wheels concealed underneath—had two sharp forks that protruded from the front like lances. It took up most of the aisle and came at them. They stopped. Alice glanced behind. There was another one coming at them from the other end. They were sandwiched between them.

Alice caught Shintaro's eye, "Over the top?"

"A foot on the fork, up on top, and then jump off the back … you okay with that Sonoko?" Shintaro asked.

She took a quick look behind at the other forklift closing on them, nodded, and muttered, "I guess so."

Shintaro successfully leapfrogged the slow-moving obstacle and waited on the other side for them.

"I'll catch you, just jump onto the fork, okay? It won't hurt you; they're just using it to slow us down," Alice said encouragingly.

She nodded.

"Chaa!" he said as he rushed the red robot. One bound, and he was on the fork, holding out his hand for Sonoko to take. "Come on."

She ran toward it, grabbed Alice's hand, and he assisted her up onto the fork. Both of them standing on separate prongs of the fork, he smiled at her, "See, just like a circus ride. Come on, over we go." He climbed up onto the flat top of the vehicle and looked down at his feet and the decal of Zen with its hexagram star logo in its menacing font. Then he simply slid off the sloping back onto the floor behind the machine.

Sonoko followed, then jumped from the top into Alice's waiting arms. He gave her a big hug, and they locked eyes … there was a little chemistry percolating between them.

Shintaro approached Alice. "I received a message from Secta. He said Anu Set is an android replicant. Be careful."

"That makes sense."

"Okay, let's move," Shintaro said and then jogged off in the direction of the sliding door exit that was only a short distance away at the end of the aisle. Alice and Sonoko trotted hand in hand after him. Before the three of them could reach the end of the aisle, they were stopped dead in their tracks by the sudden appearance of Anu Set, Kew, and Kim, who had stepped out from a stack of boxes brandishing guns they aimed directly at them.

Alice and Shintaro faced off at them. Alice let go of Sonoko's hand, folded his arms in front defensively, and snarled, "So, we meet again Kew … and you Set, what brings you to this time … need some new circuits?"

Alice was buying time for Shintaro to get an urgent message to the backup SAT team waiting outside.

"Very funny, Alice. No, we're here just for you," Kew said snidely.

"I'm such a popular guy … what's wrong Set? Haven't they written any speech sub-routines to allow you to speak?" Alice questioned scornfully.

A small plastic explosive detonated, and the big door slid open, startling Kew, Set, and Kim, who turned to find four SAT officers with automatic weapons trained on them.

"Checkmate, Kew," Alice growled.

Shintaro stink-eyed the supposed Interpol agent and snarled, "You'll keep Kim."

Covered by the SAT team, Shintaro led Alice and Sonoko past the enemy. Alice couldn't resist having another crack at Set on the way. "You were better looking when you were human."

Shintaro couldn't make an arrest even though he had them outnumbered; he knew only too well backup would be on the way. He couldn't afford to risk losing any more men.

As Shintaro, Alice, and Sonoko reached the two Bearcats, the SAT team backed up to the vehicles with weapons raised, aimed at their adversaries.

Two shots rang out, and a bullet grazed Alice's cheek. He caught a glimpse of Set holding the smoking gun just as the warehouse door closed and before the SAT team could return fire. Sonoko collapsed.

They wasted no time getting Sonoko into the rear of the Bearcat. She was bleeding badly from a bullet wound in her thigh. Alice climbed into the back of the Bearcat beside her and checked the wound … it was a through and through.

Shintaro said urgently, "There is a medical kit behind you, Alice. Get the tourniquet and the cauterising pen. Use the pen to seal off the severed artery. Do you know how to use it?"

"No," Alice admitted, getting the kit and frantically fiddling to get it open.

"Like a ballpoint pen, I think you used to call it. Find the place the blood is spurting from, place the tip of the pen on it, and click the end. The laser will seal it temporarily, long enough to get her back to the Met. Okay?"

"Yeah, got it," Alice confirmed.

Shintaro climbed into the passenger seat next to the driver, and they followed the other Bearcat out of the complex.

The wind had picked up, and the dark skies were looking even more ominous. The gate was closed, so Shintaro ordered the leading unit to bust through it. The big bulbar at the front of the leading

Bearcat smashed the gate to smithereens, and then both vehicles proceeded through.

After getting the tourniquet fastened around Sonoko's upper thigh and tightening it, the blood finally ceased spurting. Alice was relieved; it meant she wasn't going to bleed out, but she'd lost a lot of blood and looked very pale. With her blood all over him, cauterising pen in hand, he searched the bloody bullet wound in the unconscious girl's thigh for the ruptured artery.

As the leading Bearcat reached halfway along the causeway, a claw of spikes sprung up a metre high from a concealed groove across the road. The Bearcat hit the spikes at speed, and the reinforced steel sump cover under the engine was ripped open like a sardine can. The vehicle flipped end over end and through the side barrier over the side of the causeway into Yokohama Bay.

The second Bearcat screeched to a tyre-burning halt just before the spikes. Horrified, Shintaro watched the Bearcat sink out of sight in the murky dark water, taking the three occupants down with it.

"What the hell was that?" Alice screamed out from in the back.

"A barricade ... we have lost Bearcat one. Drive on," he despondently ordered the young officer behind the wheel, who had just watched his mates die.

Right then, the typhoon that had been looming struck with relentless force. A two-hundred-kilometre-an-hour gale surged through Yokohama Bay, creating a raging, churning swell of waves that pounded against the side of the causeway, breaking right across the road. The Bearcat was nearly blown over when the waves and gale hit its side.

Without a seatbelt, Alice was tossed about in the back. He hastily held onto Sonoko to prevent her head from slamming against the metal wall of the vehicle.

The driver had to lean forward, pressing against the windscreen to navigate a path through the protruding spikes, which had been bent and sheared off due to the impact of the other ill-fated Bearcat.

The rain poured down like a deluge.

"Bloody hell, what's that?" Alice shouted, but the noise of the gale drowned out his voice. He looked at Sonoko; she was very pale, her lips had turned blue—it was critical to get her a blood transfusion.

Amid the chaos, Shintaro glanced over his shoulder and saw the distress in Sonoko's face and the urgency in Alice's eyes. They needed immediate medical attention for her. He ordered the driver to enter a tunnel that connected to a series of them, forming a honeycomb beneath the city. It was the only way to avoid the mayhem of the city streets. Though it would be a longer route to the Met, Shintaro's i-Keeper calculated that it would be the quickest and safest option.

As soon as they entered the tunnel, they left the roaring, pelting rain behind.

"How are you holding up back there, Alice?" Shintaro asked.

"She's unconscious, probably in shock … lost a lot of blood. How long until we reach the Met?"

"Another twenty minutes. We need to avoid the streets; the typhoon and the fighting would slow us down. Taking the tunnels is the best option. I have alerted the police medical team to be on standby."

To Alice, it felt like an improbable escape from a certain fate. Sonoko's life hung in the balance.

Shintaro stood at the frosted glass door to the Met infirmary. It slid open, and Alice stepped through, looking sombre. Sonoko's blood was on his face, hands, and forearms, and his shirt was soaked with it. He was exhausted.

Shintaro offered a comforting arm around his shoulders and asked, "How is she doing?" He genuinely cared for her well-being.

"I think we made it in the nick time, mate."

"Thank goodness for that."

"Secta is inside helping. I'd kill for a change of clothes, a shower, and a cold beer."

Shintaro smiled, "I think I can help with that. Come on."

He led Alice through the corridor of the emergency section of the police medical division, and they boarded an elevator. The sound of the typhoon continued to batter Tokyo outside.

Two hours later, freshly showered and dressed, but still feeling fatigued, Alice sat at a table in the Met commissary, sharing a beer with Shintaro. Both of them looked worn out—it had been a long night.

Secta breezed in, pulled up a chair at the table, sat down, and said cheerily, "She'll be fine, won't even have a scar."

"How's that?" Alice inquired.

"Well, first they use a skin glue to replace conventional stitches, and then they have this fancy gadget that prints skin like a patch. There's no rejection because they dial up the patient's DNA on the VV network, configure the 3-D printer, and … Bob's your uncle, it prints out a patch of skin that melds perfectly with the flesh around the wound. Good as new."

"What has Alice's uncle got to do with it?" Shintaro asked, puzzled.

"Oh, I'm sorry, Shintaro," Secta apologised. "It's slang; 'Bob's your uncle' means 'as simple as that.' Now, who do I have to bribe for a beer around here?"

Shintaro got up and fetched him a beer from the vending machine.

"I thought you didn't drink?" Alice said, curious.

"Alice, during the surgery, you mentioned that all of the infected males at Zen walked right past Sonoko, even though she's exactly the right age for them to impregnate."

"Yes, the same thing happened back at the lab when the walker broke in. He didn't show any interest in her. What are you getting at?"

"I think I know why. Sonoko might be carrying a gene that repels them."

"Yeah, so?"

"Well, if I'm right, we might be able to isolate that gene to create a vaccine," Secta said enthusiastically. Alice knew it was the kind of scientific puzzle that excited Secta.

"Cool," Alice acknowledged.

"I've taken a blood sample from her and sent it up to Yashida in forensics to work on."

Shintaro returned with a bottle of beer for Secta.

"What's going to happen now that these bastards have killed five of your men?" Alice asked.

"Not much, Alice-san," Shintaro said, taking his seat again. "It will be up to us. High-ranking officials have pulled strings to bury the case … they want to blame the deaths on walkers."

"How convenient for them," Alice snarled.

"So, Zen Corporation wields that much political influence around here, does it?" Secta grumbled.

"They do indeed," Shintaro said disheartened.

"So, it's us against Zen, Kew, Set, and Kim then," Alice said, raising his beer bottle, lifting their spirits. "All for one and one for all!"

Shintaro and Secta raised their bottles, and the three of them toasted in unison, "Cheers."

"I could do with a little shut-eye," Alice groaned.

It was past 2 a.m., and all three of them were exhausted. The MET provided apartments for such situations, so Shintaro arranged one for each of them.

"I arranged for Sonoko to have the apartment next to yours, Alice. She's being taken there now."

Secta finished his beer, placed the empty bottle on the table, and said, "The blood and DNA test results will be ready in the morning. So, we might as well get some rest."

Shintaro led them to the elevator.

The room was small, but Alice didn't mind. All he wanted was to put his head down and get some rest, even though he wasn't looking forward to the hardness of the tatami mat. He had learned from sleeping at Sonoko's apartment that stacking a couple of towels under the mat provided some padding; otherwise, he'd be stumbling around like a walker the next day.

Just as he was about to switch off the light, there was a gentle knock at the door.

CHAPTER 23
DEOXYRIBONUCLEIC ACID

WHEN HE TURNED over, Sonoko's dark hair tickled his nose. She was curled up on the bed beside him, her face buried in her arms like a child warding off bad dreams. He kissed the back of her pale neck.

"Wakey, wakey," he softly sang.

She turned over, her hair covering her face, but one eye peeked open, and then she stretched with the lethargy of a cat.

"Are you married, Black Alice?"

He took a strand of her shiny, long black hair and twirled it with his finger. "No, and I don't have a girlfriend ... in this time."

She laughed and playfully jabbed him with her elbow. "What about in other times?"

"Yes, there have been times, but no weddings."

"Have you ever had to kill anyone?"

He flinched slightly, "That's an interesting question ... yes, but only in self-defence."

A cute, sleepy smile broke on her sweet face. "You risked your life to save mine."

Their conversation was interrupted by a knock at the door, followed by Secta's voice. "Alice, there's a meeting with Yashida at his lab in half an hour. I'll see you at the commissary for coffee first, okay?"

"Yeah, Secta, catch you there."

Yashida respectfully bowed his head to Shintaro, Alice, and Secta as they entered the lab. "Thank you for the early meeting, gentlemen. I wanted to report that I have studied the blood sample from Miss Tanaka, and it appears to be quite normal. However, I did find certain anomalies in her DNA."

Secta's brow furrowed, "Anomalies, you say?"

Yashida triggered a 3-D holographic image of Sonoko's DNA on the circular metal holo-disk flush-fitted into the cubicle. Secta approached and studied it closely.

"Hmm, pass me the remote, please?" Secta requested.

Yashida handed it to him, and Alice sat on the edge of the bench, folding his arms and looking disinterested.

"Thanks," Secta said and zoomed in on the strands of DNA.

"There," Yashida pointed to a particular strand.

"I know what that is," Secta said, handing the remote back to Yashida. "She has been genetically modified."

Alice nearly fell off the bench. "What? Sonoko? That's impossible."

Shintaro nodded knowingly, having suspected something like this.

"If you magnify further, you will see her coded ID on one of the strands," Yashida confirmed.

Secta began pacing, his hand on his chin. "It raises the question of whether she's a ring-in ... sorry, a Zen plant, if you will. Is the real Sonoko still being held captive on Zen Island?"

Alice was alarmed by the thought. "Nar mate, that doesn't make sense. If she's an android spy, why would they shoot her?" He was frustrated by the idea that she might not be human.

Shintaro had an explanation. "Either to put her above suspicion, or the bullet was not meant for her; it was meant for you, and she just got in the way. The only way to find out is through a retinal scan. That is the only way we can establish her movements in the last 48 hours."

"I don't believe this," Alice said, exasperated.

Secta placed a comforting hand on Alice's shoulder. "I'm sorry, Alice. I know how much you care for her, but facts are facts, and Zen has the android technology. Anu Set is living proof of that."

"Yeah, walking, maybe, but talking ... no," Alice growled.

Yashida was listening and zoomed in on the DNA hologram for further proof. "See, Alice?"

One strand of DNA was clearly printed with the number: #0061. "It is not just Zen with that technology, Secta. Miss Tanaka's employers produce artificial human components. She may have undergone a trial, a study, or even an experiment. It would not be unusual, especially if she had a pre-existing medical condition or a dangerous hereditary rogue gene that could have made her susceptible to breast cancer, for instance."

"I understand," Secta said.

"I will search for remnants in her blood sample to see if she did have a pre-condition. I will do it while you are doing the retinal scan," Yashida proposed.

"Good thinking," Secta agreed.

Alice whispered in Secta's ear in English, "Last night, I made love to a robot."

"Don't worry, Alice. We probably all have at one time or another or will. But she's genetically modified; we don't think it's cybernetics ... and besides, Alice, you and I are both genetically modified."

Alice considered that, somewhat easing his worry about Sonoko.

Shintaro got up from his seat. "I have made the arrangements. Miss Tanaka is being taken right now to the scan room. Does anybody wish to accompany me there?"

"I'll come," Alice said, ruefully.

"You won't need me. I'll stay with Yashida to work on the blood," Secta said. "Oh, it might be best not to mention our suspicions to Sonoko, Alice. She might not know, and the shock could be catastrophic for her."

"Why am I being scanned, Alice? What have I done?" Sonoko asked, pleadingly.

Standing in the dimly lit corridor outside the ES room, Alice wondered at her tone and the way her intense stare never left his face. Little things about her were now beginning to tell him she wasn't quite human. The warmth and compassion he felt from her earlier seemed to have faded. He couldn't discern whether her change of attitude was because an officer had told her she was required to undergo the scanning procedure without explanation, or whether he was just noticing her inhumanness now that it had been pointed out to him.

Sonoko was having difficulty understanding why Alice was all of a sudden so indifferent to her.

"What's wrong with you, Alice? What has changed?"

"Sorry, it's just that I've got a lot on my mind," he lied. "They only need to check some details of when you were on Zen Island because most of the time you were unconscious, and anything could have happened," he explained, unconvincingly.

An hour later, Alice and Shintaro returned to the Forensics lab.

"What did you find out?" Secta inquired.

"None of what I expected," Shintaro explained.

They left Yashida working and sat at a table in one corner of the lab to discuss the scan results.

"Firstly, she was not touched at all by Zen. She is the same Miss Tanaka, not a clone or a spy," Shintaro pointed out.

Alice relaxed in his chair, exhaling with relief. "Thank the heavens for that."

Secta crossed his legs and clasped his chin with his hand. "Go on, Shintaro. It seems something else grabbed your attention."

"Yes, they drugged her and took her to where we found her, but along the way, they passed through another warehouse much larger than the one we were in. Miss Tanaka's drugged vision was distorted, but it was clear enough to see that this giant warehouse housed a massive block of individual cells, like a large prison."

"Well, as a security company in our time, Zen ran prisons around the world, so that would make sense, wouldn't it?" Alice questioned.

"Well, you would think we would know about it ...We are, after all, the police. But more than that, each cell looked like it was occupied, and the occupier, in each case, seemed to be a young woman ... and from what we could make out by zooming the images: pregnant young women."

There was a pause as Alice and Secta processed what Shintaro had said. Secta was the first to react. "Is this a Noah's ark of hybrids you're describing here?"

"I think so," Shintaro admitted. "And this was only the first floor. The warehouse is at least two hundred metres long and has four stories. It could potentially hold thousands of pregnant women."

Secta was up and pacing the floor. "Unbelievable! So, we must assume they, and by they, I mean Zen, are capturing and imprisoning the women who have been inseminated by infected males..."

"But what for?" Alice questioned.

"They must be behind producing a hybrid race," Secta said, stopped, sat back down, and eyeballed Shintaro. "We need to stop the process of insemination, and fast," he said fervently.

"But how? Even if we find a vaccine, we know Zen has infected males on the island. They can just continue pumping out hybrids on their little island fortress ... no-one will stop them," Al said sardonically.

"No, after only one insemination, the male dies. We have determined that," Yashida said from his workbench.

"We've isolated the gene Sonoko has that repels infected males, and we are now trying to determine a delivery system for it. I believe we might be able to attach it to a strain of the common cold," Secta said in all seriousness.

"A virus?" Shintaro posed.

"Yes."

"That'd be the second time you've produced a virus to save the world, Secta?" Al reminded him.

"Yes, it seems I'm making a habit of it," Secta said light-heartedly.

Shintaro, of course, didn't understand what Alice was referring to. The fact that Secta had saved the world in 2087 by using a redundant computer virus to infect and shut down the mainframe computer Zen Corporation was using to trigger a dormant instruction Zen had placed in every human's ocular cochlear implant or OSCI since they were four years old. If it had been successful, it would have transformed humankind into a race of mindless drones under the maniacal despotic control of Zen Corporation and its megalomaniac master, Gorrick.

"But how would you administer this vaccine, Secta?" Shintaro asked.

"Airborne, we'd spray Japan with it, give everyone a cold."

"But for women only, correct?" Shintaro queried.

"Yes, but we think the same vaccine administered intravenously to infected males will reverse their condition. We injected the infected male we have imprisoned here with it this morning."

"Any results?"

"Not yet, Alice. We only did it twenty minutes ago while you were doing the scan. We'll check in ten minutes," Secta explained.

"How would we be able to administer an intravenous vaccine to walkers?" Shintaro inquired.

"Yashida figured the stun darts you use take 10 cc of serum. We think that would be enough to do the job," Secta said.

"Excellent. Would it take long to synthesize the vaccine?" Shintaro said, sold on the idea.

"That's what Yashida is working on right now. It will depend on how the specific gene copies. Sometimes genes mutate when they're duplicated. We'll know in a few hours."

Yashida approached them, carrying a test tube. "I have completed the tests on Miss Tanaka. Her genetic modification was for improved intelligence, good health, skin colour, athletic musculature ... a lot of blockers for diseases such as cancers, diabetes, dementia. In general, cosmetic, we call it. Most probably, one of her parents was a scientist and had it done when she was only a foetus. It is unlikely she would be aware of it."

"So, what makes her different than other genetically engineered children?" Shintaro asked.

Yashida explained, "One of her genes mutated. I do not know why, but it could have been during puberty when hormones can affect the genes, especially in females. I think we can reproduce the specific gene, but up to a point before the likelihood of mutation. Then we would have to go back to the source gene to produce another batch. That way, we would be safe. I'm going down to check on the infected prisoner now."

Secta stood. "Are we finished here?"

"Yes, we are done for now," Shintaro confirmed.

"Then I'll join Yashida. Hopefully, I'll be back with good news."

Alice and Shintaro were left talking while Secta and Yashida went to take the elevator to the basement.

It was unusually quiet at the Met due to the massive clean-up required in the wake of the typhoon. Every available cop had been mobilised to help.

"I saw on the news this morning that there was much destruction from the Typhoon," Yashida said as the elevator doors opened at the basement corridor.

"Were many injured?" Secta inquired.

"Fortunately, the curfew from martial law kept people indoors and safe, but there were some soldiers and cops hunting down walkers hit by flying debris. I think seventeen fatalities, less than expected."

They stopped at the cell door, and Secta took a peek through the small observation window. The prisoner was standing with his back to him, no longer huddled in a corner seething. Secta tapped on the window, and the prisoner turned to face him. His face had returned to normal, his eyes had lost their insanity.

"I think we can safely go inside; he looks fine," he said enthusiastically.

Yashida had a prison guard open the door, and they entered the smelly room. The prisoner immediately appealed to them, "What am I doing here? Why am I like this?" He looked down at himself and, appalled by his state, began to weep.

Secta went to the young man and sympathetically patted him on the back. "You've been through an ordeal, son. You've had a disease, but you're all right now. You're going to be fine."

The young man nodded in appreciation of the news and wiped his teary eyes and runny nose.

"We will have someone come clean you up and feed you ... I just need to take a blood sample," Yashida said, pulling a syringe from his dustcoat pocket.

They made for the elevator, very happy with their efforts.

CHAPTER 24
FAT LADY

THE DEVELOPMENT OF the vaccine couldn't have come at a more opportune time for Tokyo and Japan, given the added devastation caused by the typhoon. Conditions were rapidly deteriorating. The community was growing distressed, tempers were fraying, and radical groups exploited the curfew to protest against the military and police presence. Criminals used it as an opportunity to plunder from shops and ATMs, wherever they could find loot.

Shintaro had received orders to abandon his pursuit of Zen, Kim, Kew, and Set, and instead, focus on containing the civil unrest. But Shintaro knew better; he had witnessed Zen's criminal activities. He was in full agreement with Secta and Alice that Zen was responsible for the virus, and it had to be stopped. He understood the critical importance of introducing Secta and Yashida's vaccine as soon as they had sufficient quantities. The blood test on the young male prisoner proved that the vaccine was successful in killing the virus. Yashida set up a task force of scientists and laboratories to produce both vaccines. A group of sympathetic scientists had prepared a deposition to present to the government in order to secure funding for distributing the vaccine.

Amidst all the activity, Alice and Secta were more concerned with how Zen might counter their efforts. They were troubled by the fact that there seemed to be more to Zen's motives than just breeding hybrid children and culling young males. The real motive eluded them. Was it enough that Kew had travelled through time just to stop Alice? If it was to prevent Alice from containing the virus, then he hadn't tried very hard. They believed there had to be another reason, and Secta suspected it had something to do with the pregnant women being held on Zen Island. He was determined to find out why they were there.

Sitting in Shintaro's office, they were diligently searching for an answer.

"Why Kim?" Alice pondered.

"To focus on me, I presume," Shintaro said. "Zen had planned to have me arrest you, Alice, for the murder of Doctor Malone."

"But it backfired on them. How the hell did they manage to collect all those pregnant women? Wouldn't someone have noticed?"

"It's a valid point, Alice, but I think the women went to them," Secta proposed. "Drawn like moths to a flame."

"What, like the bell tolled, and an army of mindless zombie sheilas marched to the Zen island dome?" Alice lamented, adding a touch of gothic drama.

"Sort of, but more scientifically … you know how I can track you by the atomic marker in your DNA?"

"Yeah."

"Well, let's say Zen included a homing marker in the blockchain that impregnated these women … a marker that motivates them to mindlessly go to a specific location, a coordinate if you like?"

"Nar, people would have seen them," Alice countered.

"Curfew. There was a window of twenty-four hours before we could deploy enough army and police on the streets," Shintaro said.

"It doesn't make sense that they expect every woman carrying a hybrid foetus to make it to Zen Island. I'd say it's a numbers game," Secta proposed, "they don't care who lives or dies in the process as long as some of them make it there."

"Yeah, that's all well and good, but for what reason?" Alice inquired.

"That we can't answer for now, Alice. I didn't tell you, but while you were on the island, I had a conversation with myself in Sydney."

"You what? Far out!"

"Yes, it was … anyhow, he, I … told me to make sure Kew doesn't make it back to our time, or he will assassinate the President."

"Is the President alive now?"

"Good question, Alice. I should've asked."

"Just thinking if he is … then we succeeded, didn't we?"

Determined to appease Gorrick, Honor had devised a plan to recover the android Anu Set's body. Her plan was simple: she would set up a stakeout at the entrance to Oceana Labs, where she knew Set's body would be stored, as it was the only section of Oceana equipped with a mortuary freezer. Any lab worker finishing their shift would be the target and kidnapped. Her agents would then use the worker's ID to enter the labs, take the body on a trolley to the service exit, where a van would be waiting to make their escape.

After discussing the plan with the three agents assigned to the mission, they set it into motion.

It was 9 p.m.; the city was quiet—midweek at that time of night following the peak hour rush. One could fire a cannon down many of the streets at the north end of the Sydney UBD and not hit a soul. Oceana lab worker Haydon Reims had finished his shift for the day and was passing through the inconspicuous Phillip Lane exit to Oceana Labs, just off Bent Street. This was one of the numerous unassuming secret Oceana entry points located in various parts of the city. As he stepped out into Phillip Lane, he was jumped by two men and then bundled into the rear of a waiting van. Held at gunpoint, he was relieved of his ID and pin number and then chloroformed.

The driver stayed with the van while the other two agents returned to where the worker had exited. One stayed near the door, while the other went to the discreet entrance lobby and used the keycard and pin stolen from Reims to open the nondescript door. On the other side was an elevator. He swiped the card, and the large service elevator descended eight floors to where he'd find the mortuary.

Time was of the essence; he knew security would be monitoring him on CCTV. He found a frosted glass door with 'Cold Room' stencilled on it. Inside was a typical mortuary, though small. In the end wall were six stainless steel freezer cabinets. One was marked 'Anu Set' with a number. He pulled the drawer open. The cadaver was in a body bag that had been zipped shut. Parked against the far wall was a Rapini Mortuary Lifter Trolley designed for the movement of cadavers to and from the mortuary. He manoeuvred it up level with the open freezer door, raised the trolley bed using the pump action lever, and because the body bag was already on a bed of rollers, slid it easily out of the freezer onto the trolley.

Within minutes, he was back inside the elevator heading to the ground floor with his prize.

His partner met him at the exit, and together they quickly wheeled the trolley over to the rear of the van. There, they raised the trolley and easily slid the body bag off onto the rollers on the floor of the van. Then they replaced the body bag on the trolley with Haydon Reims, who was still unconscious.

They put his ID back in his pocket and wheeled him over to the exit where they left him.

The van pulled into a warehouse loading bay at a container wharf in Sydney's south and uploaded its precious cargo. The body bag was shifted onto an electric conveyor belt that transported it a hundred metres or so to a designated room, where Honor and her team were waiting.

The two agents were proud of how well they'd executed the plan. Honor was impressed, thrilled that her carefully designed plan had completely outfoxed her nemesis Karzoff.

As the body bag arrived on the conveyor belt, another man wearing a navy-blue medical lab coat and protective gloves positioned a single mobile mortuary freezer at the end of the conveyor, ready to receive the corpse.

"Well done, gentlemen," Honor announced with satisfaction.

"It was an excellent strategy, ma'am. As you predicted, there was no intervention from Oceana security. It went like a charm. We executed the perfect crime," the taller of the two agents claimed with a touch of conceit.

The man in the navy lab coat halted the conveyor with a remote and then opened the freezer door.

"First check, please, Doctor Hendrix," Honor ordered. The body bag zipper was padlocked. "Just cut off the padlock."

"Bring me a pair of cutters," Hendrix instructed agent Smith.

Smith darted out of the room and returned a few moments later with a pair of pliers. Handing them to Hendrix, he admitted, "These are all I could find."

"They'll have to do," Hendrix said, taking them and snipping at the zip. In a matter of seconds, he had freed the zipper from the lock and unzipped the bag. They all recoiled in shock.

Inside the bag was a female mannequin dressed in the now obsolete black dress uniform of the Oceana Secret Police. She was wearing a black wig in a bob with a crimson hair-tie, and her fingernails were lacquered silver. Each of the men stared at Honor and then back at the mannequin—the resemblance was striking.

"It's you!" Agent Smith exclaimed.

"Obviously," Honor barked, her face flushed with embarrassment.

Karzoff had won that round.

"The typhoon took out the entire drone cover of Tokyo," Shintaro informed Alice and Secta. He was seated behind his office desk, with Alice and Secta in front of him. They were working on a strategy while the science delegation proposed the vaccine delivery method to the Japanese Government.

"Surely they had ample time to move them?" Secta questioned.

"Yes, but the surveillance company that controls them claimed the curfew disrupted their roster, which left them understaffed … so it was not attended to."

"That's ridiculous," Alice growled.

"They must be automated, software-driven; everything else in this city is," Secta argued. "What's the name of the company in control of them?"

"They are subcontractors, not government … ah, let me check with my i-Keeper … Ah, that's right, Airlink Enterprises."

"Have your i-Keeper check who owns Airlink Enterprises," Secta suggested.

"Why? I do not understand," Shintaro asked, puzzled, but did it anyway. "It is owned by Partnership Z, a publicly listed company."

"Z, huh? As in Z for Zen. Better have Mr Keeper check who has the majority shareholding in Partnership Z," Secta proposed.

"You got it right, Secta … it is Zen Corporation," Shintaro said, shaking his head, disturbed by the revelation.

Alice sceptically raised the question, "Why would Zen want to blind the cops' eyes in the skies?"

While they were pondering Alice's question, Yashida burst into the room, "Gentlemen," he announced excitedly. "We got the green light!"

Secta jumped to his feet. "Fantastic!" he exclaimed.

Shintaro hopped out of his chair and rushed around it to shake Secta's hand. "You did it, my friend, you did it!"

There was plenty of backslapping. The achievement was ground-breaking; in only a couple of days, Secta and Yashida had managed to solve a problem that no other scientist in Japan had been capable of doing. The three of them turned to Alice, who raised an eyebrow, perplexed.

"And it is all because of you, Alice. The people of Japan owe you a great debt of gratitude," Shintaro said emotionally.

"Team effort, dudes … team effort. Well done to us, now let's get on with it. The job ain't done until the fat lady bursts into song. One of mine, hopefully," he said with a chuckle.

Shintaro was called to a meeting to coordinate the disbursement of the dart vaccine for males. The military would be in charge of the aerial dusting. Yashida was in charge of the production of both vaccines, leaving Alice and Secta space to concentrate on putting an end to Zen's reign of terror.

Seeing there was still plenty going on outside in the streets under martial law, they chose the commissary to brainstorm ideas. Feeling better after her ordeal with the retinal scan, Sonoko joined them.

Alice and Secta stood to receive her at their table.

"How are you, Sonoko?" Secta inquired compassionately.

"My eyelids are still quite swollen and sore, but they will recover. It is a small price to pay for the vaccine that was produced from my blood. I must ask Secta what makes my blood different than any other?"

"When you were a foetus in your mother's womb, you were genetically enhanced. Is your father a scientist?"

She didn't appear shocked, which was a relief for Alice. He worried Secta had been too forward and hadn't considered her feelings.

"Yes, my father was a genetic scientist. I always thought he used some of his discoveries on me. I am the only child; he wished for me to be just like him."

"And he succeeded, Sonoko. Without knowing it, your father manufactured a gene that will now save thousands, if not millions, of lives. You must tell him," Alice said.

"I'm afraid I cannot," she said sadly. "He committed suicide three years ago, after my mother died from breast cancer. His research into gene therapy of breast cancer was unable to save her."

Alice took her hand, gently squeezed her long thin fingers, and said warmly, "I'm so sorry."

"But there is a positive outcome, isn't there?" Sonoko said.

"There certainly is," Secta agreed.

"Would you like a coffee and maybe a biscuit?" she asked.

The guys ordered a coffee, and while Sonoko was getting it, they continued plotting.

"The UFO is due to arrive tomorrow," Alice reminded Secta.

"I can't help but think all of these events are connected with it, Alice," Secta said, his brow furrowed.

"If Zen has something to do with the UFO, it would be in their interests to wipe out all the drones," Alice mused.

"Yes, you're right. Go on, Alice."

"Well, what if it is all connected? What if all those inseminated women on Zen Island are the cargo for the UFO?"

That caused Secta to bounce up to his feet and begin pacing the floor. "Of course, of course," he echoed himself. "That's what this has all been about; it's a massive breeding program. That's why it was so important for Kew to be here—Set and Kim as well—Kim is here to distract Shintaro and the police and hopefully stop you—Kew is here to orchestrate taking us both out, with android Anu Set, the hitman. They knew Sonoko had the mutated gene; that's why they kidnapped her."

"We have to stop this, Secta. They're about to abduct thousands of women."

"You're right, of course ... but where would they be taking them, and for what reason? Why go to so much trouble when they could have simply abducted women and then over time artificially inseminated them?"

CHAPTER 25
THE SAMURAI

SHINTARO RETURNED FROM the executive meeting with excellent news; he'd convinced the Police Commissioner of Kim's complicity in the kidnapping of Sonoko and the killing of the five SAT officers. As a result, he'd won the right to track Kim's VV with the intent of making an arrest and charging him with kidnapping and murder.

It was the break they needed. Secta and Alice knew Kim would lead them to Kew and Set.

For Shintaro, it was all about face. He needed to settle the score with Kim, whose duplicity had elevated him from colleague to rival.

It was time for Secta and Alice to level with Shintaro and tell him about the destined arrival of the UFO. Sonoko had advised them to be upfront with him because his trust would be vital to their cause. She had gone on to say that Shintaro was a proud and honourable man, in the tradition of legendary Samurai warriors, and that his first name is not Shintaro; it is Atomu, which means Atom or earth, ground, or soil. His surname, Shintaro, shows his lineage to the 17th Century Ronin or masterless Samurai, Akikusa Shintaro, half-brother of the Shogun, Tokugawa Lenari.

With her advice heeded, they waited for Shintaro to finish telling them about the breakthrough before dropping the bomb.

There was a pregnant pause after the general excitement of Shintaro's news. Sonoko could see there was hesitation by Secta and

Alice to speak up. She worried that seated behind his desk, sensitive to reading temperaments, Shintaro might well be confused by their odd indecisive attitude, so she spoke up first.

"Shintaro-san," Sonoko started. "You know that Secta and Alice came here on a secret mission."

"Yes, to stop the pandemic," he said nonplussed.

"Well, there is more to it, and they are finding it difficult to tell you."

His face relaxed. "Please, my friends, we should have no secrets between us," he appealed gracefully.

"Shintaro, we have known all along that the first major contact with a UFO will occur here in Tokyo tomorrow," Alice said.

The statement appeared to go over like a lead balloon. Shintaro sat frozen in his chair with a mystified look on his face, as though he'd been asked to believe that pigs could fly.

"I know it's difficult to accept, Shintaro, just as tough as it was to believe we are time travellers from the past … but it is true," Secta explained. "We learned about it on a time travel expedition we made a while ago to 2087, but we hadn't connected it with what's going on here until recently."

"It was only today that we realised that all of this—the pandemic, Kew, Kim, the impregnated women—are all connected to the UFO," Alice continued. "We're even certain Zen knew Sonoko was carrying the mutated gene that could stop the virus, which was why Kim was involved: to win our confidence and then to kidnap Sonoko to stop us discovering the gene."

Shintaro's expression had changed to incredulous. "But why, this does not make sense?"

"We think to buy them time," Secta sought to clarify. "They even sent Kew through time after us to ensure we were stopped or at least slowed down to give them time to get enough women impregnated."

Shintaro sat forward in his seat, beginning to buy into it. "Impregnated for what though, Secta?" he questioned.

"To be taken by the UFO," Alice said. "We reckon it's the reason they're holding them on Zen Island."

"And what would aliens want with thousands of Japanese women impregnated with hybrid babies?"

"It's a good question, Shintaro, and we can't answer that," Alice admitted, nodding to Secta. "But you have to admit, it does add up."

"Wait, so let me get this straight … out of the many thousands of Japanese women who have been impregnated by infected males, Zen somehow has assembled a percentage of them for the specific purpose of sacrificing them to aliens that you believe will arrive by spaceship tomorrow? The remaining thousands of Japanese women carrying hybrid babies not held by Zen will give birth here. Are you saying the hybrid spawn will be half human and half whatever the race is on board that spaceship?"

"You would have to believe that is so," Secta agreed.

"The way you put it, Shintaro, it sounds far-fetched … science fiction, but it's not mate. We think Zen knocked out all of those drones to clear the way for the UFO to abduct these women without detection," Alice asserted.

Shintaro flopped back in his chair to contemplate the story. Alice, Sonoko, and Secta displayed tense faces, knowing that if he didn't buy it, then the mission could well be down the drain.

Shintaro leaned forward in his chair and eyeballed them. "I have no reason to doubt you … so what are we going to do about it?"

"Happening!" Alice barked, enthusiastically punching the air with his fist.

Now that he'd won the support of his superiors and with the imminent arrival of the UFO, Shintaro was anxious to strategize an achievable plan that had the lowest possible chance of failure. With loss of face and his reputation as an officer at stake, he couldn't afford to lose any more men.

"There are few options. Once we have located Kim, we have to arrest him and his cohorts. At the same time, I will have all Zen Corporation offices raided and closed down," Shintaro proposed.

"You will need the head of Zen in Japan; he'd be the brains behind all of this," Secta strongly submitted.

"He's right; take him out along with Kim, Kew, and Set, and you cripple Zen," Alice added.

"You mean Gorrick Khan?" Shintaro asked.

Both Secta and Alice were noticeably taken aback by the mention of the name.

"Gorrick? What, a tall middle-aged foreign dude with short-cropped white hair?" Alice probed.

"Yes, that is the man, the president of Zen Japan and numerous other companies. He's an extremely powerful high-roller here."

There was a pregnant pause while Alice and Secta exchanged a stupefied glance—it was all beginning to make more sense to them.

"Let me just tell you this," Secta said. "There is a Gorrick as head of Zen Corporation with exactly the same description in our time, and another Gorrick, president of Zen Corporation, again of the same description, we met in 2087. Does that not strike you as being rather odd?"

"Are you suggesting he's—"

"An alien, Shintaro, and I reckon the alien responsible for all this crap, and each time we've defeated him, he just starts up again," Alice snarled spitefully.

"He is your nemesis then?" Shintaro postured.

"More than that … a clone, a replicant … I suspect perhaps the last of an alien race intent on seeding Earth with its species of hybrids, who knows?" Secta concluded.

Shintaro sat back in his seat again. "Okay, okay … I'll put together department heads to strategize an assault. Ah, my Keeper is giving me a feed on Kim's location … he's on Zen Island."

"That should be the first cab off the rank; we hit the Island again—this time we do a job on it," Alice growled.

"I am not going to risk you, Alice. A professional tactical team will take the mission; I will lead them in," Shintaro said sternly.

"If you think you're going to leave me out, try again ... no freaking way, buddy. I didn't travel across time to be left sitting on my fat butt in an office. I'm here to stop these bastards ... now count me in, or I'll go it alone," Alice barked emphatically. By the look in his fierce eyes, it wasn't difficult for Shintaro to determine he meant what he'd said.

"I'd count him in if I were you, Shintaro," Secta said. "It can be ugly if he gets pissed off... Anyhow, just like you, he has a job to do."

Shintaro thought about it with his eyes fixed on Alice's. Eventually, a slight grin cracked on his face. "Alright, but as for you, Secta, and Miss Tanaka, I will set up a meeting for you with the head of the military space division to coordinate intelligence gathering on the UFO ... its imminent arrival represents a different challenge of a nature unknown to us."

Alice had calmed down now that he had been included in the assault team and asked, "When do you think we'd go in?"

"To hazard a guess, around 0300 hours, by chopper."

"Chopper? They'd hear us coming..." Alice complained.

"No, not in the Euro Silent Stealth they will not. It has noise-cancelling rotor blades, no thwop-thwop-thwop, like you get with traditional choppers, three decibels only," Shintaro explained.

"Unbelievable," Alice said, totally impressed. "Way to go."

Shintaro stood from behind his desk and then walked over to the large window that looked out on the CBD. Gazing through polarized glass at the cloudy sky, he said, "There is a second typhoon coming."

"You're kidding after what we had yesterday?" Alice argued.

"It often happens like that, Alice," Sonoko explained. "One follows the other, and more often than not, the second one is more powerful than the first."

Shintaro turned away from the window and faced them. "The tropical depression caused by the first one virtually sucks a second one in."

"When is it due?" Secta asked.

"Oh, about the same time as the assault," Shintaro said casually.

Fearing panic, martial law remained enforced to ensure a curfew, thus limiting the number of citizens on the street who could witness the arrival of the UFO. Otherwise, it would be panic stations.

Within hours of Shintaro's meeting with the Commissioner, the military and the police were provided with darts containing the vaccine. The hunt for infected males had changed from killing them to flushing them out and injecting them to save their lives.

At the same time, Yashida and the scientists he had marshalled had produced enough of the cold virus containing the active gene from Sonoko for the Air Force to begin spraying it on Tokyo from helicopters. However, they'd only just begun when operations had to be suspended due to wind drift. The vaccine was far too precious for it to be blown out to sea by the winds whipped up by the approaching typhoon.

There was little Secta could do for the assault planning, so he went back to the lab to help Yashida produce more vaccine. When he arrived, it was a hive of activity. Yashida had a dozen lab assistants producing the dart vaccine. The bench tops were cramped with chemistry apparatus, and there wasn't a spare seat in the room. The adjoining sterile room was brimming with more assistants, all busy producing the cold virus vaccine under aseptic conditions.

As Yashida passed by, Secta asked him, "Is there anything I can do to help?"

Yashida stopped and smiled, his face showing signs of a lack of sleep. "Thank you, Secta-san, but not really. You are free to use my office if you like … there is a desktop array there."

"Thank you," Secta said. Not wanting to get in the way, he took up Yashida's offer. There was the same hot spot metal disk flush mounted in the desk as before. Now familiar with how to work it, he decided to send his other self in Sydney a message and began typing.

Good afternoon other me, just an update. We found a vaccine for the pandemic, and we're busy reproducing it to administer to both infected male carriers and inseminated females. There will be an assault on Zen offices today to bring down the administration and arrest Kew, Set, and Gorrick. Oh yes, Gorrick, we have one here as well, apparently a dead-ringer for the one you have there and the one we met in 2087. Is there anything else you need to advise me that wouldn't breach the prime directive?

Happy with the message, he sent it to Secta's handle.

A couple of minutes later, a reply came.

Well done! Only one thing you should know; be careful not to lose Alice. Bye.

He reclined back in Yashida's big leather office chair and thought, lose Alice? That would be devastating. Does he mean lose him like dead or will he go missing?

A few hours later, Secta looked up through the office window to the lab where he saw Alice and Sonoko chatting with Yashida, and so went out and joined them.

"How's it all going Al?" he asked.

"Mate," Alice smiled. "I've done enough meetings to last me a lifetime, but we're all set to go. What have you been up to? Plenty going on here ... some of the lab assistants are Sonoko's workmates."

"Can I have a quiet word with you?" Secta whispered covertly.

"Sure."

Secta walked him to the office for a private chat. Sonoko watched them go off together and wondered what was so important that had to be kept secret.

Once in the office, Secta closed the door. "I sent a message to myself in Sydney asking if there was anything I needed to know now that the assault is on."

Alice sat on the edge of the desk. "Yeah, so what did yourself say?" He was amused by the absurdity of Secta talking to his older self.

"It's serious, Alice. He told me to be careful not to lose you."

"Lose me? What's that supposed to mean?"

"I know it's a little ambiguous ... but nevertheless, he wouldn't have warned me if there wasn't plausible danger. Just don't do anything rash, that's all, stick with Shintaro."

Alice slipped off the desk. "Nice of you to worry about me, mate, but I'll be fine. I've been through worse and survived."

"I know you have, but you'll be risking your life and—"

Alice cut him off, not one for letting the negatives get to him. "Hey, I'll be sweet, mate. If you are worried, give yourself a call and ask if I'm there ... then you'll know I made it."

Secta locked eyes with him. Both of them knew he couldn't do that; it would be in contempt of the prime directive that they had agreed to adhere to since they began time travel.

Alice broke off the stare. "Sonoko is going to treat me to a traditional Shabu-shabu at the little Tempura Bar next door ... the owner is willing to break curfew to open up just for us. Want to come along?"

"No thanks, three's a crowd."

"Alright, my friend. I'll see you when we've got this all done and dusted."

They hugged ... circumstances had made them the epitome of the odd couple. Alice, a rugged, passionate, working-class rock n roll hero ... uncouth at times, and Secta, an intellectual eccentric academic—reserved, cultured, and often aloof: the social animal and the introvert.

Alice stopped at the door and shot Secta his endearing characteristic wave, "Chaa!"

Strange things happened inside his head; Secta's words still echoing around in there while his eyes peered through the small bedroom window at the 2 a.m. Tokyo skyline.

Thundery clouds were rolling in the sky, fires were burning in the streets, there was carnage on the roads ... burnt-out cars, vandalized shop fronts ... debris from the last typhoon strewn about as though discarded by the hand of an untidy giant. His eyes blurred, and he saw a vision reflected in the glass: a tyre lever at his feet, the young feet of a teenager. A tough, coarse, three-pack-a-day voice from a burly brute towering over him challenged, "If you want to take me on ... then pick it up, son."

It was a challenge that had stayed with Alice since those days. It was about making the right choice. Back then when he was a teenager, on the first day of a new job at the mines, he had been given the choice to pick up and use a weapon to fight a man much bigger than himself, but he'd chosen not to take it … and it was the correct decision. The big man would have only risked offering him the tyre lever if he was sure of himself.

He had a nagging hollow feeling in his gut that had him torn between whether it was what Secta had said or a premonition. He'd felt it before, and more often than not, it turned out to be a premonition. But this time, unlike previously, he felt uncertainty.

He turned away from the window and found Sonoko sprawled on the tatami mat, captivating him with her beauty. He marveled at her exquisite cheekbones that lent strength to her delicate features. Her long, perfectly shaped legs were enough to make any dancer envious.

CHAPTER 26
SHIMMER

WEAPONS WERE DISTRIBUTED among the assembled assault team. This time, they were not issued with stun guns; there'd be no toothless tigers in this battle. Donned in commando grey camouflage fatigues and black berets, Shintaro and his team looked the part. He handed Alice a kitbag.

"Full commando outfit, boots and all. You can get changed over there," he pointed to a small room annexed to the large assembly area. Reluctant at first, Alice thought better of it—best to blend in, so he took the bag and went to change.

The SAT team consisted of twenty members, including commander Shintaro. Most of them wore protective helmets wired with heads-up communications that linked with their SAT dedicated encrypted VV-Intra-web. Armed with Heckler & Koch SD9 submachine guns and Nambu M90 double-action revolvers, they looked ready for action. Two specialists carried Sako TRG-66 sniper rifles slung over their shoulders.

Alice emerged from the room, outfitted in the same grey camouflage battle fatigues as the others, but wearing a black beret like Shintaro and his 2IC.

"Alice, this is my team captain Inspector Maki. We have been friends since academy days and fought many battles together," Shintaro said proudly.

Maki was a pocket-rocket with a steely look in his eyes that could melt ice.

Alice shook his hand, "Do I call you sir?"

"No Alice-san, call me Tombei," he said with a gravelly voice, his accent thick and staccato.

"It is a nickname he gave himself when he hangs around me," Shintaro said light-heartedly.

Alice could tell they were close mates.

"We have intel that Zen has an assault force of ninja assassins … they are formidable opponents," Tombei warned.

Tombei handed Alice a 9mm Glock 34 with a holster clip, and a dagger in a scabbard. Alice drew the dagger; it was flashy. "Alright," he said, admiring the craftsmanship of its shiny double-edged blade.

"A traditional Japanese hunting dagger … small enough to conceal, nasty enough to inflict serious damage," Tombei said with a macabre smile. "Sometimes, it's more useful than a pistol."

Alice clipped the holstered pistol to his belt and then wondered where to put the knife.

Tombei swivelled his body to show him his, "Conceal it inside your pants on the hip like so, is the best place."

Alice copied. Now he felt like he could take on the world. Tombei waved over an officer and had him hand Alice three full clips.

"Ammo, you will be in Alpha team … Igami here is your man should you need more ammo … he is in charge of ordnance."

A tall, wiry but rugged young man, Igami gave Alice a respectful nod.

Shintaro strode to the centre of the room, stopped, and bellowed for everyone's attention, "Okay, listen-up … I've got 0400 hours, ETD 0500 on the rooftop helipad. Three Euro Silent Stealth choppers will pick up in two-minute withdrawals. Alpha team first, followed by Bravo and then Charlie … the assembly area on Zen Island is marked point A provided on your VV digi-map."

Shintaro impressed Alice; unlike last time when he felt the assault wasn't very well coordinated, this was a totally different kettle of fish.

Shintaro was decisive, authoritative, and bellicose. His men responded respectfully.

The hour passed quickly, and Alice was soon standing with the Alpha team beside Shintaro and Tombei, watching the first chopper materialise like magic in absolute silence out of the dark, foreboding pre-dawn sky. The static electricity in the air from the coming typhoon was making the hairs on his forearms and at the back of his neck rise and tingle. Even though the sky was still pitch black, due south, he could see intermittent lightning flashes that lit up giant rolling purple thunderheads. Nervous anticipation of the daunting task ahead of him was made more ominous by the approaching storm. By the stony look on the faces of the others, he figured they felt the same.

It was only when the chopper landed and the blue-edge rotor blades feathered that the chopper made any noticeable sound at all. Sitting on the helipad, the grey-painted chopper without any livery looked like a giant insect. The side door slid open, and the seven Alpha team members quickly boarded. Six of the men took passenger seats facing each other, while Shintaro sat up front next to the pilot. The door wasn't even shut when it took off to make room for the next chopper that immediately dropped out of the darkness onto the helipad to collect its payload.

Within minutes, the three choppers were in the air in convoy, heading east towards Yokohama Bay. Through the window from an elevation of twelve hundred metres, Alice caught a hint of dawn breaking underneath the massive cloud cover. There was plenty of turbulence from the wind that was getting up to gale force, and the pockets of low cloud.

"If we had left an hour later, the choppers would have been grounded because of conditions," Tombei told Alice, who was peering out the window, pale-faced and gripping the sides of his seat white-knuckled. He wasn't a fan of choppers. Some of the bumps were serious, bouncing them about in the small cabin space like rag dolls. One jolt was so sharp that there was a loud bang from two of the men sitting side-by-side bumping their helmets together. Even inside the cabin of the chopper, it was quiet, with only the muffled hum and vibration from the engine at the top rear.

They were all pretty happy when the chopper finally touched down on the forecourt of a large warehouse. The Alpha team disembarked in seconds for the chopper to take off and disappear into the cloud base, which was now even lower than when they landed—the weather was changing supernaturally quick. Once the other two choppers had lifted off, Shintaro gave a hand signal for Bravo and Charlie teams to deploy.

Alice felt a sudden chill that had nothing to do with the temperature. He looked to the east, and something in the sky attracted his attention. The clouds were moving, rolling, bellowing, and then shimmering. He'd seen the phenomenon before, but this time the scale of it was massive: it was as if the clouds in the entire quadrant of the sky were shimmering.

"Alice, let's move!" Shintaro ordered.

But Alice couldn't move; he was stuck there, frozen. "Look at that," he gasped, pointing out the shimmering clouds.

Shintaro looked. "What the hell is that? Look, Tombei."

Tombei strode over, looked up, and said mystified, "What the…?"

"I've seen this before," Alice disclosed. "Look, there's a vortex forming in the cloud."

In the centre of the shimmer, hovering about a thousand metres directly over the Zen complex, a whirlpool the size of a small car had materialised. With its formation, an extraordinary swirling wind sprang up, lifting pieces of paper, plants, and debris—anything that wasn't tied down—up into it, much like a big tornado. The wind was so powerful that the men were battling to keep their feet.

The conditions became chaotic—the roaring wind twisting around them at gale force, lightning flashing, and thunder sounding from the approaching typhoon behind them. Then, the centre of the vortex erupted into a maelstrom of green, blue, and white high-voltage arcing electricity, accompanied by a thunderous crackling sound.

Alice could see the vortex growing, bigger than he had ever seen before. It was now the size of a football field, maybe even bigger, and still increasing. All of the men were holding onto their helmets and hats, gazing up at the massive swirling arcing eye above them in disbelief.

Alice suddenly realised what it was. "It's here, Shintaro ... it's here," he shouted to get his voice above the pandemonium.

"It is only the eye of the typhoon, Alice," Shintaro shouted back.

"No mate, it isn't. It's the UFO."

Then, the mayhem ceased, and in a blink of an eye, a massive spacecraft silently materialised from out of the vortex. It was dark grey and the size of three football fields. The vortex closed behind it, and the gigantic saucer hung suspended in silence above the Zen dome—the only sound made was from distant rolling thunder and a collective gasp from the entire assault team.

Alice presumed it must have travelled through a wormhole to get there, and he couldn't help but marvel at how big their version of Kairos must be to facilitate that.

Shintaro snapped him out of his reverie. "This is a game changer, Alice." The words were monumental in the context of the circumstances. Left taciturn, Alice could only nod, unable to take his eyes off the gigantic craft overhead.

The penny dropped, and he confronted Shintaro. "We have to attack now before whatever this thing is here to do ... happens."

"There is another chopper coming in with medical backup. I think that thing might scare them off," Shintaro said, concerned.

The sound of a servo opening something large echoed throughout the complex of buildings and broke the silence. Alice and Shintaro quickly scoured the location for the source of the sound.

Tombei called out, "There, up there ... it is the dome!"

They looked up at the huge dome that capped the main building of the Zen complex; it was opening like a lotus flower.

From the underbelly of the huge saucer, a central circular disk was opening in a clockwise iris. From within it, a bright yellow light beamed down to the core of the dome interior below. The beam was so intense it forced Alice and the others to shield their eyes.

The dome was now nearly fully unfurled. Another servo sounded, this time from the spacecraft, and a long cylindrical protrusion that looked like a massive pencil torch emerged from the open iris, with the powerful yellow light burning at its tip. Alice unshielded his eyes and watched the articulated tubular probe move as though it was organic, extending until it had stretched far enough to fit exactly into the cavity of the open dome, as though made for it.

"That's it, they're going to take up all the pregnant women through the dome!" Alice said animatedly and then glared at Shintaro. "We've got to go in ... now!"

One of the troopers from Alpha team yelled out, "Sir, the med chopper."

They all looked up at the chopper marked with the livery of the Red Cross. It was at about a thousand metres on late final approach. Then came an enormous roar as three F-26 Eagle fighter jets from the Japan Air Self-Defence Force roared out of the north in a V formation, heading for the giant saucer.

They watched the Red Cross chopper being thrown about wildly by gale-force winds from the typhoon, which hadn't hit them at ground level yet. As it neared the saucer, a silver laser-like beam shot from a node on the belly of the UFO, and the chopper was instantly vaporised. It was such a powerful explosion that there wasn't even a piece of debris left to fall to the ground—the chopper had simply ceased to exist.

The three fighter jets had seen the attack on the chopper and opened fire on the saucer with a volley of guided missiles. Three missiles exploded well before reaching the target, and in the flash from the explosion, Alice and the others from ground level could see a force field, like a bubble, that surrounded the saucer and the dome.

"Check out the force field, they won't be able to penetrate that!" Alice yelled.

A loud clap of thunder resounded, the skies opened up, and rain pelted down on them in a torrent. Gale-force winds struck simultaneously, causing the rain to strike the assault team with such force it stung like bee stings where their skin was exposed.

The leaders of Bravo and Charlie teams were with Tombei beside Shintaro, awaiting their orders.

Shintaro shouted to be heard above the mayhem, "Main attack now ... objective B, Bravo take out the doors, Charlie rear guard!"

Within seconds, Bravo team detonated charges on the locked doors of the administration building for the three teams to file through on the double, weapons ready.

The enemy was waiting in ambush inside and immediately opened fire with automatic weapons from positions on the mezzanine floor. A couple of Bravo team members took hits, but the rest of them managed to provide enough cover for the Alpha team to make it across the lobby and safely under the overhanging mezzanine.

Issuing rapid orders, Shintaro split Alpha into two attack groups, with him leading one and Tombei the other.

The thumping sound of exploding ordnance outside from missiles hitting the UFO's force field resounded throughout the building.

Alice went with Tombei to the fire exit while Shintaro took the main staircase to the elevators. The objective was the room directly below the dome, where they assumed the hostages would be assembled, ready for transport. It was three flights up.

A grenade from Tombei into the stairwell cleared the way for Alice and three others to enter. The smoke from the grenade made it difficult to see. Tombei cautiously led them up the narrow staircase and shot out the CCTV cameras high up on the walls on the way.

Alice stepped over the upright body, all bloody and torn, of a dead ninja who'd taken the full force of the grenade: it was a grisly reminder to Alice that this time, they were playing for keeps.

CHAPTER 27
THE VOW

SHINATARO SELECTED INFRARED** on his retinal imaging menu and then took out the two lights in the corridor with a laser destructor: shaped like a pointer, it was designed specifically for blowing lights. The darkness now made it easier for him to scan the area for signs of the enemy. He had only taken a few steps into the long corridor when he noticed a slight change in the light source at its end. Experience warned him that he had detected the meniscus of the heat glow around the body of a person hiding around the corner. He pocketed the laser, then fumbled in his flak-jacket pocket for a clip of heat-seeking bullets, which he quickly loaded into his Glock that was fitted with a silencer. He aimed at the glow and fired. There was slight recoil with an almost inaudible thunk as the tracer slug travelled the twenty metres of hallway and then made a sharp right turn at the end. Confident that the target had been eliminated, he signalled his men to follow and then led them at speed along the corridor, hugging the sidewall.

He found his target sprawled out on his back on the floor with a bullet hole in his cheek, dead. Two elevators were just ahead, and alongside them, the main stairs led up.

Alice was a metre behind Tombei, leading them up the stairwell. Just as he was passing the second-level door, it flew open, knocking him so hard against the wall that the jarring caused him to drop his pistol. Garbed in black coveralls with a balaclava covering his face, armed with a knife, a ninja, about the same size and build as Alice, lunged at him with a blade. Alice grabbed his weapon arm and brought it down on his raised knee, snapping the radius bone with a loud crack. The assailant let out a muted squawk.

Tombei turned, saw the clash, aimed his gun but couldn't get a bead on the attacker.

Ignoring his broken right arm, the ninja drew a pistol from his belt with his left hand. Alice went for his dagger, whipped it out, and drove it into the ninja's chest just under the sternum and then angled it up and pushed. The ninja was dead on his feet. Holding the hilt of the dagger, Alice lowered the dead man onto the ground, then removed the blade from his chest. As he was on his knee, wiping his blade clean of blood on the dead man's balaclava, he noticed the door was still ajar.

"Nice work," Tombei acknowledged from a few steps before the third landing, looking down. "You alright?"

"No worries mate!" Alice barked back. As he checked over his shoulder for the next officer below him, an arm reached out from the open door at speed, wrapped around his throat, and dragged him back through the opening. Struggling, he tried to stab his attacker with the dagger but couldn't. Through to the other side in a dark corridor, the attacker kicked the door shut and then hit a switch on the wall. There was a loud clunk from the fire door locking closed.

On the other side, Tombei had charged down the stairs and was trying to get the door open. He gave up, stepped back from it, and ordered, "Kobi, blow it!"

Kobi was a few steps down the staircase.

Alice let his body go limp, and in doing so, he caught sight of his attacker's thigh, into which he immediately drove his knife. The big man screeched and released him. Alice spun around sharply, and fired a powerhouse punch into his face. It connected big time, smashing his nose under the balaclava and making him lurch backward. That bought Alice time to whip the blade up under the man's chin and drive it upwards as hard as he could through the roof of his mouth and into his brain. Blood sprayed out from the mouth and eyeholes of the balaclava, and the luckless attacker dropped down dead.

A quick check of his surroundings for more ninja, and then with it all clear, he focused on finding a way back to the Alpha team.

A small incendiary device strategically placed demolished the lock on the door so it could be opened. When he stepped through the smoke to the other side, Tombei found no sign of Alice, only the dead body of a ninja. He immediately notified Shintaro on his VV that he'd lost Alice and was ordered to continue to the 3rd-floor rendezvous point.

Hugging the wall, Alice stopped at an intersection and peered around the corner. There was a dimly lit hallway with the second-floor entrance to the main staircase at the end. He wondered if Shintaro had gone past to the third floor yet. Inspecting the hallway before entering it, he saw there were half a dozen doors on both sides. That was a concern: a ninja could be hiding behind any of them. But his only option was to negotiate the hall to the stairs. He regretted not being wired up to the others.

As soon as he stepped out into the hallway, he regretted the move. The figures of two big men appeared three-quarters of the way down. They were in dim light, so they were silhouetted. Alice froze. One of them was aiming an automatic submachine gun at him. He knew if he opened fire, he would lose the contest.

"I want to hear your gun and knife hit the floor, Alice. If they don't, it will be you hitting it."

He recognised it was Kew. As he obliged and dropped his weapons, he kept an eye on them. They took a step forward into the light. It was Kew, all right, and beside him, with the submachine gun trained on him, was Anu Set.

The President held his mug in both hands and peered at them over the rim. Karzoff was seated in an armchair in the President's office, flanked by Viktoria and Hope.

"I would have given my eyeteeth to have seen her face when she recognised herself in the body bag," the President chortled. "Very clever of you two, you're to be commended."

Karzoff beamed a proud smile.

"I've asked the OTT team here today for—"

Hope jumped in on the President. "Sorry to interrupt you, sir, but we're waiting on Professor de Luz and Doctor James ... they seem to be running late."

No sooner had she spoken when the door opened, and Miss Vallins, looking as stunning as ever, ushered in Robert James. He approached them in a fluster.

"Sir, Mr President, I'm sorry I'm late, but I've been waiting for the Professor, and he didn't turn up at Kairos control."

"Sit down, my boy," the President said calmly. "I'm sure he'll arrive soon enough. Miss Vallins, could you call the Professor's cellphone, please?"

"Yes, sir." She spoke softly to Doctor James, "I'll bring you a coffee, decaf white, isn't it?"

"Thank you, Miss Vallins."

"Decaf? I don't know how you can drink that stuff, it's like cat's piss," the President joked.

"I have an allergy to caffeine, sir."

"You need Carbon Sixty in MCT oil, Secta put me onto it, all the allergies, aches, and pains go out the window, bloody great stuff."

"It's an incredibly powerful antioxidant, they say it rejuvenates, prevents inflammation, and protects against free radicals," Hope explained.

"Keeps you young," Karzoff said. "I take it."

"I'm not sure that's any recommendation," James said with a chuckle.

Karzoff wasn't amused.

Miss Vallins returned with a mug of decaf for James. "Sir, the Professor's phone diverts to his message bank."

"Thank you, Miss Vallins."

Hope's phone beeped. "This is probably a text from him now," she said, pulling the phone out of the side pocket of her white lab coat. "He's probably at Café Epiphany, Secta's favourite…" She stood up with a panicked look on her face, staring at her phone like she couldn't believe the text. "The message is from Honor, it says if you want to see the Professor alive again, then she'll swap him for Anu Set and Secta."

"That's outrageous! Secta isn't even here!" the President complained.

"We had to expect a reprisal," Viktoria said gloomily.

"The trouble with her is we know what she is capable of," Karzoff cautioned. Then, a wistful expression crossed his face, "I'm afraid she has us in check."

"Have you finished examining the body, Hope?" the President asked.

"I was hoping to keep it for Secta to examine, it is after all his specialty, but having the Professor back safe is of greater value. I'll run 3-D imaging of the body, organs, and brain before we hand it over. Can you help me, Robert?"

"Yes, of course."

"What are we going to do about Secta? Even if he was back here, I wouldn't exchange him for anybody," the President admitted.

"There's more to this than meets the eye. Let's do one bit at a time and see what happens," Hope suggested.

"You will be risking the Professor's life, you know," Karzoff pointed out.

"I know, but we have no other option for now."

"I agree with Hope," said the President. "Viktoria and Karzoff, coordinate the exchange of Set for the Professor, try bargaining with Secta to find out more from them," the President requested.

Hope added, "Tell her Secta is on a mission and we can't get a message to him. She'll believe that."

"Make it happen, Karzoff."

"Yes, sir," Karzoff said dispiritedly. Only minutes before he had been bathing in the glory of having defeated Honor at her own game, now he'd lost out in the end. Deep down inside, he harboured profound resentment and vowed that Honor would pay for his loss of face.

"In this age of entropy and decay, we at Zen have resisted with supreme resilience. We have vanquished our detractors with our technological superiority. You and your kind have no place in this new world. You are not even a speck of dust in the expansion of our universe," Gorrick sneered.

"For a mere speck of dust, you go to an awful lot of trouble trying to brush me off," Alice snarled.

Alice was being held between Set and Kew. They were standing at the end of a massive rectangular room bathed in lucent yellow light. In the centre of the room was a gunmetal grey tube eight metres in diameter that had descended from the saucer through the open dome to about a metre above the floor. The weird thing about the snaky tube was that it seemed alive: organic ... it looked as though it pulsed as though breathing. The bright yellow light that filled the room emanated from the end of it.

Gorrick was standing in front of Alice, straight-backed like a general inspecting a parade. By his mannerisms, it was easy to tell he wasn't impressed with Alice's arrogance.

"I don't think you get the picture, Black Alice. Your SAT team is right now being annihilated, and you are about to meet your death."

"Yeah, yeah, yeah, I've heard it all before, Gorrick ... your clone in 2087 gave me pretty much the same rave. What is it ... a prepared speech or something? You freaking megalomaniacs are all carved out of the same block of rubbish. The population of this planet has been putting up with your trash since biblical times, and you've never won, with or without your superior technology. Little ole insipid mankind seems to always knock you over, and let me tell you ... it won't be any different this time ... mark my words. You'll wish in the end that you never laid eyes on me."

"We'll see about that, you hubristic buffoon. You're not the key to the future, Alice, I am!" Gorrick snapped, overriding his preferred ice-cold demeanour.

Alice noted he'd gotten to him and so pushed harder. "Yeah right, well, tell me why you idiots needed to impregnate Earth women to perpetuate your master race ... huh? Now that doesn't sound like ye who believes himself to be an all-masterful god?"

"Shut up!" Kew barked.

"Tell him, Gorrick ... tell him you're a race of alien clones that is dying out ... huh? Aren't you? Tell him your real name is En-lil, isn't it? The older brother of En-Ki, son of Anu that you made old robot Anu Set here in the spitting image of—"

Gorrick cut him off, "What a load of hyperbole!"

Alice glared at Kew. "What's the matter, Kew, didn't you know you're working for space invaders? You're on the wrong side, pal. If Zen gets its way, they certainly won't be needing you. You're just as dispensable to them as the rest of humankind."

Alice caught sight of a line of women entering from a doorway at the far end of the hall and walking towards the mouth of the huge metal tube. They were walking dazed, mindless ... all of them pregnant.

"What is that, an oversized vacuum cleaner or something?" Alice said cheekily.

Gorrick had had enough. "Take him out and execute him," he snarled. He turned his back to watch the procession of women.

"How many alien races have been abducting our females, just you or others? What are we, a cultivation experiment?" Alice badgered.

But he wasn't about to get an answer from Gorrick; he was ignoring him. He turned away and walked off towards the chute.

Set and Kew dragged Alice backward towards the exit.

The scene shimmered.

As they reached the door, it burst open, and Shintaro entered gun up, backed up by Tombei and the rest of the SAT teams Alpha, Bravo, and Charlie.

Set swung his machine gun toward them and fired.

Everything froze except for Alice and Kew. Alice could see the vortex forming; Kew hadn't seen it; he was baffled by his first experience of seeing a time freeze. Alice ripped his arm out of Set's frozen grip and belted Kew on the chin with a perfectly executed left jab. He crashed onto the deck out cold.

The bullets fired from Set's machine gun were frozen in mid-air on a trajectory to take out both Shintaro and Tombei. Alice ripped the gun out of Set's grip and, holding the barrel using the stock like a cricket bat, bashed the bullets suspended in the air off course. He turned, took aim, and emptied the magazine at Set, making sure when time returned to normal that the bullets would obliterate his head.

"Cop that, you'll never know what hit you, but I will," he snarled, and then dumped the empty gun, ran for the vortex that had opened, and dived through it.

Kew raised himself up from the ground just in time to see Alice's feet disappear through the vortex. It was closing. He jumped up, ran for it, and dived at the swirling wormhole, but it closed as quickly as it had materialised, and he landed flat out on the floor.

Everything unfroze ... the bullets fired by Set peppered the wall right beside Shintaro, narrowly missing him, and then, to Shintaro's amazement, he watched Set's head explode as if it had taken a volley of bullets. The big man's legs crumbled, and he hit the deck, lifeless.

Shintaro looked down at Set's machine gun on the floor and realised that Alice must have had something to do with it.

"What just happened?" Tombei asked Shintaro, totally perplexed. "One moment Alice was there, and then the next, he was gone?"

"Did you see that thing? It was like a miniature version of what we saw in the sky when the UFO arrived."

"Alice must have gone through it, he called it a vortex," Tombei said.

Shintaro glared at Kew, rolling on the floor, grasping his shoulder in pain. "Arrest him. I'll get word for Yashida to tell Secta what has happened; he will advise us on what to do. Are the GPS devices in place?"

"Bravo and Charlie are just finishing activating them," Tombei confirmed.

Gorrick had also disappeared.

CHAPTER 28
SELFIE

SECTA WAS IN the forensic lab at the Met, scrutinising a holographic schematic of a piece of technology Sonoko had displayed for him.

"This is unbelievable … Yashida, have a look at this … a Core i20-67775XX organic chip, it's a twenty-core organic processor that will revolutionise processing," Secta exclaimed, entirely astounded. "The clock speed is 20.5 GHz, and because it's organic, it doesn't require liquid or air cooling. It has two terabytes of memory and can fit on the tip of your index finger."

Yashida examined the holo-image. "I had heard a rumour this was in development. Is it operational yet, Miss Tanaka?"

"Yes, I thought you would ask that … I visited the office this morning and brought one to show you," she replied, opening a small case from which she produced a minuscule cellophane anti-static packet and handed it to Secta.

"So, the body of the chip is grown?" Secta enquired, holding it up to the light.

"The entire chip is synthetically grown, and then it can be 3-D printed very affordably," Sonoko clarified.

"This is extraordinary … it is sure to revolutionise … Oh, wait a moment, I have received an urgent message from Shintaro. It is for you, Secta … it says, 'Alice disappeared into a vortex. What should we do? We are inside the Zen building where pregnant females are being loaded into the UFO positioned overhead'," Yashida relayed gravely.

Secta's face blanched. He knew En-Ki must have opened the wormhole. If Alice failed to return, he'd be stuck in 2047 with no way back ... except for one ... there was a Kairos in Sydney. He needed to speak to himself there. Alice being lost was what his other self had warned him about.

"Tell Shintaro to hold, I'll get back to him ASAP," Secta said hurriedly. He handed the chip back to Sonoko, who accepted it with an equally concerned look for Alice's safety.

"I need to send an express message to Sydney," Secta told Yashida.

Sonoko meandered over to the large window that faced east, marvelling at the sight of the colossal UFO in the distance over Yokohama Bay.

"You can see it, wow," she said, almost disbelievingly.

Both Secta and Yashida joined her at the window.

"My goodness, look at that incredible machine!" Secta gasped.

The typhoon-inflamed sky was teeming with fighter jets swooping down from on high through the thick, rolling storm clouds, firing rockets at the gigantic flying saucer. There was ground fire from tanks, artillery, and rocket launchers positioned around the foreshore of Yokohama Bay, raining down on the UFO. Each volley exploded against the surface of the massive bubble shield surrounding and protecting the craft—nothing could penetrate it.

"The bombs and rockets are like harmless insects against that technological giant. You can discern the shape of the invisible force field protecting it. There is some seriously sophisticated science behind that," Secta observed.

But there was no time to watch any more. He rushed over and sat at the desktop array, entered Secta's ID, Hud, and then typed ... UFO arrived ... Alice went through a wormhole alone ... I need to know ... is Alice there in Sydney with you?

The question would assure him Alice survived. He knew he'd survive himself, otherwise Secta wouldn't be able to talk to him from Sydney. Aware that he was pushing the prime directive and that Secta might not answer him because of that, he still needed to try.

Time was ticking away while they nervously waited for a reply … minutes passed feeling like hours … and then it came. He read it out loud, "You know I can't answer that. We are already in danger of corrupting the timeline. I will get a message through Kairos IV to Hope for her to open a wormhole for you to return home." The mention of the existence of Kairos IV excited him, but he couldn't question it. He quickly typed a response, "Why go home?"

The reply came swiftly, "You will understand when you return. Engage event opening in two hours at original arrival point. Take the organic with you. Goodbye and good luck."

The connection terminated.

"Damn, another cryptic message! Why do I always have to talk in riddles?" he grumbled out loud to himself, frustrated. "Yashida, please inform Shintaro to proceed on his mission without Alice."

Dr James was seated in the Kairos control room, almost ready to call it a day, when Kairos again activated of its own accord. The session was brief, only long enough for a paper aeroplane to pop out through the open iris in the large circular device. To Robert's astonishment, he watched the paper plane perform an awkward loop the loop and then land on the floor—it was a much better design than previous efforts, he thought. He jumped up from behind the console, raced into the studio, collected it, and then unfurled it. An expression of both excitement and panic broke on his face. He hurried back into the control room and made an urgent call to Hope.

Hope wasn't far away and got to the control room in record time.

James handed her the note and said, "It came through as a paper aeroplane."

Reading it, she chuckled, "My crazy brother ... from the future no less. Seems our Secta contacted him, so the older Secta is telling us in exactly two hours' time to open a wormhole to the same coordinates we sent Secta to last time in Tokyo ... using Secta's marker, and he signed it 'your most senior brother' ... Ha! Wait till I show this to the President."

"That's a real time twister ... want me to start prepping Kairos?"

"Yes, Robert, it's always best to do what my dear brother says ... especially this older, and I expect, wiser brother. Even if it means corrupting the timeline somewhat," Hope said with a smirk.

"Was he breaking the prime directive by contacting us?" Robert asked.

"Both Sectas broke it, yes. I'll be back," she said, racing out of the room to show the President.

She stepped out of the elevator on the penthouse level of Oceana HQ, walked briskly across the black marble lobby floor, and entered through security sliding glass doors into the President's office reception area.

The view of Sydney Harbour by night was magnificent through the eight-metre ceiling-to-floor light-sensitive windows. Miss Vallins was behind her desk. She looked up and beamed a smile at Hope.

"Good evening, Doctor, do you want to see him?"

"Yes, please. You look stunning as always, Rita," Hope said warmly.

"Thank you, Hope, same to you ... he'll see you. Go right on in, he's just reading the evening tabloid. Do you want a coffee?"

"No thanks, love."

Miss Vallins went back to touching up her eye make-up and lipstick in a compact mirror, in preparation to go home.

Hope approached the lounge setting where the President was seated, hiding behind a large open tabloid sheet. She noticed the headline on the front page:

FAILED UN PEACE TALKS ESCALATES ISRAEL
AND IRAN SABRE RATTLING

"Good evening, sir," Hope said graciously.

The newspaper lowered, and the jolly-faced president beamed at Hope with a welcoming smile. "Oh, my dear Hope, now what can I do for such a lovely lady on such a beautiful evening? Please, take a seat."

She obliged, leaned forward, and handed him the note.

"What's this? Looks like it had been folded into a paper aeroplane … I used to love making them when I was a kid … and helicopters, with a bit of folded-up aluminium foil for stability … drop them off the balcony," he motioned with his fingers like falling leaves.

Hope thought, you never can take the boy out of the man.

He read the note, "I don't understand," he said with his bushy eyebrows raised.

After Hope had explained the note, the look on his face was priceless. "That's extraordinary. It's not easy to get your head around how there can be two Sectas in the one time talking to one another, but after learning how Gorrick keeps turning up in different times, I expect anything's possible."

"We're still learning about timeline ramifications, sir. I have my doubts they could ever meet up."

"So, you think Secta couldn't actually meet his older self then?"

"No, physics suggests one would cancel the other out."

"No, can't get my head around that one either … gives me a headache just thinking about it."

Hope smiled. "We're prepping Kairos now. This gave me an idea on how to make the exchange with Honor … but we shouldn't tell Karzoff and Viktoria … they should stay focused on setting a trap to capture her."

"I agree, so go ahead and explain your idea to me."

Shintaro assembled his troops outside under cover from the torrential rain to prepare for evacuation. Under guard, Kew was handcuffed, sitting cross-legged on the tarmac with a grimace on his face like he'd bitten into a lemon. Overhead, the pandemonium of the raging battle against the UFO, coupled with belting winds and rain from the typhoon, was relentless.

"I had my doubts they would be able to get us out with this gale blowing, so I ordered a Chinook," Shintaro explained. "It will take us all at once and can hack the conditions."

"Depends on how good the pilot is," Tombei suggested.

"How many casualties?"

"Six, sir, and one gut shot. We have morphed him, but he is losing a lot of blood."

"The ninjas were a let-down."

"Yes, was not long before they retreated with their tails between their legs," Tombei said with a wry grin. They were speaking loud enough to get above the sound of the tempest and the constant thump of artillery shelling and exploding ordnance.

Shintaro glanced up at the flashes of shells and missiles hitting the surface of the bubble.

"Nothing even makes a dint in that thing," he said grimly.

"They will need to nuke it," Tombei said.

The thumping sound emitted by the two rotor blades of a Chinook interrupted them. Shintaro gazed up at it making its late final approach just as he received a message on his VV. "It is Commander Ikegami, he is the best pilot we have got ... he is requesting a rear door speed-board and take-off," Shintaro relayed.

Tombei jumped to it, lining the men up, and then marching along the ranks in the pouring rain, screaming instructions.

Shintaro watched the big Chinook battling the gale-force winds and blinding rain to make a near-perfect touchdown.

The boarding went smoothly. Inside two minutes, the Chinook had been loaded and was back in the air bound for the helipad at the Met.

Shintaro stared out of the small round window of the Chinook at fighter jets streaking by and then hitting their afterburners after releasing rockets at the target. The percussion from the exploding warheads rocked the chopper. When he looked back inside the chopper, the blinding flashes from every exploding bomb lit up the interior, allowing him to see the look of fear on the faces of his troops.

"Commander, you can give the military a message we are all clear, and GPS devices have been activated," Shintaro said through his communication link.

"Roger that," Commander Ikegami replied.

Shintaro knew that would mean the military could change the focus of the attack from the UFO, where they hadn't been able to make an impression, to the Zen complex. He hoped that it wouldn't be endangering Alice, but under the circumstances, they had no other option. They were also risking the lives of the thousands of pregnant Japanese women imprisoned on the island.

The main mission of Bravo and Charlie teams to plant GPS devices in locations in and around the Zen complex had been accomplished.

Shintaro received a message directly from military command: evacuation underway before release of a fusion bomb on the complex. He knew that the small pure fusion warhead would generate a very small nuclear yield with the advantage of no collateral damage to the rest of Tokyo from fallout. A fusion bomb doesn't create the highly radioactive by-products associated with other fission-type weapons. One of them fired at the Zen dome would take out the entire island.

Dressed in black leathers with orders from Gorrick to free Kew from the clutches of the SAT, agent Kim was on a Kawasaki 950 electro-jet motorbike speeding through the tunnels under Tokyo en-route to the Met. Gorrick was in contact with him via his VV and ordered: if escape isn't doable, then eliminate Kew. Following that, he was to eliminate Tanaka and Secta.

A professional assassin, inside his black helmet, Kim's icy expression creased slightly into a macabre smile ... it was exactly the kind of mission he relished, especially when there was the added incentive of two million crypto credits to be paid into his account upon fulfillment of the assignment.

With no traffic to negotiate, the journey was fast. As he emerged from a tunnel into the incessant rain, he missed noticing the Chinook passing overhead.

By the time the Chinook had landed on the helipad, the gale from the typhoon had just about abated, but it was still pelting rain. The rear door of the big chopper lowered, and the troops deplaned.

Two guards with Kew in tow followed Tombei inside. They would take the prisoner to a holding cell next to the scanning room in the basement of the Met.

When they reached it, they removed the handcuffs from Kew, then locked him inside. Tombei placed a guard outside and then went to meet Shintaro, who was scheduled for an online conference debriefing with the Police Commissioner and the military.

Downstairs at a side entrance of the Met used for trafficking prisoners to interrogation rooms, Kim was standing out of sight of the security face recognition camera that he knew would feed a database storing his details ... profile, image, etc. It was critical to get past it, and so he removed his helmet, took a tube of photosensitive gel from his side pocket ... shed his gloves, squeezed a wad of the clear gel into the palm of his right hand, and then smeared it all over his face. He wiped his hands clean of gel residue on his leather pants, produced a cellphone from his jacket pocket, and flicked through a series of photographs until he came to the shot he wanted and then selected it. It was a grizzly overhead shot of SAT Alpha leader Riku

Watanabe's severed head on the floor at Zen with his eyes open in a death stare. He zoomed in on it a little until it was full frame. Opening up an app, he held the phone up to his face at arm's length to take a selfie and waited; after a couple of seconds, the camera flashed.

When he stepped out in front of the security camera and looked up at the lens, it recognised the face of Riku Watanabe, and the door slid open. Once inside, he quickly peeled off his leathers, dumped them out of sight, and then made his way to the elevator. He knew Kew would be imprisoned on the basement level. The door opened, and he stepped inside, but the elevator wouldn't move until he had inputted Riku Watanabe's fingerprint into the ID security system for it to cross-reference with the photograph he had provided at the entrance. He reached into his hip pocket and produced a resealable plastic bag containing the bloody severed index finger of Riku Watanabe. Pressing it against the sensor on the floor option panel, he selected basement level, and the elevator door closed.

CHAPTER 29
ONE WORLD

MILITARY STRATEGISTS HAD computed that a GPS lock on the devices strategically planted on Zen Island by SAT would guide a fusion bomb dropped by an F-26 Eagle fighter-bomber to take out the island and possibly the UFO. All of the devices omitting the GPS signal were located outside the force field that was protecting the UFO. It had been theorised that a fusion bomb blast would take out the UFO if it were detonated directly beneath the force field bubble.

It was a risk, but one that had to be taken. The collateral damage had been estimated as low due to the isolation of Zen Island. As a precaution, civilian and military evacuation was currently underway around the foreshores of Yokohama Bay. The move would be unprecedented: a fusion bomb had not yet been used in a military attack, anywhere in the world; it was, in fact, still experimental.

Since rumours of the intended use of the fusion bomb by Japan on the UFO had gone viral, a massive press gallery had gathered on the rooftops of Tokyo buildings, a safe distance from ground zero, to capture the event. Live pictures were being broadcasted globally. Condemnation of the aggressive plan was rife, with many groups calling for communication with the aliens rather than conflict.

Contact had been attempted to no avail, but then after the UFO had made the first hostile move by downing the Red Cross medical chopper and killing the crew, followed by the shooting down of two

Japan Air Self-Defence Force F-26 Eagle fighter jets, any chance of a peaceful first contact had been abrogated.

Japan had to act fast before worldwide opinion could stand the chance of affecting the outcome. The United States wanted to intervene, but the world had become wary of that ... the UN was doing its usual thing being diplomatic while achieving very little. Right now, the UFO represented an immediate threat to the security of the thirty-two million residents of Tokyo; it was their problem, and they were going to deal with it in their way.

It was obvious by the advanced technology that had brought such a craft to Earth and then protected it so well from attack that it was expected to be capable of mass destruction on a scale never before witnessed on Earth.

The leaders of the axis countries of the world convened in the 11th hour at the UN and voted unanimously for Japan to proceed with the fusion bomb; not that that mattered, Japan was going to proceed anyway, but the rubber stamp from the UN at least gave Japan a licence to legally deploy the weapon.

With the world on the brink of a war with Iran and fighting on numerous other fronts against terrorism, the threat of the UFO had the positive effect of coalescing humanity into a common cause: an alien enemy of the people of Earth had finally united humankind into one world.

The rain and wind had ceased by the time Shintaro, Tombei, and a group of other Met officers had assembled on the Met rooftop helipad. From there they had an unobstructed view of the UFO hovering over Zen Island.

The sky was clear of aircraft, and the artillery barrage from the shores of Yokohama Bay had ceased, leaving an eerie, ominous silence.

Tokyo, Japan, and the rest of the world held a united breath, fearing the UFO could unleash a weapon of mass destruction in retaliation should the fusion bomb fail.

"The wormhole will open at your lab at Nihon Inc.," Secta told Sonoko.

"That's in Shinjuku Chuo Park … and the Skypod isn't running," Sonoko said worriedly.

"Plus, there is a curfew and a typhoon, which at least seems to be abating," Yashida chipped in.

"We need to find a way. According to myself, there's a lot depending on my return."

"When will it open?" Sonoko asked.

"In about ninety minutes."

Yashida had an idea. "My car is in the basement car park; we can take it."

"Perfect," Secta said positively. "Let's move."

On the way to the door, Secta paused and glanced out of the window at the UFO.

"The bombing has stopped; I wonder what's going on? God, I'd love a photo of that thing to take back with me." He realised that wasn't possible and shrugged off the thought, "Oh well, no worries … let's go."

The three of them left the forensic lab to take the elevator to the basement. From there, a staircase would take them one level down to the car park.

They exited the elevator, and when they turned into the corridor, they found a guard lying in a puddle of blood on the floor with his throat cut. The cell door adjacent was open.

Kim stepped out and snarled, "Well, well, isn't this convenient? You saved me looking for you."

Thinking on his feet, Yashida flung Secta his car key card and then charged Kim like a rugby player making an illegal shoulder charge.

Secta grabbed Sonoko's hand and took off for the staircase, dragging her behind.

The impact of Yashida's charge pushed Kim back inside the cell, where the two of them struggled for supremacy in the tight confines.

Kew, whom Yashida didn't realise was there, dealt him a vicious blow that knocked him to his knees.

Resentful of Yashida's actions, Kim pulled a gun, quickly fixed a silencer to the end of the barrel, put it up to the scientist's temple, and demanded, "Where are they going?"

Yashida said nothing.

"Three seconds, and I'll fire."

"Alright. Alright … they're going to Nihon Inc.," Yashida admitted nervously.

"Why? One thousand and one, one thousand and two…" Kim threatened.

"He's leaving through a wormhole, please don't shoot, I'm only a humble scientist with a family."

Kew pushed in, snatched the pistol out of Kim's hand, and jammed it into Yashida's mouth. "Why … why is he going back? Has Alice returned?" He glared coldly into Yashida's terrified eyes. "I'm going to take this out of your mouth for you to answer. If I'm not happy with the answer, you'll die, you got that?" He kept the gun in Yashida's mouth until he got a nod from him, then he withdrew it for him to speak.

"He is taking the Core i20-67775XX organic chip Nihon developed back to his time; Alice has returned already," he lied. As soon as he'd said it, he had his i-Keeper send a message to Shintaro: *Kim, basement escape 2 Nihon.*

Thunk! A bullet slammed into Yashida's stomach.

Holding onto the gun, Kew led Kim out of the cell and stopped in the corridor.

"I would have killed him," Kim said angrily.

"I have; it just takes longer being gut-shot. How far to Nihon Inc.?" Kew questioned callously. He didn't really have too much time for Kim, considered him spineless.

"Ten minutes."

"Where's your vehicle?"

"Outside."

"Move."

As soon as Shintaro received the message from Yashida, he turned sharply to Tombei and said urgently, "With me, now!" He led Tombei at break-neck speed back inside the Met from the helipad to the elevator.

"What is it?" Tombei asked while waiting for the elevator.

"Yashida messaged, Kim is in the basement."

"But how?"

He quickly had his i-Keeper access the CCTV to check entries into the Met over the last twenty minutes. The vision of Riku Watanabe entering came up … he froze the shot and zoomed.

The elevator arrived; they entered.

"He used Riku Watanabe's image and probably his body parts to gain entry to free Kew, I would say."

"How did he use his face?"

"Photosensitive gel probably. Standard in an Interpol agent's box of tricks."

The door opened, and they rushed for the cell that housed Kew. Inside it, they found Yashida sitting on the floor with his back to the wall, both hands covering a bleeding wound in his stomach.

"If I let go, my guts will probably pop out," Yashida groaned nervously.

"Have you called a medic?" Tombei asked him.

"Yes."

Shintaro put a comforting hand on his shoulder, leaned close, and asked him delicately, "Do you know where Kew and Kim are going?"

"They are going after Secta and Miss Tanaka … they have gone to Nihon Inc. for Secta to return to his time," he said through gritted teeth.

"Hang on, my friend, you will be okay," Shintaro said with encouragement. "We are going to leave you now while we go after those bastards, alright? Someone will be along in a minute to help."

"Do not let them kill Secta," Yashida said wincing in pain. "The future of mankind depends on him getting back to his time. Go…"

Tombei had already arranged a vehicle and driver to be ready and waiting for them at the main exit.

As they stepped onto the pavement out front of the Met, there was a loud roar. They both looked up sharply up in time to see an F-26 Eagle fighter-bomber flying over.

"There she goes, carrying the fusion bomb," Shintaro said.

They hopped into the rear seat of a streamlined Lexus hydrogen-powered car. Shintaro immediately triggered the Holo-TV to watch the bomb drop live.

"Shinjuku Chuo Park, code red," he told the driver.

As they sped through the deserted city, Shintaro and Tombei sat glued to the TV.

The HD 3-D picture was a wide locked-off shot of the UFO over Zen Island with an insert in a lower frame of the fighter-bomber approaching from the north. For the benefit of the broadcast, a commentator was counting down from twenty.

At ten and counting, the cloud base around the UFO shimmered. Then, when the count reached five, the UFO disappeared in a flash. The bomber continued with the mission and delivered its payload. The screen split into three, with two inserts: one a zoomed shot of the missile hurtling towards the target, and the other a feed from a camera in the nose of the missile. Two, one … there was a pause … then, Zen Island exploded into a massive fireball that quickly ascended a thousand metres into the night sky. After ten seconds, a mushroom cloud was all that remained of the event; at ground zero, there was nothing of Zen Island left, it had gone.

"What just happened?" Tombei muttered, amazed.

"I think the UFO returned to wherever it came from, taking its cargo of pregnant women with it ... and Alice," Shintaro said, disconsolately.

"Alice? Do you think that is where he went ... on the ship?"

"Sure do."

Kew was on the bike behind Kim, speeding through the city. He would have preferred any sort of getaway car rather than a 950 Kawasaki but had no option.

In the meantime, Secta, following directions from Sonoko, drove down the underground car park entrance ramp of Nihon Inc. The number plate was automatically scanned on entry. Sonoko was glad Yashida's high-security clearance got them through.

"A message from Yashida, Kew shot him ... they are following us, and Shintaro is following them. He warned us to be very careful," she said uneasily.

"We don't need those two after us," he groaned.

"The fusion bomb has been detonated; Zen Island has gone ... but the saucer disappeared just before the explosion."

Secta turned into a car space near the elevator. "That must have been the rumble we heard on the way ... The UFO disappearing was to be expected."

They hopped out of the car and rushed to the elevator. Sonoko flashed her ID at the security sensor, the door slid open, and they entered.

Inside the elevator puffing, Secta said, "Not long to go, but I think Kew and Kim wouldn't be far behind us. Will they be able to get in without security clearance?"

"Kim is an Interpol agent with priority status; that will get them in without any trouble."

"Can you alert security to slow them down ... we need to buy some time."

"Okay." She signalled security. "I will set off a break-in alert; that will shut down entry to all main floors."

"Excellent."

The elevator stopped at the designated floor. They charged out and raced along the corridor until they reached the door to Sonoko's lab. She opened the door, the sensor turned on the lights, and they entered.

Secta immediately collected a chair and jammed it against the door. "Is this the only entrance to the lab?"

"Yes."

"Good, then turn the lights out ... we'll have to sit and wait."

She went over to a panel near the door and touched a sensor that extinguished the lights. Silence befell the room ... it was an eerie silence in the dark. A light from a device in her hand illuminated Sonoko's face.

"What are you doing?" Secta whispered.

She slipped a chip into the device. "I am downloading photos I have transferred from my retinal implants to the Core i20 organic chip, along with as many schematics of different devices and software I could find ... including the one you liked of Yashida's for converting molecular structures into 3-D images ... so you can take them back with you."

"Fantastic. Thanks."

"Will you be able to take the organic chip with you? I should have asked first."

"Yes, if it's totally organic, it shouldn't be a problem. You won't get into trouble giving me it, will you?"

"Probably, but I will ask Shintaro to get me off the hook, I am sure he would do that for me..."

"If it wasn't for my senior Secta ordering me to take the organic chip back, I wouldn't do it."

"Why, because it breaks the prime directive?"

"How do you know about that? Oh, of course, Alice would have told you ... No, because if it were to fall into the hands of Zen, it would give them a very dangerous edge in cybernetics."

"Is Zen in your time as well?" she asked.

"As far as I know, they're in almost every time. They are the enemy, our nemesis."

"Secta, can I ask you something?"

"Certainly."

"Do you think Alice will come back, or was it the last I will ever see of him?"

He thought about it a moment and then said warmly, "I don't know, Sonoko. But what I do know is he is very fond of you. I can honestly say I've never seen him so happy with a woman before. His long-time girlfriend was killed not so long back, and it tore his heart out. Did he tell you?"

"No, he does not speak of such things ... he is very secretive about his life."

He gently took her hand and said tenderly, "If he doesn't come back, it would only be because he's on an important mission somewhere in some time ... saving the world ... doing what Black Alice does best."

"Where do you think he is now?" she asked, looking deep and teary-eyed into Secta's expressive cobalt blue eyes.

"On board that UFO, I'd say, doing what no-one else but Alice would dare attempt."

CHAPTER 30
FREEZE A JOLLY
GOOD FELLOW

ALICE HAD NO idea where he was. By the sound, it might have been the bowels of a ship, but he couldn't hear the lapping of water, so he ruled that out. It was pitch black, which was his pet hate. Since he was a kid, he'd suffered from Scotophobia and always slept with a light on. Now, the inky blackness of wherever he was had him breathless, sweating excessively, feeling nauseous, dry-mouthed, shaking with heart palpitations—an inability to think clearly. It was a sensation of detachment from reality and a feeling of impending doom.

Reaching out his fingertips, he touched a wall. It was cold and made of metal. He slid down to the floor, sitting with his head in his hands, eyes shut. He pictured Sonoko's face and it calmed him down. He liked being with her even more than he had with Zule, and it was different than it had been with his murdered girlfriend, Stained Class. The difference was that Sonoko somehow felt real to him, strange considering she had been genetically manipulated, he thought.

A clunk, like the sound of a corrugated iron roof cooling down at night after a stinking hot day, jolted him out of his reverie. His eyes had adjusted to the dark because now he could make out a very fine line of light from what appeared to be a gap under a door.

On hands and knees, he crawled over to the strip of light and then felt his way up the door. It sensed his touch and slid open. Once his eyes were accustomed to the glaring yellow light outside of the dark room, he made his way stealthily out into a vast room, hugging the sloping wall so as not to be noticed. There was no-one to be seen anywhere.

"Where the hell am I?" he mumbled. There were no windows, just a mezzanine floor in the round with what appeared to be several floors above it. One obvious thing he noticed was the décor, the construction materials, and then the general ambience around him—it all felt alien. Even his footsteps sounded weird; they didn't echo as you'd expect them to do in such a cavernous space. To top it off, he felt substantially lighter on his feet than normal, as though gravity was less. He scanned the room: it was circular with many alcoves in the perimeter. It reminded him of a bicycle wheel, and in the centre was what looked like an axle. Though there were no spokes, if there had been, they would have led to each of the alcoves. He made his way to an alcove and recognised it immediately. It was a cell, and the grated door was swung open. This is a prison ... but where are the prisoners? All of the cells were empty.

Being unarmed in the alien surroundings made him feel insecure. It was imperative to reunite with his Alpha unit, so finding a way out was his priority. Intuition told him to make for the mezzanine floor; if nothing else, he'd have a clearer view of the room from up there.

He scurried across to what looked like a staircase. It was a conveyor that activated when he stepped onto it. He rode it up to the mezzanine level.

A long circular corridor ran around the perimeter of the mezzanine with rooms leading off on one side. Partway along the corridor, he found another conveyor up and stepped onto it. At the top, he found a narrow hall with two doors. He tried the first door, but it was locked. The second door slid open as he reached it. Inside was a set of a dozen metal stairs leading up.

At the top of the stairs, he found a large circular control room, like that of a digital recording studio, only larger and with a lot more digital gadgets. The lighting was dim, making the vast array of tiny different-coloured lights on the console and throughout the room appear like fairyland. There were half a dozen computer terminals and an overhead console, like in the cockpit of an aircraft. Directly beyond the console was a large curved windscreen, dark; it seemed to be shielded.

Alice stood behind the console and studied the chairs and the desk. There seemed to be a seat for the captain, the pilot, and then places for co-pilots and assistants. He sat in the big comfy captain's chair. There were controls in the two armrests. He figured one of the buttons should operate the shield covering the large panoramic windscreen, so he touched one. He'd guessed right; the windshield became clear as though the polarity had been changed. What he saw through it shocked him. It reminded him of a Starship Enterprise docking scene in a Star Trek movie. He was inside the UFO, all right, at the very top in the cockpit, and stretched out majestically on the other side of the windshield was the massive grey body of the saucer. But that was only part of what had him rattled; the entire ship was docked inside a massive cavern with gigantic metal gantries supporting large mechanical arms that anchored the craft in position as though it were in dry dock.

Kim placed his Interpol ID on the glass of the Nihon Inc. main entrance doors for the security guard on the other side to read, and then he indicated that he wanted to enter. The doors opened, and with Kew at his heels, Kim confronted the guard.

"In which lab would I find Doctor Tanaka?"

Knowing it had been Sonoko who had triggered the alarm, the guard was hesitant. "She is not here at this hour, sir."

"I'm not interested in your opinion. I said, which lab?"

Kew didn't care about the guard, and he went to the reception desk, reached over, and typed 'Doctor Tanaka' into the computer. It immediately came up with Lab 177.

"Got it, come on," he snarled irritably.

"Come with me, now," Kim ordered the guard, and they followed Kew to the elevators. One of the three elevator doors opened, and they went inside.

"Level seventeen," Kew said.

Standing behind the guard, Kim ordered, "Swipe your ID."

The guard didn't like his attitude and hesitated. Kim pulled his pistol and put the silencer against the back of the guard's head.

"Swipe," he snarled.

The guard was armed with a pistol holstered in his belt. Kim kept a sharp eye on it while the guard swiped his ID. Once it was accepted, and he'd selected the correct floor, a thump sounded, and blood splashed on the closed stainless-steel doors. The guard dropped to the floor of the elevator dead; Kim had shot him in the back of the head.

"Is there a place for you to hide in here?" Secta whispered to Sonoko.

"Yes, in the cupboard under the bench. I hid there once before, playing a joke on my workmates."

"Okay, I think you better get in there now. I have a gut feeling the bad guys are perilously close. Only come out when you hear Shintaro's voice."

She looked into his eyes and gave him a big emotional hug. "I am going to miss you, Secta."

"Don't get all gooey on me now. I'll miss you as well," he said timidly.

She kissed him gently, as a family member would, and then opened the double cupboard doors under the bench, moved a few things aside, slid in, and curled up into a foetal position.

Secta held the door. "Look at you; it was made to order. Goodbye, Sonoko," he said, getting misty.

A tear traversed her pale cheek, and she sobbed a little and cutely waved her hand goodbye.

Secta was just about to close the doors when she said, "Wait," and fumbled in her pocket. She handed him the organic chip in its cellophane wrap. "I nearly forgot this."

"Thanks," he said and closed the doors. The room shimmered.

Shintaro and Tombei stopped at the main entrance to Nihon Inc. Shintaro flashed his ID at the security camera mounted above the doors, and they slid open. They rushed inside and made for the elevators. As they reached them, a door opened, and inside on the floor was the body of a guard in a pool of blood.

Shintaro shook his head at Kim's ruthlessness. "The coward shot him in the back of the head." He flashed his ID at the sensor on the floor selection panel and hit seventeen. His i-Keeper had already told him where to find Sonoko.

It was now a nervous wait for the elevator to reach the 17th floor; he didn't want to get there and find both Secta and Sonoko like the guard—with a bullet in the back of the head.

Secta remembered what Alice had told him about the moment the vortex appears during the hiatus; everything freezes, except for inoculated time travellers. The science of what caused that eluded him, but it wasn't the time to think about that. However, it was definitely the time to utilise it.

A loud crash, as Kim barged in through the door with Kew behind him, jolted him out of his thoughts. Their body movement triggered a sensor, and the lights came on. When Kim saw Secta, he immediately aimed his gun at him.

A voice shouted from the hallway behind them, "Put it down, Kim, now!"

Kim looked over his shoulder at Shintaro and Tombei, "Well, if it isn't the Lone Ranger and Tonto. Drop your weapons, or Secta gets it."

"Do as he says, cop. He means it," Kew growled.

The room shimmered again, and a swirling supernatural breeze sprang up, lifting pieces of paper from the bench top into the air, like they were caught up in a mini-tornado.

A vortex the size of a soccer ball materialized half a metre over the bench Sonoko was hiding beneath.

When Secta looked back at Kim, Shintaro, and Tombei, they had frozen, but Kew hadn't ... he quickly realised why: he had been inoculated.

Kew looked at Kim, then at Secta and chuckled, "Why have they frozen like that, some of your scientific mumbo-jumbo? Well, now it comes down to you and me, doesn't it, Doctor Secta?"

"That doesn't sound particularly inviting," Secta said, while keeping a sly eye on the vortex. He wasn't sure if Kew knew what to do about the vortex or what it was for, for that matter.

"What is that damn thing?" he said, referring to the vortex.

"Oh, just an experiment, don't get too close. It might gobble you up," he said half-jokingly but threateningly enough as a bluff. "Do you have orders to kill me?"

"No, to the contrary."

Secta was relieved, "Then what is this all about?"

"Where's the girl?"

"Sonoko? Ah, that's it. You have orders to kill her ... why, what for? Anyhow, you're out of luck; she's gone ... hiding somewhere in the building. You'll never find her."

Kew snatched the gun out of Kim's frozen hand and aimed it at Secta, "I'm not to kill you, but I can put a couple of bullet holes in you ... take me to her now, or I'll start shooting."

Secta knew he meant it, "You do know, of course, that you're a psychopath, don't you, Kew? You really do need help." He glanced up at the aircon duct in the ceiling, then back down at the gun pointed at him, "Okay, Okay, don't shoot, you've got me ... I'll show you where she is."

Kew had followed Secta's eye-line and presumed Sonoko was hiding in the air duct, which was exactly what Secta wanted him to think.

The vortex was now big enough for him to pass through. He climbed up onto the bench so he could get closer to the vortex and pointed at the ceiling to distract Kew, "She's in there ... inside the duct."

Kew moved closer, keeping the gun trained on him. Secta wasted no time and kicked the gun out of his grasp. It hit the floor and slid underneath a table. Secta put the chip in his mouth under his tongue and dived into the vortex.

Kew immediately realised what had happened, leapt up onto the bench, and dived after Secta into the rapidly closing eddy.

The vortex closed, and after a few seconds, everything returned to normal. Thinking he still had his gun, Kim swung around with his finger aimed at Shintaro and motioned for the trigger to shoot.

Three shots sounded. Kim stood numbed with a surprised expression on his face; he never expected it to end this way. His legs buckled, and he collapsed, dead before he hit the floor. Shintaro wasn't taking any chances; he stood over him, leaned down, felt for a pulse: he was dead.

"What just happened?" Tombei mumbled, as though he'd been tripping.

Shintaro straightened up and sighed, "I would say all that weird stuff was Secta going back in time."

"So, where is the other guy?"

"Kew? Must have gone after him. Sonoko, are you there?" he called out. "Sonoko, are you in here? It is Shintaro?"

A rustle came from the other side of the central bench, and Sonoko rose from behind it. Glad to be safe, she rushed over to Shintaro and embraced him in a big hug. He felt a little awkward as she sobbed on his shoulder, but he patted her on the back and said comfortingly, "It is all right, Doctor. All over now."

CHAPTER 31
FOUNDATION OF EARTH

HOPE AWAITED WITH a robe for Secta when he emerged from Kairos naked. Standing by, armed and ready, were Karzoff and Viktoria. A few seconds later, Kew popped out: as naked as the day he was born. The moment of disorientation left him lying on the floor, giving Karzoff and Viktoria the opportunity to stand over him with their guns drawn. Viktoria tossed the dustcoat she was holding at him.

"Put this on," she ordered bluntly.

Kew's vision slowly cleared, his senses returned, and he sat up, gathering the coat and slipping it on.

Hope warmly embraced Secta. "Glad you made it back in one piece."

Just as Secta was about to respond, he remembered the chip in his mouth and spat it into his open palm. "Lucky I didn't swallow this."

Kew had gotten to his feet, watching and listening.

"Hands out in front," Karzoff barked at Kew. When he complied, Karzoff efficiently snapped a pair of cuffs on him.

Doctor James's voice came over the intercom. "Shutting Kairos down now, please exit."

"We'll take Kew to the lock-up and meet you at the President's office for the debriefing in ten," Karzoff told the others, then escorted Kew out.

As Kew was led past Secta, he shot him a stink-eye. "I'll have the last laugh at you," Kew snarled.

"Goodbye old boy, enjoy your new accommodations, won't you? Here you are, the last laugh … Ha! Ha! Ha!" Secta said facetiously.

They watched him being taken away, then Hope took Secta by the arm and guided him towards the control room. "There's so much to tell you," Hope said. "And I'm sure you've got plenty to share, but first, let's get you changed. The President wouldn't want to see his time traveller in a dressing gown; it would remind him of Ford Prefect."

Inside the control room, Robert greeted Secta with a handshake.

Secta opened his left hand and displayed the organic chip on his fingertip.

"This is a Core i20-67775XX organic chip: a twenty-core organic processor with a clock speed of 20.5 GHz … and, because it's organic, it doesn't require liquid or air cooling. It has two terabytes of memory and comes loaded with the blueprint of the chip and other brilliant stuff from 2047," he said, imitating a car salesman while wearing a big cheesy grin.

Both Hope and Robert were captivated by the tiny brown chip balanced on the tip of Secta's index finger.

"Twenty cores!" Robert murmured, astounded.

"Organic…" Hope added, mesmerised. "That humble trifling thing could alter the course of history!"

"Indubitably, and put us years ahead of Zen in the cybernetics race. Things had progressed a lot in cybernetics in 2047… There were androids that made my old 2-4-D prototype guard that Alice bashed up seem like a child's toy."

"Odd you should mention that, we've got a surprise for you in the morgue."

The idea of a surprise intrigued him, but for now, he had other more important things on his mind. First, he went to his office down the hall to change his clothing. Upon entering, he went immediately to his library and his Isaac Asimov collection, selected the first addition copy of Foundation of Earth, opened it, and then carefully secreted away the organic chip inside the front cover. He closed the book and then slid it back into place with the other twenty-nine hardcovers in the collection.

Kew's OSCI came online soon after he arrived back, but he waited until he was alone in the cell to contact Honor. He filled her in on what she needed to relay to Gorrick. She was happy to hear his voice, but after the call, she realised with Kew back and in Karzoff's custody, her plan to have them swap Secta for the Professor was shot to bits. Obviously, Karzoff would now use Kew as a bargaining tool in place of Secta.

The President met with Karzoff, Viktoria, Hope, and Secta in his office. The latter had finished a debriefing of the Tokyo 2047 mission and a lengthy discussion theorising the whereabouts of Alice, and then Hope had given an account of the kidnapping of the Professor and the reason they had recalled Secta.

"You can relax Secta," the President said with a warm smile. "We won't be trading you for the Professor under any circumstances. We needed to have you back here to help with this dilemma ... we don't want to lose de Luz, do we?"

"Sir, I have an idea," Hope said with a sagacious smile. "Give me an hour alone with Secta, and we'll see if it's feasible."

As they were leaving the office, the President stopped Secta and asked, "So my friend, what was the world of Tokyo in 2047 really like?"

"Overly automated, there are plenty of good things to say about technology, but a total reliance on it is incredibly dangerous Ri."

"Yes, well, we're only just now starting to recognise that with our young folk and their digital devices, aren't we?"

"When something goes wrong, such as a major network failure or if the electricity it depends on, then all that technology, automation, communications ... is made redundant. I witnessed that in 2087, and I can now see how it came about after this last trip."

"Was that business of talking to your senior self a little unsettling?"

"Extremely weird, I only wish I'd had time to ask me more questions," Secta chuckled.

"And the organic chip you brought back with all the information on it, quite extraordinary."

"The items on it are revolutionary, but we need to be conscious of what we commercialise and what we keep for our use. I have no desire to be a hypocrite responsible for technology nimiety. But let me say this, the organic chip will put us way ahead of Zen in the cybernetics race."

The President grinned well pleased.

Fifteen minutes later, Hope led Secta into the Oceana morgue, opened a freezer, and pulled out the tray. On it was the body of Anu Set.

"Look at the work they've done on this. You know there was one in Tokyo as well," Secta said, his voice trembling with excitement.

"An Anu Set?"

"Precisely, but it couldn't speak … could this one?"

"No, and though its motions were convincing, Karzoff and Viktoria said they were just enough unnatural for them to know it was cybernetic."

Secta studied the half cavity that was once its face. One eye was in place in its socket.

"Hmm, the eye is okay … look here's what did the damage. A bullet severed the link between the power generator and the processor."

"Yes, I removed the processor," Hope said, handing him the small part.

Examining it, Secta concluded, "That's why its movements were robotic and it couldn't speak, it's only a quad-core processor. Top of the range for now but with serious limitations, I guess that's why Zen had such a big set-up in Tokyo, to develop faster chips."

"Which brings us to my idea," Hope said with a wicked smirk.

Alice lounged in the groovy captain's chair. "So, what the stuff am I doing here? Obviously, En-Ki has something in mind. It would help if I knew where this thing was parked." Just for fun, he pressed the button again on the arm of the chair and triggered the panoramic windshield to polarise back to black. He hit it again, sending it back to transparent. "What does he want me to do, save the pregnant women? Nar … kill Gorrick if he's on board? Nar. Then what?"

He was mulling over the controls, wondering whether the two throttles directly in front of him powered the engines when a chuckle came from behind.

"Are you enjoying yourself playing a spaceship captain, Alice?"

Alice swivelled the chair round to face the voice and exclaimed in surprise, "Gorrick!" Then to his amazement, two more Gorricks joined the first one.

"Damn, how many of you buggers are there?"

"Oh, about two thousand give or take," one of the other Gorricks said, in a slightly different accent.

"Okay, let's leave it at that for now," Alice said a little confused, "how about telling me where the hell we are?"

After a pregnant pause, the first Gorrick, the one with a British accent same as the Gorrick Alice had previously met in Tokyo, said simply, "Phobos."

Alice raised both eyebrows, "Phobos, like the moon of Mars?"

"Yes, we are inside it," the third Gorrick said in yet another accent, Indian perhaps.

"Are we speaking English here?" Alice questioned with uncertainty.

The first Gorrick stepped forward. "Our little chat is over now, Alice, it's time for you to say goodbye."

"Why, where are you going?" he quipped.

"Get up out of that chair and come with me or there will be trouble."

"And where are you going to find an army in a hurry, Gorrick?" Alice said cynically. He swivelled the chair back facing the controls. "Let's take this baby for a spin."

He pushed both throttles full forward.

"No!" Gorrick screamed out.

The massive machine lurched to the right side, almost throwing Alice out of the chair. The three Gorricks lost their footing and staggered about battling to keep their balance. Then came a deafening array of alarms and sirens ... with red lights flashing all over the console after external sensors had detected an imminent collision. The atmosphere had gone from sublime to ridiculous; it was utter chaos ... just the way Alice liked it.

The spraying of Tokyo had resumed, and swirling contrails of white dust descended upon the city from low-flying choppers. Martial Law would stay invoked until the military and the police were confident the streets were again safe. There were few infected males left out there; now the job was to flush out females pregnant with hybrid babies that had missed out being abducted and to take them into custody. The Government had decided hybrid children born would be raised with their mothers in a high-security institution until a study had determined whether they presented a threat to humanity or not.

It had been a day since Secta's departure. Shintaro and Tombei had arranged to meet up with Sonoko in the Tempura Bar next door to the Met. Once again, the owner was prepared to break curfew for them as he had for Alice and Sonoko only a few days previously.

Sonoko walked past the entrance to the Met and couldn't avoid seeing the graffiti 'Death to Walkers' spray-painted in black across its façade. She wondered how the graffitist had gotten away with it seeing the place was next door to the MET and teeming with cops. The frontage was decorated with bamboo and noren: long thin curtains hanging from the fascia. In the front window were sampuru: realistic plastic replicas of the restaurants' most acclaimed dishes.

Sonoko brushed her way through two long noren hanging in the doorway into the restaurant and was immediately greeted by the chef and owner Otuzu-san. He gestured for her to take a seat at the long cypress wood countertop designed and built by a Japanese shrine carpenter. She was just admiring the intricate woodwork and bamboo ceiling when Shintaro and Tombei came in and joined her. Otuzu-san served up a bottle of Nihon Sakari Gokun from Honjozo, a very fine Saké, best consumed heated.

"Speaking of Nihon ... Nihon Inc. will reprimand me for passing technology to foreigners," Sonoko said coyly.

"Ah, the organic microchip you gave Secta ... Have no concerns Sonoko you will be acquitted, I will see to it, and besides the reason we were a little late is we just heard from the Commissioner of Police that for providing the vaccine that has saved thousands of lives you have been nominated to receive a red ribbon Medal of Honor." He beamed her a proud smile.

Sonoko was surprised and humbled; she blushed.

The two men raised their cups to her and said in unison, "Kanpai!"

"The medal was first awarded in 1882 ... it is awarded to individuals who have risked their own lives to save the lives of others," Tombei explained.

"I am very honoured," Sonoko admitted bashfully. "How is Doctor Yashida?"

"He survived the bullet wound though it probably means early retirement for him with a sizable golden handshake, but I do not think that bothers him so much. He is also getting a Medal of Honour," Shintaro said.

"Yes, a blue ribbon, for individuals who have made significant achievements in the areas of public welfare or public service," Tombei added.

"And what of you two, surely you must be honoured for your bravery?"

"We were just doing our job," Shintaro said humbly. "Besides, it is Alice and Secta who are most deserving of a medal, do you not think?"

"I agree," Sonoko said. "Let' us toast them … to Alice and Secta."

They raised their glasses and took a sip.

"I wonder what happened to Kew when he chased Secta back through time?" Tombei queried.

"And what of Alice? I wonder if we will ever hear from him again?" Shintaro ruminated.

"I would like to think so," Sonoko said, tears welling up in her brown almond eyes.

The chef served up their meals and said, "The whole world is going crazy with the news of alien invasion. Did you see the UFO?"

The three of them exchanged a wry smile.

CHAPTER 32
SEND IN THE CLONES

THE SPACECRAFT HAD minimal thrust. It relied entirely on a wormhole generator to transport it through space and time. There was a small nuclear reactor in the core that provided power for the anti-gravity field, used for hovering when on a planet with gravity, and for all internal power requirements, including force field generation.

The saucer's outer perimeter was fitted with retro rockets. These were for manoeuvring the massive craft when docking or departing, providing only minimal thrust but in any direction. It was the forward-thrusting retro rockets Alice had engaged.

Alice was expecting the craft to whip into warp drive, with a massive starfield shooting at them at hyper-speed like an all-encompassing big bang. Instead, the big machine just lumbered slowly to the right, taking the huge gantries and gigantic clamps that were securing the craft with it. It was heading for the huge wall at the entrance to the natural hangar it was moored inside and, by Alice's reckoning, destined to make a mess of it when it collided.

The Gorrick with the British accent managed to regain his feet and immediately took a dive at Alice. He landed on top of him and began wildly waving his hands about, trying to reach the throttles on the console. But Alice had them covered. He grabbed Gorrick by the throat and head-butted him in the face. Alice's forehead split Gorrick's eye open, and blood gushed out of the deep cut. Three short right-hand jabs had Gorrick's face looking like a bashed crab. He was out cold with a facial makeover. Alice irreverently cast him aside and then looked back through the windscreen at the mess the giant lumbering craft was making of all the surrounding docking equipment. Sparks were flying everywhere, there were small explosions, then the entire ship began to shudder.

Another Gorrick came at Alice, this one armed with a small chair, which he tried to hit Alice over the head with, but Alice ducked, and the high back of the captain's chair took the hit.

Alice looked about for a weapon to arm himself with, grabbed the right throttle, and wrenched it out of its housing. He jumped up and clouted Gorrick in the face with the chrome-plated metal T-bar, sinking it deep into his eye socket, rupturing his eye, and shattering the cheekbone. He then laid into his face using the T-bar like a hammer. It didn't take long before his face looked like minced meat. That Gorrick dropped to the floor beside the previous victim. With blood spatter on his shirt, face, and hands, Alice pointed it at the remaining Gorrick.

"Come on, you freaking turd!" Alice snarled loudly to get above the ruckus of the explosions and sound of the craft crashing into the docking.

Four more Gorricks arrived, all of them dressed the same, all clones.

With the opposition increasing, Alice cursed, "Hell! You reproduce like rabbits!"

With his back to the windscreen, he noticed a look of abject fear break on the faces of the Gorricks.

He whirled around and found what was freaking them out: the craft had collided with a gigantic crane, the impact causing the huge arm to swing across the front of the saucer, skidding off the sloping surface and headed directly for the bridge.

Alice didn't know if there was an atmosphere outside; he didn't think so ... and by the faces of the Gorricks, the windscreen wasn't going to withstand the impact of the crane, so he had to assume it was probably going to take out the entire bridge turret.

He settled back into the captain's chair and muttered, "So this is it, my final performance. Hmm, not even a decent audience."

Gorrick wasn't impressed that Honor had concluded a deal to accept Kew in place of Secta in the swap of Set's body for the Professor.

"What Secta has is worth more than a million Kew's," he shouted, prowling about the luxurious living room of his Point Piper home like an agitated cat.

She decided on a mode of action, slowly pirouetted, and then walked towards him with bedroom eyes.

"Your human depravity has no effect on me, Honor. I am not equipped with the necessary parts to appease your lust. I have no sex. I feel nothing. You have a term for my kind ... it's genital aplasia: a lack of gender organs."

Honor was perplexed. "But ... but, how do you reproduce?"

"I do not. I am a clone from the same host stock: the original Gorrick, if you like."

"Ah, I see, zat explains why Black Alice said he met you in ze future."

"That is correct."

"How do you get rid of waste?" she questioned, with a furrowed brow. "You eat, I haff seen you."

"By osmosis, I eat no animal matter and require very little to sustain me."

"Are you an alien?"

"To humans, yes, but to me, you are the alien."

Mind-blown, she sat on the arm of the lounge, "Where are you from?"

"That's a very long story, but the long and the short of it is my kind is dying. We cannot sustain any more cloning because the genes are beginning to mutate, and the mutation results in an inferior species. Within a century, we will be gone if we don't act now."

"How did you end up like this?"

"Forty-thousand years ago, there was a planet like Earth in the same Milky Way galaxy. The people were territorial and hostile, just like humans ... eventually, this led to war and, then, once they had evolved to nuclear capability and beyond, they eventually annihilated themselves and destroyed the planet. But not before exploring other planets such as Earth. It was the time of Neanderthals, Cro-Magnon, and other human sub-species on Earth, so these people genetically altered the humans for them to mine the Earth of gold, which they needed to power their ships for intergalactic travel."

"Slaves."

"Yes. Over time, the humans evolved and then revolted against their masters. There were those who supported the humans and those who wanted to exploit them. Soon, these two factions went to war over it. Their genetic experimentations had led to the creation of the perfect being: one that could live for hundreds of years, a being of superior intelligence, and could be reproduced by cloning, so gender wasn't necessary. The two factions eliminated one another thousands of years ago, leaving behind only the clones."

"You."

"Correct."

"And now you need to add fresh DNA to your genome to survive. Is zat vot this is all about? Zen, is ze vehicle for you to achieve zis?"

"Simply put, yes. But there is a little more to it. The organic processor Secta brought back with him from 2047 will give Oceana superiority over Zen in cybernetics. That cannot happen; we must possess it at any cost."

"So, zis has been ze plan all along, to have Secta bring ze chip back from ze future for you to take and ... produce smarter androids to take over ze planet?"

Gorrick's thin lips curled into a smug smile. "How perceptive of you, Honor ... something like that. Now, do you see the relevance of snatching Secta from their grubby little hands?"

"For zis organic chip?"

"Correct."

"I'm sorry, if I had known..."

"Yes, you're right; it is my mistake for not taking you into my confidence before this. Nevertheless, the damage is done. Make the exchange and devise the means to get me that chip. At least we'll have Set back before Secta has a chance to steal our technology. When is the exchange to take place?"

"Tonight at 2300 hours..." she quickly checked her wristwatch, "in four hours, sir."

"I will be in my office; bring Kew and Set to me."

"Yes, sir."

What he'd confided to her had her worried. It was exactly as Alice and Secta had claimed; Gorrick was indeed an alien. Thoughts flashed through her mind: does this make me a co-conspirator in an alien coup d'état to conquer the human race? Will Zen simply discard me when I am no longer of strategic value to them? The last thought worried her the most; without Zen, she would be left with nowhere to go.

While she was standing at the patio doors, staring at the view, mulling these thoughts over in her mind, Gorrick went to the small bar and poured himself a glass of Chardonnay.

"You have doubts now that I have confided in you."

She remained facing the window and said, "I must admit I was not expecting such a disclosure."

"Does that change anything?"

She turned and faced him. "It causes me to question my value to Zen and ze security of my position."

Gorrick moved to the white leather lounge setting, took a seat in an armchair, and crossed his long legs. "Do you believe that because I am not human, you cannot trust me?"

"Trust comes from experience, which is something zat I lack ven it comes to aliens."

"I think what you need to consider is that had I not told you I was of another species, then this conversation would have no relevance, would it?"

Honor thought about the statement for a moment and then countered, "We are well past zat point now, Gorrick. It would be appropriate for you to tell me truthfully about yours or Zen's plans in order to restore my confidence."

He knew she was being crafty and using the situation to gain more insight, but he could handle that. "Very well, take a seat. What I am about to tell you will imbue you with a sense of purpose such as you've never known before."

Honor took a seat, all ears.

Absolute pandemonium had broken out on the bridge. Convinced he had set the destruction of the UFO in motion with the swinging crane, now only seconds away from smashing through the windscreen, Alice swivelled the seat to seek a way out. The entire bridge shimmered, and then all movement froze. The huge crane stretched out like the arm of a robotic giant, was less than five metres from smashing through the ten-metre windscreen, and shearing the bridge right off the top of the saucer. The leading edge of the saucer had collided with the wall of the cavern. Alice could now see the huge craft was definitely inside a massive hollowed-out space. It reminded him of the huge cave he experienced on a previous mission, where he'd met Zule and the Vixen.

The collision with the wall was in the process of ripping an enormous gouge in the saucer body. The rip would split all the way through the craft once it continued to plough into the wall. Explosions were erupting all over the saucer body from metal fractures severing power lines inside. Once the crane wiped out the bridge, the loss of atmosphere would likely cause a massive implosion, which would lead to a breach of the nuclear reactor, resulting in a thermonuclear explosion.

Alice hopped out of the chair and walked over to the Gorricks. He could see in the hallway beyond there were even more Gorricks frozen on the run ... it seemed the ship was manned only by Gorricks. He wondered where all the pregnant women were and then noticed a side window on the bridge where he could possibly get a different view of the dry dock. He rushed to the window and looked out. There was a twelve-story building beside the craft, conjoined by several air-bridges. Each floor was glassed in, and he could make out what appeared to be body bags hanging in rows behind the glass, hundreds on each floor.

It dawned on him, "It's a gigantic incubator; these aliens are using the pregnant humans to make babies, and then they'll die." Then he noticed that one of the huge gantries that had been supporting the saucer was crashing into the far end of the building, smashing the windows and the atmosphere escaping. He knew that when time returned to normal, the entire building was doomed, as were the abducted surrogate mothers. He felt sorry for them but figured it had to be. This must have been what En-Ki wanted from him ... to destroy Zen's base and their propagation program. In his mind, he was wondering why there wasn't another way to achieve the same goal without such a terrible loss of life. Obviously, there wasn't, but he found it difficult to reconcile that he would solely have to carry the guilt of causing the accident that would kill thousands of women and their babies for the rest of his days.

After that sobering thought, he felt it was time to leave.

CHAPTER 33
TIME BOMB

SONOKO TUNED IN to the Holo-TV in her apartment just in time to catch the evening news. After the report of an explosion on the moon base and its impact on the Mars colony, the broadcast was filled with local stories. There was graphic footage of the UFO and the destruction of Zen Island, along with information about the plague that had infected Tokyo. Politicians were patting themselves on the back, trying to gain political mileage from the success of the vaccine. Choppers were shown spraying the city, and people were seen catching colds for the first time in their lives, and they were happy about it.

She watched the footage of police shooting infected males with darts, and then interviews with formerly infected men now cured. Disturbing images followed, showing pregnant women being herded like cattle into buses to be taken to secret containment camps.

The devastation caused by two typhoons and the chaos of martial law were horrifying, and it would take years and millions in crypto to rebuild the worst-affected areas of the city.

Sonoko thought to herself that the loss of Zen Island was an improvement for Yokohama Bay. The fusion weapon used had precisely targeted the island without causing damage to the surrounding areas. Tests had proven ground zero safe from radiation.

The death toll from the pandemic was estimated to be over thirty thousand, with many people left unaccounted for, the majority of them being women. Sonoko knew that many of those women were alien abductees. It was evident that the news was being censored due to the persistent fear of riots while martial law was still in effect.

She was massaging her tired feet when another news item caught her attention.

The newsreader said, "Reports are coming in tonight from Astronomers around the globe of a gigantic explosion on one of the moons of the planet Mars. Scientists have stated that the explosion was probably caused by the impact of a meteor in the massive crater of Stickney. The explosion was confirmed by the Mars colony, which reported no ill effects from it.

"There are two moons of Mars, Phobos and Deimos, both named after characters of Greek mythology. Phobos means panic or fear while Deimos means terror or dread. They accompanied their father Ares, god of war, into battle... Ares was known as Mars to Romans. In the late 1950s and 60s, the unusual orbital characteristics of Phobos led to speculations that it might be hollow. Around 1958, Russian astrophysicist Iosif Shklovsky studying the secular acceleration of Phobos's orbital motion, suggested a thin sheet metal structure for Phobos, a suggestion that led to the speculation that Phobos was of artificial origin. This Night Tonight asked chief astronomer Professor Tatau Suzuki from the National Astronomical Observatory of Japan to explain."

The regal figure of a scientist in his sixties with bushy grey eyebrows and longish grey hair stood at the entrance to the Tokyo observatory, speaking like a Japanese version of David Attenborough. "Was Phobos some sort of engineered alien outpost, as some would suggest? Was it created by an advanced Martian civilization that inhabited the red planet in another epoch? These are just some of the questions that have been spinning around Phobos in the last few decades. According to scientists of note, including Doctor S. Fred Singer, a special advisor to a former President of the USA, Phobos might be an artificial satellite launched into orbit around Mars a long time ago by a highly advanced Martian Civilization. Russian astrophysicist Shklovsky based his theory of this on a long study of Phobos' peculiar orbit, which other astronomers have also noted. The Russian calculations and those of earlier astronomers prove Phobos cannot possibly be an ordinary moon. So, the world of astrology watches Phobos tonight through the lens of incertitude ... was it a meteor impacting Phobos, or was it an internal explosion?"

Sonoko couldn't help but feel deep down inside that the explosion on Phobos was somehow connected to Alice.

It was time for the exchange. Karzoff was driving a black Renault Trafic van, with Viktoria in the passenger seat, and an agent on either side of Kew, who was handcuffed on the second-row seat. Set's body was in the rear, inside a body bag.

The exchange had been prearranged to take place at 2300 hours, on Hickson Road, Dawes Point Reserve, right next to the southern pylon of the Sydney Harbour Bridge.

The van crawled along the empty road. The reserve and street were well illuminated—it was quiet there at that time of night.

"Are we early or something?" Karzoff queried.

"No, we are right on time. She is late, as to be expected," Viktoria said, expressing her distaste for Honor.

"She will not be here; she would not be brave enough," Karzoff said. "Look there..."

A grey Ford Transit Custom was travelling towards them. The two vans parked on opposite sides of the road.

Karzoff checked the magazine of his Glock 19 pistol and then slipped it into his side jacket pocket. "You cover me; I will do the talking," he said.

He stepped out of the van and waited for someone to emerge from the Ford Transit. A man in black coveralls with a black balaclava got out, went around to the rear hatch, and opened it. Another man dressed the same emerged from within, escorting the Professor.

Karzoff opened the door of the Renault, and an agent brought out Kew.

Karzoff pulled his pistol and pointed it at Kew's ribs. "One false move out of you, and it will be the last move you make, understand?" Karzoff snarled, his face and tone indicating his eagerness to harm Kew.

"Sure," Kew said smugly.

"You two get Set," Karzoff ordered the two agents, and they moved to the rear of the Renault.

They opened the hatch, pulled out a trolley with the body bag on it, folded down the legs, and then wheeled it over to Karzoff.

"Kew will wheel the trolley to you ... send the Professor to us," Karzoff shouted at the opposition waiting a few metres away on the other side of the road.

The exchange went without a hitch. Once both vehicles were loaded, they sped off in different directions.

The President, Hope, and Secta were seated in the OTT monitoring room in front of a wall of monitors. Karzoff and Viktoria entered from making the exchange.

"How did it go?" The President asked.

Karzoff held out a hand to usher the Professor into the room.

"Like a charm," de Luz said, with one of his customary chuckles.

Hope jumped up and gave the Professor a big hug. Once she'd let him go, he shook hands with Secta.

"Glad to see you made it back in one-piece old buddy. Where's that goddamned Alice?" the Professor asked.

Secta's gaze dropped with dismay. "We don't know where he is my friend. He didn't make it back."

The happiness evaporated from the Professor's expression. "Oh, I see."

"Are you all right, de Luz?" The President asked.

"Sure, nothing to complain about, they treated me well enough."

As Secta was talking to the Professor, he failed to notice one of the monitors flick on.

The Professor caught it and said, "There's something on screen."

The others turned back to the monitor. The Professor, Karzoff, and Viktoria took seats.

The picture on the monitor flicked on and off, from black to video noise. Then a picture of something flicked on for a couple of seconds, then off ... it was difficult to make out what it was.

"Tell us what we're looking at here, Secta?" the President questioned.

Secta raised a small remote and turned the sound up.

"Against all odds ... given the time we had, Hope and I managed to fit the android Set with a new processor that we pre-programmed to perform specific tasks. We used the quantum chip I brought back from 2047. For your benefit, Vic, the processor is a twenty-core organic processor with a clock speed of 20.5 GHz."

"That's unbelievable, how did you manage to bring it back through the Kairos?"

"It's organic, I held it in my mouth when I passed through the vortex."

"Incredible."

"So, are you telling us Set is active, alive?" Karzoff asked.

"Yes, and I can control him using this remote via satellite," said Secta, holding up the small remote.

The picture on the monitor cleared, and a heads-up display became apparent.

The President reclined in his chair and crossed his legs. "You never cease to amaze me, Secta."

The picture flickered a little, but this time it stayed on.

"Right, let's just sit back and watch what happens," Secta said.

A Chinese face appeared on the monitor.

Doctor Xiang Chu had opened the body bag and was looking at what remained of Set. He and Doctor Lissy Li were responsible for the cybernetics that made Set a functioning android and had been invited by Gorrick to join him, Honor, and Kew in his palatial office to make an assessment of Set's condition, now that he had been returned.

"Plenty damage but only superficial," Chu told Gorrick in broken English. His prognosis was promising, and Gorrick liked that.

"But we need to inspect him closer to make certain nothing has been removed," Doctor Lissy Li added, in less broken English.

Gorrick rose from his chair and moved in for a closer look. As he leaned over the body to look at the battered android's face, a hand reached up and fastened tightly around his throat. Set's strength was ten times that of a normal human.

"You know your problem, Gorrick ... some of your pages are stuck together," Set snarled, his vice-like grip choking Gorrick so hard it was making his eyes bulge and the veins on his temples dilate.

"You spoke!" Gorrick managed to say, gripping Set's wrist desperately trying to wrench it free of his throat.

Set reached up his other hand as he rose into a seated position and then with one violent action tore Gorrick's head clean off the shoulders. Both Chu and Li recoiled in shock.

Set held up Gorrick's head.

Kew and Honor were struck dumb by the act. They couldn't believe their eyes; it was so outrageous, so impossible, it was difficult for them to process what they had witnessed.

Set climbed out of the body bag and then slid off the chrome trolley, holding Gorrick's severed head in one hand like a deranged axe murderer from a B-grade horror movie. But it wasn't a movie, and Honor knew it ... she felt nausea rising in her oesophagus and a wave of uncontrollable panic about to overwhelm her.

The seven-foot monster dressed in white coveralls tainted with Gorrick's blood glared at Honor, and then he bent ever so slightly and bowled Gorrick's head along the ground to her. It rolled like an uneven bowling ball, leaving a trail of blood on the timber decking, and stopped at her feet with its soulless eyes glaring up at her in a vacant stare of death.

Fearing she'd be next to have her head ripped off, Honor looked fearfully at Set, almost beseeching him not to do it. Half of his face and head were missing, and the huge dark cavity left behind was filled with wires and metal. One eye was somehow fastened in place in the cavity, still managing to move about in a macabre motion, while the good eye was locked on her in a deathly stare. He was an awesome spectre that shouldn't be alive.

"Guess who has the last laugh now, Honor?" Set said.

Physically shaking and about to collapse with shock and fear, Honor recognised the voice and slowly backed away, disbelieving.

"I know that voice!" she almost screamed.

"Yes, Honor, it's Secta, your old sparring partner," Secta said into the microphone on the bench-top in front of the monitor. All of the others in the room were sitting captivated by the images they were seeing through Set's eyes.

Secta glanced at each of them one at a time—the President, Karzoff, Viktoria, Hope, and finally the Professor—checking their expressions, searching for vindication for what he was about to do. He found it.

He raised the small remote he held in his hand, showing it to them before pressing a button. The screen on the monitor went blank.

"What just happened?" the President asked, bemused.

Hope chuckled wickedly and said, "An android bomb, sir ... Secta just triggered it."

"But that would mean the organic chip has been destroyed?" the President questioned.

"Yes, it has, but we have the specifications to build more," Hope said.

"I would have given a year's wages to have been there to see Honor's face when she realised she had been had ... again," Karzoff admitted, shaking his head.

A loud alarm was resonating throughout an office that was no longer palatial. As the smoke from the explosion cleared, the place looked more like the aftermath of a train wreck than Gorrick's base. Human body parts were scattered all over the floor. The once elegant white-painted arched wooden bridge over the moat, a feature next to the lounge setting where the meeting had taken place, was now nothing more than smouldering charred firewood.

As he was nearest to Set, Doctor Chu had taken the brunt of the explosion and was instantly killed, blown to bits. The force of the explosion had blown Doctor Li across the floor, but she had been lucky and shielded from shrapnel by Chu's body, only sustaining superficial wounds.

Kew was sitting on the floor, stunned, his face and body peppered with shrapnel, the wounds bleeding badly.

Honor was sprawled face-down on the floor, not moving.

Ignoring her own wounds, Li rushed over to Honor, knelt down, and then very gently rolled her over to assess her condition. Honor's face was totally unrecognisable. Li checked her pulse ... she was still alive.

CHAPTER 34
THE GUARDIAN

ALICE FOUND HIMSELF once again in the same strange place he had been before when he first met En-Ki, or at least an orb that suggested inside his mind that the presence he was communicating with was called En-Ki. He had no reason to doubt it. The procedure was much the same as previously: he found himself standing alone in a featureless room with no obvious source of light other than a glowing orb floating a metre or so above the floor. Low skeins of chilly mist were drifting through the room, reminding him of a Hammer Horror film from the 60s. At any moment, he expected Christopher Lee to come charging out of the darkness with arms extended and his Dracula teeth gnashing, with Peter Cushing as Doctor Van Helsing hot on his tail. But no, he wasn't on the set of a movie ... it was real enough.

"You're having a crisis, Alice?" a gentle male voice said as he approached the orb.

"You might say that. This quest sending me through time to kill innocent people has me feeling I'm nothing more than just a time-travelling hitman."

"I can understand that, Alice. Elaborate a little on why you feel that way?"

"Was it the object of the exercise for me to kill thousands of pregnant women and their babies? It was an action I think, in retrospect, could have been avoided."

"How is that?"

"I could have gone to 2047, identified the problem, then returned to my own time and made plans to prevent the problem from ever happening. Then I wouldn't have this bloody guilt trip weighing on my conscience."

"There was no time for that, Alice. The event took place twenty-seven years after your time, too long. It had to be dealt with in real time. You saved millions by sacrificing a few thousand ... such is the price for the security of humanity."

"You're saying that's my gig: a time-travelling executioner?"

"No, I am not saying that, Alice, but you will be called upon to make such choices of life and death again. Alice, I assure you the choice you made on board that craft was the correct one."

Alice thought about it. Though his instincts were telling him he was talking to an orb that was communicating with him inside his head, he brushed it aside because his gut told him the quest he was on was critical to the survival of humankind. That fitted perfectly with Alice's egalitarian ethos, his personal mission statement—freedom from suppression was in his songs and in his psyche.

"What is it with this plague of Gorrick clones?"

"Produced in the likeness of En-Lil ... yes, by now I expect you know they are clones. There were two thousand; now only fourteen hundred remain. You exterminated six hundred of them on Phobos, Alice. Humankind will not be safe until they have been eradicated, every last one of them. Know this, there exists the source, the one prime being from which all the clones were cast. Only when he is exterminated will it end."

"Right, En-Lil. How could he have lived that long?"

"I suppose I should not be speaking ill of my brother Alice, but there is good and there is evil, En-Li is the latter. He has lived longer than me because he killed my physical being. My consciousness and memories are preserved in this orb. En-Lil has the technology to allow him to live for another thousand years."

"Why don't you just send me to him and be done with it?" Alice complained.

"I would if I could, but he is far too clever. Only in time will we uncover his lair. Somewhere along the line, one of the Gorricks will turn out to be him."

"A bit like the lottery of life," Alice quipped. "What's the story with the hybrid breeding program then?"

"Different species have been abducting female humans from your planet for centuries. En-Lil's cloning program employed the same concept but on a much larger scale. It was designed to rescue his bloodline. When he reached two thousand clones, there was a genetic aberration, a mutation that resulted in an inferior being. So, through Zen on Earth, in different times, he has been trying to use both hybrid production and cybernetics to solve the problem. Inevitably, all the clones will die because the mutation exists on the timeline of every one of them—it's only a matter of time. The hybrid-breeding program in 2047 was his grand plan, but you crippled it. In 2087, you also crippled his cybernetics program, and now you're dealing with his android program. All of it is a means for him to create his own master race to dominate Earth."

"Is the quest for me to kill En-Lil?"

"No, but it is certainly a component of it."

The thought was mind-boggling for Alice: fourteen hundred Gorrick clones, and any one of them could be the original. It would be like finding a needle in a haystack.

"There must be something to distinguish En-Lil from all those Gorricks. A birthmark, a tattoo, a twitch, a stutter ... some way of recognising him?" Alice argued.

"He and only he is the guardian of the Tablet of Destinies, and we must possess it."

"Why don't you tell me where this damn tablet is then ... or better still, where your brother is ... why don't you kill him?"

"I can't, I only exist in this form, Alice. He killed my physical form thousands of Earth years ago. If I knew where he was or the location of the Tablet, I would tell you. I know this much ... you first need to locate the Cyrus cylinder or a transcript of the cuneiform text. You will find it on a cipher that you will need to decode. It holds a key that will allow you to identify En-Lil. The cipher exists in your time."

This was something completely new; it was the first time En-Ki had given Alice a definitive task, and it made him feel a whole lot better about things. The quest was beginning to take shape.

"We went through all this shit before with the Ark of the Covenant, and it only amounted to a hill of beans. If you know there's a cipher, then you must know what's on it ... let's stop all the bullshit and just tell me."

"No, Alice, I don't know what it says, only that there is a secret code in the text. In days gone by, there were no computers to decipher such a code; only now in your time can it be done. As far as the Ark is concerned, you protected it from falling into the wrong hands. Don't get discouraged."

"Why don't you just get a copy of the text and use your magnanimous brain to decrypt it?"

He was waiting for an answer when he realised he wasn't there any longer. He was standing with his back to a window, looking down at Sonoko sleeping in her apartment, and he was overcome with the sensation that a great burden had been lifted from his shoulders.

He crawled in beside her under the bedcovers and wrapped his arms around her petite warm body.

Even in her sleep, she knew it was Alice holding her, so it didn't disturb her; she had been expecting him. She took a deep breath of his distinctive odour and then snuggled into his embrace.

Sleep would come easily for Alice now that he had his girl in his arms, and En-Ki had freed him of his guilt. He knew it wouldn't be long before he'd have to leave her and return to his own time, but for now, he felt that by being sent through time to be with her again, En-Ki was rewarding him for what he'd achieved.

He was awakened early morning by a gentle shake from Sonoko, kneeling beside him garbed in a flowing white yakata.

Martial Law was over, and Tokyo dwellers were slowly finding a way back to normality. When Alice stepped out of the apartment with Sonoko, he was surprised to see they were so efficient; all of the debris in the streets had been cleared. The Skypod still wasn't functioning, but knowing the Japanese, it wouldn't be long before it was up and running again.

"No more walkers?" Alice questioned.

"I spoke to Shintaro about it yesterday; he was hopeful they got them all. Let's go to Henri's, where we first got to know each other. It is close by, my i-Keeper said it is open."

Alice found the brisk walk in the cool morning air to Henri's invigorating.

Over breakfast, Alice recognised that Sonoko had a look on her face as though she wanted to ask him something but didn't quite know how.

"You can ask me anything, Sonoko," he said, to put her mind at rest.

She looked worried. "Um, I just wanted to know what is going to happen with us, Alice?"

"Us? You mean as an item?"

"Yes."

"Well, soon I will have to go back to my time, but once I'm there, I plan to return here in due course with the serum, so you can then return with me to my time. Would you like that?"

"Yes, Alice. When do you think that will be?"

It was a difficult question for him to answer; he really had no idea.

"I still have a mission to complete, depending on how long it takes, I'd hope to return to you after it's done."

He was saved from an awkward situation by the surprise arrival of two familiar faces and jumped up from his seat exclaiming, "Shintaro ... Tombei!"

There were loads of hugs and backslapping, and then they eventually took their seats. Catching up on all that had happened since they separated on Zen Island took some time, but when they were finally up to speed, it all seemed like the plot of a science fiction movie ... the only difference being it had actually happened.

It had been over a week since the successful attack on Zen, and still, there was no sign of Alice. The OTT team members were becoming increasingly worried about him. There had been no repercussions from the attack on Zen that had killed two, including Gorrick the company president, and injured three others, and that was odd ... in fact, what was even more odd was there had been no reports of the explosion in the media ... it had been hushed up.

The OTT team had no idea who had survived the attack. Karzoff was keen to know if his nemesis Honor remained a threat and whether to keep Kew at the top of his list of terrorists.

In the meantime, Secta was enjoying being back in his own time and was quietly confident that Alice would eventually turn up. Just like Alice, he was enjoying a hiatus from the chaos of his world and others.

But it was time to get back at it, and he arrived at the scheduled monthly OTT meeting at Kairos refreshed and ready for the next challenge.

After getting through all the usual updates: a Kairos status report from Robert, a security brief from Karzoff and Viktoria, with the issuing of a high terrorist alert for an expected reprisal from Zen to the attack, it was time for Secta to speak. He rose to his feet and began pacing the boardroom, holding his chin.

"We need to create a wormhole detection network to alert us to incoming UFOs or if per se Alice was to return some place other than here."

"I think I can help with that," the Professor said confidently. "Picking up quantum signatures is the key."

Karzoff instinctively knew the meeting was about to denigrate into a quagmire of scientific hyperbole, well at least to him, so he raised his hand.

"I cannot contribute anything to the science of wormholes, so I will take my leave, but before I do, have we decided on the next mission if Black Alice fails to return ... and, how long do we give him?"

Hope wasn't impressed by what she felt was Karzoff writing Alice off. "Before we commit Alice's ashes to the depths, I think we should first exhaust all measures of confirming that he is lost," she said emphatically.

There were nods all round.

"What do you have in mind, Hope?" Viktoria asked.

"I would think the obvious would be to contact Sonoko in 2047 to find out if she knows anything about him. You'd expect, under the circumstances, she'd be the first to know."

"Yes, well, at least that would eliminate 2047 from the search area," Secta agreed.

"Can you not just open Kairos and scan time for his atomic marker?" Karzoff posed naively.

"Ha! That's easier said than done," Robert said, writing off Karzoff's suggestion to absurdity.

"But not illogical," the Professor submitted.

Karzoff smiled, pleased with himself that even in his academic ignorance, he was able to contribute something to the scientific discussion.

The President took a sip of wine. The view of Sydney and the harbour was amazing from the balcony of his palatial penthouse apartment. Out there in the sparkling grid of lights, there were those who wanted him dead.

He lurched back inside through the open sliding glass doors to the lounge room that was dark. He'd been standing on the balcony watching the sunset, oblivious to everything else around him. He noticed the silhouette of a man sitting on the sofa. He'd not seen him when he came in.

"Some people never change," the man said. "Creatures of habit."

"I see nothing habitual about coming home after a day at work and admiring the view. Who are you?"

There was a chuckle, and the man leaned over and turned on a table lamp beside him.

The President peered at the intruder aghast.

"Kew? But how?"

"I wasted your bodyguards ... it wasn't very difficult."

The President sat in an armchair opposite Kew, put down his glass of wine, and said casually, "Have you come to finish what you failed to accomplish last time?"

Kew collected the Glock 19 from the sofa beside him, reached into his side pocket, produced a silencer, and slowly screwed it to the barrel of the pistol. "A gun is like a god, it determines one's fate ... don't you agree, Mr President?"

"No, you've got that totally wrong, son, the gun doesn't pull the trigger."

"So, I'm the one with the power over life and death?"

"Wrong again, that would be Zen, they issued the wet job for you to pull the trigger, so in effect, you're no better than the gun."

"They say there is nothing when you die, how do you feel about that ... you're about to cease to exist?"

"Oh, death is just another leg of the journey ... another part of life, I'm just going back to where I started," he said philosophically.

Kew was dressed like an undertaker in a black suit, white shirt, and a pencil-thin black tie. His face was battle-scarred by the remains of the explosion of only a week previously.

The President knew his time was up. He was prepared to die comfortable with the belief that he had achieved a lot of good in the fifty-five years of living.

"Get it on with Kew, I'm ready," he said resolutely.

Kew aimed the gun at the President and fired three shots in slow succession. The first shot hit him in the stomach, the second in the chest, and the last, just as he was slumping forward, in the forehead.

CHAPTER 35
PRESAGE

ALICE AWOKE WITH a start. It had been a nightmare. Seeing the President killed in cold blood made him think, was that a dream or a premonition? He'd had dreams of such portent before. There was no denying it ... the dream was telling him he had to return to his own time.

A sweet voice came from the darkness, "Were you dreaming?"

"Yes, Sonoko, go back to sleep. I need to think something through."

He leaned across the tatami mat, found her delicate face, and gently kissed her ruby lips.

It took him seconds to dress, and he was at the door when her small voice stopped him, "Goodbye my love. I will wait for you, no matter how long," she said warmly, knowingly.

Oh, how he hated goodbyes. He opened the door and slipped out into the corridor knowing the vortex would be there waiting for him. He took a moment watching it form and then, making up his mind, went quickly back inside the apartment, rushed into the tiny bathroom, found Sonoko's red lipstick, went over to her, found her frozen in the act of crying, lifted her flimsy nightdress, and wrote 'I love you' in lipstick on her belly. Happy, he dropped the lipstick and told her, 'Chaa!' and then went back out through the door into the hallway where he stepped into the vortex.

Robert was finishing up after an exhausting day of maintenance on Kairos. He was in the server room and was switching off the main XC-70 Supercomputer about to leave when it rebooted of its own accord. Thinking it must be a glitch caused by the maintenance, he returned to it and tried to shut it down a second time. Again, it rebooted. Then, he heard a familiar sound through the air conditioning duct to the adjoining studio room—Kairos was booting up. The panel next to him lit up with green lights blinking on the patch bay, and that would announce only one thing—incoming.

He rushed back inside the control room and flopped into his chair in front of the console. Sure enough, his computer monitor was confirming incoming. Even though it was two in the morning, he had no choice, he picked up the phone and rang Secta. It took a while for him to answer, but his reaction to the excitement in Robert's voice was to get there as quickly as possible. He knew it could only mean one thing ... Alice was coming home.

Secta came flying into the control room dressed in a velvet navy blue dressing gown, over red silk pyjamas, and wearing UGG slippers. Robert was in one of the high back chairs behind the console, and seated in the other chair that had swivelled round to face Secta was Alice, wearing a huge grin.

"You didn't have to get all dressed up for me mate, I didn't ... again," Alice quipped.

They'd only just finished a big friendly hug when Hope and the Professor came in, the pair of them panting out of breath like they'd jogged from their apartments.

After a heartfelt welcome, it was time for a recap, so for the next hour, Alice told them the incredible sequence of events leading up to, during, and then beyond the Phobos incident.

Secta was most intrigued by En-Ki's intervention, especially this time having given Alice a directive instead of the usual cryptic puzzle that required hours of decoding.

It was late by then, so they agreed to call it a night and to meet up later in the day to inform the president and discuss the way forward. There was still plenty for them to tell Alice about that had happened in his absence, but it would have to wait until then.

Secta offered Alice a ride to his apartment. At that hour of the morning, there were few cars on the road. As Secta's 1967 avocado green VW beetle tottered along Park Street bound for Kings Cross, Alice wound down the window and took a whiff of Sydney's fresh morning air.

"Argh, it's good to be home. I didn't know you had a car Secta, thought you cabbed it around like me."

"I've had it forever ... Yes, I do prefer to cab it," Secta agreed.

The interior of the car was a cesspool of junk food wrappers, empty milk cartons, and general rubbish.

Alice kicked some of it out from under his feet, "Some of this stuff you've got in here is as old as the bloody car."

"Yes, I must get round to cleaning it someday. Oh, that reminds me, open the glove box, I put your keys in there ... I think."

Alice pressed the button on the glove box, and it burst open, overflowing with parking citations. He dug underneath them, came up with the keys, and then struggled to jam it shut again.

"So, the vaccine did its job. There was a report just before I left Tokyo there were no more walkers," Alice said, slipping the keys into his pants pocket.

"Great news. How was Yashida? Kew shot him ... Kew who, by the way, made it back ... jumped into the vortex after me. We had him prisoner but had to trade him for the Professor after he'd been kidnapped by Zen."

"Yeah, Sonoko told me about Yashida ... he's bad news that bastard Kew. Yashida survived okay, Shintaro reckons he'll retire with a gold watch and some sort of bravery award from the government, Sonoko's also getting one."

"She didn't get into trouble from Nihon Inc. for giving me the organic chip, did she?"

"Yes, she did, but Shintaro straightened it out for her."

"Good on him, good bloke that."

Alice went quiet, as though in deep reflection. Secta noticed it and tentatively asked him, "How are you feeling about it all?"

"Like I've become a time-travelling bum," Alice admitted.

"Peripatetic?" Secta enquired.

Alice automatically searched his translation database for the word and found the definition. "A migrant ... nomadic, yeah, that pretty much sums me up. I offer the world and deliver an atlas."

"I think you might be missing someone," Secta said with a knowing glance and a raised eyebrow.

"Yeah, s'pose so ... she got to me all right. I promised her I'd return with the serum to bring her here."

"Hmm, now that would certainly wobble the foundations of the old prime directive," Secta said gravely.

"Wouldn't be the first time we've given it a shake," Alice scoffed.

"True, but she wouldn't need to be given the serum. You could just get her a message to go to Sydney, meet up with my other older self, and have me put her through Kairos IV to here."

"Kairos four?"

"Yes, older Secta let it slip, I expect it would be pretty refined by then, probably no need for the serum, I suspect it would be a wormhole generator ... you'd just dial up the coordinates and step through to wherever ... So, all we'd need do is get a message to older me to set it up, and that wouldn't be too difficult."

Secta could tell by the look on Alice's face the idea had elevated his spirits.

"Did you get a message to Karzoff to put an extra guard on the president?"

"I left him a message ... you know my older self warned me to make sure Kew didn't come back because he'd kill the president."

"Yeah ... then it must have happened."

"Hmm, didn't think of it like that but you might be right. Anyhow, we'd better make sure it doesn't happen ... maybe that's what he intended by telling me. So, tell me more about this Tablet of Destinies that En-Ki was on about?"

Alice was staring out of the window thinking of Sonoko and his premonition.

"Uh," he snapped back, "Oh, the tablet, yeah, he didn't say much more except that we need to get it off Gorrick ... the real Gorrick that is, En-Lil. But to do that, we first have to locate a thing called the Cyrus cylinder; he reckoned that'll help us identify the real Gorrick from the fourteen hundred clones."

"Fourteen hundred? I thought you said there were two thousand?"

"I killed six hundred on Phobos, remember?"

"Right, so the Cyrus cylinder?" he said, pulling into Challis Avenue and double-parking outside Alice's apartment block.

"Yeah, it's here somewhere ... I mean in this time, we don't need to go on a mission to find it," he said with a yawn. "Let's leave it to talk about later, I'm knackered."

"Okay, midday at OTT then."

Alice got out of the VW, stretched, and then watched it totter down the street and turn left at the end into Victoria Street. When he turned to enter the gate to number 4 Challis Avenue, he could see the sky getting lighter in the east: the sun wasn't far off rising. It reminded him of the hundreds of times he'd rocked home at that time of the morning from gigs. He opened the grey wrought-iron gate at the front of the three-storey federation terrace with its faded yellow façade, walked up to the dark-painted front door, and opened it.

There were gloomy faces all around in the OTT boardroom when Alice cruised in looking all recuperated, carrying a mug of steaming coffee.

"Hey dudes, what's with all the doom and gloom?" he said jovially, taking a seat.

Karzoff was the only one standing. He turned from the window. "Welcome back, Alice, unfortunately, it is not a good day. The President was found dead this morning in his apartment ... murdered."

"Argh, don't tell me ... three bullets, one in the stomach, one in the chest, and the last in the forehead ... right?"

"How did you know that, Alice?" Viktoria asked with a shocked expression, flicking a 10x8 photograph across the table for him to see.

Alice looked at the gruesome picture of the dead president slumped in an armchair. He pinched the bridge of his nose between his fingers and squeezed his eyes shut. "Damn! It's exactly as I dreamt ... it was the reason I returned when I did."

"And I should have treated the warning my older self gave me with more alacrity. Karzoff didn't get my message until it was too late," Secta said dispiritedly.

Alice jumped up and paced about angrily. "It was bloody Kew, I know it!"

"Well, that answers that, we have been studying the CCTV footage and have not been able to identify the assassin," Karzoff said. "Now we know he survived the blast, we have to assume maybe Honor did as well."

"It's a goddamn tap-back for killing Gorrick," the Professor grumbled, his Texan accent accentuated by his anger.

Hope was in tears. Secta stood up and placed a consoling hand on her shoulder. "This teaches us an invaluable lesson, we cannot afford to ever again ignore any of Alice's premonitions. This isn't the first time one has come to fruition."

Alice straightened up with an idea. "Why can't I just go back in time to the president's pad just before he gets whacked and bump off Kew?"

"No, Alice, we can't go down that road, we need to stick as closely as possible to the prime directive," said the Professor.

"But the bloody prime directive is from Star Trek, made up by the screenwriter Gene Roddenberry," Alice argued.

"But that doesn't make it wrong, Al ... the timeline of history must be preserved at all costs ... the ramifications if it's not could be catastrophic," the Professor said forcefully.

Alice flopped into his chair annoyed and snarled, "So, where does that leave us ... and the project?"

"Nothing will happen to the project ... it was black-budgeted by the president before we built Kairos, but we will be getting a new boss. The country will be going to the polls."

"I don't think the republic will vote in another dictator ... it's sure to return to a more conventional stable leader," Viktoria said emphatically.

"We better make sure whoever it is, he's or she's the right one for the job, Karzoff, there's far too much at stake here," Secta said, eyeballing Karzoff and then the others in the room one at a time.

"And we need to get rid of Kew," Alice snarled, bashing his fist violently on the table.

He got a solemn nod of agreement from each and every one of them.

There was a strong reaction from the public to the news of the President's death. It then snowballed when speculation of foul play was circulated.

As head of the Government Security Directive, Karzoff called an emergency meeting with state police commissioners to plan for all possible outcomes, including riots. The country had been on the brink of revolution for some time, and the angry voices of the rank and file had only recently been calmed by the appointment of Mal Function, in Alice's absence, to the leader of the Octagon Peace

Movement. Because the President had changed the system of government from the original democratic system when he gained power a few years back, opposition parties or candidates for the presidency were few and far between. In fact, the only real opposition party was the Octagon Peace Movement.

When Alice learned from Hope that Mal had been shot and was in the hospital, he immediately went to visit him.

Walking down the street towards the hospital, Alice had forgotten that now he was back in his own time he would be recognised. It seemed to him that with the President's death, and him being the former leader of the Octagon, people were happier than ever to see him. So much so that when he reached Mal's hospital room and the gaggle of reporters and cameras waiting outside it for an interview recognised him, they swamped him with questions. He 'no commented' his way through them and then past the security guard on the door to Mal's room. Alice was no stranger to press harassment.

"Hey dude!" Alice said on entering.

Sitting up in bed, Mal returned a broad smile. "Well, if it isn't the main man! Al."

Alice went to the bedside. "I'm here to bust you out ... if you're anything like me, you hate hospitals."

They hugged, and then Al sat on the edge of the bed.

"No mate, I won't be going anywhere for a while. See all this crap?" Mal said, referring to half a dozen tubes leading from under the bed-sheets to an array of bottles suspended from overhead stands. "That's my digestive system. That woman, Honor, shot me in the gut ... it'll take forever for it to heal. In the meantime, they have to feed me directly and then take all the waste away through these tubes. I feel like a lab rat with all this stuff hanging out of me."

"Yer poor bastard."

"I heard the news," Mal said gravely.

"Yeah, terrible. Poor bugger, I was getting to like him."

"Yeah, me too. When'd you get back?"

"Last night."

"You'll have to tell me all about it," Mal said excitedly.

"Yeah mate, will do. How's the food in here?"

"Sucks."

"Who's depping for you in the band?" Alice asked.

"Rastus, remember him? Used to be Wally in Wally and the Nomads?"

"Yeah, you mightn't be able to get your spot back, unlike you he can sing," Al joked. "Listen, in all seriousness, there's something we need to have a yarn about."

Mal struggled up a bit higher in the bed and winced in pain as he did it. "Alright, go on mate."

A few minutes later, the press gallery made room for Alice when he came out of Mal's room. Microphones on booms and handheld devices were immediately jammed in his face. Every single one of the reporters shot him rapid-fire questions all at once. He wasn't having a bar of it and held up his hand to shut them up.

"Hey! Get orderly!" he snapped, and they obliged. "I've got something to say, if you're here to get a scoop then here it is ... Mal Function, leader of the Octagon Peace Movement, is considering running for president of Oceana at the coming election."

It was massive news.

"Why not you, Alice!" many of them asked in unison.

CHAPTER 36
CYRUS CYLINDER

WHEN THE NEWS reached Kew that Mal was considering running for the top position in the country, he was far from impressed and immediately went to the infirmary to tell Honor. He found her sitting up in a hospital bed with her face entirely wrapped in bandages, leaving only a small hole for fluids and speaking, and a tiny slit for one eye.

"Have you heard the news?" Kew said, taking a chair at the end of the bed in the small, well-equipped room. The Zen infirmary was on a mid-floor in the Zen building in Sydney. Gorrick's former office on the top floor had been all but gutted by the explosion.

"No, what news?" she said, her voice muffled by the bandages and an inability to move her lips properly.

"Mal Function is going to run for office now that the president is dead."

"Dead?"

"Yes, he stopped three bullets early this morning."

"So, you squared things up then?"

"You might say that."

"Mal Function, I thought I killed him." There was anger in her tone.

The door opened, and Doctor Lissy Li breezed in, garbed in a white medical dustcoat, her long black hair worn up, a black knee-length tube skirt under the open coat with a white blouse, and wearing horn-rimmed glasses on her almond-shaped face. There were no signs on her face of damage from the explosion.

"Ah, Kew, glad you here. Have you heard the new Chairman is arrive from New York in hour or so? He will want to speak with you. I have report in my office for you to show him," she said in slight broken English, dropping some of her prepositions.

"Okay, so what's the status of the patient here?" Kew asked.

The slim, attractive Chinese doctor's thin, red-painted lips curved into a small smile. "She is doing well. Skin grafts have taken, no-one will recognise her when the bandages removed, she will not recognise self."

"You mean I will look like ze creature from ze black lagoon?" Honor grumbled.

"I am proud for my work," Lissy said hubristically.

"Doctor Li is the foremost cosmetic surgeon in China, Honor. You can be confident in her skills," Kew said, eyeing off the doctor's shapely legs while she leaned across the bed to check beneath Honor's facial bandages.

She straightened up and whispered to Honor. "Healing fast ... you will look better than before, promise."

Kew stood up. "Okay, just thought I'd bring you the news, Honor. I'll go get ready to meet the new boss."

"I come too," Doctor Li affirmed.

"I'll drop in tomorrow, Honor," Kew said.

"Unveiling will be sixteen hundred hours tomorrow. That something you look forward to?" the doctor said, applying her thumbprint to the digital chart that hung at the base of the bed.

It was welcome news for Honor; ten days in a hospital bed was about as much as she could withstand. At least now, with the bandages coming off, she could envisage light at the end of the tunnel.

Kew accompanied Doctor Li out of the room, along the corridor, and into the elevator.

"Has Doctor Chu's body been returned to China yet?" Kew asked politely, after the elevator doors closed.

Lissy selected a floor. "Yes, go China two days ago."

The elevator doors opened on the Doctor's floor. They exited, and after a short walk, they came to the frosted glass-panelled door to her office. She opened the door, and Kew followed her in. They passed the young receptionist and entered the Doctor's office through a mahogany-panelled door. Once inside, she stopped, turned, and they caressed passionately. They had been having a surreptitious affair for quite a while. It was the secrecy that turned them both on. Though she had been betrothed to Doctor Chu and Kew was supposed to be an item with Honor, passion had superseded convention.

A few minutes later, Kew strolled out of Doctor Li's office as though nothing had happened. He acknowledged the young, plain-Jane Chinese receptionist Suzy and headed for the elevator.

A few floors up, he exited the elevator and entered his own office.

There was no receptionist to greet him; his office was just a hole in the wall, and that's all he required. Most of his meetings were held in boardrooms, and the majority of his work was in the field, so there was no need for a big office or a receptionist. Just as he sat behind his desk, he received a notification via his OSCI to attend a meeting in the boardroom. He expected it would be to meet the new boss.

The wounds on his face from the explosion had healed but had left a few more scars to add to the collection. He checked them out in the small round mirror on the wall. "The scars give you more character, buddy," he mumbled to himself happily. There was no reason to be dour; he was going to meet the new head honcho and was feeling positive. He straightened his thin black tie, ran his fingers through his short-cropped brown hair ... he was ready to rumble.

Alice went directly from the hospital to a boardroom meeting with OTT members at Oceana HQ. They were all seated, waiting for him when he breezed in.

He stayed standing and announced to them all, "Mal has accepted to run for President."

The news lifted the spirits of the entire team.

"That is excellent news, Alice. How long do you expect he will stay in the hospital?" Karzoff asked.

"It's still painful when he moves, so another week, I reckon," Alice said, pulling up a chair at the big black boardroom table.

The window was west-facing, so the afternoon sun was glaring into the room. Viktoria noticed it and pressed a button on the table for the windows to polarise.

"Much better, thank you, Viktoria," Secta said.

"We will need to increase security for Mal once this is made public," Viktoria said sternly.

"It would be well and truly public by now ... I was bombarded by the press hanging outside Mal's room and gave them an exclusive: too good an opportunity to miss. It'd be all over the news already," Alice explained.

Viktoria stood and said, "I'll make arrangements for added security now ... we must assume Zen will try to take him out once they know."

"I think he should be brought here where he can be kept under surveillance," Karzoff stated.

"Good shout, Karzoff," Al said. They all nodded in agreement.

"I'll look after that," Viktoria said on her way to the door to leave.

"We need to focus our attention on the quest. I discussed it with Alice and then sent each of you a report this morning ... did everybody get it?" Secta looked around the room for acknowledgement. "Right, the first part was an account of the last mission, but it is section seven we need to focus on now." He pressed a button on the desk, and a plasma screen rose out of the boardroom table. "On the screen is the text ... Alice said En-Ki told him the following: 'First, you will need to locate the Cyrus cylinder, or a transcript of its cuneiform text. On it, there is a cipher you will need to find and decode. It will hold the key for you to identify En-Lil from the Gorrick clones. The cipher exists in your time.' Hope, I know it was short notice, but have you managed to locate a transcript of the Cyrus cylinder?" Secta asked.

Hope looked at him over her horn-rimmed glasses. "Yes, I have. There's a fair bit to go through, everyone, so you'll need to be patient."

She produced a notebook from the pocket of her white dustcoat, opened it, and read, "To quote the British Museum, currently in possession of it: The Cyrus cylinder: a clay cylinder; is a Babylonian account of the conquest of Babylon by Cyrus in 539 B.C., and his restoration to various temples of statues removed by Nabonidus, the previous king of Babylon, and of his work at Babylon. The cylindrical form is typical of royal inscriptions of the Late Babylonian period, and the text shows that the cylinder was written for burial in the foundations of the city wall of Babylon. It was deposited there after the capture of the city by Cyrus in 539 B.C., and presumably written on his orders. The text is incomplete. It is written in Babylonian script and language and records that Nabonidus, the last King of Babylon (555-539 B.C.), had perverted the cults of the Babylonian gods, including Marduk, the city-god of Babylon, and had imposed labour-service on its free population, who complained to the gods. The gods responded by deserting Babylon, but Marduk looked around for a champion to restore the old ways. He chose Cyrus, King of Anshan (Persia), and declared him king of the world. First, Cyrus expanded his kingship over the tribes of Iran (described as Gutians and Ummanmanda), ruling them justly. Then Marduk ordered Cyrus to march on Babylon, which he entered without a fight. Nabonidus was delivered into his hands, and the people of Babylon joyfully accepted the kingship of Cyrus. From this point on, the document is written as if Cyrus himself is speaking: 'I, Cyrus, king of the world...'. He presents himself as a worshipper of Marduk who strove for peace in Babylon and abolished the labour-service of its population. The people of neighbouring countries brought tribute to Babylon, and Cyrus claims to have restored their temples and religious cults, and to have returned their previously deported gods and people. The text ends with a note of additional food offerings in the temples of Babylon and an account of the rebuilding of Imgur-En-Lil, the city wall of Babylon, during the course of which an earlier building inscription of Ashurbanipal, King of Assyria (668-627 B.C.), was found.

The interesting part that seems to relate to what En-Ki told Alice concerns the rebuilding of Imgur-En-Lil and the famous Balawat Gates ... I'll read on...

Balawat is an archaeological site of the ancient Assyrian city of Imgur-En-Lil, and the modern village in Nineveh Province. It lies 25 kilometres southeast from the city of Mosul and 4 kilometres to the south of the modern Assyrian town of Bakhdida.

Now this is very interesting: The meaning of Imgur-En-Lil is 'En-Lil agreed.' Note that there was also a wall in ancient Babylon named Imgur-En-Lil.

So, I'll read on: The city of Balawat lies near the famous site of Nimrod. It is a land that was an archaeological paradise centuries ago. During their excavations in the area, some researchers unearthed the remnants of magnificent gates that were made during the Assyrian golden age. It was through the work of several archaeologists, historians, and conservators that the famous gates of Balawat were brought back to the world.

Let me show you the restored wall of Imgur-En-Lil."

She pressed a button on the table control panel, and the large monitor displayed a panoramic picture of the restored ancient brass gates.

"You can see that most of the figures on the bas-reliefs appear to be warriors at war, but when you zoom closer to the lower section, like so..."

She pressed a toggle on the panel, and the picture on the monitor zoomed.

"You can see a line of men walking out from some sort of strange-looking cabinet object, and standing right next to the cabinet is a solitary man holding two long levers, one in each hand, that connect to spiked wheels at his feet. Immediately beside him is some sort of strange-looking apparatus. Now let's look even closer ... see that all the men coming out of the strange cabinet are the same ... they have the same face, the same clothes ... they are identical."

Alice leaned forward for a closer look, "Clones ... they're Gorrick's with beards coming out of a cloning machine!"

"Exactly, now look above and beside the man holding the levers who seems to be creating these clones of himself ... there are inscriptions. I haven't found any transcript of them. I think archaeologists and historians have simply dismissed them as merely war stories ... but I don't believe they are. With what we know, I think the man holding the levers isn't the god Marduk, as is claimed ... but En-Lil—in fact, Marduk might well be En-Lil."

"And the cuneiform writing around him?" Secta asked.

"I think it could be what En-Ki wants us to decode," Hope concluded.

The Professor chimed in, "We must remember that these gates were unearthed in 1878 and only recently restored. Most of it was kept in the Baghdad museum, which was looted in the 1990s during the Gulf War, and much of it destroyed since."

It made complete sense. They all sat staring at the images of the brass bas-reliefs on the screen.

"This was after my old buddy Nebuchadnezzar then?" Alice queried.

"Yes, this was after his son who took the throne was murdered, and then the next king Nabonidus was usurped by Cyrus, who then spent most of his life searching for the Ark of the Covenant ... unsuccessfully, I might add."

"Well, we all know why he couldn't find it," Secta said with a chuckle.

Alice sat back, folded his muscly arms in front of him, and declared with a grin, "Coz I'd already buried the bugger."

"Oh, and one final thing ... I researched the Tablet of Destinies that En-Ki mentioned to Alice," Hope said.

"Did you get any sleep last night?" the Professor quizzed her compassionately.

CHAPTER 37
CHANGING OF THE GUARD

HOPE FLICKED OVER a few pages of her notebook and then continued to read out loud to the others: "The Egyptian Book of Thoth is similar to the Tablet of Destinies in that it holds the secrets of the Earth: the secrets of the gods themselves. Even if you're dead, you may walk the Earth as if living when in possession of it. With the Tablet of Destinies, the Anunnaki are believed to have been able to see the Universe as it truly was. The Tablet of Destinies is attached to the breast of the holder. Destiny conjures up fate ... the future ... events that might or could take place to determine one's eventual life. The three discs of the Tablet represent past, present, and future. These discs can prolong and redirect your life course, depending on which disc is used. The discs hold enormous power for the holder.

"Wait, so there are three discs that you wear on your chest?" Secta asked.

"Yes," Hope said. "I'll go on ... The 3 discs have a hole in the centre, and this would indicate that the real purpose is to have them on an axle, and spinning as a wheel. From these discs, the fate of man can be altered. So, where are the Tablets today? Is it believed that the Tablet of Destinies is the real power behind the Tablets that Moses returned with from Mount Sinai? The question is: Are they one and the same? To cut to the chase: Cyrus entered the great ancient city of Babylon, without a shot being fired, and went directly to the

Treasury. Upon opening it, he finds, to his consternation, that many of the great iconic pieces he was expecting to find there were missing, including the Ark of the Covenant."

Hope studied the faces in the room; all of them were captivated by the story.

Secta spoke up, "Excellent research, Hope. To recap, Marduk is possibly En-Lil ... he was banished from Babylon ... stated symbolically as though Nebuchadnezzar and his successors had quashed the worshipping of Marduk as a god."

"Let me butt in here," said the Professor. "This kind of misinterpretation is very common in archaeology; rarely is ancient text or art taken literally, mostly it is considered myth. I'm reminded, as an example, of the Trojan Wars and the city of Troy, believed to be a myth by historians and archaeologists until Heinrich Schliemann followed a dream he'd had and discovered Troy in north western Turkey."

"What, he dreamed it?" Alice asked.

"Apparently, some sort of premonition," the Professor qualified.

It was something Alice could relate to completely.

"The bottom line is we need to have that text on the bas-reliefs transcribed," Secta said.

De Luz half raised a hand, "I have a buddy at Harvard, a professor of ancient text and linguistics, I could get him onto it, unless you have another option, Hope?"

"No Professor, please go ahead ... that would be perfect," Hope conceded.

Viktoria returned with Miss Vallins. She was devastated by the death of her boss and friend.

Hope stood, put an arm around the shoulders of the distraught woman, and said warmly, "Oh Rita, we're all so very sorry. He was our friend as well."

"When he said goodbye after work last night, it was in a manner he'd never used before ... it was as though he knew," she said, drying her eyes with a petite white-lace handkerchief.

Alice got up and gave her a hug, then held her at arm's length, "We need you to be strong, Rita. You know more about running the office of the president than anyone; you're going to need courage to handle it until there's a newly elected president."

"I heard Mal Function will run," she said quizzically.

"Yes," Secta said, standing and then taking her hand. "And a fine president he will make as well."

"Let me get you coffees," Rita said with a slight whimper.

"No, sit down, we can get our own," the Professor said kindly.

"No, I insist ... I need to do my job," she said with a sniffle and then left to get the drinks.

Kew was sitting alone in the boardroom. The panoramic view through the windows under a clear blue sky was stunning. But after twenty minutes, the only thing that was keeping him from getting up and leaving was his interest in the movement of ferries and small craft on the sparkling Sydney Harbour waters.

The door opened, and six people filed into the room. A short young guy he'd never met before, with a panicked expression on his round face that matched his austere dull grey suit, seemed to be in charge of them. Kew wondered if he was the new boss, then dismissed the notion.

"Please take your seats," Lane said and reached out a small hand for Kew to shake. "You must be Kew, I'm Bernard Lane."

It was a dead fish handshake, which to Kew summed up the man's personality or lack thereof.

"Apologies for being late, but there was an unavoidable delay at the airport," he carried on. "These people are department heads. Oh, someone is missing ..."

The door opened, and Doctor Lizzy Li breezed in and found herself a seat.

"Doctor Li, glad you managed to make it," Lane said facetiously.

The Doctor ignored his tone, straightened her glasses ever so slightly with her forefinger, and then glared at Lane with annoyed narrowed eyes and tightened lips.

He cleared his throat, conscious that his jibe had ruffled her feathers, and was about to sit down when the door opened, and in walked Gorrick. They were all stunned: he was an inch-perfect replica of their previous six feet five boss right down to the hairstyle—everything.

"Good afternoon everyone," he said, with a rich New York accent, the only point of difference from the last Gorrick. "My resemblance to your previous boss may be disconcerting to some, but it will make the transition easier in the long term, as will my name, Gorrick. Think of it as though nothing has changed. Now, I asked for a meeting with Kew, is there more than one Kew as well?"

No-one was sure if it was a witticism or not, so no-one laughed except Kew. This was the third Gorrick he'd worked for. It didn't matter to him whether they were clones or aliens ... as long as he got paid plenty. He was a mercenary, and that translated to giving his allegiance to the highest bidder.

"Sir, I figured you would want to meet the department heads," Lane said with a puzzled expression in his beady eyes. He had a face most would find difficult to warm to.

"Is your job description to think for me, mister ...?"

"Lane, sir, Bernard Lane, company COO."

"Yes, you were ... now take all of these good people out with you. Kew, you stay. Oh, and Doctor Li?"

She was standing ready to leave, "Sir?"

"You stay as well," he said brashly.

His manner might have been assertive, bordering on impudent, but he certainly commanded obedience. Once the others had left the room, Gorrick sat down.

"I've downloaded details from my predecessor's memory to my OSCI, so I don't need a heads-up on the events leading to his death. But there are some questions following the explosion that I need answered; for obvious reasons, those memories weren't retained. Firstly, did Honor survive?"

"Yes, she's in the infirmary under the care of Doctor Li here," Kew answered casually.

"And what's the status of her recovery and damage, Doctor?"

"She make a full recovery. I reconstructed her face; bandages removed today," she said curtly.

"Good. I presume Doctor Chu's body has been returned to China?"

"Yes, sir," Li said, her face displaying a little false remorse.

"We will need to find a replacement for him; I intend ramping up the cybernetics project and downscaling the android programme. We'll leave that to our Japan chapter; they're more advanced on android technology than we are, as can be evidenced by the failure of Set. Send all of our development data to Japan, please, Doctor."

The news bothered her; together with Chu, they had spent years developing the prototypes that ultimately led to the creation of Set.

"Sir, Set was state of the art ... not our fault he was captured and compromised," Li argued vehemently.

"The fact that he could be compromised is where the failure lies, Doctor. No, the future is the development of the RF series of Cyborgs," he said firmly.

Li stood, her thin lips in a concave meniscus, her eyes narrowed, incensed that her project had, in the stroke of a pen, been made redundant.

"Then, no further need for me here," she said crustily.

"I didn't say the android program would end; I said it would be downscaled. The project will still be yours; in fact, more so now that Doctor Chu is no longer with you. You must understand the commercial reality of Zen. My job is to increase profits, to that end, the Cybernetics RF program numbers add up. I want to introduce the first RF Warbot to the Pentagon within the year. The R&D is complete, so the time has come to perfect and fine-tune a working model."

Placated, Doctor Li sat back down in her chair and said, "Sir, we need integration between android project and cybernetics division for perfect mix. While are separate, development is decelerated."

"You're absolutely right, Doctor; uniting the projects would certainly increase productivity."

Doctor Li was aware that Chu's stubborn opposition to the united integration of the android and cybernetic departments had been an issue. Now, with Chu out of the way, with her in charge, the challenge of the venture was much more appealing to her. The thin-lipped meniscus on her mouth had changed to convex, and her eyes widened with excitement.

Gorrick noticed the positive change in her, and that encouraged him ... he was after all only just getting to know them and knew only too well from previous experience that creative intellectuals posed a problem due to their oversensitive and sometimes self-indulgent nature. Dealing with this came with the territory, but he was content with how it had panned out. He focused his attention on Kew.

Gorrick glared unblinkingly at Kew, "Two things worry me, Kew: the breach of security that got Gorrick killed, and the failure of the mission to 2047. What have you got to say about that?"

Kew was noticeably uneasy. He knew the responsibility of the failure rested on his shoulders; he was answerable on both counts.

"Want me to hand in my notice?" he said unemotionally.

"What is it with you people, are you all quitters around here?" Gorrick snarled. "I would have fired you on the spot if that's what I wanted. No ... you used your initiative to take out the president ... that was commendable. You tick all the right boxes ... I just think you've been poorly managed, along with the rest of this chapter, and that caused mistakes that should never have occurred. I'm going to need a right-hand man, are you up for it, Kew?"

"Depends on what it entails," Kew said coldly.

"I want a lock-down on security ... I want the blueprint of the organic chip ... I want to get rid of this thorn in my side, Black Alice. You've got 48 hours to come up with an MO. Can you buy into that?"

"We're on the same page, Gorrick, yes," he said with a callous look in his eyes.

"Good, as for you, Doctor ... find me a replacement for Professor Chu. I want a Cybernetics genius ... tap into your contacts in China, Russia ... Korea ... get me a shortlist within 72 hours. Get Honor up and about ASAP; if your work is as good as they say, then she will play an integral role in getting us the chip and bringing Black Alice down. Deal?"

"Yes, sir," she said enthusiastically.

"And Kew, put someone good onto digging up all the dirt you can on this Mal Function running for president."

Kew and the Doctor sensed the meeting had drawn to a close and so got up to leave.

"Oh, by the way, Doctor Li, what is your professional opinion of chief scientist Professor Adamski?"

She thought about it for a moment. "He is young ... quite brilliant; like anyone, it will depend on the assignment he is given. Can I be direct?" she said cautiously.

"Yes, that is what I demand of my staff."

"He's not challenged, finds job boring."

"I read his dissertation entitled 'The Casimir effect of transcendental bijection of the spacetime continuum or asymptotic projection of the Calabi-Yau manifold manifesting itself in Anti-de Sitter space.'"

Kew raised his eyebrows ... it was all mumbo-jumbo to him, but nevertheless impressive.

Doctor Li was also impressed. "Yes, it difficult to find someone more informed on exotic matter," she said, testing Gorrick, whom she figured could simply have read the information from his heads-up OSCI display.

"Wormhole theory, well, I think his skills will finally be utilised, send him to me."

After the meeting, Li and Kew were waiting together at the elevator.

"So, what do you think of the new Gorrick?" Kew asked Li in a low voice.

"Different than last one, this one intellectual."

CHAPTER 38
SAVING FACE

ALICE CROSSED THE street and stopped at the intercom to the Coogee Beach Apartment block. He checked the slip of paper he was holding, confirmed the apartment number, and reached out a finger to press 701. He stopped short, then, after a contemplative pause, pressed it. A static-enriched female voice answered.

"Hello, who's there?"

Alice chickened out, turned, and hurried away. He stopped at the promenade, gripping the railing as if he were about to fly off into space, cursing himself. What sort of gutless wimp are you? He looked up into the night sky, shaking his head at his ineptitude. Grumbling to himself, he stormed back across the road, marched up to the buzzer, and hit it again. This time, an irate female voice answered.

"Who is this?"

Alice grimaced, figuring it wasn't a good start. "Um, yeah, is Wyetta there?"

"This is she, who is this?"

"Your brother."

The buzzer punctuated the statement, and Alice entered the building.

About to knock on the door of apartment 701, Alice did a double-take when it opened. The person on the other side was almost a female replica of himself. He froze, transfixed by the tall girl with a long black mane, shaved up on the sides, big almond-shaped brown eyes painted with heaps of mascara, eye shadow, and eyeliner, a pear-shaped face, high cheekbones, full lips—painted black—garbed in a black singlet that sported the Black Alice blood logo. Her body was ripped, her left arm tattooed to her fingertips in a sleeve, the most prominent illustrations: a pentagram, a skull, a black rose, and a snake wrapped around the tree of life. Her skin was darker than Alice's; her ethnicity on display more than his. In black leotards, combat boots, and no bra, the package presented wall-to-wall Goth, but to top it off, she exuded a razor's edge steely vibe.

"Well, are you going to stay there undressing me with your eyes, or are you coming in?" she said sarcastically but in a way that Alice figured it was the sort of thing he'd say. He pushed past her. "You're a goth or something?"

"More goth than something," she retorted.

Alice stopped and took in the Spartan living room. "Yeah, well, we've got that in common," he said, looking through the glass patio door at the view of Coogee Beach.

"Nice spot."

"Didn't wear the T to impress you?" she said, sitting on the three-seater lounge.

Alice turned to face her. "I wear them myself."

"You're a bit of a legend, aren't you, Rob?"

"You can drop the Rob bit; I left that behind centuries ago. Just Al."

"Please yourself ... Al. Park yourself."

Al sat in the only armchair and folded his arms defensively. "How long have you been in Sydney?"

"A week."

"On your own?"

"This sounds like a first date. Yeah, no obligations if that's what you're asking."

"So, you're training for a gig with OTT ... what are your skills?"

"Martial arts instructor."

That caused him to raise an eyebrow. "What makes you think we're related?"

Vee mirrored him and folded her arms. "You asking me that because you're famous, and chicks will use anything to hit on you?"

"Nup."

"Tell me, where did you get the name Black Alice?"

"My dad was a proud Indigenous feller; he'd been taken from his mob and raised in a reform school in Alice Springs. The other kids called him Black Alice."

"Unbelievable, I didn't know that about Dad. He passed, and I never met him. I mean, I know I've got native blood, but hey, my skin's darker than yours … you'd never know looking at you. Does all this feel awkward to you?"

"My oath."

"Yeah, me too. Shit like this doesn't come with a manual," she joked.

"You sounded just like Mum when you said that."

They exchanged a long, deep stare that confirmed they were indeed siblings. Then tears welled up in Vee's eyes, and her voice trembled as she emotionally said, "It's wonderful to have found you, big bro."

She stood up to take a tissue from a box on the coffee table. Alice jumped out of his chair and embraced her. They both cried as Al muttered in her ear, "Yeah, touché, sis … touché."

Honor was counting down the minutes. The whole day had been a nervous wait. Nearly blind due to the heavy bandages, her other senses seemed to have intensified. Her sense of smell and hearing were both more dependable than ever before, and she had even developed a sixth sense for when something was about to happen— and she was getting that now, in droves. She could discern Doctor Li's footsteps in the corridor outside her room, and that started her heartbeat racing. The footsteps stopped at the door … a shuffle, then she heard a second set of footsteps, a man's: Kew's. They also stopped at the door. Then she heard a kiss. She tried to push the idea out of her mind but couldn't. She had to stop it. This was her time, not theirs. There was a glass of water on the table beside her, so she purposely knocked it onto the floor, and it shattered. There was a pause, and then the door opened.

Kew entered first and came to Honor's bedside. His shoes crunched on the broken glass. "There's broken glass on the floor," Kew complained to Doctor Li as she entered the room.

"I accidentally knocked it over," Honor lied.

Doctor Li strode back to the door, opened it, and called out into the hallway, "Nurse, bring broom and pan!"

"How are you … excited?" Kew asked.

"Yes, but maybe not as excited as Doctor Li," she said facetiously.

It went right over Kew's head … he missed the implication by a mile. A nurse came in and followed the Doctor's pointing finger to the shards of glass on the floor. Kew moved away to let her sweep it up. "How you feeling?" Doctor Li said.

"I could ask the same of Kew or you for that matter … I've learned a lot laying here. I'm ready," she said tersely.

Once the nurse had left the room, Doctor Li moved in to remove the bandages. It took a few minutes to remove the outer layer, then came the finer gauze or lint, which the Doctor sprayed with an oily solution to make it more pliant. They were in six-centimetre square patches covering all of her skin, including her scalp, ears, and neck. This was such a delicate operation it took some time. Kew was trying to see Honor's new face, but Doctor Li was in the way.

Eventually, Li moved away, and with open hands, she announced with the excitement of someone showing off a newborn, "Voilà!"

Kew just stood there, staring at Honor, totally thunderstruck. Doctor Li removed the thirty-centimetre square mirror hung on the wall and handed it to Honor to check herself.

There was a pregnant pause while Honor held it face down on her knees, and then, after mustering the courage, she turned it over and held it up in front of her face.

Her eyesight was still hazy, but as it cleared, so did the image in the mirror. After a long pause, Honor calmly said, "I will need a new name to match my new face ... an entirely new identity ... I have been born again." Slowly she lowered the mirror and then glared at Kew narcissistically.

The shock of her complete facial transfiguration had rendered Kew stupefied.

Three days later, Alice visited Mal in the temporary hospital room set up at Oceana. "Hey dude, you're looking like you might live," Alice said, as he cruised into the room in his customary upbeat manner.

"Thanks Al, yeah, I think I'm ready to break out of here. Had a few walks over the last couple of days, and all went well ... I'm even on solid foods ... look, all the tubes have gone."

"That's what I came to tell you, they gave me word you'll be released this-arvo."

"Yeah man, unreal!" Mal said happily.

Al sat on the edge of the bed. "But listen mate, things are gonna be different for you once you're outa here. First of all, there will be heightened security on you because Zen would want you whacked ... then all the bullshit to do with running for president."

"I'm up for it, Al ... had plenty of time to think about it, and yeah, I dig the challenge. But listen, I'll need to change my name ... I cringe when I think of posters that say Function as President."

"I dunno mate, sounds kind of funky. What's your real name?"

"Get this—Malcolm Low ... about as charismatic as a toothbrush. Mallow is a herb with a hairy stem ... think of what I copped at school when kids found that out," he grumbled.

"So that's what made you tough, mate. Listen, it sounds like a president's name to me." He stood up and waved an arm as if he were ushering a head of state into the room. "Ladies and gentlemen presenting our new president, Malcolm Low…"

"Yeah, maybe, but people already know me as Mal Function."

"Yep, but we can easily change that, just like changing a band's name … the punters don't care as long as the music's still good," Alice said, walking towards the door. "You'll be staying with the Professor for the next few days; he's got an apartment nearby that's easy to secure … but for now, tell no one. I'll send Karzoff down to talk security with you."

"I'd prefer the big South African chick," he said, trying to think of her name.

"Viktoria? Okay, no worries, I'll send her … Oh, and thanks for your help with Vee; we met up the other day."

"Excellent. You reckon she's your sister?"

"Could be," he said in a non-committal fashion, then waved. "Chaa!"

He left the room and took the elevator up to OTT. There was a new girl at reception. He cruised over to her, sat on the edge of her desk, and purred lewdly, "And whom do we have here?"

The petite girl with pink short-cropped hair and a plunging neckline on her white silk blouse that fought to hold in boobs that were larger than to be expected from one so small offered up a broad smile filled to capacity with perfect teeth.

"Candy Trette … and you're Black Alice," she said with a cute trill voice that had a slight lisp that Alice found super sexy.

"Your parents were very creative naming you Candy Trette," he said, unable to resist using a flirtatious tone.

"Thank you," she said coyly, impressed at meeting the famous rock star. "Who would you like to see, Mr Alice?"

"Just call me Al … I'd like a word with Viktoria, please."

"She's in with Karzoff … you can go in, they're expecting you."

"Thank you, Candy." By the time he got out of the two-hour meeting with Karzoff and Viktoria, the sun was setting. He wasn't impressed with having as many bodyguards on him as Mal was about to inherit, but at the same time knew they were for his safety. A message left with Candy at reception inviting him to band rehearsal had him change his plans. Originally, he was going to catch up with Hope at her apartment for a happy hour drink and decided to put it off until 9 p.m. That would give him time for a blow with the boys— he felt he owed them that much after being absent for so long.

It was a rehearsal room he hadn't used before located in Alexandria on the fringe of the Sydney CBD. Having two bodyguards was a whole new experience for him, and he got on with them fine.

Enjoying the plush comfort of the Range Rover SUV rear seat and listening to one of his own albums on the quad sound system, Alice figured he could get used to being chauffeured about. "Hey Alex, pull up at that bottle shop over there, I'll get a slab of piss for the boys," Alice said to the driver.

"Sure boss. Give Tiny the bucks; he'll get it," he said with a strong East End London accent. He was referring to the big oaf in the passenger seat next to him. Tiny was a great nickname for a bloke so big he had to keep his head permanently bowed in the car to keep from banging it on the roof every time it went over a bump.

The black Range Rover pulled up outside the Cauliflower Hotel in Waterloo. Tiny struggled out and went inside. He lumbered out of the pub a couple of minutes later, carrying a slab of two-dozen cans of Toohey's Extra Dry beer tucked under one arm. Alex leaned over and opened the door for him to climb in. With the slab secured on his lap, they drove off.

"You'll be able to dine out on the story of getting a slab of piss for the great Black Alice for years, won't ya, Tiny?"

"I don't dine out much, Alex," the big man muttered.

It wasn't long before they arrived at the gates of Warehouse Complex 51 to 57. It comprised six warehouses in a gully with a narrow driveway leading down to them. The entire industrial estate consisted of rows of warehouses, most of them former wool stores built just after WWII.

A single light up high on the warehouse closest to them was all that illuminated the access road. The rest of the complex was in complete darkness.

"I don't like the look of this," Alex warned, turning down the volume of the music and hitting high beam.

Alice sat forward in his seat, "Nothing unusual, mate. Rehearsal joints are always in dingy dumps like this; it's because there are no noise issues. Drive down, mate, look for a light inside one of the warehouses ... that'll be it." Alice urged.

Against his better judgment, Alex complied, drove the Ranger Rover down the steep driveway, and then along the narrow lane that ran in-between the warehouses.

"There's a light inside the end one," Alex said.

"That'd be it," Alice said, still sitting forward on the seat for an unobstructed view through the windscreen.

The vehicle stopped at the last warehouse. Just beyond it was Alexandria Canal, which became obvious to them by its pungent aroma as soon as they got out of the car.

"Phew, it's a bit whiffy." Alice complained.

"We better check ahead," Tiny growled uneasily.

"Nar, come on ... it'll be fine," Alice said, brushing off any need for concern.

Tiny shot Alex an anxious look when Alice strode off toward the warehouse entrance door. Just as he reached it, Alice's cell phone rang. He whipped it out of the pocket of his black three-quarter coat and answered, "Yeah?"

"Hey Al, it's Ratsso ... heard from Mal you're back. Listen, the boys were thinking of rehearsing tomorrow ... you up for it?"

Alice's face froze, "Did you leave a message for me at Oceana?"

"Nup."

"Okay, sure mate, what time and where?" he said, waving Tiny and Alex over.

"Say four in the arvo at the usual haunt in Clovelly."

"Okay Ratsso, see you there, chaa!" He terminated the call just as Alex and Tiny reached him and said with a grave expression, "It's a set-up, fellers. Just heard from my band … rehearsal's tomorrow, they hadn't left a message for me at Oceana."

Both bodyguards immediately drew guns from their shoulder holsters and held them in both hands pointed down, ready for anything.

"Back inside the car, boss, I thought this was on the nose," Alex snarled on edge, his eyes flashing about at the terrain, on the hunt for assailants.

As Alice turned to leave for the car, he noticed movement in the darkness at the corner of the adjacent warehouse.

"Alex, over there at 11 o'clock," Alice said sharply.

A shadowy figure slipped into the darkness and disappeared. Alice felt they had walked into a coordinated ambush. The only cover available to them was the Range Rover, either that or they'd have to hit the toe.

A noise came from the roof of the warehouse behind which the shadowy figure he'd seen had vanished.

Alex raised his Glock 19, taking aim in the direction of the noise. A small red laser dot from a night-scope appeared on his forehead. Alice and Alex saw it, but it was too late. There was a muffled crack from a gun fitted with a silencer, and Alex's legs crumbled from under him … he went down.

Alice peered down at the neat bullet hole in the forehead of his dead bodyguard, exactly where the laser dot had been. He looked up in time to see movement on the rooftop … the sniper had to be there.

"On the roof above the other dude," he warned Tiny, and then he bent down and snatched the Glock out of Alex's open lifeless hand … he wouldn't be needing it any longer.

A voice called out from the shadows, "Throw down your guns now, Alice, we have you surrounded."

Alice recognised the voice. "Kew, come out in the open and fight like a man!"

As Kew appeared out of the shadows, Tiny took aim, but before he could peel off a shot, a red pin spot flashed on his chest.

Alice saw it and quickly fired two rounds at Kew to try and draw the sniper's shot, but it was too late … Alice heard the thud. The big man staggered about like a drunk and then went down hard.

"Oh, no…" Alice moaned, looking down at Tiny face down on the deck. Pissed, he yelled out venomously, "I'm gonna kill you, Kew!"

A red laser spot flashed in Alice's left eye.

CHAPTER 39
DIXIE

SECTA'S CELLPHONE RANG; now it was a matter of dragging himself out of bed and traipsing naked to the lounge room to fetch it from where he'd inadvertently left it. Fortunately, the phone was turned the right side up for the screen to guide him to it in the otherwise dark room.

Grumbling, half asleep he checked the caller ID and then answered, "Hope?"

"Alice was supposed to be here for drinks at nine … that was three hours ago, I'm worried Secta, it's not like him to stand me up."

The distress in her tone woke him up. "No, no, he would call … he was issued a new cell phone, wasn't he?"

"Yes, I've tried the number, but it just goes to message bank."

"Wait a second."

Secta returned to the bedroom and the buxom naked woman waiting for him in bed, and said, "Alice didn't turn up at Hope's three hours ago, can you call his bodyguards?"

Viktoria hopped out of bed, retrieved her phone from the pile of clothes on the floor, and speed-dialled Alex.

Secta waited.

"No answer," she reported, "I'll try Tiny." After a few seconds, she looked at Secta and said gravely, "Message bank … tell Hope you'll get back to her, I'll use your computer to put a trace on Alice."

"Hope ... there's no response from the bodyguards, so we're going to trace Alice's phone."

"Is Viktoria with you?"

"Yes."

"Oh, good," she said. "Um, can you call me back when you know something?"

"Sure, bye."

In robes, Secta led Viktoria into his study that was annexed off the living room. A sensor light switched on when they entered. He went to his desk and booted up the laptop and then turned it over to Viktoria. She sat down in his office chair, while Secta took up vigil standing beside her. With her fingers speeding across the keyboard, she punched details into the dark web the security agency used. Once logged on, she input Alice's cellphone number, sat back, and folded her arms. After a few seconds, a response came, "No signal. I'll check GPS location of their vehicle."

She keyed an ID number for the Range Rover. The coordinates were triangulated and then displayed on-screen with an approximate address.

"The vehicle is inert at a warehouse complex in Alexandria. I need to call Karzoff," she said urgently.

Within an hour, four OTT agents in a Range Rover SUV drove in through the entrance gates of the Alexandria Warehouse Complex. Karzoff was driving with Viktoria beside him navigating, and two agents were on the back seat. The GPS signal on the dashboard computer was showing the target vehicle as a blinking red dot.

At the bottom of the dark descending driveway, Karzoff flicked the lights to high beam and then drove slowly along the lane between the warehouses. They sighted the abandoned Range Rover in their headlights and parked beside it. When they got out, they immediately found the dead bodies of Alex and Tiny sprawled on the ground. Tiny was face down, and Alex on his back with his head in a pool of blood.

Each of them was armed with a gun and a highly-powered torch, so they split up to scour the area. After fifteen minutes, they reassembled, having found no sign of Alice.

Karzoff gave a heads-up. "Okay, the abandoned vehicle, two dead agents, and no Black Alice. He was here for a band rehearsal according to a message he received yesterday from OTT receptionist at 1800 hours. It was a phone message, a male caller who identified himself as Ratsso, the bass player of the band. I checked the server, and the call originated from an unregistered cellphone, so we can assume the rehearsal was a set-up."

They heard a groan. They all swivelled around at once to see where the noise had come from and found Tiny, still alive.

Viktoria quickly snapped digital photographs of the crime scene, and then it took the four of them to load Tiny into the rear of the SUV. Karzoff and Viktoria would rush him back to the Oceana infirmary for urgent medical attention, while the two agents would be left at the crime scene to wait for forensics.

"You'd have to say Zen has Alice," Viktoria told Karzoff.

Running red lights, Karzoff was occupied with getting to Oceana as quickly as possible.

"If they had killed him, they would have left him behind," he said.

"Not if they want to turn him into an android like they did with Set."

Karzoff glanced at her, knowing she could well be right. "Perish the thought."

Fortunately for Tiny, there was no traffic at 2 a.m., and as a result, within twenty minutes of leaving Alexandria, they had him in the safe hands of the medical team Viktoria had put on standby to tend to him.

After an hour in ER, Tiny survived to fight another day. But Karzoff and Viktoria were still in a dilemma as to the whereabouts of Alice.

It was several hours before Tiny, whose real name was Timothy Specht, came out of anaesthetic and was able to be questioned. Karzoff had waited all that time in the infirmary and was snoring soundly when a nurse gave him a nudge to let him know Specht was conscious. He was given five minutes with him.

Specht was in bed with tubes in his nostrils and mouth and an array of beeping machines connected to various parts of his body.

Karzoff leant over him and said gently, "Tiny, are you there?"

The big man's eyelids slowly opened as though they had been glued shut. He stared at Karzoff and then nodded his head ever so slightly. He was naturally very groggy.

Karzoff pulled a chair up beside the bed and sat. "You will live, my boy. The bullet missed all your vital organs … you are very lucky indeed. Can you tell me what happened?" he said, and then waited patiently for an answer.

His mumbling reply interfered with by the tube in his mouth was still understandable to Karzoff; all he could say with his eyes squinting angrily was, "Kew."

Karzoff stood, kindly tapped the back of Tiny's big hand, and said graciously, "Get well, son. We will need you back on deck as soon as possible."

Though pain was evident in the big man's eyes, he still managed a faint smile around the tube in his mouth.

Karzoff immediately took the elevator up to the OTT offices. It was too early for Candy to be at reception, he took a peek inside Viktoria's office and saw she was curled up on the two-seater lounge asleep and so went to his own office and phoned Secta.

"Secta, sorry to ring so early, but it is important … I spoke with Tiny when he came out of anaesthetic just a few moments ago, he said Kew took Alice."

"Had they shot him?"

"That he was not sure of, he had passed out."

"There's a chance he's alive, meet me at Kairos in two hours. Is Viktoria with you?" Secta asked.

"She is asleep in her office."

"It's been a long night … wake her in an hour or so and bring her along. I'll arrange for Hope, the Professor, Robert, and Candy to be there as well. We need to work on this as a collective."

A state funeral for the President was due to take place in Sydney the following day, so Karzoff had his work cut out for him. A large turnout was expected for the procession with all its pomp and ceremony. The President had ruled out a religious service: only a parade through the city will be conducted should I die while in office, which of course he did.

It was deemed the perfect time for Mal to make the public announcement that he was running for office, and even though it had already been reported in the media, it was still necessary for Mal to deliver it to the nation personally.

At a meeting of the Government Security Division, police, and military chiefs, headed up by Karzoff, a few days prior to the shooting of Alex and Tiny and the abduction of Alice, it had been determined that following the funeral of the President, Mal Function would make a public announcement that he will be running for office. The broadcast was scheduled to take place from a secure television studio at Oceana Headquarters.

Gorrick was seated on the balcony of his palatial Point Piper apartment, enjoying the view of Sydney Harbour bathed in the early morning sunlight. In the distance were thunderheads: a storm was brewing in more ways than one. On the table was a report he'd only just finished reading. It stated that tomorrow following the state funeral of the President, Mal Function would make a public announcement that he will be running for office. Gorrick knew if he was to let that happen, then trying to eradicate him once he was in campaign mode, or even worse … elected … would be made far too difficult. They needed to strike before the announcement goes to air.

Honor walked out onto the balcony with shaggy blonde hair and garbed in a flimsy red silk Chinese robe.

"Good morning, Honor, they told me you were here."

She looked long and hard at Gorrick, trying to detect any perceivable difference between him and the former Gorrick, but there was none to be seen. "Good morning, sir."

"I know what you're thinking, and no, we Gorrick's are identical … the only difference is the brain function, each of us has a varied social upbringing and education, thus though we look identical, we think differently."

She sat down. He looked at her pale shapely legs showing from under the robe as she crossed them.

She mentally noted that was already a difference: the previous Gorrick showed none of that.

"You have an American accent," she said.

"Yeah, New York … Harvard … and all that. You know, I can only tell what your appearance was like from the few photos I've seen of you, and you look nothing like the former Fanny Honor, you're much more attractive."

She feasted on the flattery. "Yes, funny … I have spent a lot of time this morning looking in the mirror trying to come to terms with my new face. Doctor Li even did something to my tongue that has completely altered my accent."

She no longer pronounced the as ze; her Eastern European accent had been totally neutralised.

"A skilled surgeon, Doctor Li."

"I have to agree with that."

"Annabel?" he called out, and the maid appeared as if out of nowhere.

"Yes, sir?"

"What would you like for breakfast, Fanny?" he asked.

"Eggs Benedict," she said.

Annabel waddled off to fetch the order.

"I have a job for you when you're fit and well. It will require a temporary change of your name."

Honor reclined in her chair and smiled smugly, "I'm ready for anything. Though a few things will take a little while," she said, and then leaned forward and removed the shaggy blonde wig she was wearing.

He studied the fine lines of her clean-shaven head.

"Not a scar to be seen anywhere, quite remarkable. Your hair will grow back soon enough … for now, you will look just fine with any colour or style of wig you wear."

"Can you brief me then, sir?" she said, putting the wig on the table and enjoying the tingling sensation of the morning air on her naked head.

"The objective is to possess the powerful organic chip Secta brought back from 2047. You know of it?"

"Yes, we believed he fitted it in Set, that's what enabled him to speak."

"Correct. Well, I want that chip. Last night Kew captured Black Alice, but I'm not about to trade him for the chip as my predecessor would have done; that's not my style."

"Good … What do you intend doing with him then?"

He thought for a moment and then said, "I'm thinking of setting Doctor Li on him, perhaps to produce a more dynamic version of Set."

"An android, perfect … if we had the chip then he would definitely be dynamic."

"No, the chip is for a new series of RF Cyborg Warbots. Doctor Li strongly believes she will be able to unleash the many talents of our Professor Adamski to produce a working model sooner rather than later."

"So, what do you have in mind for me?"

"We've had surveillance on Professor de Luz's apartment for the past few days, and we've learned about all of his personal habits, plus we suspect the person chosen to be the next president is holed up there."

"And whom might that be?"

"Someone I believe you thought you'd wasted, Mal Function."

Her face soured. Detecting her distaste for the man, he carried on, "It seems the Professor has a penchant for massage … and to that end, has regular night-time visits … do you get my drift?"

"How about Dixie?" she said, with her lips pouted and then added suggestively, "She gives excellent massage."

CHAPTER 40
CAUGHT IN THE ACT

ALICE HAD SPENT hours tied and gagged in a dark room. He had no idea where he was. All he could remember was the red laser shining in his eye back at the warehouse and then seeing stars. Someone must have crept up from behind and whacked him over the back of the head with a piece of four by two. His mouth felt as dry as the floor of a parrot's cage. Unlike last time when he woke up in a dark room on board the UFO, this time there was no ribbon of light under the door to dispel his fear of the dark. He decided to distract his mind and so imagined that Sonoko lay beside him.

Just then a door opened and light flooded in, blinding him. Shadowy distorted hands reached out of the light, dragged him to his feet and then manhandled him out through the door into a brightly lit room. Before he could recognise anything, a hood was pulled over his head and he was led out of the room and into an elevator. He looked down from under the hood at the floor. There were three pairs of men's shoes and a pair of female feet in sandals. They were pretty feet, well-manicured red-painted nails. It was silent, only the sound of the elevator mechanics.

The door opened and he was bundled out along a corridor into another room and then into a final room where he was made to sit in a chair. The hood was removed. He looked about … it was an executive office. Someone behind him handcuffed his wrists to his chair and then removed the gag. He heard water being poured and then the woman wearing sandals appeared in front of him with a glass of water, which she held up to his mouth to drink. It was refreshing. He drank it down and then studied the woman. She was Asian and she was wearing a white lab coat.

He straightened up in the chair just as Kew came into view. "Alice, what were you saying back at the warehouse … you were going to kill me? Not this round old son," Kew scoffed.

The door opened behind him and someone came in. "So, I finally get to meet the notorious Black Alice." The speaker moved into Alice's field of vision and he recognised him. "Gorrick … ha! which one are you, I'm losing count? I've killed so many?" Alice snarled.

Gorrick sat in a chair opposite Alice.

"We haven't met previously. I'm the replacement for the Gorrick your associates murdered."

"Let's not go there Gorrick … all this shit about who murdered who and for what reason really pisses me off … it's boring mate … just get on with it … why am I being held captive, what do you bunch of freaks want?"

"That's not very polite language for a man in your position Alice, you don't mind if I call you that do you?"

"You can call me whatever you like pal, and who said I had to be polite?"

"Doctor Li," he called, and she came to his side. He took her hand. Alice studied Doctor Li's face. In her early thirties it was a pleasant almond shape with her long back hair drawn back into a bun showing off her slender neck. He was certain that beneath her lab coat dwelt a sexy petite body, similar in shape to Sonoko's but that was where the comparison ended … Doctor Li had cruel eyes … the eyes of a masochist, and thin deceitful lips. This was a dragon lady in the making, cold, callous and self-important.

"What would you like to do with Alice here?" Gorrick asked her.

"I think he make very good android," she said grabbing Alice's face and prising open his left eye wide to check it. "Only use some parts but yes, perfect."

"Good, it's settled then," Gorrick said. "Take him away and prep him immediately. I have nothing more to say to the rude bastard."

"Been there, done the I'm going to turn you into an android thingy before. So, hey Gorrick, go to hell ... oh that's right, that'd be home to you. Hundreds of you bastards couldn't beat me on Phobos, I killed them all ... what makes you think you can beat me now ... huh?"

Gorrick nodded at Kew. He stepped forward, smiled at Alice, and then belted him on the jaw with a powerful right jab that knocked him out cold.

Doctor Li felt Alice's jaw. "I hope you didn't damage him, Kew. That was not necessary."

"Who cares," Kew barked sneeringly.

"What percentage will be human?" Gorrick asked Li. "Set was forty-five percent, I think half in this case is perfect because no physical damage. A lot will depend on the processor speed I have. The more actuators used for movement, the more processor power required ... and so it goes," Li explained.

"A new chip five times more powerful than what you used with Set will arrive today from Tokyo. It's nowhere near as powerful as the organic chip," Gorrick said.

The news transformed Li's expression from morose to excited. "Five times, excellent, that will enable speech sub-routines."

Gorrick said on his way to the door, "Let me know when you have him prepped."

The next time Alice opened his eyes, he thought he was dreaming. There were flashes of light flicking past him every five seconds ... and he could hear the sound of wheels moving on a floor and rattling. Squinting, his eyes finally focused, and he realised the flashes were oyster lights in a ceiling, and the noise was from the hospital gurney he was on being pushed along a narrow corridor.

Raising his head, he looked at the theatre nurse pushing the gurney. He was wearing a white facial mask, a hair cover, and a green operating gown. Then it all became clear: he was on his way to be prepped for conversion to an android. Panic set in, and he tried to raise his arms, but they were strapped to the side bar of the gurney, as were his legs.

"Hey mate, stop for a minute, I need to take a leak," he urged the nurse, desperate to try anything to get out of his predicament. But the nurse paid him no attention.

With a sudden jolt, the gurney careered through flapping plastic swing doors and came to a halt inside a pre-med room. The nurse quickly checked the fastenings that anchored Alice to the gurney were tight enough and then disappeared.

"How are you going to get out of this one, buddy?" Alice mumbled.

A few moments later, Doctor Li came in. At least she's not in an operating gown, Alice thought, as though it was a reprieve.

"Alice, we have a little wait for processor to arrive from overseas. It will be your new brain."

"Listen, I don't need a new brain, I'm happy with the one I've got, thanks."

"You will make fine android, Alice, better than Set, you will be able to talk."

"I can already talk … look, let's cut a deal, whatever they're paying you we'll pay you double … and I'll get you the organic chip … there is no faster chip not for another twenty years … now doesn't that turn you on?"

She leaned close to his face and pecked him on the cheek. "Sorry Alice, but life would be over for me if I double-cross my boss, you know that."

"You must want something … name it, anything," he was beginning to panic.

She produced a syringe. "No Alice, I am happy with what I have. Now, a little jab and you can sleep a few hours."

"No, I hate needles," he protested. But it was too late she injected his bicep. Within seconds his eyes rolled back in their sockets and he was out like a light.

Doctor Li left Alice to sleep, and on her way along the corridor toward the elevator met up with a short man in his late thirties with a seriously receding hairline that made him appear much older than he was. It was Professor Adamski, born, raised and educated in Russia, brought to Australia by Zen to head up the RF Cyborg R&D program the previous Gorrick had instigated some ten years previous.

"I have just come from a meeting with Gorrick," he said with a sense of urgency in his strong Russian accent.

"Good … he outlined new project?" she asked.

"Yes, and it is very exciting, I must thank you. Along with the merger of our cyber/android projects he has also given me the opportunity to design a wormhole generator."

"A wormhole generator … time travel? To compete with OTT?"

"I think so, he said we will require technology from the future to keep our projects on the cutting edge."

"Wise thinking."

"Is the patient prepped?" Adamski asked.

"I knocked him out … I am waiting for new processor from Japan. Once it arrive I will prep him … should be later today. You will assist the operation?"

"Yes, just let me know what time. Thank you again Doctor Li, I owe you one," he said with a smile.

Lissy pressed the service elevator call button, the doors opened, she stepped inside.

Kew was waiting impatiently at the sixth-floor service elevator door. The elevator stuck on the 2nd floor was making him late for a meeting with Honor. Finally, it arrived, and the door opened. Inside were Doctor Li and Professor Adamski and they appeared to Kew to be somewhat flustered. The doors closed.

"Lissy, Uri, everything all right?" Kew asked pressing the button for the 18th floor.

"Yes, just dropped Alice to pre-med," Lissy said calmly.

"Ah, that would explain the hold up with the elevator."

The elevator stopped at the 15th floor for the professor to get off.

"Let me know what time, Doctor," Uri said on his way out.

"Yes, professor," she said.

The doors closed.

Kew entered the 18th-floor boardroom where he found Honor seated at the long table.

"You're late," Honor snarled, facetiously. "Why, have you been with Doctor Li?"

Kew ignored her jibe and sat down. He had to brush aside that during her stay in the infirmary she could easily have worked out he was having an affair with Doctor Li.

"Gorrick briefed me this morning about your discussion with him over breakfast," Kew said.

"Yes, that is why we are having this meeting," she said curtly.

"He said you've decided on a new name for the operation."

"Yes, Dixie."

"Good, I interviewed Professor de Luz's Tuesday girl about his habits."

"Tuesday girl?"

"Yes, he has the same masseuse every Tuesday and another every Saturday. She said sometimes he likes to try someone new but mostly sticks to regulars."

"How do they get through Oceana security? When I was there such things were handled by Viktoria."

"I think she still handles it. We can simply swap you with Tuesday girl inside his apartment building. I have a photo of her so you can mock-up like her to fool the CCTV."

"What will be expected of me?"

He looked at her and felt a pang of yearning. She looked much different, more attractive by a country mile.

"The girl always arrives at the same time, 1 a.m., he takes her to his bedroom where she massages him."

"Is he masochistic or a submissive?"

"Submissive I think, he's not into pain."

"That's all very straightforward," she said churlishly.

CHAPTER 41
ZENESIS MAN

THE OTT TEAM was together in the Kairos control room. Candy was serving coffee, while Secta was pacing the floor. Hope, the Professor, Robert, Viktoria, and Karzoff were sitting patiently, waiting for Secta to begin.

Secta stopped pacing but was still holding his chin and said, "We have a problem we need to solve, and quickly—" He stopped abruptly when the door opened, and to everybody's surprise, Mal entered.

"Sorry to burst in on you all unannounced, but I heard they've got my buddy, so I'm here to help."

To Mal's surprise, Hope led a round of applause. When it stopped, Secta said, "You wonder why the applause? Because you feel exactly as we do. We want Alice back unharmed, and we'll do anything necessary to achieve that."

They couldn't help but cheer ... it was a rousing moment, so much so it brought tears to the eyes of many of them. Hope gave Mal a big hug, as did Viktoria, and then he sat down to listen.

"When Tiny came out of the veil of unconsciousness this morning, he managed to tell Karzoff that Alice had survived the ambush and had been taken by Kew ... we expect, to a Zen safe house. I fear because he's the outright nemesis of Zen, they will do to Alice what they did to Set ... transform him into an android. It very nearly happened to him before on the mission to 2087, but that's another story."

A rumble of disapproval came from them all.

Secta continued, "I don't think we've got much time, so I'll get on with it ... we need to come up with a plan to snatch him from their clutches."

"But first, we need his location," Hope added.

"How can we do that?" Karzoff questioned.

"By using the same means you found him before ... his atomic marker," the Professor pressed.

The idea stunned them; it was so obvious.

"Of course, an ILDD," Secta said, pacing again.

"Yes," Hope said, getting up and rushing out of the room.

Viktoria whispered to Karzoff, sitting beside her, "What's an ILDD?"

"An isotopic labelling detection device," Karzoff whispered in reply. "It can locate an atomic marker Secta implanted in Alice's DNA up to a distance of ... Hmm, you know I am not sure of that part." He spoke up, "Secta, what is the range of the ILDD?"

Hope returned thirty seconds later with the handheld unit and passed it to Secta.

"A radius of about ten kilometres," he said, switching a dial on the unit.

"You'll need to take it outside, Secta; there's RF dampening in here," Robert advised.

"Of course, best we go up to the rooftop," Secta urged.

Hope led them to the service elevator, and all eight of them squeezed in.

"Let's hope he'll be in range," Secta told the Professor on the quiet.

"If he's not, what's the back-up plan?" de Luz asked.

"Take an ILDD each, split up, and scour Sydney. But time is of the essence; if they were going to ransom Alice, they would have made an approach by now."

"I hear you," de Luz said gravely.

The elevator doors opened on the 27th floor, the rooftop. Hope led them up the short staircase, through a fire door, and out onto the roof. They were immediately bathed in sunshine, and the ILDD instantly responded with a reading.

"I've got him!" Secta said with alacrity.

"Does that mean he knows where he is?" Candy asked Karzoff.

"No, it means he has a signal, and that Alice is within sight of the device. Now he will try to determine the direction."

Candy was watching Secta with her mouth open in amazement, like a school kid.

Secta turned in a slow circle, holding the ILDD out in front of him, and then stopped when he found the exact direction of the signal.

"There, that's the direction," he said, holding the device steady, then turned the calibration dial to narrow the field. "That building ... the tall grey one in Macquarie Street at Circular Quay, I'd say." He moved the device ever so slightly left and then right to test the strength of the signal. "Yes indeed, that's the building, all right."

"Zen Headquarters," Karzoff said soberly. "We will need more than a search warrant to raid it, and we would require a small army."

"I don't think so," Robert said as he wandered over to Secta like a man on a mission.

Alice wasn't in any position to do anything; he was still flat-out on his back, on the hospital gurney in pre-med, unconscious.

Doctor Li entered, garbed up for the operation but without a surgical mask. Adamski followed her, also suited up and without a mask.

Li checked Alice. "He should be coming around ... I ordered the anaesthetist. In the meantime, come with me to prepare the OR."

As Adamski followed her through the hermetically sealed doors into the OR, the lights blinked on, and he said, "I ran a simulation of your transmutation of Anu Set; it took fifteen hours. Quite an operation."

"Yes, but he was a mess, shot at close range, and it caused serious physical damage. Alice is clean slate ... it will be much faster."

The theatre was equipped more like a laboratory than a conventional OR. It was necessary for Li to walk Adamski through all of her specialised equipment.

"I will have an assistant ... of course, I was an assistant for Doctor Chu in the Anu Set procedure," she admitted begrudgingly.

"Yes, I know. By the way, Gorrick ordered me to use our newly perfected cybernetic joints for the wrists, elbows, shoulders, hips, knees, and ankles."

"Yes, he sent me a note confirming that."

"The parts are already in the sterile zone," Adamski said.

"Excellent. Do they function hydraulically like some of the android components, or will they require a specific liquid such as ethylene glycol?"

"No, they are not hydraulic at all; they are self-lubricating, requiring no pump or feed from a reservoir. Made from lightweight shape-shifting metal produced from the isotope Helium 3 from the moon. No human physical rejection problems ... I designed and built them myself, and they are fitted very easily," Adamski said excitedly. "The centralised mechanics are 3-D printed."

Doctor Li was astounded by the concept of shape-shifting metals used in such a manner. If commercialised, she knew it would revolutionise bionic implants. It now made complete sense why Gorrick had claimed the future was in cybernetics. This new technology would definitely open up the opportunity for the creation of a perfect cyborg.

"You realise this union utilising our ingenuity will produce from Black Alice the first of an entirely new species ... I call it Zenesis man," Li said proudly.

"Yes, Zenesis, good call ... a species we will ultimately fit with the groupthink mental processor I am developing."

"What is the groupthink processor?" she queried.

"Put it another way ... the hive mind. You see, the aim is to build a wormhole generator through which we can send cyborgs to explore other worlds."

"Fantastic," Doctor Li said excitedly, the adrenaline pumping through her veins.

An unexpected voice called from the pre-med room, interrupting the conversation.

"Doctor Li?"

"That sounds like Gorrick," she told Adamski conspiratorially.

They ventured back into pre-med where they found Gorrick waiting.

"Ah, there you are," Gorrick said. "I understand the processor has arrived; are you close to getting underway?"

"Yes, sir, we're just waiting on the anaesthetist and my monitoring assistants," Li confirmed.

Just then, Kew joined them.

"Ah, Kew, is everything in order with Dixie for de Luz's apartment tonight?" Gorrick enquired.

Acting as though he was still unconscious, dazed but cognizant, Alice eavesdropped on the conversation.

"Yes, operation dethrone is go," Kew said seriously.

"Aptly named, I like it, how many of you?" Gorrick queried.

"I'll only need one with me."

"Good ... Now, Doctor Li, we're not getting any younger waiting for you to begin. Call me when you're ready; I'll be in my office ... come on, Kew, you can bring me up to speed on the game plan."

Alice listened to Gorrick and Kew's departing footsteps, echoing and fading into the abyss of the corridor. Their continuing conversation had become inaudible, so he focused on the doctors' chitchat. He figured his best chance of escape would come if and when they decided to free his fettered arms to remove his clothes for surgery. His hope was that they would do that with him conscious.

Doctor Li approached Alice and prised open his left eye with her long, thin fingers to check the pupil. If it were dilated, she'd know he was conscious.

"Doctor Li?" A voice came from behind, distracting her.

She straightened up sharply without checking Alice's pupil and exclaimed, "Ah, finally ... Doctor Uri Adamski, this is Doctor Dunlop, our late anaesthetist," she said facetiously.

Alice was relieved she hadn't checked his pupil; there was still a slim chance for him to escape.

Dr Dunlop was a middle-aged, good-looking man with receding short-cropped salt-and-pepper brown hair. Attired in a beautifully tailored navy-blue business suit, he said apologetically, "I'm sorry, my dear, but the cursed city traffic held me up coming from Citizen's Hospital."

"We were about to give up on you," she joked. "We'll prep him now while you change into a gown."

"No problem, just give me five to scrub, and then set things up. Do we have assistants?"

"Yes, three ... traveling."

Just as the anaesthetist left for the scrub room, footsteps belonging to the three assistants resounded in the corridor. The footsteps were quickly overpowered by chatter and giggling as they approached.

Doctor Li looked sharply back at Alice, "Quick, get him out of clothes before he regains consciousness. Undo the straps."

The nurses arrived, and Doctor Li, unimpressed by their tardy behaviour, shot them a disdainful glare and snapped angrily, "Nurses, sit the patient up and remove his clothes! Nurse O'Brien, get gown for the patient."

The nurses exchanged a sly aggrieved glance out of Li's view and then got on with the job. Doctor Li had the reputation of a draconian taskmaster.

They untied the straps, then they professionally manoeuvred Alice into a sitting position. He played along, enjoying all the attention, though through squinted eyes, he was watching and waiting for the right moment to make a move.

Nurse O'Brien returned with the gown for Alice. The nurses got his shirt off, removed his boots and socks, and were opening his pants when Alice noticed everything in the room shimmer. His pants were slipped off, then his underpants ... he was naked. At first, he figured the shimmering might be the effects of the narcotic they'd used to knock him out and was just about to jump up and start throwing punches when everything shimmered a second time, and then time began to slow down, down, down ... until everyone in the room had frozen mid-action.

Alice struggled out from under the nurse's hands and slid off the gurney. He observed Doctors Li and Adamski frozen in conversation, and the anaesthetist mid-stride on his way back from the scrub room. There was no way he could resist having a bit of devilish fun, especially being in the nuddy with all the people around him fully clothed ... it was unfair. He went to Doctor Li, unbuttoned the front of her operating gown, and peeled it off ... he unzipped her tube skirt and found she wasn't wearing knickers.

"Hmm, naughty doctor," he snarled in her ear.

He looked up at the vortex forming and knew from experience exactly how long he had before he needed to enter it. Ignoring it for the time being, he continued stripping Doctor Li until she was standing naked except for her white theatre shoes. Then, he quickly moved on to Doctor Adamski ... opened his gown, unzipped his pants, and pulled them down around his knees, then pulled down his underpants and left them around his ankles. He stood back and checked him out, "Hmm, not very impressive professor Scungeface."

Full of mischief, he moved quickly over to the nurses and stripped them of their gowns and skirts, and then pulled their knickers down around their ankles. Job complete, he stood back and took in the scene. Three nurses of varying proportions dressed only in their tops with their knickers around their feet bare-arsed. Doctor Li standing mid-conversation in her birthday suit next to Doctor

Adamski, also naked. He thought of getting up to some more trouble but decided he was running out of time. The vortex was at its maximum, as he moved towards it he heard footsteps approaching. He knew they could only belong to one person, only Kew could avoid being frozen. When Kew appeared in the doorway, Alice barked at him, "I'll catch you later! Chaa!" and dived into the vortex. It immediately dawned on Kew what was happening, and he raced for the vortex that was closing fast.

CHAPTER 42
BOY'S TOYS

GORRICK STEPPED OUT of the lift and hastily made his way along the corridor to the pre-med room, furious that Doctor Li hadn't notified him of the operation commencement time as they'd agreed. When he reached the room, he found utter chaos. It was like a Roman orgy; nurses were in the nude ... Doctor Li was standing completely naked, trying to cover her genitals with her hands ... Doctor Adamski had his pants around his ankles, hopping about on one leg trying to pull them up. Doctor Dunlop was standing there trying to deal with a fit of hysterics, and there was no sign of the patient.

"What the hell do you think you're doing?" he complained and then noticed there was someone sprawled out on the floor trying to get up. At first, he thought it was Alice, but then realised it was Kew.

Alice popped out of Kairos, executed a perfect forward paratrooper roll down the sloping padded ramp onto the event room floor, and into the waiting arms of Hope holding open a lab coat for him. Karzoff and Viktoria were standing nearby with guns trained on Kairos, ready in case Kew appeared.

"Kew won't be joining the party," Alice mumbled somewhat dazed. "He got left at the barrier."

Karzoff and Viktoria holstered their weapons. Secta, the Professor, Mal, and Robert joined the others to welcome Alice. This was the first time the OTT team had managed to pull off matter transfer within the same time frame.

"Glad you were able to work your magic, mate," Alice told Secta, "but I tell you I was expecting to be talking to a pulsing orb, not you blokes."

"It was experimental, but then I expect you're getting used to that," Secta suggested jokingly.

"Yeah, but listen, you've got to solve this arriving buck-naked thing, it's bloody embarrassing," Alice complained.

"Yes, we're onto it," the Professor admitted, scratching his head as though the answer to the problem was still eluding him.

"Now ... what's a bloke gotta do to get a feed around here?" Alice grumbled and then sighted Mal and cackled, "What are you doing here, you low dog?"

Mal sniggered, slipped an arm around Alice's shoulders, and walking him towards the exit said, "Come on, buddy, let's get you changed, and we'll go find us a burger."

A little while later, they were jammed round a table in Café Epiphany on Bent Street, not far from Oceana HQ. Karzoff and Viktoria insisted on coming along to guard over Alice and Mal.

Alice was busy hoeing into a burger, while Secta was feasting on his favourite dessert: banana bread with butterscotch sauce.

"I don't know how you can eat that and stay so skinny, Secta," the Professor said jokingly.

"A high-speed metabolism, my friend ... that's the key to skinniness," Secta returned serve.

"He's always had a sweet tooth," Hope divulged.

"Think I'll try it as well, it looks scrummy," Robert said, licking his lips.

Karzoff was happy with his chocolate donut, and Viktoria content with her coffee. Mal, on the other hand, was busy scoffing down French toast drenched in maple syrup.

"I don't get why they're so intent on building an android ... what's the diff between a bloody android and a cyborg anyway?" Alice asked the scientists, hoping for an understandable explanation.

"Okay, let's look at this in the context of androids versus cyborgs," Secta said like he was lecturing students. "Doctors Li and Chu were working on building an android ... that's essentially a robot with human appearance... Doctor Chu was eliminated, so the program was probably terminated because he was the brains behind it. Now, the other scientist you came across, Adamski, whom I've read about and is quite brilliant, he's been working on Zen's cybernetic program ... an entirely different ball game."

"Adamski is also noted for his paper on Anti-de Sitter space, which is basically wormhole theory," Robert said informatively.

"I see ... I didn't know of his interest in wormholes, but that now adds a whole other dimension of concern for us ... hmm, anyway ... we know Zen's cybernetic program takes over from the android program because they ultimately develop the RF series that we encountered in 2087," Secta said.

"Seems to me the new Gorrick has merged both departments," the Professor supposed.

"For sure, so is it human/machine integration they're wanting to develop?" Alice speculated.

"Ah, yes," Secta agreed, knowing he was being brought back on track. "Because it's a shortcut ... building an android with consciousness, capable of speech, is incredibly difficult ... but by utilising part human components, they can achieve that much quicker."

"Why haven't you gone that way instead of building the 2-4-D android?" Alice queried Secta.

"Rejection problems," Hope answered for him.

"Zen has obviously solved that, Set was a walking example ... I knew Adamski was working on it, but I didn't know that he'd cracked it," de Luz said.

"Karzoff, where's Mal staying tonight?" Alice asked.

"At the Professor's apartment, it is our safe house for the time being," Karzoff said.

"I'll tell you what I overheard Gorrick and Kew talking about," Alice said prudently.

The seriousness of what Alice reported to them had Karzoff hopping mad, and the Professor perplexed.

"So, they've been spying on me! I thought you had that covered, Karzoff?" the Professor complained.

"No good complaining about it now ... this is not the place to discuss any of these security matters, we need to go back to OTT right now to formulate a plan," Karzoff said emphatically.

They knew he was right; they could easily be under surveillance by Zen spies. They finished up and filed out of the café bound for OTT.

It was 1 a.m. The Professor was in a blue satin dressing gown tidying up his bedroom when the video intercom rang. Humming a happy tune, he left the bedroom for the kitchen to answer the unit on the wall. As he entered, sensor lights illuminated the kitchen; the entire apartment was sensor light-activated.

"Hello?"

A pretty face wearing dark wraparound shades came on screen and said, "Hi there, Professor."

"Hey Sandy ... come on up, darling," he said, pressing the buzzer.

"Who was that?" A male voice called from inside the second bedroom.

"Just my Tuesday girl. Good night."

He cruised back into the bedroom to finish tidying up while Sandy travelled up in the elevator. A few minutes later, there was a knock at the front door, so he went to let her in.

When he opened the door, the young lady he found there surprised him. He looked her up and down—she was wearing a striking red three-quarter length single-button Cashmere coat with matching red gloss lipstick. She had a shaggy platinum blonde hairstyle, bare legs, and red high heel pumps. For the Professor, women don't come any more seductive than that.

"You're not Sandy?" he quizzed, congenially.

"No, I'm Dixie. Sandy couldn't make it tonight ... am I pretty enough for you?"

"No, I mean yes," he stammered, "you're stunning, but—"

Biting her bottom lip provocatively, she put down the red patent leather bucket bag she was carrying, then used her long slender fingers in thin black kid gloves to slowly, sexily, unbutton the single button of her coat, and then she gently opened it.

His eyes opened to the size of dinner plates to feast on what was before him—she was wearing a very brief string bikini under the coat.

"To your taste?" she asked, and punctuated the question with a foxy smirk.

Mesmerized, he drifted aside to allow her entry.

A gruff voice again called out from the guest room, "You sure you're all right, mate?"

As the Professor ushered Dixie into his bedroom, he called back, "Yeah, no problem, good night," and closed the bedroom door behind them.

"Who was that?" Dixie asked.

"Oh, a guest."

"Will he want to be massaged as well?" she asked.

"No, no ... he's very tired."

She sat on the edge of the King-size bed and patted it for him to join her.

"What's in the bag?" he asked.

"My favourite toys."

He rolled his eyes. He couldn't help but sense there was something familiar about her, but he wasn't sure, and so he let it go.

"Now, lay face down on the bed."

He obliged her with a sigh. She furtively reached into her bucket bag and produced a syringe.

Unable to see what she was doing, he said, "I like oil ... do you have Jasmine?" His face in the pillow muffled his voice.

"Yes, I have everything, Professor," she said testing the syringe. Then she jabbed it into his gluteus maximus.

"Hey?" he complained, trying to sit up but couldn't; she was holding him down.

"Shush, dear, it's alright ... just something to relax you," she said warmly.

He sank back down onto the bed and within seconds was off with the pixies.

Job done, she dropped the syringe in her bag, put on her shoes, stood up, and put her coat on.

"Sweet dreams, baby," she muttered, and then crept out of the room.

The lights came on when she entered the kitchen. She pressed the access button on the intercom and then went to the door, opened it very quietly, and waited.

After a few minutes, two men dressed in black cat commando suits came to the door.

"Now don't you look a sight for sore eyes," Kew whispered.

"Your eyes are probably sore from all the attention they give Doctor Li. Good luck, Kew. Bye," she whispered, bitterly.

He grabbed her arm to stop her leaving, "Go out through the basement just in case there are guards. We already took care of the two down there."

She wrenched her arm free of his grip and then irately set off for the elevator.

Kew's accomplice was bigger than him with a big square jaw, Russian facial features. Both of them pulled their guns: Glock 19's.

Kew whispered, "I'll go in first, Timur; you back me up close behind. Hold your fire, leave the mark to me."

A nod from the big brute, and they stealthily entered the apartment. In commando technique, Kew, holding his gun up with both hands, went to the door of the Professor's bedroom, which Honor had purposely left ajar. As he entered, Timur stopped to cover him.

Kew went over to the Professor sprawled out on the bed and prodded him in the middle of the back with his pistol. He didn't move. Satisfied, he quickly prised open one of his eyes and checked the pupil; it confirmed he was out cold. He looked back at Timur and nodded.

Leading the way, Kew approached the guest bedroom door. Timur backed up close behind while Kew gently turned the doorknob, gun ready.

The bedroom door creaked open, and he stepped inside. The only light was from a lamp on the bedside table. There was no-one in the bed, just the impression in the duvet where someone had been. He moved quietly into the room with Timur as before, stopped at the door providing cover.

Kew spotted a light under the en-suite bathroom door. The toilet flushed ... it had to be the mark ... Mal Function.

CHAPTER 43
CHEAP SUIT

THE ROOM SHIMMERED. Kew paid no attention and aimed his pistol at the door, committed to kill Mal.

Then the room shimmered a second time.

A voice began singing a tune inside the bathroom.

Kew went to the bathroom door gun up and ready, leaned on the lever handle and gently pushed the door open.

A vortex was forming in the room.

An unexpected fist exploded out from behind the bathroom door and collected Kew right on the button.

He reeled backwards, holding his nose that was streaming blood and snarled, "You!"

Dressed in a navy-blue singlet and black track pants, Alice roared out of the bathroom, throwing punches that hammered Kew to his knees and jolted the gun out of his hand.

Alice kicked the gun out of Kew's reach and then looked sharply towards Timur, who was standing frozen with his gun still aimed at the bathroom.

He checked the vortex. It had fully formed, ready to take a traveller and would soon close.

Kew struggled in an effort to get up, spied the gun on the floor, and dived for it. Alice reacted quickly and gave him a swift kick in the gut, then smashed him with a savage barrage of jackhammer punches that ripped open Kew's lips, obliterated his nose, and split both his eyebrows. Alice was all over him like a cheap suit. It was no contest, the ferocity of the attack had caught Kew unawares ... he was done and dropped limply onto the floor, his face a bloody mess.

Alice rolled him over, sat him up, bear-hugged him under the arms, and then dragged him over to the vortex. Then, he changed for a better grip and using all his strength, picked him up and bodily threw him into the vortex. Kew disappeared into the void, leaving his clothes floating to the floor like formless ghosts.

Alice collected Kew's gun and then went over to take care of Timur.

"Hmm, what a big mug you are ... let's see what I can do here," he said with a cheeky grin. He took the big man's gun, removed the clip, flicked out fourteen of the fifteen 9 mm rounds, and dropped them into his hip pocket. With one round left in the clip, he slipped the clip back into the butt of the Glock 19 and locked it into place. Next, he devilishly moved Timur's left hand in front of the barrel and closed his palm around it. Then gripping Timur's gun hand forced his index finger to pull the trigger.

Job done he cast his attention to the living room. Karzoff was standing frozen with his gun aimed at Timur's back. He had been hiding in the lounge-room all the while Dixie was there.

Alice moved quickly, the vortex was closing, Karzoff would soon unfreeze. Full of mischief, he undid Karzoff's belt and pulled his pants down. Then he flopped into a lounge chair, crossed his legs, set to enjoy the scene of Karzoff snapping out of his trance and Timur shooting himself in the hand.

From his position, he could see the vortex through the bedroom door. It disappeared, and a gunshot sounded immediately followed by a scream from Timur.

Karzoff snapped out of his trance with his gun still on Timur and instantly felt a chill. He looked down surprised to find his pants around his ankles.

Not knowing whether to keep his gun trained on Timur or to pull up his pants, he saw Alice sitting on the lounge-chair grinning like a Cheshire cat and yelled at him knowingly, "Alice!"

With a hole clean through the palm of his left hand dripping blood, Timur pulled the arm tight against his body, gritted his teeth, and turned sharply to aim at the voice he just heard.

Karzoff saw him turn and aimed at him, so he dived for the ground to avoid the bullet.

Timur pulled the trigger and kept pulling it, but it just clicked.

Karzoff was about to return fire, but Alice stopped him. "No Karzoff, it's okay … drop your gun, feller, or Karzoff here will put some more holes in you. Speaking of holes…" he got to his feet gun in hand and gave Karzoff a hand up. Then he walked over to Timur keeping his gun on him, "You're bleeding all over the carpet, mate, the Professor ain't gunna be happy about that."

Karzoff hitched up his pants, "Did you do that?"

Alice shot him a cocky grin over his shoulder, "Nar mate, you need a new belt."

Kew rolled awkwardly out of Kairos, his face a bloody mess, naked, he dazed up at the half dozen armed agents surrounding him. The closest of them was Viktoria with her pistol aimed at his head.

"Just give me a reason to take you out, Kew," she snarled.

He struggled to his hands and knees, with blood hanging in long strings from his mouth and muttered through shattered teeth, "Go to hell."

Mal walked out from behind the agents and stopped just short of Kew.

"You piece of rubbish … you murdered the president and wanted to kill me … well, it backfired … this time no-one will be releasing you because Zen will never know how you disappeared."

"You won't survive, they'll just send someone else to kill you," Kew groaned.

Mal wasn't going to take any more and let fly with a powerful right boot to the face. The blow broke Kew's jaw and knocked him out cold.

Mal stormed out.

"Cuff him and lock him up," Viktoria ordered her agents.

Later that day the OTT team were assembled in the boardroom watching the State funeral of the President on a new eighty-two-inch flat screen that had descended from a concealed housing in the ceiling. The procession had snaked through the city and had just come to an end at the Martin Place Cenotaph.

"So, Professor, when's your next visit from Dixie?" Alice jibed.

"You know there was something odd about her," de Luz admitted.

"Yeah, she jabbed you in the bum!" Hope said with a snigger.

"Shush! … shush!" Viktoria said, using the remote to turn up the sound on the TV.

Mal came on screen. He cut a striking figure with his platinum-blond short-cropped hair, a dashing bright royal-blue suit, a white shirt, and a thin blue necktie with white polka dots. He was standing at a lectern in front of the Oceana insignia on a dark blue curtain.

"Doesn't he look the bee's knees? Hope said.

"He looks like a president to me," Al agreed.

"Hear, hear!" Karzoff and the Professor said in unison.

They hushed to listen to Mal's speech.

"Hi good people of the nation … you might know me … some of you might like what I've stood for over the years with the Octagon Peace Movement, while others might not, but that's fine because isn't that what democracy is all about? I'm known as Mal Function … in fact, that's my stage name, my birth name is Malcolm Low, and it will be Malcolm Low who will run for candidacy as President of this great nation. Today we mourn the loss of President Ri Smith, a fine man … yes, there were times when we didn't see eye to eye with policy, but he was a wise enough man to make amends and set us on a strong path into the future. So, what can I offer? Simple, a voice … your voice … a younger voice … I will listen to you and act. Anyone who knows anything about me is aware I am a doer, not a sayer, definitely no spin-doctor. I proudly hail from a working-class background, I have a successful career in entertainment, and I am the leader of the largest Peace Movement in the nation … I believe I can relate to the electorate. Vote for me in the coming election, and together we will bring about the best of times for Oceana. Thank you."

Alice leapt out of his chair and fist-punched the air, "Yeah Mal … excellent."

The others applauded. There was jubilation. Mal had performed just as Al had expected, with dignity and intelligence.

Candy came into the room, had a quiet word in the Professor's ear, and then left.

As Alice sat back down, the Professor stood and said, "Everyone … Candy has just informed me the transcription of the cuneiform stele from the brass Gate of Babylon has just come in from my Harvard Professor friend Gill Delgado."

All eyes were cast on the large TV screen that flicked from the news broadcast to a video file. An elderly man with receding white hair and wearing a brown corduroy jacket and glasses—an academic archetype—was seated at a messy desk littered with papers and books looking down the barrel of the camera.

"Vic, I hope my little video here finds you in the best of health old friend," Professor Delgado said with a rich Bostonian accent. "We all missed you at the annual SSRA convention last month … hard to believe you've moved down under. But hey, good for you … change is good, yes? I've got to say in your usual fashion that we've come to expect from you, the text you sent me to transcribe turned out quite fascinating from two standpoints. Firstly, you were right, no-one has ever transcribed that particular block of text before, God knows why not ... and secondly, it said the most peculiar things. At first, I thought it mere gibberish ... sometimes you get that with Assyrian cuneiform, especially with battle propaganda ... but the images threw me because they weren't telling the story of a battle ... they were telling the story of the creation of mankind. I've emailed you a document containing the full transcription, there's no point going into it all now, but because I was so intrigued, I wanted to run past you some of the more mysterious moments, so to speak. The stele dates to around 556 B.C. at the end of the reign of Nabonidus, the last king of the Neo Babylonian Empire. It is suspected he built the En-Lil Gates of Babylon, but his successor Cyrus the Great, known to have buried the infamous Cyrus Cylinder at the gate, which I might add is on display at the British Museum and I've transcribed, altered the stele because Nabonidus had got it wrong. Now what's strange is one particular part of the text."

The screen cut to a still photograph of the section of the stele the professor was referring to, just above the head of the character using the levers to produce clones of himself. An animated red line encircled the section of text, and Professor Delgado continued. "The section circled states mene mene tekel pharsin. Now, we know this phrase from the book of Daniel in Daniel 5 ... the phrase appeared on the wall in the palace of Belshazzar, the acting king of Babylon, he is regarded as the son of Nebuchadnezzar, although he was not Nebuchadnezzar's immediate successor."

The picture cut back to Professor Delgado. "At the risk of boring you, let me read you the biblical reference ... Daniel 5 tells the story of the Babylonian ruler Belshazzar, a rich and debauched king, who gave a banquet to his court. During the drunken party, the sacred vessels from the Jewish temple, stolen by Nebuchadnezzar in 587 B.C., were used in a blasphemous manner. At the height of the festivities, a man's hand was seen writing on the wall the mysterious words mene mene tekel pharsin. The king was terrified. But no-one could understand what the words meant.

"The king summoned enchanters, astrologers, and diviners. Then he said to these wise men of Babylon, 'Whoever reads this writing and tells me what it means will be clothed in purple and have a gold chain placed around his neck, and he will be made the third highest ruler in the kingdom.' Then all the king's wise men came in, but they could not decipher the writing or tell the king what it meant. So, King Belshazzar became even more terrified, and his face grew pale. His nobles were baffled. The Queen, hearing the voices of the King and his nobles, came into the banquet hall. 'Don't be alarmed! Don't look so pale! There is a man in your kingdom who has the spirit of the holy gods in him. In the time of your father, he was found to have insight and intelligence and wisdom like that of the gods. Your father, King Nebuchadnezzar, appointed him chief of the magicians, enchanters, astrologers, and diviners. He did this because Daniel, whom the King called Belteshazzar, was found to have a keen mind and knowledge and understanding, and also the ability to interpret dreams, explain riddles, and solve difficult problems. Call for Daniel, and he will tell you what the writing means.'

Daniel was given wisdom from God to read and translate the words, which meant "numbered, numbered, weighed, divided." Daniel told the king, 'Here is what these words mean: Mene: God has numbered the days of your reign and brought it to an end. Tekel: You have been weighed on the scales and found wanting. Peres: Your kingdom is divided and given to the Medes and Persians.' Peres is the singular form of pharsin. The Bible never identifies what language the words were in. The handwriting on the wall proved true. In fact, it proved fatal for the dissolute Belshazzar. Just as Daniel had said, the kingdom of Babylon was divided between the Medes and Persians, and it happened that very night. Belshazzar was slain, and his kingdom passed to Darius the Mede."

Professor Delgado looked up from the book he was reading, removed his glasses, and squinted. Then he put the glasses back on and looked back at the camera.

"Vic, the stele states that the appearance of mene mene tekel pharsin on the King's wall is a reminder that whatever we sow, that we will also reap and that it does not pay to ignore the handwriting on the wall. This is a very odd statement, and I don't believe it was a prophecy, I think it is some kind of code but I have no idea what. Well, that's about all I can go into now, read the transcript and keep me informed of your research … you're always onto something unique Vic, and we all love that about you. Take care."

CHAPTER 44
THE WHEEL OF FORTUNE

HOPE PRESSED THE button on the control panel in the boardroom table for the screen to ascend back into the ceiling, and the big windows facing Sydney Harbour polarized back to opaque. The room flooded with natural light. All of them seated around the table were in deep thought after the video.

"Well, that was enlightening," Vic said.

"It was an excellent idea getting him to do the transcript," Secta confirmed.

Hope stayed standing and said, "If Cyrus added this text to the stele, then I think it was because he was Chaldean. All of the rulers of Babylon were Chaldean, with the exception of Nabonidus, which is possibly why Cyrus figured Nabonidus had got it wrong."

With a wrinkled brow, the Professor slowly nodded his head. "Yes, Hope ... I think you're onto something there ... go on."

"Well, the Chaldeans either invented numerology or, as some suggest, were gifted it from the god Marduk who we believe was En-Lil ... remember the gates are actually called the En-Lil Gates ... the name was changed by Cyrus from the Gates of Babylon to the En-Lil Gates ... he would have done that for a reason."

"What are you suggesting, Hope?" Secta queried.

"What if mene mene tekel pharsin means something in Chaldean numerology and like Professor Delgado suggested, is a code?"

"What if it's the code En-Ki told me about? The key to picking the real En-Lil from the other Gorrick clones?" Alice said, excitedly.

"Give me a couple of hours to consult my Chaldean numerology references," Hope requested.

"Good, we'll reconvene at 2 p.m. after lunch," Secta said. "Oh, and Karzoff, both Kew and Timur would be fitted with Zen OSCI's, we'll need to shut them down pronto," Secta said.

"Yes, we have them in RF lockout rooms at present," Karzoff said, standing ready to leave.

"Who can disconnect their OSCI's?" Viktoria asked.

"Get Doctor Skinner from the infirmary, she has a mastoid OSCI removal map I sent her a while back, she can do it," Secta affirmed.

Gorrick was sitting behind his office desk at Zen, livid. The door opened and Honor came in. She was wearing a simple black ASOS A-line dress that showed off her figure in fine form. This time with her hair in a black bob, like she used to wear, the graceful line of her thin neck accentuated.

"Sit down Honor, I'll be with you in a second," Gorrick said, his voice lacking any warmth.

She sat in a lounge chair and casually crossed her long bare legs.

"You sound a little moody today Gorrick," she put delicately so as not to ruffle his feathers.

He stood up from the desk, made his way to the lounge setting and sat in an armchair opposite her. "You obviously haven't heard the news ... Mal Function, now known as Malcolm Low just announced his candidacy for president."

"What? But we—"

"Neither Kew or Timur returned from the mission ... it failed ... again. Why he felt he could succeed with only one accomplice I have no idea."

"The bigger question is how did they know we were coming. I saw no signs of an ambush, I left as planned with de Luz out cold on the bed. I didn't even encounter agents entering the apartment block or leaving it."

He stared long and hard at her, mulling over in his mind whether she was completely trustworthy or not. Is she complicit: a double agent? He pondered the notion ... and then dismissed it; no-one would have gone through what she had after the explosion if she was playing both sides.

"Then we must assume Oceana is holding both of them," she said. "What do you intend to do about it?"

"Not a thing. It's time to move on ... I want you to put together a new covert security team. I don't care where you get them from as long as they are loyal and skilled. I want unmitigated background checks for the highest level of clearance. You got that? Ex-Navy Seals, SAS, mercenaries ... I don't give a damn ... but they need to be ruthless and committed."

"How many, sir?"

"Half a dozen."

"And what is the objective?"

"To finish what Kew failed to do ... I want Black Alice and Malcolm Low eliminated and it needs to happen before the goddamned election!"

She wasn't used to seeing Gorrick show emotion; he was typically cool, calm, and collected. But this guy was very different from the last Gorrick, and that excited her.

The OTT meeting reconvened at 2 p.m. on schedule, with Hope last to arrive. She was looking a little flustered. They all took their seats while she remained standing. She pressed the button on the control panel for the monitor to appear, the windows polarized, and lights dimmed.

"You can see on the screen the breakdown of Mene, Mene, Tekel Pharsin using Chaldean numerology ... a sacred number is attributed to each letter so, mene is 4555 which adds up to nineteen, which added together comes to 10 then 1, tekel is 45253 which also adds up to nineteen resulting in 1, and then pharsin is 8512315 which adds up to 25 which equals 7. When it is totalled, it comes to 10, which in the book of Chaldean numerology is the wheel of fortune. Now, you might well ask what all that means, well..." She pressed the button on the panel to get rid of the TV and threw some light on them, and then she opened a book on the table in front of her. "Ten is symbolised by Osiris. A number of rise and fall according to personal desire ... it goes on but what's important is the reference to the Egyptian god Osiris who to the Assyrians is En-Lil. So, there we have it, the magic number is 10, and it means the wheel of fortune which is symbolised by Osiris who is En-Lil. And..." she held up a piece of A4 paper upon which was a photo of the selection of stele that had been transcribed. "You see the man standing there working the lever, what is that above his head? A disk with 10 spokes, a wheel of fortune. It is saying that the person below it cranking out clones is no other than En-Lil."

Alice jumped up excitedly, "And, check it out ... the ten spokes ... connecting them up and what do you get?"

Hope pulled a pen from her pocket and drew the ten spoke wheel of fortune on the opposite side of the A4 paper and held it up with an amazed look on her face, "A ten-point star! A pentagram and an inverted pentagram inside a circle."

"The Zen logo!" Alice snarled.

Hope sat down and skimmed madly through a book looking for something. She found it and read it out. "Here, the ten-pointed star is an upside-down pentagram on top of a right-side-up pentagram which is the symbol of man as a star being perfect in god's eyes to having sovereignty over the earth and all the beasts of the fields. The circle around the outside of the star symbolises unity. The entire symbol is also related to the tree of life from which Adam took the apple. An apple sliced in half reveals a beautiful five-point symmetry—a star formed by the seeds inside. In fact, each of these five seeds may be seen to contain a symbolism of its own mirroring the spiritual aspects of this universal symbol: idea, sustenance, life, secret knowledge, and the hidden mysteries within the earth. The apple signifies hidden knowledge, which was forbidden to humankind."

"That ties in with your hypothesis about the tree of life being the DNA helix. So, if we think that through, it begins to make sense ... it's all symbolism ... En-Ki using DNA to create a new race of humans in his own image ... using the tree of life—DNA. En-Lil doesn't agree and seeks to destroy En-Ki's DNA modified humans using the great flood, etc., etc., ... and an intergalactic war. En-Lil kills En-Ki, then En-Lil creates his own race of clones to finish the job of annihilating mankind over time," Secta hypothesised.

"So, Hope ... Secta ... what is the hidden code that will allow us to detect the real En-Lil from the Gorrick clones?" Alice asked.

"It's the numbers," the Professor said vaguely. Then as though it all came together in his mind, he stood up and said excitedly, "The numbers, the spokes, the pentagram ... the number ten is on the body of every clone except En-Lil ... probably in the form of the encircled ten-point star."

"And how would we find it on their body?" Alice questioned, as the Professor sat back down.

"It might not be on the clone's body, maybe it is in the DNA, like the atomic marker in Alice's DNA," Karzoff theorised.

They all looked at Karzoff wide-eyed as though he'd had a stroke of genius.

Secta jumped out of his seat and began pacing the floor faster than any of them had ever seen him pace before. "Karzoff, you're brilliant ... you're brilliant ... that's the answer ... that's the code ... we've broken it!" He stopped and glared at them. "The marker is in the DNA!"

"That's exactly what the stele is telling us ... the ten-pointed star is above En-Lil who is holding two levers that look like a double helix ... it's saying the–marker–is–in–the–DNA," Hope summed up.

"And it's with the DNA En-Lil has the problem of not being able to clone any more Gorricks, that's why Zen was trying to create a hybrid race in 2047," Al added.

"And the reason they're now trying to create the perfect cyborg," Secta concluded.

"So, Al, all we need to do is analyse a sample of Gorrick's DNA to determine whether he's a clone or the real deal En-Lil ... the real En-Lil won't have the marker," Hope concluded.

"Yes, but we all know that would be cumbersome, Hope. The process of analysing DNA is complicated, Alice needs a means to easily detect a clone so he can determine on the spot if it's the real En-Lil or not," Secta explained.

"Wait a minute, you said ten is a magic number, didn't you, Hope?" The Professor asked.

"Yes, in Chaldean numerology," she agreed.

"Well, there are two other options as I see it. The atomic number 10 on the periodic table is Neon because the electron shell has 10 electrons circling the neon atom. What if Neon is the valency of the isotope in the DNA?" the Professor suggested.

Secta continued pacing the floor, holding his chin. It was another option to consider.

"What if it's the Schumann resonance frequency of 10 hertz?" Robert proposed.

"Of course, a 10 Hz rhythm is present in the occipital cortex when the eyes are closed." Hope said, accessing the information on her handheld device. "Alpha waves ... the 10 Hz frequency fulcrum is proposed as the natural frequency of the brain during quiet waking, but is replaced by higher frequencies capable of permitting more complex functions, or by lower frequencies during sleep and inactivity. At the centre of the transition shifts to and from the resting rhythm, is the reticular activating system, a phylogenetically preserved area of the brain essential for preconscious awareness."

"What's all that supposed to mean, Hope?" Alice asked.

Secta stopped pacing with an idea written all over his expression. "What she is saying, Alice, is the clones might operate at 10 hertz, in other words, in an alpha brain wave state at all times ... unlike us. If we were to couple that with what Vic is proposing ... that Neon could be the atomic element in the clone's DNA, we should be able to calibrate two detection devices. The ILDD we use to detect your atomic marker, Alice, calibrated to detect the Neon atomic molecule coupled with an electroencephalogram EEG to cross-reference the occipital alpha rhythm and we'd have it."

"When we can get a DNA sample, a mass spectrometer reading will do the trick, it uses electric and magnetic fields to measure the weight of the charged particles. It's used by forensics to analyse blood found at a crime scene. Neon fluoresces red," the Professor added.

"So, let me get this straight, we can calibrate an ILDD to pick up a clone's Neon signature, then cross-reference that with an EEG to confirm it. But if we have blood from a clone or En-Lil, we can use an Ultraviolet light to check for Neon because it glows red under it," Alice summarised.

"Exactly, Alice. In fact, I will be able to build an EEG into the ILDD specific for the purpose," Secta added.

"But how can I take an ILDD through Kairos?"

The question had them stumped.

But then Robert jumped out of his seat excitedly. "I've got it ... Graphene smart contact lenses ... they give you thermal infrared and UV vision and ... get this ... they're organic ... I only read about them last week. By sandwiching two layers of graphene together, engineers at the University of Michigan have created an ultra-broadband graphene imaging sensor, it can capture everything from visible light all the way up to mid-infrared and can see far into the infrared spectrum, plus it operates well at room temperature."

"You reckon I'll be able to wear these lenses to see Neon?" Alice questioned.

"No, you wear them and then when you shine a light on blood your lenses will allow you to see the red Neon fluoresce in the same way that Luminol fluoresces blue when it detects traces of blood under ultraviolet light," Robert explained.

"Will I need a sample blood from a Gorrick to use it?" Alice asked.

"Yes, but only a minute. At least if you're on a mission, all you need to do is get some blood from a Gorrick, and a light source, a torch or something to test it for Neon," said Robert.

"Yeah, yeah, that'd work." Alice agreed.

"Alice, I received a report from the Department of Immigration this morning that the Gorrick you heard speaking at Zen Headquarters is a replacement from New York," Karzoff said.

"Well, that gives us a target to test these new devices on ... better get them ready boffins, I think this is the way ahead for the quest. First cab off the rank, capture a Gorrick to test," Alice snarled.

Secta sat down and said, "Once we've produced the organic chip from the blueprint we will be able to upload the basic mechanism of an ILDD on it so a detection device can also be taken on missions. With luck, we will be able to connect it to our version of the OSCI that Alice and I are currently fitted with for language translation."

"Absolutely," Hope said enthusiastically.

They were distracted by a knock at the door. It opened, and Viktoria led Mal in fresh from his national television broadcast. All of the OTT members stood and applauded and congratulated him.

Secta had one last surprise for them. "Listen up everyone, there's something I want to show you so that you can grasp the enormity of what Alice here achieved in 2047." He pressed the button on the table for the TV to lower from the ceiling.

Mal sat down to watch.

When a still photograph took up the big screen, they were all awestruck by the intensity of the image. It was the photo Sonoko had taken from her retinal imaging through the lab window of the UFO hovering over Zen Island that she'd loaded onto the organic chip. The night sky had been split by a flash of lightning that had lit up the massive thunderheads of the typhoon ... in the dark sky were blazing fire streams from the afterburners of Jet fighters that had fired missiles at the UFO then rapidly climbed to get the hell out of Dodge ... Dozens of missiles and bombs had exploded and illuminated the enormous force field bubble that surrounded and protected the gigantic spacecraft, and directly below it was the dome of Zen.

Secta used the remote to zoom on the dome. He stopped the zoom at an encircled ten-pointed star on the top of the dome—the Zen insignia underpinning the resolution of the discussion they just had on the meaning of the sign.

Oceana was about to turn a new leaf. The people would soon go to the polls to elect a new President, and very little of Oceana would ever be the same. Whether it would be a better place, only the future would divulge, but there were none better than a time travelling team to have the ability to know that, and then do something to make it right.

Should Mal Low be elected president, as opposed to someone else less familiar with the secret workings of the OTT? Mal would at least be able to preserve the status quo the previous president had given his life to secure for Oceana. The most important thing was to keep OTT funded to further their exploration of time.

As for the quest, the OTT team was pledged to continue pursuit of it. Akin to the search for the Holy Grail by the Knights Templar or those of Arthurian legend, the quest would lead them on an unpredictable journey into an uncharted future. Like a blind man given a window seat in an airplane, Alice had no idea where the quest would lead him next, only that the journey was necessary for the survival of humankind.

EPILOGUE
BOOK 5
AL AND THE ID

THE **ALL-POWERFUL OCEANA** chapter of Zen Corporation, under the governance of a new Gorrick, wasn't about to tolerate any more interference from Black Alice. So Gorrick issued an edict to Honor, director of the newly established security division, ZEO (Zen Espionage Operative), to eliminate Alice once and for all and to destroy Kairos, the Oceana Time Travel wormhole-generating teleporter. A megalomaniac, Honor would pull out all stops to carry out the order, determined to succeed where her predecessor and former boyfriend Zanza Kew had failed. Gifted with a new face from cosmetic surgery performed by Doctor Lizzy Li, who had been appointed director of Zen's cybernetic development division, Zenesis, enabled Honor to be in disguise, which would better help her settle the score with the members of the Oceana Time Travel Division ... in particular her nemesis Black Alice.

The shadow of a laugh is not distinct from the shadow of a scream of terror, but the reality of it is. A hunted man, Black Alice, lifted his blood-drenched hands and stared at them, wondering whether it was his blood or someone else's—he had no idea—he had only just regained consciousness. The only sound audible to him was a high-pitched whistle. Then the pain came ... letting him know the blood was definitely his. He followed the crimson rivulet along his right forearm in search of the source and arrived at a deep gash in his bicep oozing blood.

Sound returned to normal, but the whistle was replaced by a much more sinister noise: the sound of crushing metal. He scowled, where the hell am I? It was dark, night ... he was behind the wheel of a car, and it was moving ... How the hell did I get here? But he wasn't driving it—the engine wasn't even running—the car he was on a conveyor belt. He glanced out of the shattered driver's side window; hmm, maybe that's how I got cut? I've got to get out of here. A feeling of dread was tying his stomach in a knot; he had to follow his instincts. He tried the door handle ... but the metal wall of the conveyor channel prevented him from opening it wide enough to get out. He looked through the windscreen ... there was a car ahead of him on the conveyor being fed into a crusher. It took only seconds for the massive metal claws to compact the car into a neat cube—his car was next.

Favouring his injured arm, he swivelled in the seat, brought both feet up higher than the dashboard, and then, glad he was wearing his Cuban heeled boots, let drive with a massive double-footed kick. The windscreen shattered, showering cubes of glass onto the bonnet. He was through it onto the hood in a flash, and then just as the metal claws opened up to consume him and the car, he jumped.

The two-metre jump was jarring, but his ankles and knees handled it. However, his jaw didn't handle the left hook he was greeted with on landing. The punch caused his knees to buckle, but driven by a powerful instinct to overcome adversity, he straightened up, looked his opponent square in the eye, and let fly at his face with a barrage of blows. The first two connected, but then a gunshot caused him to freeze mid-punch. His opponent hit the deck, cuffing a shattered nose ... blood streaming through his fingers.

Unarmed, Alice knew it was a contest he'd assuredly lose if he were to continue the fight, so he slowly turned with his arms raised in capitulation.

There were three Zen agents, all armed.

"What's the beef?" Al snarled. He could tell by their calm, stony-faced behaviour they were mercenaries; he'd come across that look plenty of times before. It wasn't difficult to tell the objective was to execute him.

The guy with the broadest build, a six-foot-six commando type with a square jaw, eyebrows back-slashed with battle scars, and blond hair in a regulation army crew-cut, stepped forward with an automatic revolver held at his side. Obviously, the top dog, he strode over to Alice and, towering over him, glaring with abject disdain, growled, "On your knees."

"If you insist," Al said compliantly. He knew the next step in the deadly game would be a bullet in the back of the head.

With his fingers locked together behind his head, Al sank to his knees, wondering how the hell he was going to cheat certain death this time...

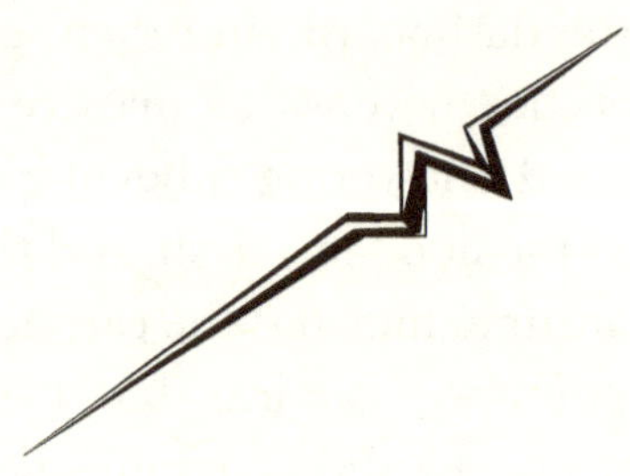